# Chronicles of Galaxy Osmaron

# Infilates

'This is the V-Room. Here almost any pseudo reality may be experienced.

'Would you like to join us in a game? Perhaps we could do ancient Rome today.

'We have thousands of worlds to choose from including historical periods and scenarios from ancient Greece to the Wild West. As a matter of fact, any good book can be turned into a virtual program by the Game Macron in much the same way as a movie is made.

'The Macron simply creates the actors and scenes, and will compile the whole thing in a matter of seconds, instead of months or years as needed by film companies. Here, you can become a real actor and play yourself as one of the dominant roles in every scene.

# The Chronicles of Osmaron Series

Chronicles of Galaxy Osmaron - I am Shadite

Chronicles of Galaxy Osmaron - The power of One

Chronicles of Galaxy Osmaron - Escape from Andromeda

Chronicles of Galaxy Osmaron - The Solarian Empire

Chronicles of Galaxy Osmaron - Fertilates

**Chronicles of Galaxy Osmaron - Infilates**

Chronicles of Galaxy Osmaron - Son of Destiny

Chronicles of Galaxy Osmaron - Jull, the Supreme Patriarch

Chronicles of Galaxy Osmaron - Battle for Andromeda

Chronicles of Galaxy Osmaron - Battle for Osmaron

## *First Edition*

# CHRONICLES Of OSMARON VI

## INFILATES

Earth has been contaminated - Almost everyone will die

By

# Adrian Graye

Nutralian Publishing
http://nutralianpublishing.com

*nutralia*
An imprint of Nutralia Publishing
5 Brayford Square, London E1 0SG
http://nutralianpublishing.com

This paperback edition 2010
B00005555

First published in Great Britain by
*Amazon KDP* 2024

## ISBN 978-1-0687902-5-6

Printed and bound in Great Britain by Amazon KDP Publishing.

A CIP catalogue record for this title
is available from the British Library.

This book is dedicated to friends and animal lovers

&

To all those who believe in universal existence and appreciate the lowliest of life, for like babes, they are the beginning.

## *The Anachromagnon - The book of final light.*

The wisdom of these words, herein, shall be like a sharp sword whose thrust will sever the hearts of all idolaters and fornicators. Those that worship in the names of pleasure and wealth at the expense of suffering; for they are the true corruptors and predators of worlds.

Let these words hitherto shine through all corridors of darkness and show all superior intelligence throughout the Cosmos the way towards their Final Goal.

### *By Siend Seno of The Plains of Herron.*

# THE PAINFUL RACE OF LIFE

On every living thing a little rain must fall,
And every drop will help, even the smallest tree grow tall.
For even in the darkest night,
The stars above will still shine bright,
And if we stay until the morn,
A glowing sunrise may adorn.

So trust in God, but do your best,
And with strong endeavour you'll win the test.
For life's a race only few attain,
So even if you fail, try and try again.
Because the entire point of life,
Is within the Eternal Race we strive.

**Victor Ernest Roche**

# TABLE OF CONTENTS

# Prologue: A major discrepancy

### GALAXY ANDROMEDA... Earth Time 2042 CE

The swarms of Nano-bot Javols had destroyed almost every civilization within the galaxy of Andromeda. They met little opposition during their outward thrust from the galactic centre. Their orders were to destroy or enslave all advanced primal species that posed the slightest threat, so they did as ordered by their MasterMind.

What they did not consume immediately was frozen and stored on cold uninhabited moons for later use. Their progress was relentless and their quantities too numerous and powerful to challenge.

Although composed mainly of heavy metals, they also needed biological tissue rich in certain chemicals and metals for their own metabolism. Plants and their offerings were not suitable for that purpose, only those life-forms with blood and minerals pumping through their bodies.

After having ravaged most of the galaxy in the intervening 3000 years, several of their scouts had arrived within the Andromedan Precinct Seven, once the seat of the greatest galactic empire when ruled by the Ancients.

All the planet's original near-human Ancients had been destroyed 3000 years before. The more recent human inhabitants knew nothing about the Javols nor of their rapacious nature.

With the help of the most advanced Osmaronites, the Ancients had set a complex survival plan in operation that would be enacted over the next few millennia.

When the Javols returned 3000 years later to harvest the remnants, several scouts were sent in advance of their main assault troops. They had reported many systems rich and ready for harvesting, but on arrival their rich and live crops of humans had vanished. Somehow they had been warned of the Javols impending visit to decimate their populations.

All the Javols could observe were the remains and ruins of a once thriving civilization. Cities and industries had wilfully been laid waste by their original occupants months before. They searched the local planets but could find no remaining life in all the local systems.

The numerous bird people on planet Coln had also vanished and so did more than ten million on Caefon. Then there was the report of an explosion close to the inter-spacial vertex, also within the perimeter of those systems. That enormous explosion had destroyed more than two hundred thousand Javols, including one of their massive carrier ships, not to mention a small unknown one near the vertex. Somehow, things did not add up.

They searched the system again but could find no trails or evidence of a mass exodus. There had been no reports from their many waves of assault troops now on their way to the local galaxies.

As always, one of the Javols' leaders, Lupher, was not pleased with the data received and called his brother, Dracma, to confer.

'I found a major discrepancy in our harvest records returned from sector fifteen of precinct seven. The population there have simply vanished!' Lupher exclaimed in bewilderment.

'Or they were eaten by one of our more unscrupulous commanders and his underlings. Check staff records to see if their numbers tally. If they have trebled their numbers that can only mean they have eaten a surplus,' Dracma replied, unconcerned.

'That has been done. I have been assured that it is not the case. I don't know how or why, but those primal civilizations have left our galaxy.' Lupher appeared quite concerned. If such behaviour could be attributed to such demonic beings.

'Perhaps it's just an error in the data you received. It could also be due to renegade units or perhaps, that area has already been harvested and records not updated. Our commanders can sometimes be negligent in their duties and responsibilities, to say the least.' Dracma was ripping apart a female's leg. He swallowed the chunks of meat whole, followed by a crimson glass of her chilled blood.

'Now, that really hit the spot!' he burped loud and hard.

'Where are my slave girls. I need entertaining!' In walked a row of Timit women for entertainment and sacrifice. But Lupher continued his discussion.

'That can't be. The systems in question had been scanned by five of our best scouts several months before. Furthermore, most of their cities and towns have been left in ruin. They set explosives before their timely departure to a place or places unknown.'

'And you think they have escaped to one of the local galaxies?' Dracma was now a little more concerned.

'What else is there to believe. A thorough search had uncovered not the slightest fragment of evidence that there had been an exodus to any outside system. Yet they are nowhere to be found,' Lupher replied.

'All you can do, Brother, is give instructions to our intergalactic voyagers and wait.'

'What if they have discovered some new means of travel that can take them to the local galaxies in months instead of centuries. How would our voyagers detect such fast moving craft and if they did, we are able to do very little about their passage before they warned the other galaxies?'

'You worry too much. No primal with basic technologies could have left our galaxy by such means without detection.' Dracma was currently munching on a large human bone trying to get at the rich marrow.

'You remember the abomination. It was not a natural phenomena. We have found large parts of a device used to create it. I'm sure such an engineered wormhole could be used to transport ships to another galaxy,' Lupher replied.

'Yes, but the device was destroyed well before they disappeared. If that is what really happened.'

'Frankly, Brother, I am concerned, and there is the matter of a super-fast ship that exploded in the vicinity of the worlds in question near the abomination. That happened just after our secondary scouts entered their system. I am sure both events are connected. I think there is a greater mind at work here.' Lupher suddenly grabbed a large raw leg from the table and quickly absorbed the meat from it. To be followed by a large mug of cool dark blood.

'Nice vintage. It tastes much better when we starve and dehydrate our Timit Women.'

'Pity we have to sacrifice so many, but we have to break eggs for the proverbial omelette.' Dracma said, but Lupher continued.

'I realise I can be too scrutinising in this matter, but I sense trouble.'

'If, as I perceive, our troops have already eaten the evidence and the primals have left for another galaxy, we should make our own preparations to do likewise. Our home galaxy, Triangulum, should be reward enough for our long stay in this virtual prison and on this desolate place among these microid idiots,' Dracma replied.

'I keep telling you, we cannot leave this place right now! We require the higher orders at the galactic centre to sustain our elemental structures and can only get such energies close to the nucleus of a galaxy. Preferably, within the vicinity of a black hole like this one. We may travel only if we can store and shield the higher and more volatile fifth order energies,' Lupher replied.

'In that case you must get your MasterMind on the task of finding the escapees. Because if they get to their destination, I am sure others will follow and we might never leave this place, ever!' Dracma shouted somewhat enraged.

He signalled to the smallest Timit woman and she came forward. He carefully tore her head off with a single turn of his hand and lifted her greenish body so the spray of her blood was focussed on his mouth. When the spray had died down as her heart stopped beating, he continued sucking at her neck until he drained almost every drop. The other Timit women began to shout.

Gracious Lord! Gracious lord! Gracious lord!.... Please send us to paradise!' Then Lupher did likewise. This time he hugged the body and put much more effort into his meal.

'Brother, we now have these idiot Javols under our control through our MasterMind, which I have created. A task I thought would be impossible, knowing their pathetic dispositions. Now we can use them to conquer the universe for us. Let them eat all remaining primal life throughout the universe if they so wish. We can always have our fair share of sport with the remaining Timit slaves. In the mean time, I can focus my attention on new technologies, including a new intergalactic drive. One that will take us both to Triangulum in safety,' Lupher was blooded by his ravenous feast. All surpluses being devoured by scavenger bugs they carried around on their person. All Javols were contaminated with those pests.

'But Brother, if that happened and every intelligent species got eaten, there would be few pleasures left for us in an almost empty universe, filled with ignorant Timits and disgusting Javols. Then there would be no one to assist us with more advanced technologies. No one to learn and copy from,' Dracma replied, perplexed by his brothers words.

Since the release of both Hexolyte demons from their eternal confinements in their containment tanks by the Javols, they had ruled over them. That accidental encounter was in one of the Patriarch's prison caves in Andromeda.

It was more than two billion years ago when they were trapped and contained and if not for the Javols' visit to that moon and their overwhelming curiosity, they would still have been contained within that prison. Dracma and Lupher had subsequently taken control of the Javols through MasterMind, which was a large computer they designed for that purpose. Using their MasterMind those two clever demonic Hexolytes had deceived the Javols into thinking they were of their own kind.

Because of their manner of escape they were partly Javol in form. Elementals like Hexolytes could only possess other life-forms if not contained within their own shielded tubular metallic body. However those specially designed bodies were not available in Andromeda and perhaps not within the present universe. A universe that had evolved and drastically changed since the Hexolytes existed in number more than two billion years ago.

Since that time the universe had grown much older. The rear higher dimensional elemental energies needed for their sustenance were presently well below their normal levels of survival. At this time they could only survive close to the nucleus of galaxies where the stellar densities and such energies were somewhat higher.

Nevertheless, while using the bodies of Javols that they possessed, they could survive for much longer periods without that type of elemental energy.

Their only real chance of a freer long-term survival was to visit one of their ancient caves in Triangulum and find a suit of encasement. One that would prevent the continual leakage of their elemental energies. However after two billion years the chance of finding such a suit was highly unlikely. In the mean time the Javols would continue their unimpeded conquest of Andromeda and within a few centuries reach the local galaxies, including Galaxies Osmaron (our Milky Way) and Triangulum. On their arrival, decimating and laying waste beautiful planets like Earth and Eden in the process. Nevertheless despite that looming spectre of death and destruction, with the arrival of Lumak the Shadite on Earth and the Ancients on Eden, the chance of their conquest had been inexorably diminished.

The Grand Lord of our part of the universe had put certain plans in motion to secure the survival of all primal life and that plan was being followed by the Plorans and several of his servants called Shadites. Even so, Earth had to undergo a transformation in technology, population and government before she could partake in the final battle against the Javols. That transformation had begun several decades before, with Lumak as the intrepid Professor Jeffery Longhurst. Now it would be Mallory's turn and then the Son of Destiny.

# BOOK 1

# Return of the Patriarchs

CHAPTER 1

# Sylon on Tuil

Earth Time... AD2061

Place... the city of Sylon, on planet Tuil somewhere within the galaxy of Triangulum.

The new city of Sylon on planet Tuil had expanded in leaps and bounds since its inauguration fifty years before. Unlike Pron, which was over a thousand years old, with its constant congestion, unhealthy smog and quaint means of vehicular transport, Sylon had been specifically built around the latest portal technology that was based on many new concepts found on Eden. Eden was presently the seat of power of the vast Solarian Empire within the galaxy of Osmaron, known to many as the Milky Way. That vast empire included many worlds and others were constantly joining. Currently the Tuillians, although in a different galaxy, were keen on joining before the Javol's invasion. Empress Sarah also wanted footholds in Triangulum and Andromeda via long-range portals. That way she could establish a base in anticipation of the future battle on several important fronts against the Javols. Lumak was under similar orders from Grand Lord Gerra, supreme ruler of the seventh part of our universe .

The Tuillians had designed their ancient cities in the ways of their ancestral architects; two thirds underground and the remainder plus additions and extensions towards and above the surface. The most critical areas were deepest underground. That way they avoided the previous high death rate from the occasional meteoric bombardment every third year of their worlds progress about its parent star.

During the past century they had installed many orbiting satellites for early warning and matter diversion. There were also several orbiting platforms with mounted plasma projectors and deep penetration missiles. Those would intercept the meteors and in the process create large super heated craters and jets of matter, to alter their orbits. The smaller ones would be vaporised by missiles. That was if they were detected in time. However they were not always that lucky.

Most of those new technologies they had gained from the Octans in Osmaron. Presently they were the real technologists of the Shadites who were committed to assist worlds like Tuil from impending disaster. Lord Faemon, the Ploran, was presently in charge of that side of business within the Greater Purpose.

As a result, all those recent introduced technological measures now protected Tuil from those past dangers, making it possible for its civilizations to live on their planet's surface even during the third year of the expected bombardments.

'Sire, we have received warning of a meteor in sector nine approaching from deep space,' Nogad informed through implants.

'Set seven scanners to keep an eye on its current position and I want a complete analysis in composition, spin, and approaching velocity. Set the primary drones to intercept at one hour before critical distance,' Cleman replied, unperturbed.

'All data has been entered in the targeting computer,' Nogad continued, while Cleman checked the flat screen monitor at his position.

'Dam it! Five croes (6 miles) across, It's as big as Mount Seribos. And 100,000 croesons (110000 miles per hour). If she strikes, that monster will put pay to most life on our world,' said Cleman, scratching his forehead in distress.

'Sire, we have little or no choices. It's too massive for our usual weapons. They will not put a significant dent on that moonlet,' Nogad informed after completing some minor calculations on his terminal.

'But Sire, we have never used that weapon before. I'm not sure it will work!'

'Do we have a choice?' Cleman replied.

'This is definitely not a normal one. We've never before registered one with such a high velocity before. Not in the last 1000 creons (1600 years). I wander where it came from?' he said still scratching his forehead.

'Sire, it's approaching critical distance. Shall I give the order,' Nogad said.

'I suppose you'll have to, it's our only choice,' Cleman replied. Then Nogad pressed a red button on his panel and the secondary screen came to life showing the large lump of rock rotating about a common axis and determined to do the most damage to his world below. It followed its course with many other companions, some as large as buildings. The large space station on which they stood began to rotate and move to a more suitable position in space. It had to be in line with the trajectory of the target to be most effective and at light speed it soon arrived at that optimum position.

'We are on target, Sire!'

'Weapons primed and ready to fire. Graviton beams ready on primary station to collect debris!' the screen said.

'I Think it's time I said a prayer in case things went wrong and there is no need for those beneath us to know about the evil one that approaches,' Cleman advised.

Then he knelt for prayer, but in silence. Suddenly the orbiting station rocked and objects flew about everywhere. She was hit by a smaller part that lay waste the main control room. Nogad was thrown across the room and Cleman was left with a large gash on his right side from flying debris.

'Go, Nogad! Go and do it manually. You are the only one left. You must save all our lives!' he said and passed out. As he felt the air sucked out of his lungs he forced himself and entered a small sealed room where he painfully squeezed his body into a sealed suit.

Nogad was damaged but knew in such a situation his life was unimportant. Even at the risk of his own survival, he realized he had no time to waste. He slid down the almost vertical stairwell and entered the master control room. That weapon was supposed to be automatic, but he found a transparent container with another red button to be used in emergencies. He broke the glass and pressed the button just in time. There was a massive roar which shook the station and in an instant the large moonlet was as hot as the centre of a star. It and its companions had vaporised in an enormous explosion. Then once more everything went still, including those on that faithful lookout station.

'Thank God for that unknown weapon! Thank God for those incredible Shadites like Lumak and Gemmi!' Nogad whispered as he fainted from his wounds.

That accident occurred several years before and Lumak remembered he was the first one on the scene to rescue Nogad. But no other individuals on that station had survived that faithful day. It was always a risk faced when placed in the path of such bodies. They always followed with companions and some moved quicker than the target. That is what the Gravitons were used for, to alter the course of the lighter objects away from the main path. Lumak saw the weakness in their system and had modified their main weapons to include his own designs. After that, they never had the same problems again. He had also introduced a range of other technologies to that world.

Since then they had utilized micro robotics in many of their cities' functions and utilities, making the new environments more comfortable and pleasant for its many citizens. However, only their better citizens were allowed within its heavily secured enclosures, and those most trusted senior members of their society were issued with special portal passes for that purpose.

Sylon had been constructed within a transparent and sealed dome, acquiring virtually nil pollution from the filthy atmosphere of the industrial planet outside.

It was the first dome city to be built in that manner and if found satisfactory, the process would be replicated throughout the planet. Such dome habitats would be built everywhere, until all its occupants, including wild life, were isolated from the poisonous atmosphere. Then the complete biosphere would be slowly cleansed and detoxified over a period of several generations.

The gigantic machines for that purpose were already being constructed on designated sites throughout the planet. After their completion, almost all industrial processes would be sited elsewhere on barren worlds. For such were the process of planetary re-modelling when large indigenous populations could not be evacuated elsewhere.

The new portal technologies had allowed them a way out of their problems of industrial pollution. With Lumak's ingenuity and assistance, they were finally able to transpose their operations to many regions of space well within their lifetimes.

Unlike Earth's conversion, which had mainly failed because of its severe overpopulation, their planetary ruler, Toccor IV, passed laws prohibiting any form of unprotected coupling for the purposes of procreation. By so doing, only those with a procreation license could produce offspring.

The penalty for breaking that law was banishment to the hostile penal mining world of Tribor IV within their system. That method of birth control was preferable to seeding their planet's environment with bio-engineered bacteria as with the Terminal Disease on Earth, or the use of sterility drugs. Everyone of age would be issued protective kits and informants given extra privileges.

His people would be judiciously informed of all the facts and lawbreakers would swiftly suffer the consequences of their impetuous actions. It was during that time that they were informed of the dreaded Javols and that gory transmission further shocked them into a correct decision.

Once the majority accepted their present course, the process of population reduction would continue until there was a planetary safe balance. During that period some parent-able couples would be randomly selected for procreation, giving every obedient family the same chance.


## GEMMI DOFF

Shadite Gemmi Doff surveyed her new apartment in Sylon and was amazed by its many spaces, but bemused by all the modern appliances and equipment. She strolled unto the circular cushion and felt more comfortable than she had been for ages. She had only recently arrived to her home world from yet another mission for her Grand Lord.

She was presently a Grade 3 Shadite and had been assigned to many important missions for the Greater Purpose, including the present one on her home world. Of all, the most memorable was with Lumak and Plato. That was during the evacuation of the Feloween from their nova catastrophe on Misoran II to Romera IV. Although she had met Lumak several times since, he had always been on urgent missions.

She pondered those thoughts and soon fell into deep slumber. Then she found herself in a falling nightmare. Just before she crashed unto the ground below, there was a burring noise in her head which took her out of sleep. She realized it was her brain implants informing her of an incoming call. She allowed the communication, while struggling from her bench to select her favourite beverage for that time of day.

'I must have been under for five hours. I didn't realize I was so tired,' she thought.

'Gemmi! It's me, Lumak. I decided to pay you a short visit. Nothing urgent, but I might need your assistance for something important,' he said and she was utterly surprised. After all, she hadn't seen him in years.

'Lumak! What a pleasant surprise. I was just thinking of you and Plato, during the Misoran tragedy. I'm in my new place, so make it soon,' she said and down-loaded the address information.

His incredible ship materialized in a myriad of multi-coloured lights just outside the main building and many of its brave local inhabitants, including their little children, went to view the strange inexplicable occurrence. Soon there was a large crowd of Speell on the scene to observe and comment on the strange aberration.

They were a very inquisitive race and relished a journey into the unknown. However, the shock of the alien human figure walking through the walls of a ship without a doorway was to them truly gross and beyond reality. Many took to their multiple heels from that unexpected shock.

Since changing into the human form many decades before, Lumak had adopted that one on a more permanent basis. He didn't relish the process of changing into an alien form every time he visited a different world. There was also the relearning of all those sensual perceptions and the evolved modes of travel and manipulation. He would only forego those transformations if the environment was not a natural one and he required those changes to survive like its inhabitants over a lengthy period.

He knew their language well, so he released his hood behind his neck to reveal his human features and called them to him.

'My beloved friends of Sylon, there is no need for fear. I am Shadite, and I am here to visit an old friend. She is Siend Gemmi Doff, and I am told she lives within this local building,' he said.

'He is Shadite?' one of the local ones shouted and many began to murmur amount themselves.

'Where is he from?' shouted another.

'I am from the galaxy you call Fondle, and we call Osmaron,' Lumak replied.

'All the way form Fondle. Is that really possible?' the first one exclaimed.

They halted their progress in the direction away from the ship and began to get close to observe the strange alien form.

They had heard of the Shadites and knew they were messengers of a higher order within the universe. Anyway, that is what they were thought in school, but other than their own Gemmi Doff, they had never seen such a strange one before.

After spending time with the large crowd and answering their many questions, he took a local portal and were transferred to Gemmi Doff's apartment.

'Woo... What a surprise! A human surprise!' Gemmi Doff greeted. Despite her initial foreboding, she had grown used to the human form over the years. She herself had tried it during her visit to Eden in Osmaron, for her implants, and had found it quite acceptable.

Seeing him completely vertical, while being horizontal in her large caterpillar-like form, made her think how dissimilar both species were. Yet, the human one was a lot simpler and being vertical, found it a lot less cumbersome in getting about. Also, they took up a lot less space in crowds. Yet their voices and some facial features were similar.

'We have an important trip ahead of us. For that one you must become human again. I shall take you to Eden, where you will be transformed and briefed. From what little I have been told, your galaxy and its peoples are in immediate danger,' he said. She closely observed his human features and realized he was not his usually happy disposition.

'That bad, eh!' she replied.

'Do you remember that time we visited the barren world of Riporan III? It was the planet with the strange Hexolyte underground installations,' he said.

'Yes! I do! It was the one with the good demons, and I wanted to complete that mission to see where it led,' she replied.

'I said we would take up that quest again, at some future time when we were not on urgent missions. I have now been given the go-ahead by our Grand Lord himself and after all this time, would like you to be my historian and archaeologist once again. Plato is also part of this campaign and will join us later, after he has completed his current mission,' Lumak said.

'Well, my humble person is at your command, Sire. But I must first inform my cousin Prann. He can take over in my absence,' she replied, in her usual humorous manner.


Gemmi knew she would be very well cared for at Sarah's palace, as on her previous visit. But she took along a few carvings and perfumes as gifts. Anything else would not have been relevant in her new human form.

Several hours later they arrived in the palace grounds on Eden and were received by Sarah.

After a brief rest, she was taken to the Macron, Mac, where she was transformed into a most beautiful woman with more advanced brain implants.

## CHAPTER 2

# The ancient Hexolyte base

It was not long before Lumak and Gemmi were summoned to the beautiful diamond satellite of Little Osmaron to be in the presence of the Grand Lord of the seventh part of the known universe. They transposed through the magnificent crystal enclosure and found themselves in a brilliantly lit room. Presently that satellite moonlet orbited planet Eden and remained perched above Eden City.

'I brought you here to inform you of certain changes within the master plan. One of the Javols leaders, the Demon Hexolyte, Dracma, is on his way to Triangulum with the intention of reviving his kind to plague the universe once again. He will use whatever means available for that purpose. You are to locate all their main bases within the local galaxies and install hidden H-wave communicators so that their progress may be monitored,'

'Will do, My Lord!' Lumak replied.

'I have decided to promote you, Gemmi Doff, to grade 2. You may leave your original cloak and collect your new one on your way out.' The brilliance faded, leaving them in a different room with a large table on which was a black container. She removed her original cloak with hesitation and fitted the new and more advanced one to her human person. Those black cloaks had the powers to adjust themselves to the shape of any life-form.

The Grand Lord realized how attached Shadites were to their old cloaks, so they were kept within a special museum within the orbiting crystal city of Little Osmaron, which formed a major part of the Greater Mind.

They filled their special super fast reconnaissance and surveillance ship with all the provisions it could hold and were on their way back to Galaxy Triangulum. This time they headed directly to its nucleus to investigate a red dwarf. That one had been pinpointed on the alien's map several decades before during a previous excavation.

'How do you feel with your new body and its superior implants,' Lumak asked, knowing it would have taken several days for her to recover from the system shock and get used to her new human body.

'Just a little strange and groggy. I'm afraid, this time it's more intense. I'll need some more sleep than anticipated, so I hope you don't mind if I remain inactive for a little while. Otherwise I might not be of much use to you for a couple days or so,' she replied.

'Using just LPDs, it will take us three days to get to where we are going and this ship is on automatic, so you can sleep as long as you wish. When we get to our destination I will give you a nudge. I have placed you in virtual, so enjoy some restful music and images with a little tranquillity while you rest,' he said and she nodded and fell fast asleep, to be subconsciously awakened into a virtual world of an Alice-in-Wonderland adventure.

She had taken special booster drugs to speed the process of humanization, but those also had the side effect of making its subjects sleep during the re-configuration and learning process. However, the virtual program was also designed to enhance the drugs by placing her new human mind in simulated adventures, many of which were survival oriented. Original herbivores and non-predatory life-forms always had problems when changing to predatory types like humans. It was partly to do with the balance of hormones in such systems. However, once the change was made they grew to like the social experiences in that body format.

Lumak had on board an analytical computer that he programmed for the specific purpose of plotting that area of the universe in space and in time. By so doing, he could find the precise location of any known stellar body up to tens of billions of years in the past.

That computer was linked to the ship's own navigation computer and Lumak's brain implants.

After another three days, they arrived at their destination within the nucleus of Triangulum.

'You can have it! You Hexolyte bastards!' Gemmi shouted, with sweat pouring from her face. But she slowly opened her eyes to view the strange cabin with Lumak at its controls.

'Sorry captain. I just had a fight with a few Javols and a couple Hexes. You took the Javols out and I terminated their superiors,' she added.

'Ah! You are finally back with us. Those were the final images in your conversion program. They were meant to kick start you back into the real human world,' he replied, smiling. She awoke from her deep sleep with much better coordination and an appetite to match. Her implants were also more finely tuned and could now be linked with the ship's computer. Feeling somewhat guilty for her absence, she decided to assist, but she soon found there was nothing to do with Lumak's brand of advanced technology.

'How long have I been under?' she enquired, still in a slight daze.

'Only two days. We have about another to go,' he replied, while she viewed the enormous galactic bulge through her linked implants.

'Commander, do you think there is intelligent life in this part of the galaxy?' she enquired.

'It wont be natural. The radiation levels out here are far too intense for natural evolution. Too many heavy nuclei and cosmic rays shooting about. Any life out here will be robotic, microid or perhaps an elemental form.

Javols would relish this part of the galaxy. However, they also require a constant supply of primal life for their sustenance. So they would prefer an area just outside the nucleus. But they are also able to breed other life-forms in isolation, so even this location would not stop them.

'You know, evolution has very little to do with random radiation, which if anything, impedes the process. Evolution has purpose and is more to do with the will of a self-aware entity, desperately wanting a specific change to enhance its survival causation, while being driven by environmental changes. It might take numerous generations to attain a specific goal and pass it, but it is never random. Well, not random in the long term. If a condition is not suitable for us we will not remain under those conditions but move to another more acceptable environment. That applies to all life-forms, even microbes. They will continually move away to more acceptable environments and will themselves to adapt. Therefore, it's a strong will that matters.

'It's like a constant wanting to climb a mountain or fly from branch to branch. Only those specific muscles and bones would be developed and shaped for that purpose. Radiation could not assist such a process because the parts of their genes relevant to those muscles and bones would not be specifically targeted by random radiation. That wanting, to get away from a predator or even to get a prey, would over many millennia change the life-form into a more suitable type for that wanting during its survival causation.

'A planet does not evolve life. Only life evolves life. A dead planet, even with an active atmosphere, will always remain a dead planet. However, the moment life is introduced unto that world evolution will begin. Life is usually introduce when certain building blocks like proteins and nucleic acids fall unto the planet from outer space when the planet is young and relatively stable. The stellar processes involved are quite complex. Nevertheless, this incredible process tells us that every complex living thing holds a special living entity within its person which makes it self-aware.

'In the case of prey and predator. The prey will sense its natural enemy and attempt to device a better method of survival, by better protection and defence and finding a better means of escape. The predator will devise better weapons and skills to locate and consume its prey. By so doing, a balance is met and both prey and predator survives together and in balance,' Lumak said, while Gemmi listened attentively.

'If that is the case, where did the original life come from to seed the planet and begin the process?' she asked.

'Like the heavier elements, the building blocks of cosmic life begins with a supernova or a giant star blowing off parts of its atmosphere. You know, giant stars exist as life givers. Anyway, during that time many of the heavier nuclei come together to form complex proteins and nucleic acids. Those in their many variety are distributed throughout space and are scattered everywhere within the galaxies by cosmic winds, meteors and comets to seed all worlds. However, only suitable parent worlds with a correct environment can nurture primal life,' he replied.

'Where does the entity come from,' she asked, out of curiosity.

'Some think that a living entity is an indestructible bubble of space-time, which existed since the beginning of the Cosmos. They were the first building blocks of the Cosmos, which encompasses and permeates all things, being inter-dimensional. It was during that time that order came to exist out of chaos. That was even before matter and time existed. So you see, our innermost beings or identities are the oldest living entities in the Cosmos. Nevertheless, there are numerous identities and many that are non-corporeal exist within what we call the Nexos. However, many also exist within the City of Gohenna or Goh. Every thing that exist and can be given a name has an Identity associated with it.

'To further understand, you must think of an entity as a prime number. A number is unique in that it cannot be removed or destroyed. Can you destroy the number 4. If you could, no one would be able to add 2 and 2 to make 4. As a matter of fact, the whole system of numbers would collapse.

'In a similar manner, an Identity is unique and cannot be destroyed, but its inter-dimensional matrix can be enhanced through experience. That is because, there are numerous amounts of such individual entities in a body, thus forming the complete life force. Once they form a suitable cognitive matrix, the spirit in that form can continue its explorations to eternity. Like the numerical system of numbers, every Identity in the universe is needed to make it complete.

'You should further realize, that the whole Cosmos is composed of Identities and groups of Identities. Whether they be groups of atoms to form a particular substance or a group of sub-atomic particles to form an atom, and all those will have their own Identities. Since every Identity is unique, only one type of the same can ever exist within the Cosmos. That is why everyone of us are so unique. Even if an identical clone was made of you at this moment, your Identity would not be in it and it will have its own identity, simply because every atom in its body will be different to yours.

'Space is filled with visible matter and a similar amount of invisible entities which cling to ordered strains of matter. The more ordered, the more they cling. So I suppose certain types must prefer the symmetry of a DNA chain. Apparently, because of their self-awareness, there is an inbuilt desire to explore and modify. So evolution must begin with the smallest protein chains.

'Further, such an Entity or Identity has the strange ability to modify its environment by a strong desire or wanting. You know, all life is capable of altering the chaotic nodes of matter by thought. This is also the process used in evolution, a form of altering ones own matter to enhance its survival causation. In other words since all matter is composed of waves, something only becomes real by observation. Therefore, because of those reasons we exists within our own Virtual Universes, Time Lines and Space-Times,' he replied and she was surprised by his detailed knowledge of such unknowns. Their small ship suddenly appeared above the planet but did not release its shields to become visible.

'We must not leave evidence of our presence on any of the worlds we visit. That means we cannot disturb anything, not even the dust within their installations.'

'Whatever you say, Boss!' she replied, nervously, but he continued while she listened.

'Our cloaks must be fully vectored and surveillance units placed withing solid rock or within the walls of their enclosures.

These small surveillance units are held within specially phased containers which will materialize minutes after they are activated. Three will be placed within each installation, although only one is required. Then we place micro probes in orbit about this world to relay the information.

'Because Hexolytes do not use electromagnetics, all links from their installations to our orbiting probes will be of that type. However, the probes are both electromagnetic and H-wave.

'Once the probes are initiated, they will transmit all received data to one of several randomly selected repeaters. That way, they will not be able to locate any of our collection bases within this galaxy. The ancient Patriarch's bases must also be probed in a similar manner,' Lumak advised.

'Ok, Boss. Lets do the work!' she replied and they both vectored their cloaks and floated out of the ship's wall towards the planet below. Being almost massless and unaffected by the remaining atmosphere of the planet, meant the special LPDs could automatically propel them at incredible speed toward their destination.

They selected a warmer area of the frozen planet. That area was the most turbulent and with a large gradient in temperature. Those conditions were good evidence of an ancient underground fusion reactor that utilized hot plasma from the planet's core. That method was common with Hexolyte bases, since such installations tended to utilized hot matter for the fabrication of atomic elements used in manufacture and repairs of their maintenance robots.


'Be careful! Parts of their bases can be booby-trapped, so seal yourself into your suit!' Lumak advised through her implants. Anticipating the worst, she had already selected that mode.

Lumak soon located the main door to the outer cave. That entrance was on a steep rock face overhanging the sunken plateau. The flat rectangular area of grey sand he called the sunken sea, but there was no water in that area, just a dense mist that covered a thick layer of sand.

On analysis, the sand was found to contain particles of debris from an ancient city. Over the aeons it had been reduced by the turbulent weather into a wavy surface of thin sand.

'To avoid any of their more subtle traps, I think we should follow their natural routes and entrances until we find the door to their main control room,' Lumak said.

She followed him until they came upon the massive door with a perfectly flat surface, but with no orifices, handles or projections. It reminded her of the similar one they had encountered on Riporan III and she cringed with horror when she remembered the sight of the rows of human skeletons on the other side of that door. Not to mention her experience with the demon Neramon probing her mind. However, she was now Shadite and could introduce a mental block to prevent that problem.

From previous knowledge, Lumak knew the code they used for

such locks and had fabricated a suitable electro-magnetic key.

He pointed the small device, pressed a button, the catch released and the door slid opened vertically. That was the only way they could enter without tripping the many sensors. After all, it would have been the natural route taken by any one of its previous occupants. However, Lumak and Gemmi would have to normalize their bodies before entering and vectorize once inside. While normalized, they would be vulnerable, so only one would enter and vectorize before signalling the other at the rear. As always, Lumak took the lead while a very nervous Gemmi followed at the rear.

Without disturbing any of the local debris just inside the door, he vectorized and Gemmi followed in his steps precisely. She was a trained Shadite and knew the processes involved.

That entrance led into a small area with three corridors that diverged into the distance. From what they could observe, that underground facility was endless, with an assortment of many containment tanks and numerous connecting pipes of all shapes and sizes. At that level there was no illumination.

Lumak viewed its immensity in infrared with awe and realized it was probably the main part of their universal factory for mass-producing Hexolyte soldiers. At least that was their intentions before their plans were disrupted by the Patriarch Masters aeons ago.

Nevertheless, despite its dormancy, that base had been kept in better condition than the others visited. Judging from the cleanliness of the place, it had an active contingence of robots that came alive frequently to service the equipment and their environment. Such robots were advanced enough to create and replace other robots or even to alter their designs to more efficient models.

'We must locate their main portal. Judging from the way the rows are organized, it could be directly below us, but we should enter via their trap-door. There is usually at least one on every level,' he said.

After an extensive search at that level, they found the hidden door. It was on the same level as the floor and relied on two near human weights on either side in order to be released. They had to normalize and face the dangers of whatever traps had been set in that area.

When they entered that area there was a whir as the trap-door lifted and the area began to move beneath their feet. That whole area moved downwards to the next level and stopped. Despite the scare, they did not re-vectorize their cloaks in case the process relied on their joint weights, but did when the platform completed its descent. So far they had encountered no booby traps in that part of the building. Perhaps it was because those areas were more frequently used by personnel and robots. At least those areas were dimly lit.

They took the local stairs to yet another level and found themselves close to one of the ancient hexagram portals. It was a large area with the floor surface engraved with the hexagram and circles. Above their heads were the many rods and amplifiers used by such ancient portals. There were several attachments that linked with the portal to receive material or make connection to other similar portals on distant worlds. All being part of a massive production plant, perhaps intergalactic in scope.

'This place is more extensive and larger than any of our previous visits. I hope there are no more of their elemental demons down here,' Gemmi said, but Lumak did not reply.

They approached the first of many hexagram circles along the straight and narrow middle path. That one led as far as the eyes could see. The circle they beheld were enclosed by five small tanks along its outer periphery. Several lines radiated from the centre to the tanks and cris-crossed into the sign of a star. On either side of the large circle were massive pillars which could be circumvented by small zig-zag routes around them. Those two routes bypassed the circle but were not the easiest. The shortest and easiest path was directly through the centre of the circle.

## CHAPTER 3

# Within the limits of Hades

Their cloaks were fully phased, making them immune from any physical dangers, so they decided to take the easiest of the three routes which led directly through the pentagram. The moment they entered that area it became active and they found their forms being pulled by an irresistible force into the unknown. For a brief moment they were in complete darkness.

'I don't know where this is going to take us, but we must always remain close together!' Lumak shouted through his implants. He then retrieved a climbing line from his cloak and quickly linked it with hers. The vertex was long and dark and during their transit through it to places unknown they were virtually helpless.

On arrival they came to a sudden stop on a firmer surface within several large pillars. The blackness became a reddish sky with many flames and fires burning in the distant horizon. Yet, the place was not alive. No life energy could be detected anywhere, not even their own.

'Where do you think we are?' Gemmi inquired.

'One thing I know, it's no where I've been before. This place does not appear to abide by our natural laws. It could be another completely different universe and one where life hasn't yet evolved,' Lumak replied.

While they walked in the opposite direction, the fires diminished and they found themselves in an ancient place or city. But the strange city contained boxlike buildings, many of which were twisted and contorted, and was devoid of all life. The many stacked box-like enclosures were of all shapes and sizes. Within the distance they could observe several dragons blowing what appeared to be blue flames of light at others. Using their inbuilt LPDs, Lumak and Gemmi took to the air and were on the way to where the dragons were. However, they took cover behind a large square pillar until that area became uncomfortable. Then they decided to move again. This time they were exposed to all and sundry.

'Keep close to me. We should try to make it to the hills yonder,' he advised through implants.


A large and fearful dragon-like creature flew towards them from another direction and silently settled on the route in front of them, blocking their path and halting their progress.

'If you wish to survive their chambers of pain, quickly get on my back!' it yelled. Utterly confused by all the strange occurrences about them, they mounted its back. After passing many large mountain ranges, it approached a cave that was sited close to the apex of the largest peak. That cave could not be seen while the dragon was in the air above the mountain.

Within that cave was many of the dragon-like creatures, but there were a few aliens and humans. Lumak soon realized that he could no more communicate with Gemmi, so he quickly released his hood and attempted to breathe the air. After sampling and testing, he gestured to Gemmi and she released hers.

The dragons spoke without moving their lips.

'I am Algo.

'You have been transposed to a place between universes. This is a link between ours and yours and a type of prison created by our superiors. Only the vilest of creatures are placed here, within the shadows of Hades. This place was created at the beginning of time by our forefathers, better known to you as the Mesotrenes. We are what you would consider the better part of our species and are now considered dangerous rebels by our so-called masters,' the creature, Algo, said.

'I am Melfa,' continued another more powerful dragon with a bluish crest.

'You are lucky we sensed and caught you in time or you would have0 surely been devoured by Kator. He is in charge of this place and will shortly be searching for you and your companion. He can sense all new entities within this plenum and no one ever survives his gaze. However, you will be quite safe with us for now,' Melfa added.

'I am Lumak, and this is Gemmi my close companion. We are also of the good part of our universe. That part we call the

Greater Purpose and we stand for life, freedom, and order within the Cosmos, if those attributes also hold in this place. We were investigating one of the Hexolyte bases within one of our galaxies and found ourselves falling within this trap. Could you tell us of a way out?' he said. There was a deep silence, then Algo spoke.

'To our knowledge, there is no way out of this cursed place or we would have taken it aeons ago. This scenario is constantly changing. Whatever plans were made seconds ago will not hold in the future. The fabric of this place will soon change to another, so it is not easy to create a fixed and stable form from its substance. Further, within this realm, time constantly repeats itself in one continuous loop. However, the temporal loops, although continuous, will exhibit slight variation to cope with new unexpected changes within this continuum.

'Our cave here appears to remain constant in time only because of a spacial generator. This device also prevents our enemies from locating us, because it shrinks our space and places us ahead of our enemies in time, but we are not completely outside of the temporal loop. Everyone of us wears the special headband which links our bodies with the device and to our own engineered continuum,' he said.

Lumak was surprised by his present ordeal. He had no idea that the Mesotrenes were dragons who existed in another, but not parallel universe. Neither did he know that the majority were not nice creatures. Their universe appeared to be the exact opposite of all things natural. With its own type of order. Even the substance of that plane was different, with the ability to shrink and enlarge.

When their universe clashed with ours many aeons ago, they had obviously created a hyper-spatial link between both universes, but it had since been removed from their end as part of an ancient agreement with our seventh universe.

During that period of upheaval and their negative effect on our seventh universe, they were given the necessary technologies to enhance their survival and asked to move on. But they were very ancient and may have existed in a very strange universe which made them little suited to ours. Since the Grand Lord ruled the seventh part of all seven universes, Lumak thought that Grand Lord Gerra would be somewhere involved in the bigger picture. However, that place called Hades was within the sixth part of the sixth universe and was not under his lord's jurisdiction.

'It appears that a link still remain between our universe and yours, but not the other way around. I wonder why that is the case,' Gemmi asked.

'It was a condition met for services rendered many aeons ago. However, there was no requirement to remove the link at your end. Nevertheless, others may have found a way to use it for their own purpose,' Algo said and licked his leathery lips with his forked tongue, as if to lubricate them.

'Perhaps it might be possible to re-establish a link at our end for your safety. Since it appears to me that we fight a common foe. At least, it will release you from eternal bondage. Is there others like us on this in-between world?' Lumak asked.

'Since the beginning, many have been sent here, but few like you. Some have found ways to survive and others were absorbed into the whole. However, ones like you still remain within Hades. They are too powerful for Kator and have built their own defences against him and his hordes,' Algo said.

'Where do you think they came from?' Gemmi asked.

'I don't know. Many could have used this place as a type of eternal prison from which no one could ever return,' Melfa replied.

'Can you take us there. I mean, to the ones like us,' Gemmi inquired.

'They will not accept outsiders. They trust no one. Not even us. That is the reason why they have survived this long,' Melfa said.

'Is it possible to communicate with them?' Lumak asked.

'Only if we share the same time and space. That will mean releasing our spacial generators, and leaving us open to the mercies of Kator and his demonic hordes. Only then can you communicate telepathically with them through one of us,' Algo said.

'In that case, let us assist you towards our common goals and perhaps in a little time we shall find an answer to our dilemma,'

Lumak replied and they agreed.

Both were taken to a lower level within the apparently large cavern within the mountain. Then they were issued their own neck-bands which linked them to the causal generators. That way they would exist just outside of Hades time and space, but with the occasion phased cyclic temporal connection at the start of each time cycle.

## CHAPTER 4

# Jot, the Inter-dimensional Entity

Jot had existed within Lumak's mind since their meeting decades before. That strange occurrence took place while on his way to rescue the Feloween. After his wanderings from his own dimension, Jot was cast out from amongst his own entities because of irreversible changes to his being. That was due to his acquiring certain dimensional viral attributes that he had unknowingly collected during his wanderings outside of his domain. Like any contagious virus, those irreversible changes could have become dangerous to his own kind if he remained among them.

After rescuing Lumak from their strange dimension, the only way he could survive in the material universe was to possess part of Lumak's mind. However, although Lumak had given the entity permission, he had hypnotized Lumak into thinking he did not exist. So Lumak awoke thinking it was just a dream. However, since that time he had assisted Lumak in many of his scientific projects without his knowledge.

Jot had learnt much over the decades and because of his capabilities, knew infinitely more than Lumak about inter-dimensional structures or the lack of them. Because of the strange qualities of their new dimension, Jot could now survive outside of Lumak's person.

To make himself visible, he became a small point of light which increased in intensity to a small radiant blue ball. He bobbed up and down on the flat surface of rock they used for a table. He floated through Lumak's head and in an instant Lumak knew who he was.

'Jot, what are you doing here?' Lumak asked and Gemmi looked at the strange light on Lumak's head with utter surprise.

'Do you both know each other?' she asked, perplexed.

'I met him before I arrived on Trom. That was during the evacuation of the Feloween. It's a long story and I will tell you all about it one day,' Lumak replied, but he had his mind on more important thoughts.

Foremost in Lumak's mind was how to find a way out of the strange in-between world. If only he could communicate with others like him from his own universe? If those other humans in Hades could resist Kator and his hordes, also meant they were superior beings and could aid in their release from the Hexolytes' super-trap. But if they were that good, wouldn't they have taken the quickest route out of their eternal prison long ago. Or had they chosen the Hades path for themselves, because it was safer than some other choice. Lumak pondered those ideas until a thought began to grow in his mind.

'I've got it! I've got it! I think I have found a way out of here,' the thought said and by its mode and inclination he knew it was his old friend, Jot.

'What have you found, my friend?' Lumak asked.

'This place is between universes, which are themselves different planes of existence. It shares the laws and substance of both, albeit in a more chaotic manner. Being intermixed, their effects are reflected in the strange environment observed within this sub-plane called Hades. By unravelling and isolating those attributes, it will be possible to escape.'

'Are you sure?'

'Yes! It should be possible to isolate substances here of our real universe. Then with that substance we can create an environment similar to our own universe which is very different to this one. By so doing, we will be rejected by this one. In a not too dissimilar manner in the way I was rejected from mine,' Jot said and Lumak smiled at the ingenuity of his little pal.

'That's an intriguing hypothesis, but risky. What if the ship blows up during the process of rejection,' Lumak replied.

'That is not possible. If it blows up, even more unwanted material will be present and the numerous fragments would be infinitely more difficult to remove from the system. Such substances cannot be created or destroyed, only transferred to other places and certain substances will follow the more natural course to blend with others of their own kind,' Jot said. Lumak was finally convinced that Jot was on the correct track in finding a way of escape.

'Could you get Algo and his friends to design such a device?' Lumak asked.

'I am sure I can, with what little I've learnt from their type of technologies,' Jot replied.

'Well if you can do this, Pal, you will have me as your best friend for eternity.

'However, I must locate the others from our universe before we can leave this place,' Lumak replied.

Because their human form hadn't changed significantly since their arrival, Lumak and Gemmi thought the only way they could make contact with the other humans was to merge with the original Hades and take their chances with Kator and his hordes. However, once that step was taken they could only find Algo and his other companions again by merging with their space-time coordinates. That meant he had to take along an arm-band for the convertor that would be linked at the appropriate time. He also realised that all those in the proximity of the arm-band would be similarly transposed to the new temporal parameters. Nevertheless, only when they approached the position of the cave could they be converted to the new microscopic dimensions.

They informed their companions of their intentions and leapt towards the southern regions. That was the place where the humans they sort would be found amidst many dangers. Apparently, their fortress occupied the southern part or south polar region of that strange in-between world. Their few Mesotrene enemies occupied the northern or northern hemisphere and Kator, its northern polar regions.

The world itself was barely ten kilometres in diameter. Worlds within the Mesotrene universe were somewhat smaller and there were no stars or galaxies, just planetoids of immense mass floating about in an ocean of a less dense and transparent medium. At lease that was what Lumak and Gemmi observed.

Beyond the spacial curtain of the in-between dimension of Hades were those cratered worlds that extended to infinity. Mesotrenes existed in a myriad of different sizes within that universe, for that was the only species that could evolve within its strange domains, and they took sustenance directly from the medium while travelling through its vastness. Yet, they were ancient and each species attained the knowledge of all others at the time of birth. It was as if the universe itself was a living entity and the perpetual ocean was a multiple of substances, including an interface for the universal mind.

There was a strong telepathic link between them and the universal medium, which permeated everything for its own survival causation.

'Siend, I never thought such a place could ever exist out of the weirdest nightmares and here we are,' Gemmi complained.

'I must agree, it's one of those experiences better done without, but we Shadites are constantly tested,' Lumak replied.

Lumak wondered about the strangeness of that world and could not fathom its depths. Neither did he attempt that course of action in earnest, because the process sickened and irritated him. After all, the environment was so utterly boring to any creature that needed the experience of beauty and variation in all their many shades. However, the Mesotrene's real universe existed within their minds. They were highly creative and had conceived their own universe within a world of abstraction. That was because, in their real universe they had little else to do or appreciate.

Jot gave instructions to the friendly dragons for the types of enclosures he wanted and they were built in sections. The special field convertors were designed to change one of the structures to the precise material of the seventh universe. A second one of equivalent mass was to be configured in a different manner. That one would be left behind as its doppelganger. Only in that way could their bodies be transferred safely to their home dimension.

With spiritual entities like Jot, the process did not matter, because he was almost compatible with both universes and for long enough periods. Nevertheless, he could not survive within the seventh universe on his own for very long without Lumak's assistance.

'Do you think the device will be ready by our return,' Lumak inquired.

'It will be ready by anytime when you return. This is because you will be outside of our time and we can adjust our temporal loop to contain those events,' Algo said.

 'Stranger and stranger!' Gemmi replied and left their presence.

## CHAPTER 5

# Passage through Hades

Lumak felt completely helpless in the in-between dimension of Hades. It was apparent from the time of their arrival, that his Shadite's Cloak, including all his weapons had stopped functioning. And that was not all, their forms were slowly changing to the stronger elements of that strange dimension.

The more natural dragons of that plane were favoured with a bluish flame, which they utilized to reduce their enemies. By blowing the flame on their victims something was taken from them and they reduced in size. Whatever it was, gave the larger creatures greater powers over their minions. But they never carried the process to termination, for their victims were better alive than dead. After all, they could grow again and be further harvested, while they in turn would harvest those beneath them, ad infinitum. That was the only way they took real power from that dimension. But they could also draw energy from the strange spacial substance that propagated everywhere. Occasionally a dragon would acquire greater powers by chance and begin to dominate the others. That process of prey and predator within that singular type of species must have continued to eternity.

They had each been handed a special net by Algo.

'This will protect you for a while as you travel southward. It will prevent them from extracting your elemental energies. Try not to get too close to the large ones. Their powerful breath can tear the net and constant attacks will diminish its protection. When you approach the southern fortress, switch the communicator fully on. It will amplify your thoughts and link you with the other humans,' he advised.

For that important journey Lumak and Gemmi had transformed their bodies into the natural Hades types and had taken the eight kilometre route to the southern fortress. According to Algo, that area was filled with the smaller of his species and they would not pose a great threat in themselves. However, whatever they observed would be instantly relayed to their superiors, who would soon be on their way to investigate. Even so, those dragons would not have entered a three mile limit imposed by the southern citadel. Nevertheless, the two Shadites would be exposed to unwanted encounters during the first four kilometres of their journey.

Once they were released to the natural environment of that place, they walked with difficulty along the surface of the strange and rugged world. The dense atmosphere was similar to that encountered at the bottom of a deep ocean, with its many obstructions and changing currents. When they tried to increase their speed, their bodies slowed and when they slowed below a certain level their bodies speeded up. Nothing remain still in Hades. Not even the world they were on, for it constantly rotated. Like a gigantic ocean, the energy medium was meant for swimming, so Lumak sent a telepathic thought to Gemmi and like fish they both took to the dense water-like medium. The medium was perfectly transparent and colourless.

'I didn't realize we could float in this substance. Travelling this way is a lot faster but not as quick with wings,' Gemmi said.

'That's why the dragons are so nimble. Their bodies have been specifically designed for this environment,' Lumak replied.

They could watch thousands of dragons floating about and moving hither and thither. Ever so often a larger one would pounce on a smaller one and absorb its energies until it became a tiny spec. However, by that action it would have stirred a much larger one into action. Then that one would pounce to absorb its newly claimed energy, leaving it with an equivalent size of its previous victim. That way some form of order was maintained.

Lumak pondered the thought, that if they got larger and larger to infinity, why were there not giant dragons within that world and how did the little ones come into existence in the first place, since they all appeared to be of a single sex or perhaps even sexless.

The little dragons constantly moved their small wings for speed, with their webbed three fingered hands and tail for guiding them through the medium.

'I don't think they can harm us. We are not like them and are not composed of their strange chemistry. I think we should ignore them and carry on as if they didn't exist,' he said. But soon after they were observed by a large one several times their size and like a desperate shark he moved towards them at great speed.

They dodged and darted hither and thither, trying to shake off the creature, but he persisted and kept on their trail. He might have considered them to be something special. A new type of living energy in his dimension to be sampled. After all, how often in his whole existence had such a lucky chance morsel occurred.

As they approached the southern region they could observe a ring of blue flames encircling that area and the once desperate dragon made a sudden last-attempt and dived towards them. He missed and in an instant changed direction and vanished. Not a single dragon could be observed within that region of Hades and the medium was perfectly clear.

'Oh! That was a near miss!' Gemmi exclaimed.

'I hope those here are more friendly,' he replied.

Lumak switched his communicator on and sent a thought.

'I am Lumak the Shadite and have come from the primal universe of humans and others. I was brought into this strange in-between world of Hades by a Hexolyte trap. We are the new guardians of the seventh universe and need your assistance. There is much we can learn from you and we have information that will interest you. Can we discuss these matters?' he said.

They felt a rumble within the spacial medium and a narrow passage formed within the local flames, but there was no reply.

They propelled their way towards the narrow opening, trying their hardest not to miss their landing at the neck of the dangerous flames. They assumed the strange flame had something to do with the energy elements of the Mesotrenes' universe and did not wish to experience its clutches at first hand.

Lumak was the first to land. Once he had gained a foothold, he guided Gemmi to his position.

'That was another close encounter. I just missed it by a foot. Did you know, this flame has no warmth or heat. It just penetrates and absorbs,' she said.

'How do you know?' he inquired.

'I felt it in my innermost senses,' she replied. Then he realized it was probably a mental thing.

They followed through the centre of the narrow passage with menacing flames on either sides and above, which were assisted by more wandering currents that tried to move them either way. Despite their protective nets, the flames seemed to penetrate the core of their very beings. Yet, their protective nets held. Those flames seemed to engulf the complete area of the south polar region.

They soon realized that only human forms with the ability to walk could enter that area. One had to be firmly anchored to that type of terra firma to manoeuvre themselves through the narrow passages, and those dragons without any hind legs, had little knowledge of the concept of walking and could only float in the deadly inferno with its much slower currents.

## CHAPTER 6

# Patriarch's City

As they approached the end of the path, the area about them began to fold and they found themselves falling into a bright light, not too unlike the sensation felt in an intergalactic portal. Suddenly they found themselves in an enclosed place with a large door. On the door was inscribed many ancient symbols that had been engraved unto it. The entrance opened to reveal a large transparent sphere amongst an infinity of Mesotrene worlds. The sphere itself contained a large city with many diverse life-forms. Even Mesotrenes could be observed within its large transparent bubble. There were numerous such bubbles containing their own cities, which were unlike the boxlike structures encountered on their arrival in Hades.

Like an immense bubble, the local city floated within the medium as if completely isolated from its influences and that area outside the city contained many dragons, but they were all of similar size and did not prey upon each other. One approached the couple to guide them into the city.

'I am Malfor! I shall guide you into the city of Gol. Our masters would like to meet you,' the creature said telepathically and they followed.

A voice thundered into their minds.

'You have been transposed to the seventh part of this universe of the Mesotrenes. This part is within what you call the Greater Purpose, and we have been informed of your timely arrival,' the voice said.

Suddenly, Lumak felt more at ease within himself and sensed the dangers felt since his arrival in Hades were dissipating. However, he would have felt a lot better within his own universe, even with lurking Javols and Hexolytes about. To him, Hades was the eternal hell, where his type could never fulfil a truly creative dream. Here, there was no beauty, no colour, no trees or other forms of life. He also wondered how any life-forms could live an eternity in such a vacuous environment.

The dragon took them to the only entrance of that transparent world.

'You must wait here for your guides. They will take you to our Master's citadel within Gol,' it said and departed. Soon thereafter four creatures of light came forward. They were like large fairies, but appeared to be composed of light energy. They held Lumak and Gemmi by their shoulders and lifted them toward a distant palace.

'We approach the citadel of our masters. Clear your minds and prepare yourselves, because he will see through your every thought,' one of the beings said.

'The master awaits your presence,' another one said and dropped them in the middle of a white floor in the centre of the building. Then their guides left via one of the many entrances. There was a blinding light and from it walked an ancient Patriarch.

'I am Aron. You have been specially chosen to take us home. The Hexolyte's base was rigged to bring you to us at an appropriate time. I am afraid, it was the only way,' he said. Then Lumak realized the cleverness of such a device. It was the perfect path to their world, since only the right ones with good intentions would have found their way through. All others being taken to the worst places of that universal dimension.

'I thought you had died many aeons ago, but you live?' a surprised Lumak inquired.

'We all live. This is a place of eternity. Within its boundaries no one ever dies. We had to take this path without making our enemies too suspicious. We knew we would have to return in later times to secure our universe, and could not have taken any chances in case our enemies caught on. Neither would they have been suspicious of the use of their own base for our purpose. But we have also learnt of changes in our original universe.

'We can no longer exist within your universe in our original forms. However, we have designed special containers that will hold our beings until the appropriate time of release, when we are given new bodies. Our Grand Lord has made the necessary arrangements for us.'

'This is most incredible!' Lumak said, while Gemmi nodded in agreement.

'At this time, only six of us will return with you. Myself and Jull, my eldest son; Melka, my youngest son; Corra, my eldest daughter and Balla my beloved wife. The other eight will remain behind to control and maintain this part of this universe until the time is right for them to join us,' he said.

There was another flash and all his remaining family members appeared as if from nowhere. They were indeed very powerful beings and were twice the size of an average human. Their thick eyebrows lifted upwards and their foreheads were slightly bulged and more circular. Yet, their eyes were intense and piercing.

'I am very happy to have been given this great privilege and will always remain your humble servant until our safe arrival back within our home universe,' Lumak said and bowed.

Soon they encircled him and Gemmi, observed their strange attire for a while. Then they offered their powerful hands in friendship.


Lumak told them of his universe, and the way it was today and they were happy that the majority of predator species had disappeared, with the exception of the Javols, whom they had not met. He also told them of the rebels Algo and others, who had assisted him in his quest.

'Algo is also one of us. His task is to remain hidden and watch for all new arrivals. Shortly, he will lend his skills to our departure.

'Your companion Jot has done well in designing a suitable containment vessel for our journey. A more detailed knowledge of which has been departed to Algo.

'Since you have initiated the doorway, no longer are we to remain prisoners within these realms beyond Hades. Nevertheless, we must not get carried away and allow the Mesotrene masters to possess this knowledge, or they could try to re-establish a link with the Hexolytes or another predator species as in ancient times.

'Their minds cannot penetrate beyond the bubble. It is like a separate universe within the Mesotrene's one.

'It is their way, you know, and the way of their universe. They are not at fault, for everyone must be allowed free will to evolve in its own ways, as with prey and predator. Even the aging star must be allowed its freedom to explode into a nova and destroy many of its innocent children. That is the way of the natural order and we cannot change it. However, our duty is to uphold law and order and to prevent the strong from taking advantage of the week. Assuming the process does not threaten the long term survival of either by so doing,' Aron said. And Lumak realized the wisdom of his words.

'Lumak, our time here has not been wasted. Knowing our stay would be long, we decided to create our own temporal and spacial configurations. Once we had achieved our goal and were secure from the predators of this universe, we turned our minds towards unravelling the secrets of the Cosmos.

'During that process, we have achieved much and are better beings because of it. Believe me when I say, we are a lot more than what you see. This is only a representation of our former selves. Our persons have evolved well beyond form, but in a universe with little in common with our originals. That is the reason why we have to attain the new material substance of your present universe before we can exist within its domain. In fact, we must be born again,' Jull said, and Lumak understood his words, for they were within his own concepts.

'I just realized. I haven't eaten a thing in weeks,' Gemmi said and he realized he was not hungry.

'While here we are always eating. The energy you require for sustenance is always present everywhere and permeates all things. This whole universe is a living organism,' Jull said and Lumak realized that most, if not all universes were alive, with their own internal organs like galaxies, stars and such like.

In the case of his own primal universe he thought it was more like a tree with branches of galaxies like leaves on some incredi-ble multi-dimensional tree.

Lumak transferred most of his knowledge to their minds and very soon that area of the citadel changed into a place similar to Sarah's palace on Eden. They had created it for Lumak and Gemmi's comfort during their brief stay within that city bubble they called their world.

He soon learn they had become powerful beings and could at a moments notice translate their universe into any comfortable type. However, they had to obey the laws of all natural universes and could not change their attributes or substance. But it didn't prevent them from altering their own bubble, since it had been created by them and obeyed their rules.

## CHAPTER 7

# The way out of Hades

They had to choose a precise time to leave that universe. First of all, they had to pass the roaming dragons that fed on all others, then avoid Kator and his evil hordes, and once in the protective cave, choose the precise time of temporal alignment between both universes.

This time they took a new route to the hills of Hades. It was completely different to their first and avoided the larger dragons. Nine large dragons follow to protect Lumak and Gemmi from the largest predator types within Hades. Those dragons held weapons that could repel any advances from would-be predators. Lumak and Gemmi held the six vials containing the entities of the six chosen Patriarchs within their cloaks.

Because of their incredible knowledge and powers, the Patriarchs were considered Grand Lords of the Cosmos. However, during the journey within universes they were vulnerable. They had to follow the same dangerous route out of hades as had been taken by Lumak and Gemmi on their way in. That journey would begin where Algo collected Lumak and Gemmi on their arrival and at that time no one could protect them from the wicked Masters of Hades. This whole process was precisely timed to the second.

Algo had moved his caves to another mountain closer to the exit plains. He could view that area directly and tell when the time was right for their departure. He also wanted that new position in case their original one had been found and reported by Kator's sympathisers.

Soon after their move he realized that it was indeed the case, when the dreaded Kator came thundering in with fifty of his best and most feared. They trampled and flamed that mountain until it was unrecognizable. Then thinking they had destroyed the minutest of their enemies' bases, moved on to reap more havoc elsewhere. That way Kator was always noticed and feared by his underlings.

The whole performance would be repeated on a daily basis, until some other sequence of events occurred during that exact time period and replaced it. However, all other causal sequences within future time periods would remain as before. Even their conscious memories would repeat. Time in Hades always repeated with the rotation of their strange worlds.

Only the most advanced Mesotrenes could overcome that time repeating problem by creating their own worlds within their minds, and Kator was young and not yet that matured in his nature. It required much endeavour and training for anyone to gain powers over the natural environment of that world.

Lumak and Gemmi's arrival had altered the normal course of events on that world. It was as if they had taken a causal something with them from their universe which permanently changed everything. And while they remained, those changes would continue to affect the natural order and in the process change them to fit the newer one, so they had to leave as soon as possible before those changes became permanent.

That problem did not occur within Algo's cave nor Aron's fortress. Those places were technologically controlled and followed their own temporal loops. It only occurred when they were synchronized with the more natural and raw energies of Hades. But as it changed so also did they change to confirm to the new parameters.

They had been given the new location of Algo's cave and had arrived without any problems on route. The time chosen coincided with Kator's meditation period. During that time, Mesotrenes were dead to their physical universe.

'Your special cloaks are being rejected by Hades. From what I have sensed, total rejection will ensue within two rotations of this world. We must therefore leave this place before then,' Jot said.

'Is everything ready for our departure?' Lumak inquired.

'We have been unable to test the process. Only by our successful journey can this method be fully tested. However, if everything goes to plan, we should arrive at the original point of departure, within the Hexolytes' base and at the exact time that you left. To prevent a repeat operation of the trap, I have arranged for an immediate displacement away from the circle when we materialize.

'From that moment on, you and Gemmi will not remember your experiences within this world. Neither will the transportation vessel remain. Only I and the sealed entities will retain that knowledge. However, with your permission...when I return within your mind again, you will be reminded of your mission and given a strong desire to return to Eden. At that time, the entities and their containers will be removed from your cloaks without your knowledge,' Jot said.

'Wow! You are something, Pal. In the name of our Grand Lord, do what you think is right to get us home and well away from this place,' Lumak replied.


The transportation vessel was securely fitted to Algo's large back. Lumak and Gemmi was harnessed to Melfa's back. That way, if things got rough they could remain on board during their short trip.

The moment they left the hidden cave and their spacial generator bands released, they were joined with Hades. Everything was timed so that the moment of their arrival at their point of departure coincided with the correct time within the temporal loop, so they had little time to spare after their arrival.

While Algo settled, Melfa carefully lifted the transporting vessel off his back and placed it within the area of the four pillars. Then Lumak and Gemmi released their harnesses and landed within the area. They quickly entered the vessel and sealed the entrance. Once that was done, they switched their control hand-bands, which in turn did something to the vessel's controls. In an instant they had materialized within the ancient Hexolyte base on a world close to the centre of the Triangulum galaxy.


Lumak stopped for a moment and realized he had completed his mission at that base. For reasons he could not understand he was unable to remember his recent past or of the previous steps he had taken. Yet, they were on their way back to the ship, so he assumed his mission within the base was completed and the detectors laid.

'You know I have the strangest feeling I've been somewhere and accomplished something significant, but for the life of me, I cannot remember,' he said while Gemmi patiently listened.

'I have the same feeling and think it was meant to happen that way. Perhaps we are not meant to remember,' she replied.

While they climbed the stairs they could observe many tanks opening to free the robotic guardians holding powerful defensive weapons and realized they had to make a swift getaway. Their suits were still vectored and they remained invisible. However, they must have done something to trigger their awakening. It was as if they were being chased out of the place for some greater purpose.

'Something must have tripped their sensors. We must get out of here immediately,' Lumak exclaimed.

'Those strange rings in the portal could have sensed our presence,' Gemmi replied.

Either way, they were not going to remain and find out. Hexolytes were clever and would not have laid such obvious traps. After all, at that time in their ancient past they were waging a war with superior beings.

They couldn't be sure what other traps awaited their escape, so they took the shortest route out of the area, which was vertical.

After laying the micro-probe in orbit about the planet and testing the system, they left in a hurry.

'We are to return to Eden before continuing with our present mission,' he said.

'Is there a reason?' Gemmi asked, realizing the unpredicted change in his transmitted thoughts.

'I don't know. I just have that feeling. There must be an impor-tant and overriding reason,' he replied and she understood. Jot had reclaimed his territory within Lumak's mind and had done his job by reminding Lumak of immediate changes to his plans.

As always, Gemmi made the perfect Shadite companion and both understood each other like brother and sister. That was despite the fact they were from completely different worlds and the most alien in origin to each other.

When they arrived on Eden, the Grand Lord sent his messengers to collect the six small containers from their cloaks while they were asleep. Yet, Lumak and Gemmi had been none the wiser of their unscheduled visit to Hades or of the small containers that were safely hidden within the weaves of their cloaks.

# BOOK 2

# Mallory and Roseanne holidaying on Eden continued

CHAPTER 8

# Mallory on Planet Eden

Because of the Terminal disease which separated humanity into two races, Fertilates and Infilates, Mallory had recently formed his organization of warriors called Specials. Their purpose was to combat crime and protect the few remaining human Fertilates from violent Infilates globally. He had acquired acknowledgement at the highest levels and the guaranteed assistance of the President of the USA, in promoting his special force in Congress. As far as President Arnold was concerned, Fertilates were the future of all nations that required extra security. Therefore it was in the best interest of those nations to favour Mallory's independent outfit.

At that time every government on Earth wanted an independent organization to combat lawlessness. There were numerous criminal gangs on Earth that comprised both sections of human society. Those criminals were involved in every type of illicit acts, from child kidnapping and smuggling to organ theft for transplant. Those they would sell on the black market for enormous sums. In some instances organs would be removed from donors while walking the streets. And usually those poor victims were still alive while their vital organs were painfully removed. Police were untrustworthy and would sometimes turn a blind eye for a price.

Mallory realized if he was to fight the mounting crime and violence on Earth, it was essential that he located better weapons and protection for his Specials. He knew Professor Khan (Ben) and his people in Solarian Banking. They were the most advanced on Earth and were also interested in Fertilate safety. Therefore it would be in their best interest to assist his campaign.

Nevertheless, the main purpose of his present visit to Planet Eden was for his honeymoon, and he didn't want any disasters during that distant holiday, with so many unknowns. Although a military pilot in previous years, he'd never travelled interstellar distances through portals before, and that alien concept of travel worried him. His unwilling wife Roseanne was even more traumatized by the ordeal. She considered all such methods of transport with dread and dismay.

Despite their original fears, after their arrival on Eden, they were overcome by the beauty and intoxicating environment of that world. The place was utterly astounding in every conceivable way. Many times they thought they had died and were in a perfect heaven of immortality. They were indeed correct in their assumptions, with one exception; they were not dead. They were presently on the most perfect world in Galaxy Osmaron. One that was run by powerful Headrons and Macron computers. One where all its citizens, including robots and androids were treated as equals. They worked for the common good of their Galactic Federation and Eden was the main governing world in that Federation of Worlds. On Eden, the main world of the Solarian Empire, every human lived forever and never got ill.

**Earth Time.... 2062 AD**

Presently, Mallory and Roseanne is in Sarah's beautiful golden palace on Eden enjoying their honeymoon. They are learning the ways of the Solarians, which hopefully will be put to good use after their return to Earth.

That poor planet, Earth, with its present human overpopulation in dire straights with unprecedented variations of Global Warming. Where everyone faced the worst-case scenarios of climate change.

With severe overpopulation, there were constant food shortages, riots and revolutions. Utilities usually down for days on end. Over ten percent of the planet's surface had already been lost to the rising oceans and global temperatures increased by close to 5 degrees centigrade from previous centuries. Mankind was in for a most painful and unproductive future, with no where to go. No one outside of Solarian banking knew of the existence of the Solarians. They had the technologies to change Earth, but would not, until its human population dropped below 500 million.

The Terminal disease was the doing of the Solarians. They had introduced the inhibiting virus to stop mankind having more children. They realized all the problems of Earth was due to human population growth. Those drastic steps were meant to save the planet at the expense of humankind.

Within a few decades there would be no more Infilates. Only the few selected Fertilates, who were constantly administered the antidote. They would survive the turmoil. After that, out of a population of over 10 billion, lest than 500 million humans would remain.

CHAPTER 9

# The great ships visit Tarran

### Earth Time... Summer of 2062 CE

Lumak hadn't revisited his home world, Kanaefon, since he left several decades before for Earth. During that special mission he had transformed his body, from its original bee-like Semonite, to the human form. Although he was always Lumak, the Shadite, he had taken the credentials of one Professor Jeffery Longhurst while on Earth.

Now on the day of their departure from planet Eden, he wondered whether his human wife Sarah would take to his people as he had to humankind. Nevertheless for that extreme alien adaptation they were required to transform, from human to the Semonite form. It was a giant bee-like creature that was as alien as anyone could imagine and become.

Because of cultural differences, Sarah could not become a female queen, so they decided to become sexless worker members of the hive hierarchy for the duration of their stay. There could only be one dominant female in each colony. That single female was the local queen, and any more competing queens would not be tolerated by the Duty Queen. She would insist on that queen leaving the colony to form her own hive within a new part of their territories.

Queenship also included marriage to a drone of their choosing that could not be with those already married. Neither could any such decisions be made without the approval of their Duty Queen. Their complex society was thoroughly controlled for population and hive structure and their families were the main pillar stones of Semonite society.

Lumak had explained the situation to Sarah as best he could and she had accepted the transformation as she had with other forms on other occasions. At least it was not too undignified, like being changed into the opposite sex which she abhorred. At least workers were sexless and the most superior below the queen. Sarah's only real disappointment was that she was unable to take her younger son along to see his grand parents.

'Now, knowing everything there is to know about my people's customs. Do you still want a holiday on my home world?' Lumak said.

'If anything, it will make a pleasant change from human culture and allow me to view the universe in a different light,' she replied, unconcerned.

'That's my beautiful queen, speaking. Even when you are a worker Semonite you will still be my most beautiful queen!' he said and kissed her.

'I just hope I'm able to fit into such a complex society without too many mistakes.'

It was then that she realised how alien some intelligent life-forms were from a human cultural viewpoint. She also understood how Lumak's mother, who was also a Shadite, must have felt when she had to transform into other species like human. At least, she was a duty queen and had a greater choice in such matters. Not like Lumak, her husband, who was born a sexless worker and had to learn from scratch the concepts of maleness and sex when he was transformed into a male human.

In the mean time her son would remain behind in the palace on Eden, until his mother returned and visited him in human form and as a woman on their return.

During their special trip to Kanaefon, Lumak decided to use his Shadite's powers for her protection and wore his black hooded cloak. That was only a precautionary measure as Sarah had a range of her own special powers.

On the day of their departure Sarah was wearing a tight fitting and highly reflective outfit that was designed to protect her body from most dangers. On her head was a jewelled headband that could shield her complete body from all forms of projectiles. Around her waist was a metallic belt with a small nuclear powered plasma gun. The Federation insignia was boldly displayed on her left lapel. That was also a communication device. However, her Brain Implants could be directly linked to any Federation world for the relay of information.

They transposed from one of the palace's portals to Venusa's ship and while there awaited the arrival of Jon, Lira and the other young Andromedans. Then they waited for the arrival of princess Bawaki of Tarran. Some of her male students from Tarran, still in their cat forms, had completed their six months training course in the university and were returning home with her.

Princess Bawaki was presently in human form and soon to visit one of the Megotron transformation chambers. During that process she would be completely changed from her adopted human form to her original catlike one and become a most ferocious hunter. Hopefully, she would retain most of her original psychological profile, but with different instincts and emotions to face a harsher world.

Tarran was Sarah's first port of call and she intended to spend a few days on that world with Bawaki and her mother. Bawaki's mother had remained queen of their Marawi clan for many decades. During her brief stay Sarah would observe its varied life-forms and their cultures before travelling on to Kanaefon. Her visit to that world would be done in human form. She didn't like the idea of changing into too many forms, with the resultant after effects and lengthy adaptations, on this mission.

On her arrival to that world, Sarah knew she would be treated like a stellar empress, being highly respected by everyone within the federation of planets.

Nevertheless it was her first visit to the Tarranian System and she had come prepared for almost any eventuality. Since Venusa-Bawaki and her friends' experiences on that harshest of worlds, she realized there was always going to be unforeseen dangers on one of the deadliest worlds in the galaxy.

Both giant ships transposed from the space port near Eden City and within minutes had arrived above Marawi City on the distant planet of Tarran. Roseanne, Mallory and Jerry were watching their departure from one of the palace's high balconies on Eden, when to their amazement both ships simply disappeared, leaving behind a small dust storm, as air rushed in to fill the vacuum left behind. Soon after, Jerry took them to a viewing room where they could observe the world of Tarran and the great ship's through sensors and Sarah's brain implants.

'My god, it's disappeared in a whist of dust, and has already arrived!' Roseanne exclaimed.
'We don't use rocket-ships anymore. All our space-ships have powerful inter-dimensional drives which can take us across the galaxy in seconds, but our portals are much quicker,' Jerry said and Mallory remained silent and in awe of their technologies.

On arrival on Tarran, the ships travelled eastwards, just beyond the ancient Marawi city and landed in a region close to the Sadana sea. That place was where they intended to build the new city of Ziona. Sarah, Lumak and the others accompanied Bawaki in a small shuttle to the city and landed just before the main southern gates. As they left the shuttle became airborne and returned to its mother ship in view of all the welcoming committee.
They cautiously walked through the gates among assembling crowds of cat-people, cheering in their cat-cries. Bawaki and Sarah walked ahead with Lumak and the others in tour while following a tight group from behind. Even further behind were the group of male cat students, wearing their uniforms and Federation insignias, and walking proudly with their heads held high.
The male cats were almost half the size of the females. Females were the most dominant sex that were accustomed to treating the males as inferiors. Yet, that attitude was slowly changing. They realised their males were the most industrious and technological of the species that had ideas for changing some areas of their hostile world into better places to live with the help of the Solarians.

It was noon when they arrived on Tarran. Its atmosphere was hot and misty, and two suns were present. The second was just visible through its dense canopy.
Despite Sarah's inbuilt refrigeration and highly reflective attire,

she felt stifling hot and wondered how any life could exist comfortably within such an extreme environment.

At that time of day it was over fifty-five degrees Celsius in the shade and much higher elsewhere. Even so, cat people did not sweat or show any outward signs of discomfort or exhaustion. Their bodies were designed by nature to conserve water, with circulating systems within their thick isolating skins.

Its main sun appeared four times more massive than Earth's, and was of a deep yellow that appeared to boil with much sunspot activity and many more prominences. It was not as old as Earth's sun, but was more massive and as a result had used up its resources at a much faster rate. While they walked through the narrow streets they were engulfed by thick stone walls on either side. Those included many small square windows that looked unto the streets below. The place was very similar to ancient castles on Earth during medieval Europe.

The windows themselves were access points from which they could dive unto would-be invaders below. Instead of such ferocious encounters, today they were cheering and chanting at Bawaki and the silvery figures that approached.

Several guards soon came forward and bowed in front of Bawaki and her companions. Then they guided them towards the palace in the centre of the small city. When they entered, it was somewhat cooler and Sarah breathed a sigh of relief.

Queen Rowani and her company could not have prepared a reception in advance. She only knew of the possibility of their visit in late spring. However, she had made standby arrangements and it was not too difficult to prepare a small one at short notice.

This was the first time her world had confronted supposed alien gods from another world in human form. They had never seen the like of humans before and did not relish the occasion out of fear for the unknown.

Sarah had learnt the main tongues of those local clans, with their different dialects and had their complete vocabulary within her language implants. Therefore with the exception of facial hair and hand movements, she could communicate effectively. Their verbal language was rich enough for conversation without the use of gestures and suchlike, which was mainly used during hunting.

That was when a noiseless repertoire was essential for tracking and stalking.

The queen sat on her padded throne and two of her male advisers came forward and bowed as the group entered the quaint room. That room contained many decorated jars and oil lamps of a medieval design.

The queen rose and went towards Bawaki and the strange visitors. For a brief moment she stared at her daughter before turning towards the visitors and kneeling before them, while showing Sarah the respect that could only be bestowed upon a goddess.

Sarah placed her hand on her shoulder and said in a gentle voice,

'Please stand, Queen Rowani. You may call me Sarah and may I introduce my companions. Then we can sit together and speak like ordinary friends.'

The queen was dressed in strangely knitted cat fur, and her longer whiskers were curled into vertical spirals on either side of her nasal cavities. Her headdress were of mullok's shell. They were cut in strips and mounted unto a circular wooden frame. The strips panned out to resemble a great mother-of-pearl's array, and added stature to her poise.

She was adorned with many beads, large bangles and anklets on her furry hands and feet. Her claws were manicured to remove their sharpness and those on her feet were cropped for wearing the thick leather sandals more comfortably.

Despite the hardships of her world, she was very dignified. Nevertheless she was a most vicious cat-woman through and through.

CHAPTER 10

# Harshest of worlds

Tarran had not changed significantly since Lumak's first visit to that desert world several decades before. At that time Princess Bawaki was just eighteen Earth years old. Presently the world was changing in leaps and bounds by the introduction of new technologies from the Solarian Federation. Now, there were two large water filtration and sewage plants on the shows of the Sadana sea and the old city was a lot cleaner than it had ever been.

The giant Bat-vultures and other scavengers no longer loitered close to the city gates in anticipation of the occasional free scraps and small animals. There was now a fenced area west of the city where they were occasionally fed.

A large area north of the ancient city had been cultivated with Socria. A giant beetroot type plant with celery-like stocks and leaves that could be used for spinach. That highly nutritious vegetable captured and stored lots of water from the surrounding dry soil, and its roots could be fermented into the most delicate wines. Due to the harshness of their world, cat people had a mixed diet. Being about 40 percent vegetarian, with meat forming the main course.

Because fruits were unknown to Tarran, several like apples, citrus and dates had been bio-engineered specifically for their climate and later introduced by Solarians. They were cultivated in northern fields. Many were used to make juice for the indigenous population and their occasional human visitors.

Sarah had planned daily visits for many cat-people onboard Martia's ship. That way, it was hoped they would learn more about the positive effects of advanced technologies and not shy away as they had done in the past.

Meron and his planetologists were set on changing the whole of our Osmaron galaxy into one large forest where all life-forms could evolve naturally and coexist together, with relevant measures taken to isolate the very dangerous predators from the mild herbivores whenever necessary.

New plants and animals were constantly introduced to those planets to improve their biospheres. When normal life could not be used, others could be specifically engineered for those worlds, taking into consideration the indigenous flora and fauna.

The Solarians had become so advanced that virtually any type of life could be created by their powerful Macrons, once the size, bone structure and other parameters were given. Those very same animals or plants could exist and live in a Virtual World for as long as needed to test their suitability. Their existence could also be speeded up a thousand times for quick analysis. Once the life-form had passed all their necessary tests in the Virtual World it could then be made real and transported to its destination world.

It was estimated that most of Tarran's indigenous life would disappear within a million years or so. While preventing those extinctions, it was necessary to assist the lower life-forms in overcoming the survival pressures. In alleviating such problems Solarians had bio-engineered what they called a meat plant. Although it didn't supply real meat, the fruit grew a menacing face and included meaty and bone-like tissue, with juices that resembled and tasted like real blood. It could even pretend to be prey by certain motions. Those plants required lots of water and nutrients to grow, so large pumps and sprinklers had to be installed in desert regions before they could be cultivated. Once the wild life became accustomed to that fruit, their numbers would increase and they could then provide the food chain for the larger animals and monsters.

The Solarian's plan was a truly ambitious one. As Senots, they considered themselves caretakers of our galaxy Osmaron and for them, all life was to be saved and allowed to evolve naturally whenever possible.

The desert mulloks were to remain in the deserts of Tarran and live as they had done in the past, only being occasionally harvested by hunters. There would be no intervention of technology to either produce or harvest them in greater numbers.

Solarians considered it a sin against nature to artificially produce or harvest any natural evolving life-form that had of its own volution formed a survival niche. All such methods of factory farming destabilised eco-systems and helped to create and propagate new dangerous strains of disease, not to mention detrimental changes to well established and closely linked systems and cultures. Those methods also caused the most predominant species to multiply without limit. This could occur in much the same way as mankind had done on Earth, with disastrous consequences.

All lower species needed a restraining influence on population growth, either in the form of predation, disease, regular wars or a level of difficulty in attaining their food supplies and resources. Although the occasional disease and acts-of-God played a major role, such factors were considered incidental and too random. The balance was met somewhere between the predictable hardships and other extremes.

Obviously, such rules didn't apply to those who could wilfully control their future by powerful and complex computers and associated machines. In this regard Solarians were advanced enough to desist from all forms of child bearing if at any time their population growth went above expected levels. This was because, in essence, their society was controlled by super intelligent Macron Computers. They always had the final word in human population growth. After all, they were always correct in their analyses and predictions.

If Tarranians used similar methods to those by humans on Earth, their world would have had less than a thousand years before all life became extinct, leaving behind a few of the most dominant life-forms. With the loss of the lower part of their food chain, those would in time become fully dependant on advanced technology in order to survive.

Sometimes, nature took millions of years for its creatures to adapt to slowly changing conditions and habitats. Even the most carefully bio-engineered strains could require several thousand years to adapt to a suitable survival niche within those extreme climatic conditions. Psychological changes were also a major part of the complex survival scenario.

With those parameters in mind, most of Tarran's conversion would be carried out by robots and androids. They were not affected by its climatic conditions and contained their own energy supplies in the form of small nuclear power packs that lasted for decades.

During the remainder of her brief stay, Sarah had decided to remain on board Venusa's ship. She found the planet too uninviting, with an overwhelming odour that persisted. It reminded her of an old pig farm she once visited on Earth belonging to Jerry. That was when he was President of the USA. She also didn't want to stretch the capabilities of her immune system with so many yet unnamed bacteria and other invading microbes, even when they could be quickly isolated and removed by the Megotrons.

Therefore Venusa's ship would be her place of residence from now on and everyone would visit her there. She arranged daily trips to Martia's ship and evening parties on board Venusa's ship.

The larger almost human bipedal female cats observed the delicate fabrics and furniture, the beautiful and magical lights, which to them resembled stars and they wondered how it was possible for light to come from such an enclosed sphere. Then they watched robots assembling machines and even other robots at incredible speed. Finally, they were taken through a shopping precinct and into a large theatre where a show was in progress. The large orchestra played classical music that was previously unheard by their sensitive ears.

After those visits to the giant ships, they didn't feel like continuing their present dangerous way of life like hunting in the hot and dangerous deserts and scratching the land for a pittance. They were signing on in droves to be trained as engineers or to partake in the servicing sectors of the new city.

During the remaining two days of her stay on Tarran, Sarah visited the vast deserts to observe mulloks' swarms laying their eggs. Then she went to see the scaly monsters in a few of their still existing habitats.

'What a beautiful species. They will make ideal specimens for our new habitats on Tyrrel II,' Lord Meron commented.

'They appear to be the most ferocious monsters in the universe,' Sarah replied and he smiled.

'Perhaps we can armour them to fight Javols!' Lord Meron said and she smiled.

When she had seen enough of that world, she held a farewell party and invited every leader on Tarran. Then the shuttles went out to collect those that were in the most inaccessible regions of the planet.

After dinner, Bawaki gave one of her important speeches to all in attendance. Then Sarah added a few words of her own.

'Beloved friends and colleagues of our Solarian Empire, may we always strive for peace and perfection in all things throughout our empire,' she said and they cheered.

Most of Bawaki's friends and family were there and sitting at her table. They included Siri, Biluchi, Caldi, Matbi and others. There were also the Zadi's queen and many of her seniors.

Bawaki would remain on her world until the city was built and that part of her world successfully converted into a more pleasant environment. Then she would once again be available to the Greater Purpose; for she followed the path of a Shadite.

CHAPTER 11

# Beautiful Kanaefon

After the three days on planet Tarran had elapsed and Venusa's ship unloaded, it was time for Lumak and Sarah to depart to the globular cluster of Kalboron. It was one of the larger globular clusters that orbited Osmaron. Sarah said farewell to Bawaki, her mother and friends and their ship simply vanished from Tarran. A short time later it arrived on Kanaefon, in one of its many docking ports.

That world was another most beautiful world, but filled with strange monstrous creatures like flying dragons on land and Leviathans in its seas and oceans. Most of its expansive waters were covered with floating forests that moved with the waning and waxing of her two satellite moons. Everything on that world was large in comparison to those on Earth. That same pattern of evolution made the Semonites, a bee-like creature, over 5 feet tall.

Sarah removed all her jewellery and entered one of the many Megotron chambers as a nude human. Her body and mind were thoroughly scanned and recorded, then her present matrix transformed into a Semonite life-form, but with her existing brain implants. However, she retained her original personality and memory, but her senses, instincts and emotions were changed to reflect those of her new form. The scanning process would always ensure that she left in the same human body in which she had arrived. Solarians could also use that method to create another body if the original had been damaged beyond repair. That way they could live forever.

As advised by her husband Lumak, she struggled for a while with her new sexless form, to learn the use of its many append-ages and limbs. Then she practised her pheromones sensors until she could detect every material in her vicinity. It was a strange sense indeed; for she could now smell metals, including composi-tion and hardness. It was like being able to observe purity in matter for the first time. Even germs and bacteria could be clearly observed in their different colours. It was then that she realized how inadequate her human senses were.

When she was sure that she had a modicum of control, she put on the skirt and little cape with insignia on part of her upper torso. She was finally ready to meet her reception committee as a neutral hive worker. Despite all her intensive preparations she was still worried.

'Darling, do you think I appear normal?' she asked Lumak telepathically through her implants.

'You look exactly like one of my brothers. I wonder where Venusa got the template for your form?' he replied with sarcasm, but nodded his head to mean everything was quite acceptable.

Kanaefon was indeed a world of contrast, from cities with spires into the clouds and shuttles serving off-world freighters, to portals invisibly moving people about even to the most distant outposts. However, despite their advanced knowledge and technologies, the Semonites still retained most of their ancient ways and customs. They considered themselves to be just another of that worlds more advanced insects and went out of their way to maintain the ecological balance.

On that world many separate species had evolved to high intelligence. The only reason why there were no serious conflicts was because each species was so different from another and they filled different niches. For instance, the Semonites and Lamphis were giant insects who had evolved on nectar and berry juice, while the Petan Dragons were more reptilian. They had evolved along the shores and lived mainly on fish. However when their fish stocks reduced in certain areas, they turned to nectar and berry juice. These days they had a more varied diet. The giant monsters of the sea, called Laviatans, were also equally intelligent. They were built more like giant octopuses, and unable to move freely out of their oceans and seas.

Venusa's ship had transmitted their estimated time of arrival before they left Tarran. There were many senior Semonite scientists attending at the dock. They all knew it was a senior Federation figure that had been transformed for the duration and treated her with great reverence. Although she was a pretend worker Semonite, those were at the highest level below the queen and weighed high above the drones in the hive hierarchy. After all, they were the ones who brought benefit to their world through farming and technology.

When they arrived, it was nighttime on Kanaefon and the sky was flooded with light which seemed to be everywhere. Just above her head she could observe the bright outline of Galaxy Osmaron, known to many as the Milky Way galaxy.

The globular cluster of Kalboron was just beyond the rim of Osmaron. It orbited about 100,000 light years from the galactic nucleus. From Kanaefon the whole of the galaxy could be seen worming its way across the sky with its brighter central bulge below the planet's southern pole.

While they came forward to greet her with special scents and clawed arms, she attempted to respond in like-manner, but found her motion and senses uncoordinated. However, Lumak did most of the communicating while she bowed, showing respect with the occasional claw-shake. Most of those attitudes and customs had doubtlessly been adopted with space travel. She was introduced as Siend Sara from another similar world to avoid complications.

As customary, she was taken by portal to the main tower and shown the expansive city with its many buildings, powerful installations, historical anecdotes. Then they were taken back to Venusa's ship and shown around.

The whole ordeal was extremely tiring for Sarah and she prayed for a moment to herself in private, to sleep off her transformation and awake with better sense control and limb coordination.

'My Dear, it's never easy for first-timers. It's mainly because our senses are quite unique and takes a while to become highly tuned,' Lumak said.

'I find it all to be an incredible experience, but I require a little rest to sort things out,' she replied and they retired early while still on Venusa's ship. However, she wasn't sure how she was going to do while living among them.

The following day Lumak communicated with his mother's palace, but she was still away and would arrive in two days, so he decided to take Sarah to his town house. He had always kept that place for himself and his Shadite friends on short visits. His mother and her staff had always tended to its upkeep in his absence and ensured it was regularly stocked with nourishment and other essentials.

To Sarah it was a very strange building that was built on an hexagonal format, almost no furniture was included and there was a small cubicle with a strangely shaped toilet that was level with the floor. There were no urinals. Semonites had a single back passage and did not pass liquids, just small lumps of faeces. Neither did they eat solid food. Their main diet was nectar and a rich protein mixture that was obtained from the juice of special berries. They sucked those juices through an orifice in the lower part of their head.

Semonites were as alien as anyone could get and didn't compare well with any life-forms on Earth, except wasps and bees. Nevertheless, they were beautiful to watch, with different hair colours throughout their bodies. Those of a specific type, were coloured similarly for identification and special clothes were worn to denote profession or seniority in rank. They were one of the most intelligent and technological species within Galaxy Osmaron proper.

She had much to do in getting used to her new surroundings, yet, she saw the planet of Kanaefon through new senses. Those were much more highly tuned than the human type and she were initially overwhelmed. The pheromones and scents alone carried their language, songs and poetry and she could sense all kinds of different feelings on the wind.

Her eyes could see warmth well into the infrared and covered a visual spectrum from there to the ultraviolet region, with multiple lenses that could contract and expand to focus and magnify a distant object in myriads of spectacular colours. Her new view of their world was sharp and in incredible detail. However, her sense of touch was not as unique, because humans with fleshy skin covering had many more nerve endings, while Semonites used body hair and whiskers for the same purpose.

They had several ways to communicate, but the most commonly used type was speech. It was less polluting than scent and used less energy for a given sentence. However, it was more limited in range because of the high frequencies used. It was also more directional and very private. Their natural speech was almost inaudible to humans and consisted of noises that included hisses similar to that of bats. However, the process could be altered to become more audible without much difficulty.

Scent was generated by special glands close to the neck and did not always occur in sympathy with speech. Most of the time it was switched off and tended to carry emotive feelings like joy, hate, love, danger and suchlike. But it could also be used for tracking and locating others of their kind and predators.

Sarah was exhausted and hungry when they entered his home.

'Darling, I am so hungry! When are we going to have some food?' She inquired.

'Our new bodies can go for months without any nourishment. You must be having slight withdrawal symptoms from your original human form, combined with travel exhaustion. I know, I am also quite tired. It is all quite natural for first-timers to this form. It's a reaction between your original subconscious and the new.'

'Really? But it's so strong and real!' she replied.

'In this form, we only take fluids like nectar and berry juice. Come, let me show you,' Lumak said and took her to a small private feeding room. There were four large transparent containers with green, yellow, red and clear liquids in a large metallic tray. Each container had tubes linking them together and there were others leading from each container to special feeding nozzles.

'Darling, they can be mixed to your choice, or taken separately. There is also water for dilution, if required. Put any of these nozzles to your mouth and suck,' he said and she did, hesitantly at first.

'The green one is very delicious. Shall I try them all?' she said.

'That's the general idea, Love. You can have as much as you like. They are just ordinary nutritional juices with no detrimental additives. The colours represent different flavouring, to give us greater variety. These four basic ingredients are all we need for sustenance.'

'That's all you have?'

'Yes. Unlike humans, with an incredible variety of food, our culture is very simple and efficient. Food is considered a precious, but basic commodity and strictly for sustaining life. We are not as self-indulgent as some other species and concentrate mainly on more cosmic issues,' he said.

She tried them all and found she was soon fully satisfied. Then she didn't feel like having another meal for months.

'Now, I would like to take a nap, Darling? Where is the bedroom?' she asked.

'There is no bedroom here. We can sleep on any surface. Personally, I prefer the area close to the window, over there. Why don't you take the other window? Also, it doesn't matter whether you stand, sit or lay flat on the floor,' he said. Sarah couldn't believe that there wasn't any beds on Kanaefon. However, Semonites did not have fleshy tissue that felt discomfort or pain while resting on solid surfaces. With the exception of small hairy areas and joints, most of their bodies were protected by a thick solid outer layer or skeleton.

Sarah did as he asked and had a most enjoyable sleep with no discomfort, whatsoever. Yet, she had difficulty in getting used to the bareness of the place, for there were no chairs, tables or beds. However, there was something similar to virtual image television and she spent the best part of the morning viewing one of their programs.

She soon realised the Semonites concentrated on mental development and very little on their bodies and material things. After all, there was little need for improvement in that direction. They were seldom ill and lived for several thousands of Earth years. Even without the use of any techno-rejuvenators.

They used many technologies that included methods for personal safety, but never took pleasure by pursuing matters for personal gain. After all, they worked for the common good of the hive hierarchy. Here, individuals were counted for very little in their matriarchal society. Only the queens were free to do as they pleased and they followed the same pattern of conservation and tolerance in all things for the benefit of their children.

Soon she began to admire their culture, not because of the plenty, but because of the absolute purity and simplicity of their lives. When she tested the scents, she seldom felt senses of hatred or remorse, for they all worked together and took the credits together.

That day was the beginning of their major full moon. The minor moon was in the same quadrant in the sky. That was also the time of highest tides on that part of the world. Lumak took Sarah to visit the Great Chasm and observe the extensive waterfall. They heard its thunder across the Great Wall as the waterfall from the upper sea began to cascade and flood the lower canyon. It soon became one gigantic waterfall some seventy eight miles long cascading from 7 miles high into the dismal abyss. It panned out on either side of them as far as the eye could see and they were awed by its power.

The foaming waters fell seven miles into the deepest chasm, forming dense black clouds with perpetual rainbows along its length. There was thunder and lightening everywhere across the canyon walls. The experience was nerve shattering, but most exhilarating when felt through Semonite senses.

'Darling, this place brings back many sad memories of adventure, friendly dragons and others since departed,' he said.

'You speak of your adventures with Stikol? Perhaps you could take me to their main city, to meet his grandchildren. I've also brought them a present,' she said.

Chapter 12

# Celebrations

That night Sarah had only a few hours sleep and was soon up and about, with nothing to do. Despite the extensive use of automatons and technology on Eden, where in her usual human existence was always much effort due to human complexity, here, everything was done as and when required with minimal effort. There were no beds to make, no breakfast to prepare and no houses to clean, etc, etc.

All remaining minor tasks were carried out by the Lamphis and their eager robots. They were the natural labour force of the Semonites. The giant beatle-like Lamphis had evolved with the Semonites and had been built by nature for physical effort. Presently, they controlled the most advanced robots in all Semonite society.

At dawn she could smell all kinds of strange pheromones and scents on the wind. She realized that particular day was going to be different to any other she had experienced before. She also realized one day on Kanaefon was just over 38 hours of Earth's time.

Lumak sensed her restlessness and rose from his preferred corner in the small room. He took a gentle sip from of the bluish nutrient.

'Something strange is happening and I don't know what?' she said.

'You will not be able to interpret the meanings of pheromones until you select the correct menu within your brain implant,' he replied.

'She remained silent for a moment, while staring at him and was suddenly aroused. She had turned the interpreter on.

'Carnival celebrations! Your mother is back and we are going to have some major celebrations today!' she shouted in Kanei. Suddenly her features lit up with excitement.

'Yes, Dear, I knew all about it. But it was meant to be a surprise. This is the beginning of another of our Lyran cycles. At the beginning of each moon cycle we celebrate and give offerings to our Lord.'

'Are we going to see Petan dragons on parade?'

'Yes, and my mother, the Duty Queen, will also be back today from yet another of her special missions. So her subjects are preparing the greatest celebrations of all time,'

'Sounds fantastic!'

'The following day we hold a memorial to celebrate the passing of Obe, Aurlsba and ... Longe... they were my dearest friends,' he said with sadness.

'I would like to wear something special on that occasion and perhaps place a wreath?' Sarah said.

'That's already taken care of!'

'Anyway, The Grand Lord said they would return at the appropriate time,' Sarah replied.

'I know, but corporeal existence may take many forms. No two bodies can ever be the same after such a long passing. I just hope they return as Semonites, Humans or even Petans,' he said with sadness.

'So you knew all those plans without telling me?'

'I Know! I didn't tell you before because it was meant to be a surprise. This was also because I wanted you to taste the rougher edges of our culture and show how basic we can be. Then you could learn to appreciate our existence from both sides of the survival spectrum,' he said.

'I suppose you know best! But remember, I now have my implants on pheromones,' she replied and he smiled in Kanei.

'Today we shall have a most fantastic time. So please wear the Federation tunic I had specially made for this occasion. Also, as a visiting dignitary, you may wear your special headband and wand of office.'

'There is more you are not telling me?' she inquired.

'Much more. My mother and the Petans' king have decided to add our world to the list of Federation worlds,' he said.

'That's incredible news! I always wondered when such an important world like yours would join us. It's about time. Now we can place an interstellar portal on this world and visit any-time,' a happy Sarah said.

'Today you will be received by our government and queen as a most important dignitary from Osmaron. My people have always loved and respected the Grand Lord, who left our world for yours, so they wish to complete the link. That way they may visit Eden anytime to show their homage and respect,' Lumak said.

'Don't tell me, we also have to build a commemorative square and monument in Eden City for the purpose?' she inquired.

'It doesn't have to be in the city centre. I will design and build it myself,' he said and she agreed.

'There is one more thing!'

'Only one more?' Sarah inquired.

'I thought, perhaps, we could build a monument on Eden for Obe-chopter in memory of Obe!'

'Your great spirit of Obe needs it?'

'It will make Eden my permanent home. I can always visit here through portal when the need arise,' he said.

'So be it! You have your wish, Shadite!' she said, with a Kanei smile.


The real celebrations began soon enough. It was led by a mile long procession. In front were a semonite musical band with drums and tubular wind instruments. Then there were the Petan Dragons beating their own type of massive war drums. They were followed by numerous Lamphy and their robots playing instruments akin to xylophones. Following behind were the different professional groups, from scientist to farmers. Those comprised all types of workers that went in separate groups. All showing the implements and products of their trade. They were dressed in the most beautiful uniforms and in perfect step to the beat of the Petan drums.

As they approached the main pavilion the procession turned their heads to address the duty queen and other dignitaries. Sitting on the main elevated platform was Lumak's mother, Queen Ushaia, and two of her subordinate queens. Drones including her husband were in another group. Next was the Petans' King. Then Lumak, Sarah and other dignitaries were on either side.

The procession soon broke up and each group took their places in front of the large crowds, while the bands took up position just in front of the elevated platform. Suddenly many Petans rushed unto the surrounding field and began to play their own type of football, to the surprise of all. The game was quite rough and resembled a cross between American foot ball and Soccer. The Petans' King and Lumak cheered.

After the games were over, the Duty Queen stood up to give her speech. Although she spoke in Kanei, devices similar to our microphones received the information and passed it over to translators. Translation was mainly for the benefit of the Petan Dragons, who communicated very loudly and boisterously like humans.


'My dearly beloved, I am back! Back from another of my important missions for our Grand Lord. This one was in Triangulum. I am also happy to say that my most beloved son, Siend Lumak is also back from Osmaron. He has been away for many cyclons now and we are very pleased in his return,' She said and everyone cheered, but she stretched her massive hairy claws forward to calm the mixed crowd.

'That is not all. Amongst us today is one of the most important people in Osmaron. She changed form to show us even greater respect.'

They were surprised and cheered.

'My beloved people, this day marks a changing point in our society as people of one world. I have taken the advise of our Grand Lord to become a member of the Federation of Worlds. Once we are members we may trade freely with every civilization within Osmaron, our galaxy. We may also visit for long periods and experience the whole of our Osmaron Galaxy. Those freedoms will be for all of us of every different culture, form and race. Now I would like to introduce all our people to the Queen Empress of the Solarian Empire, Originally human, but now as a beautiful worker,' she said.

It was a most beautiful day in that part of Kanaefon and everyone was excited.

Sarah stood up and bowed in each direction of the large crowd.

'Most lovely people of this incredibly beautiful world, I am happy and pleased to be here with you on this auspicious day. Siend Lumak told me so much about you and your incredible world, that I had to visit. However, my main reason for being here today is to sign the relevant documents and treaties that make you a part of the greater whole.' They kept cheering so she brought her arms forward to quiet them.

'Once you become members of our esteemed Federation, you will become part of a much larger galactic family. If for some reason you required our help in any matter, we would always be there to assist. That is what family and friends are for. We also have much to trade with you, to promote health, happiness and well being. Furthermore, our universities are free for all within the Federation.' They cheered loudly again.

'We now face a great threat from the invading Javols. They will visit your world within 100 of your cyclons. They have devastated the whole of the Andromedan galaxy and hope to do the same with ours. Therefore we must prepare to fight as one people against a common foe.' This time they remained quiet.

'There are many fantastic projects we can plan and build together for the common good. Therefore, I would like to take this opportunity in welcoming you all into our esteemed federation,' she added. They cheered and cheered. Even the powerful Petan Dragons could not stop and began to beat their chest. The uproar was deafening. The Duty Queen soon stood up and waved her arms to calm them.

'I know how you feel. The last time we had such an uproar was when the Grand Lord arrived in the form of Siend Obe. Our world has never been the same since and will never be the same again. Every step we take in the right direction gives us even more freedom. This step takes us towards the centre of Osmaron and adds more friends and families to ours. We will also be much more prosperous and safer as a result. Thanks again my people!' she shouted. After more acrobatics and games, Sarah and the other dignitaries were taken to a local portal to the queens palace. While there they would sign the relevant documents and treaties.

CHAPTER 13

# Paradise World

Back on Eden Mallory and Roseanne were enjoying their honeymoon holidays. Jerry had shown them around his own palace which was a few kilometres north of Sarah's within the Garden of Eden State. That palace reflected Jerry and his wife's attitudes in its design and decor, and reminded Mallory of the president he once knew. Yet, no pigs could be found anywhere within palace grounds.

'What have you done with Podgy and Misty?' Roseanne asked and he was surprised she knew about his two adorable Vietnamese pot belly pigs.

'It's great you asked about those two. I passed them and their litters over to Madeline on our farm near Sol Newtown. I am able to visit the manor every month to see them,' he replied and Roseanne realized many on Eden still visited Earth, but kept well away from its virus ridden populations.

Jerry had decided to take them to Eden City and for that visit they were to wear their special robes of office which gave them seniority and greater respect within the Solarian society.

After several transits through the portal system, their initial fears had dissipated, in much the same way as country bumpkins boarding their first train.

They had taken one of the local portals and arrived in one of the city's main portal stations. There were portals everywhere, with people entering and departing the city in their multitudes. Such travel was processed in much the same way as a busy railway station on Earth. It was then that Mallory realised how difficult it would have been for them to return to the palace by portal since there were no visual instructions associated with portal travel. There were no announcements or indeed any visual annunciators or displays. He realized this lack was due to strict security, whether from in or out.

Passengers were guided through the system by the Transport

Macron which read their travel cards while in transit. They could read and modify those cards at anytime without the passenger's knowledge and could also give verbal and visual instructions when necessary.

People came from all over the planet and wore every conceivable type of attire. To Mallory's amazement some of the young wore multicolored hair styles of the most bizarre designs which may have been considered outrageous in some places on Earth. They were very friendly, even when asked directions to special places of interest.

From what he could observe, the city was just like one of the cleaner Earth cities, but without the level of intimidation or violence. Cruelty was unheard of and ill considered in their society. As a result, everyone was quiet and pleasant. There were many android guards throughout, making their presence felt by their special uniforms. They made a particular groan which when heard ran shivers down one's spine. That particular noise was generated to instill fear and that it did with little misgivings. However, those androids carried no weapons and could reprimand or arrest any lawbreaker at a moment's notice.

'What do people do in this place and remain so pleased with themselves?' Mallory said.

'We have numerous friends to visit, careers, creative outlets and games to play. When we become bored with one type we soon move to another. Also, there are competitions for the best in every conceivable field. In other words, Mal, our lives are completely filled. If for some reason we are having problems it will be detected during our next visit to our local shrink and we can modify our lives to suit. Even so, we have much leeway in any rehabilitation and it's usually a joint decision. Finally, there are Virtual Games where we can immerse ourselves and become anyone and choose to experience any environment,' Jerry replied.

'This is truly incredible!' Mallory was speechless.

Every inch of the city was observed at all times. All data being fed into the Security Macron for analysis. However, the city's population and its visitors were never conscious of the ever present security system. It functioned invisibly behind the scene.

Roseanne was curious about the level of security in such a peaceful city.

'Why all the guards and security in such a peaceful place?' she asked.

'It's to do with certain long term procedures that have to be maintained for the benefit of all. Human nature takes a while to adapt to such stringent measures, unless when it persists. We must also be prepared for the first Javols,' Jerry replied.

'You think they are close?' Roseanne asked showing concern.

'We expect the first in about 100 years and there could be a few ahead of our predictions. Therefore we must be prepared,' Jerry replied.

'So all this is about approaching Javols?' Mallory asked.

'No, not all. Our present levels of security is just a computer procedure based on statistical analysis of human behavioural patterns. To them, I mean our Macrons, Earth is a constant reminder of the effects of runaway violence and lawlessness, and prevention is always better than cure. Once violent trends are started, they soon become the fashionable norm, leading to an ever decreasing and worsening spiral. Although the Andromedan humans are different to Earth's, there are many people from Earth on Eden and they have plans to bring a lot more of Earth's uncontaminated young to live with us.' Jerry replied.

'That's fantastic!'

'It's all Sarah's doing! Although the final population of Earth will be 500 million, Sarah has exempted over 100 million of the young below 20 years of age. So that final survival figure is really over 600 million. This is taken care of by the selection Macrons on Earth,' Jerry said and they were happier by that knowledge.

'What a great woman you are, Empress Sarah!' Roseanne exclaimed and the others agreed.

'She is the Greatest!' Jerry replied.

'It's great giving some of our young people a chance. After all, it's not their fault, for Earth's problems,' Roseanne said.

'Yes. We need them in our Federation where they will undergo the necessary training. To us councillors and Macrons, prevention is always preferable to sickness and then cure. That way our system remain highly efficient and healthy, without the costly overheads of crime and other antisocial behaviour which tends to feed on itself.'

'I see what you mean. You guys are always planning well ahead,' Mallory said.

'Further, Mal, one expects unrest, coup de tats and even wars during the life of every civilization. If not from within, from without. The Macrons simply works out worst case scenarios. Somewhat like a possible invasion from Earth within the next fifty years, or from the Javols within one hundred years. Either way, it is necessary for the society to be kept alert, prepared and practised in such methods of security, defence and survival.'

'Yea, but things that go on in people's heads are very difficult to predict. I might without a moment's notice decide to leave you and go somewhere else. How can anyone predict random thoughts?' Mallory said.

'That's why we always have to be prepared. But there is also defence of another kind. Certain weak strains of bio-engineered bacteria and virus, like the common cold are deliberately added to our water from the purification plants to maintain a strong immune system in the population. It also prevents biological regression and decay. For similar reasons, mixed marriages are frowned upon.'

'Why would you require such methods when you can live forever?' Roseanne asked.

'We live forever simply because we do not take Mother Nature for granted. That way we may enjoy and suffer just like any other. If I pass my finger across a sharp object will I not bleed? We live forever because we are in perfect sync with nature. Further, if we travel to Earth or other worlds our immunity should be strong enough to cope,' Jerry replied.

They took the moving walkways which travelled throughout the length and breath of Eden City. There were two sets of routes and each comprised fast and slow speeds in opposite directions. Ever so often the walkways would come to an abrupt stop near a beautiful fountain where robotic venders handed out drinks, snacks and sweets freely. Then travellers would join others for new destinations. The pillars were each marked with a type of symbolic language that changed for each traveller, but there were instructions in smaller English scripts. They could also observe several Christian churches and temples while on route. Those images made Mallory and Roseanne feel much more at home. Despite their agnostic leanings, religion symbolised freedom to worship and wherever there were several together, there was also people freedom.

The LPD cabs flew to and fro throughout the complex city like darting fireflies. They appeared to be the fastest means of transport for those in a hurry. Apparently, such vehicles were not owned by anyone and were driven by uniformed androids that spoke to their passengers like normal people. They gave useful information and made them feel more at ease during each trip.

There were no lamp lights on poles anywhere in the city. Five large rings of light floated above the city at night showering it with light which was adjusted in brilliance to suit the occasion and time of night. They returned to their respective perches on the top of the highest buildings at the beginning of each day. Local filtered light came from the side of walkways and only where they were needed.

Most buildings had their own internal power sources in triplicate and a common electrical power grid was not used. However many basic appliances also contained their own nuclear power sources. That way, the system could hold no one to ransom when there were power cuts.

Food and other essential commodities were supplied randomly through small secured Kitchen Portals for each individual. Those portals were just untraceable numbers in the computer system, and only the Macrons knew who they represented. All the major decisions were taken by Councillors and Macrons for the benefit of their society.

Eden City was within Sarah's Protectorate State and she was therefore their Lady Protector and Chief Councillor. However, there were many subcommittees, committees and sub-councils before any complaints got to the Grand Council of Protectorate Lords and Ladies.

Although democratic, their society was probably the only true technocratic one in existence and it worked only because of the minimal requirement of money. It was also based on robots and androids which serviced the masses at little cost to anyone. In such a society everything was easily obtainable and available to everyone and they had a complete galaxy of worlds from which to choose.

The population was controlled to just two children per family. Anymore was usually frowned upon, although no positive steps were ever taken to chastise the offenders. It was just common sense to have small families. Most people were genetically similar and almost identical anyway. Why have more of the same for the sake of some basic primordial instinct?

Any law or rule could be changed by a majority vote of the Grand Council and corruption was nonexistent. They were all owners of their world and the system did not lend itself to those practices because of the random nature of distribution and other methods of supply and demand.

Those found abusing the system were promptly stripped of their seniority and placed at the bottom of the ladder, and that was not a considered alternative because of their lost privileges.

Where there were many intelligent life-forms, there had to be a structure or very soon chaos reigned and the weaker was usually the first to suffer. On Eden things could never have progressed that far. They were all too happy and content with their modus vivendi.

Their society was mainly Andromedan and ran on similar lines to the way life used to be on Caefon before the Javols destroyed it. It was a way of life based on their great prophet Siend Seno of Mond and their main religion was Senorian. It's main followers were called Senots.

Yet, it was a proven way of life and an alternative that worked successfully with great freedom and respect for all. Everyone was only expected to work for the good of the state during three months in each year. After that time they would pursue their own business and hobbies.

'We have heard a lot about Central Macron. Is it really a

powerful computer that governs all?' Mallory asked.

'By the way, Mac is not an object, she is a living, breathing entity. Since you are so keen on meeting her, why don't we pay her a visit,' he said and they were both intrigued.

Jerry decided to take them to the administrative block in the middle of the city. While they travelled, they could observe many pedestrians, but none were more than thirty-five years old. Physically, Mallory was probably the oldest person on Eden.

'This world has certain rejuvenation properties. However many also take special drugs every six months to renew their metabolism. That way, they never age physically. However, there is always the Megotron for a complete transformation. You both should consider that alternative while you are here. Why die of old age when there is always so much for your capable minds to achieve. You must think seriously about what I've just said and let me know your decisions before you leave,' Jerry said.

When they got closer to the city's centre, they could observe many theatres and cinemas, and Mallory wondered whether they showed any of Earth's violent films.

'What type of films are shown here? Are they violent?' Mallory asked.

'No! My friend. Those cinemas are for children, and they are not violent. Just lovely stories with a good moral topic. A few Earth films are also shown, but they are thoroughly censored. Here, grown-ups use more realistic Virtual Image Projectors in their own homes. During such Virtual Interactions we can feel real pain and experience every feeling as if we were in that world and at that time. Films are just 2D visual images and do not effect our senses in like manner.'

'You are talking 3D with special glasses?' Roseanne asked.

'No! Our systems are much more advanced. We can create any country or place, along with its people and their troubles, from ancient Greek to the second world war and it can all be extremely violent and bloody. We can also become part of that society interactively to such an extent that we become part of them. It gets bad feelings and frustrations out of the way and we experience the true reality of pain and suffering in all its forms. When we get home, I shall arrange for one later this evening,' Jerry said.

'I will look forward to that new experience,' Mallory replied with curiosity.

'I'm not so sure?' Roseanne became worried.

'Be brave, Woman!' Mallory jested, but she briefly changed the topic.

'Are there no hospitals on Eden?' Roseanne asked.

'No! My dear. Every individual carries a card and some like me, with special Brain Implants. Over the years everyone has been tested and scanned by Megotrons. The resulting data and DNA groupings are held in central Macron. She is also tied into Megotrons that are situated throughout the city and elsewhere on Eden. There are also accident cubicles in every building where anyone can be administered first aid. For more serious accidents, like the loss of a limb, they would be transferred by local portal to a Megotron chamber where a new limb can be regrown. In the unfortunate incident of death, the same process will be used to create a new heart, plot new blood vessels, or whatever is required. Because of the ubiquitous citing of these portals, the service is almost instantaneous,' Jerry said.

'That is incredible. You are all truly immortal,' Roseanne replied.

'I suppose... Given the choice, not many would take the alternative of death. If one is tired with their present existence, they simply visit a psycho councillor, who may advise them on whatever changes are required in their lives. That change could be anything from a different lifestyle to a new wife, mutually agreed, of course.

The children from that failed relationship would be given to a more senior councillor for safe keeping until their problem is resolved. Here, children belong to the society and are allowed to live with a married couple who happens to be their parents. Even so, they can have their own or other children back when they remarry and lead a more stable existence. A form of re-adoption, if you wish.'

'What a strange method. I suppose governments always have the final say, even on Earth,' Roseanne said.

'Here, marriage only last for nine years, and can be renewed or re-licensed on a five-year basis. Yet, there are not many contract defaulters or unrenewed licenses,' Jerry continued.

'Freedom of choice in the long term. I suppose lots of people change with experience. Also their circumstances change in unpredictable ways. That method can relieve such problems and give them a fresh start in life,' Mallory said.

'Many of the children you saw at Sarah's palace are adopted in that way. To them she is like their real mother and they consider themselves to be very lucky while living among such a great woman. Their original parents may see them on neutral territory from time to time, until the situation is resolved on a more permanent basis. Here again, it is all geared to the benefit of the child,' Jerry said.

They soon arrived at the Admin Block and ported to his office in the main section. Jerry then introduced them to a few of his loyal assistants and fellow councillors, before taking another portal to Central Macron. That one he called Mac for short. There were many androids in that area, all handling numerous amounts of data in every form, but many were guards specially designed to secure and defend their central brain.

'Our Central Macron is equivalent to several hundred million of the best human minds working together in parallel. Mac is fully self-aware and conscious, but exists within her own universe. It's a different type of reality to our own that encompasses all possibilities. To her, our three-dimensional universe is but a small part of the complex whole and is of little interest on its own. She is perfectly safe here and can transpose to a safer place on Eden if her existence was endangered,' Jerry said.

It was not what Mallory and Roseanne had expected. The main peripheral of the complex system was a most beautiful female android that was wearing a white suit. She was the human link between the machine and was also a senior councillor. However, there were also several privileged human assistants and bird people who had been given special brain implants for the job. Those could communicate directly with Mac telepathically at thousands of times faster than normal people to save time.

The computer itself was a large sphere and its outside consisted of several blinking blocks. Many of those blocks were for bulk information storage, with individual capacities of billions upon billions of terabytes. They were linked to the central processor unit which did the thinking.

'Please meet Petra. She is a chief controller,' Jerry said and she came forward to greet them. There she stood in all white and wearing a bold federation insignia on her broad lapel.

'I have been looking forward to meeting you and Madam Roseanne, Siend Mallory. I trust you are enjoying your stay on our pleasant world?' she said, with a mild but almost hypnotizing voice.

'Yes, Lady Petra, we are having a great time,' Roseanne said to the beautiful and powerful female android, for she was nothing less than human.

'You must visit us again soon before you leave our world. I enjoy a little gossip with visitors from Earth. It is such an intriguing world,' she said, genuinely.

'Perhaps we shall,' Roseanne said.


That day they visited many places and seen many things in Eden City. Everything necessary was automatically recorded within the small computer they were each given, including catalogues of appliances and clothes, from which they could directly order items.

After visiting a restaurant in the city centre, and having had a most enjoyable pizza with glasses of the local lager and wine, they took the nearest portal for Jerry's home.

## CHAPTER 14

# A universe of games

Later that evening Jerry took them to the projection room in his palace. The room was padded throughout with a white material that displayed strange patterns.

'This is the V-Room, here almost any pseudo reality may be created!'

'What a strange place!' Roseanne commented.

'Would you like to join us in a game? Perhaps we could do ancient Rome today.'

'You mean an actual Ancient Roman!' Mallory was intrigued.

'So real, you couldn't tell the difference. We have thousands of worlds to choose from including numerous historical periods and scenarios from ancient Greek to the Wild West. As a matter of fact, any good book may be turned into a virtual program by the Game Macron in much the same way as a movie is made.'

'Really?' Roseanne was fascinated.

'The Macron simply creates the actors and the scenes, and compiles the whole thing in a matter of seconds, instead of months or years as needed by film companies. Here, you may become a real actor and play one of the dominant roles in every scene.'

'This should be interesting?' Mallory couldn't wait.

'There are hidden portals throughout this area that can be manipulated by the Macron to give the impression of infinity in every direction,' Jerry continued.

The light dimmed and a beautiful sunset filled the area they observed.

'The landscape you now observe in this small area is limitless. Like Alice in Wonderland, you could take that route over there and walk to infinity over the hills and vales. Any world and its historical periods can be simulated in this large room, including its varied life-forms. By so doing our perceptions may be carried to an interactive level of reality that can deceive anyone, including ourselves. It becomes one with the player and can be a lot more realistic when the players wear Brain Implants. With this unit I do not need a Golf Course, or in fact any type of stadium or arena. They can be created by the Macron with audiences if required.' Jerry said.

'You are telling me, you can create any environment with real talking players?'

'Yes, and a lot more besides. Once the game begins, your parameters are fed into the Macron and from that moment on you and every one of your senses become part of the scene. This includes weather conditions, smell, touch and pain, including all associated dangers and pleasures.' Jerry continued.

'As real as that?' Roseanne was hesitant and wanted to leave.

'What would you like to become? Emperor, centurion, guard's, captain or some other character? You will have to choose your clothes and weapons from the panel over there,' Jerry said.

'We could go Roman if you like,' Mallory said with hesitation and foreboding in his voice, so Roseanne remained.


Suddenly the scene changed into dusty streets bustling with pedlars and Roman soldiers. They selected their clothes and suddenly found themselves in different areas of the scene. To make the game even more interesting, the Macron made unexpected changes of its own to the game while being played.

Instead of being the loyal wife of one Marcus Pyrinius (Mallory), Roseanne was a captured slave on her way to the slave market. Marcus was on his way to that same place to buy new slaves. He was presently a trader in such novelties. She was shackled with nine other slaves. Two guards with whips made sure the slaves kept pace.

Marcus never liked to see his female slaves beaten by sadistic guards, because it left bruises and cuts that could reduce their market value. Nevertheless, although he found such violence repulsive, he didn't mind if he was the potential buyer, since their bruises worked in his favour for a good bargain.

He expected to see a few of his enemies and friends at the government auctions in the main square, where the Greeks and other captured slaves were put on show.

Roseanne was now Helen, of Greek descent. She couldn't believe that she was a slave and at the head of her pack on the way to market. She had a strong impulsion to escape, but to where could she run or hide. After assessing her situation she decided to remain with the group and take her opportunity when the time came. She would never be a slave again for anyone and those Roman dogs will pay dearly for what they had done to her master.

She had been confiscated along with many of her master's possessions for tax evasion purposes. At least that was the meagre excuse given by the Plebeian dogs. He was setup and put to the sword after a manufactured scuffle. After that encounter all his possessions were confiscated.

Marcus soon overtook the group of slaves. He was eyeing the women in his usual manner, looking for deformities, cuts and bruises, before they were put on show. He had been taken once before, when he was new and green in the slave market, but he swore, never again.

The slaves were unshackled and placed on a large viewing platform that was surrounded by many guards. The area was well lit with oil lamps and the wealthy tribune, Palodius, was there to oversee the proceedings. That arrogant tribune had thick gold rings on every finger with larger ones on his blue and red toga. On his head he wore a golden band of olive and laurel leaves and in his right hand an Egyptian staff with the head of a bird carved from ebony.

He was sitting on a wide ornate chair and signalled the slaves to come forward. The guards soon set them in line and he observed them individually from their teeth down to their fingers and nails. Then he returned them to their original positions.

Marcus was suddenly nudged from one side.

'I wager you twenty talents that Palodius gets the beautiful one on the right. She must be worth fifty at least,' he said.

'And I bet you, Casius (Jerry), that I get the maiden for another thirty talents,' Marcus (Mallory) said, as they greeted each other.

'She is the slave girl of Ludni Demitrius, who was himself a slave trader like us. From what I heard, they killed him and took his home for supposed tax evasion, but I think it was all Palodius-'s doing. He has always been a treacherous one. You must watch your step with that one. However I think his days are numbered. He has too many enemies among us. One of these nights he will be greeted with a lance between his ribs and a dagger in his neck,' Casius said.

'I know, I have done business with Ludni in the past. If what you say is true, he will pay dearly for taking one of us so blatantly,' Marcus replied indignantly.

'I think it all started several months ago. That was when Ludni outbid him for the beautiful female. He went twenty-five over the odds to make sure he didn't get her. Anyway, he's been plotting against him ever since, with the help of a few of his friends in high places. They will each get a share of Ludni's property, one way or another,' Casius said.

'Scum like that should never be made tribune and given power over our poor plebeians. Perhaps we shall play him a little game of our own,' Marcus said with that familiar look in his eye when he targeted a wager.

'She is the one that he wanted then, and I am sure that his desire has not waned a bit since, brother Marcus. Luckily she was not one of Ludni's household slaves. Then by law she could not be resold in the market, and by so doing become the legal property of Palodius by default at half her usual price, if unsold. Today of all days, she will cost you at least seventy,' Casius said.

'You can make it a hundred, for all I care. He will not have her, and that is that,' Marcus replied, defiantly.

'And have your property repossessed, including your slaves?' Casius warned and Marcus remained silent for a while, calculating the odds and checking whether his tax payments were up to date, and they were.

As always, the bidding began from left to right and she was the last in line. Marcus had only bought one of the slaves, saving his purse for the one on the right, in case he would have to outbid Palodius.

'I bid fifty for this tempestuous and unhealthy looking wench!' Palodius shouted.

'Sixty!' shouted someone from the crowd.

'Seventy!' Palodius again attacked.

'Eighty!' Marcus shouted, getting into the bidding and Palodius viewed him with what could only be considered utter contempt. Palodius again outbidding with ninety.

'One hundred!' Marcus shouted, with a grin of satisfaction and there was a row of laughter among his colleagues that was focussed towards Palodius. From that moment Palodius features turned to boiling anger and hatred for Marcus. He tapped the armrest with his weighted fingers to release some of his pent-up fury.

Turning to Casius, Marcus whispered: 'I wish I didn't wager that girl with you, then I would have let the fool take her at three hundred.' Realizing he would have to hold some money back in case he lost to Palodius. Several of his friends overheard his words and once again there was a roar of laughter from among them.

The bidding went on up to two hundred, amidst much laughter and cheer from Marcus's following. At that point Palodius gave up, feeling somewhat belittled by Marcus and his gang, and walked out with his company in tour. Then there were more laughter and jeering from the crowd, who had by that time caught on to the amusement. Palodius would have her one way or another, and the other way wouldn't have been to Marcus's liking, or so he thought.

When it was all over, Casius paid Marcus his fifty talents. Helen was taken to Marcus's house, fed, bathed and clothed. Then she joined his other slaves in their compound. He would have to watch his back from now on, because he didn't know what cunning scheme Palodius was plotting against him.

Soon the word had got around about what had happened to Ludni and the traders visited Marcus's house to discuss a mode of action against Palodius. They argued that Palodius did not play fairly, always wanting the best slaves for himself, and that any of them could follow the same course as Ludni.

'We must set a snare to catch a fat rat. Leave it with me for now. I shall try to figure out a plan,' Marcus said. Then they sneaked away in the dead of night without arousing any suspicion.

Later that evening he called the slave girl, Helen (Roseanne), to his private quarters.

'You paid way over the odds for me today, you know. I hope I am worth it,' she said.

'I just wanted to teach Palodius a lesson for what he did to your master. He was one of us and I will sign you as one of my house slaves, so you needn't worry about going to market again. What we have to do is wait for his next move. By that time we should have a few of our own worked out, but you are not to leave this house in the mean time,' Marcus said.

'Tell me what I have to do to help you? I don't want you to follow the same faith as Ludni, and I need some payback,' she said.

'Just remain here and do as I ask, and pray to Jupiter and Juno for me,' he said.

'I shall go to the temple and pray to Juno, if anyone can help, she can,' she replied.

'I have given the matter much thought and can find no neat way to deal with this matter. He has too many powerful friends in high places, and I don't want news to get around that I am after him. I shall have to call him out. Call him a useless scum-bag in front of witnesses. Then he would have to fight me on a one to one basis, I being a senior and a well-respected merchant,' he said.

'But he will cut you to pieces. He is one of the best with a sword, you know, and such a challenge might give him great pleasure in cutting you down to size, and I mean that literally,' she replied.

'There is no other alternative. In any case, I will have choice of weapons, which for me has always been the mace and dagger. I used to be one of the best in that form of combat once and trained by a master gladiator. All I need is a little practice before I make the challenge. Let's pray that he doesn't attack us before then,' Marcus said.

Marcus knew where Palodius was to be found, so after he had explained his plan to Casius and a few others, he stopped him in the street.

'Palodius, I think you are a gutless rat for killing my friend Ludni and I intend to give you a good whipping like you deserve,' Marcus said. Palodius looked the smaller man over with sarcasm and scorn.

'In that case, why don't we make it official. I hereby challenge the fool Marcus to a fight to the death. Let it so be written, most useless idiot!' he challenged in front of his companion.

'I accept, you Palodius moron!' Marcus replied and Casius, Marcus friend and witness, accepted to be his second on the day.

'You being the challenger, gives me choice of weapons,' Marcus said.

'Have whatever you desire, trumped up Plebeian fool. It will do you no good against my sword. You will pay dearly in blood for past insults,' Palodius replied.

'Shall we say at noon tomorrow, in the old arena? You bring one observer and I shall do likewise, and no hidden snipers, please,' Marcus said and strolled away.

Marcus had several hours practice before his meeting with Palodius, but was not happy with his technique. Nevertheless it was now too late, so he practised a few of his better moves and power strokes with the mace.

The following day they met each other in the arena as planned and their companions made sure their suits were tightly fastened, then their helmets went on. Marcus held his shield in his right hand and mace in his left. That was the way he was trained to combat and confuse sword users.

The first swipe came unsuspectingly from Palodius and took Marcus by surprise, which almost made him stumble behind his shield. He dived and parried another powerful blow with his mace, then countered.

It was not the fight Marcus had expected. At his greater age, the ordeal was tiring and Palodius was not even showing the slightest signs of fatigue. He would have to find a weakness soon in his technique and exploit it, or so Marcus thought.

Another blow was struck by Palodius. This time Marcus countered with his shield and returned with his mace, to be again similarly countered. However, this time Palodius shield had a dent and the man struggled backwards under the force of that blow.

'So your weakness is one of balance,' Marcus mumbled to himself.

'You should be thankful I am yet playing with you, swine!' Palodius barked, but Marcus remained silent, concentrating on his every move and blow.

Despite Palodius's greater agility, Marcus was much heavier and firmer on his feet and could put much into his heavy mace. Palodius, was fast and agile with the sword, but was not very strong on his feet.

This time Marcus put as much as he could into his mace, and went into Palodius's shield, but took too long in forming the blow and Palodius swiped him one across his left arm. It was not a deep wound, but the smell of his own blood reminded him of worse things to come. The recoil of his own blow was too much for Palodius and he dropped his shield. It was then that Marcus went after him, tooth and nail, until his sword was discarded by a powerful swipe from the mace.

Once Marcus had gained the advantage, he just gave it every-thing he had and like a tornado, went about Palodius without relent. Then it was Palodius's helmet, as he crashed unto the stone of the central arena. The mace had crushed his skull and there he lay shivering uncontrollably while life drained from his body. He was left in his blood in the field of battle and Casius moved towards Marcus, in sympathy.

He then aided Marcus out of the arena and towards their cart. There waiting was a worried Helen. She had run all the way from his house to assist with more remedy for his wounds.

'I told you to remain home. You should not be seen out here with us!' Marcus complained.

'Remain still while I check your wounds. What does it matter now, anyway? The disgusting traitor is dead. I watched the whole thing from beyond the last row and cheered when the pig fell. I wanted payback and I got my fill of it, thanks to your courage,' she said.

'This day, my friend, you had both Juno and Jupiter on your

side. I thought you would never make it after he cut you. It seemed a nasty one at the time. Let's have a look at that one. I also took along some special remedy and tools,' Casius said and they slid his armour off and tore his toga to get a clear view of the wound before cleaning it with oils and applying herbs and a black ointment.

'It's only superficial and unlike Palodius, you'll live to see another day. However, you will have to hide for a while until the heat is off, and that wound is a dead give away. I took care of his friend and hid him in the bushes, so we shouldn't have problems from his friends for a while,' Casius said, now very happy that Marcus was temporarily out of danger. Then the arm was bandaged.

'If I go into hiding now, they will think I am guilty. Just do a good job with my shoulder and Helen can dress the wound occasionally. In the mean time I shall have to concoct a good alibi,' Marcus said.

When he arrived home that day, he told no one about the fight and those who knew had taken an oath to preserve the silence.

The following day several soldiers arrived at his house and began to search his armoury and weapons for traces of blood, but none could be found. They had already been discarded in a local pond.

'You haven't heard the last of this, Marcus. We shall be back,' the captain said with little uncertainty in his voice.

'I told you, I had nothing to do with any fighting or whatever you think I have been up to, and I don't even know the fellow, Palodius. I only saw him a few times from a distance at the slave auctions,' Marcus said, innocently, never showing any discomfort from his still painful arm. Then the captain ordered his men to leave and he hoped the worst was over for him.

The scenes changed briefly into another as if moving in time towards the future, and they found themselves back in Jerry's V-room, back in their original clothes and without a scratch to mind or body.

'What's happening... It was all so realistic, Jerry, and my cut is gone. I thought I was really in ancient Rome and you, my dear, was my own slave and my arm was really in pain. We were then struggling to survive one Palodius who I slew in battle. How can any show be so realistic?' Mallory said, as he slowly recovered from the change.

'Subliminals, are also transmitted during the projection. They hypnotise you into the scene. Once you are caught into the action, they are reenforced by your emotions like fear, love, loyalty and so forth, for those sensations are what mankind is all about. Then you become so involved and absorbed by the story that you cannot doubt its reality. It could even be a lot more realistic if you both had implants. You should also realize that unlike 2D movies, our senses like smell, and other environmental stimuli are present to reenforce those sensations,' Jerry said.

'With such a device like this, one could train armies without even getting out of the building. One could relieve all pent-up feelings and desires, never to practice them against real people on the streets. What a place this Eden really is,' Mallory said.

'Now you know why we don't use cinemas or theatres on Eden,' Jerry said and they smiled at his relaxed attitude to all things.

# A decision for the new


They took the portal from Jerry's palace back to Sarah's and after spending some time with the children, retired to their bedroom. The couple had experienced so many new things during their brief stay on Eden that it took them a while to absorb it all.

On Mallory's mind was the Roman experience in Jerry's V-room and whether or not they should take the implants and other advantages freely offered by Jerry, Sarah and others.

'Why are you so quite, my beautiful Helen of Troy?' Mallory inquired playfully. Roseanne turned her head around from the large mirror to face him.

'Darling, I'm still recovering from slavery. It was so real I'm having withdrawal symptoms. It's like I was in a previous life,' she replied.

'Yea, but it helps us better face reality, while those 2D movies assist in inciting us to do terrible things without feeling the true consequences of our actions,' he replied and she was satisfied with his answer.


All the people he observed on Eden were very happy and contented with their way of life. They were not like the technological zombies that he and Roseanne had expected. Even Jerry appeared to be more of himself than when he was President of the USA. Admittedly, it was a technological society, but one geared to the happiness and nourishment of that society with everything being supplied freely. That was with the exception of a few dangerous pursuits and luxury items that many did not require anyway. It was truly a unique society that any parent would relish for bringing up children. Mallory and Roseanne pondered those thoughts.

Nevertheless, they were told by Jerry that the addition of Brain Implants would be a simple transformation in the Megotron chamber, which also included a Psyrotron for scanning one's mind to record their thoughts. During which time his body and mind would be scanned and genetically replicated to another parallel casket, with the micro devices or implants already transposed into his brain and connected to the relevant information centres. The implants themselves did not require any external power source, as they had micro batteries and could use certain chemical changes in the brain for maintaining their own power. However, they could be recharged with an external microwave transmitter set to the relevant frequency when necessary.

He was also told that those implants would increase his mental powers some tenfold, giving him access to all types of new data, including the ability to communicate directly with other implant holders and Macrons in a Virtual Universe of the mind. He could then become several doctors in many subjects. They were completely transparent to the host's mind and could be switched on or off by certain thought codes, visual image sequences and suchlike, but it also included a death signal that was transmitted to Central Macron in the event of his death.

The Megotron would then use the previously recorded information on his original body to begin the process of creating a new body for him, or to revive the old one.

In the first case, his new body would lose all memory between the time of its last mind recordings and death. That was one of the reasons why it was necessary to go through the scanners at least once a year. For that system to work it was imperative that a special portal was installed at Mallory's house on Earth. Therefore many things had to be discussed between them and Central Macron (Mac) before that step could be taken.

After diving into their comfortable bed that night they spent a little while discussing those issues.

'Love, what do you think of this place? Could you make it your second home?' Mallory asked.

'I could make it my first if you were here with me and I knew I could visit Earth whenever I wanted,' Roseanne replied.

'I never thought this world would ever get to you this way. Remember that time with Ben, when you thought the whole thing was a big joke. Now you are purring like a little kitten,' he said and showed a big grin.

'I know, cynical me. That's the reason why I came along. I wanted to prove you wrong. Now that I am here, I can't see any harm or problems associated with this world. You know, talking to the palace children has shown me the true nature of Solarians. Young kids never lie. You can always see the guilt and unhappiness in their eyes, or they would show extreme antisocial behaviour, but those here are just great kids, full of innocent love and kindness,' Roseanne said.

'I never thought this place could be so rich in everything, but it is. You know, when people talk of heaven and perfection, one always thinks of eternal boredom, but here, even the most painful and dangerous can be experienced in the V-room. How would you feel if you were put in the most beautiful flower garden, forever? I don't know much about you, but if I was not a botanist I would get bored after the first day.' Mallory said.

'I see your point!' she replied.

'We humans need a great variety of change over a wide spectrum in order to be happy and my variety might not be your cup of tea. Here, however, one can experience any change without involving or sacrificing themselves or others in the process. You know, I felt like I never been before when I fought Palodius for you and for what I thought was right. I had the feelings of satisfaction and happiness after we won, although they were just images created by a clever computer,' he said.

'I know how you feel. Don't forget, I was that unfortunate slave-girl. Although I once doubted you and Ben about life on Eden, now, I don't even want to return home. I think we should seriously consider their offer, and have the implants, with a suitable reduction in age before we return to Earth. I don't think we should reject immortality, providing we keep it a secret from our families and friends on Earth. Most won't believe us anyway,' Roseanne said.

'And there are the wicked Javols after our blood. I don't want any of them to visit Earth or Eden!' Mallory replied.

Once again, the furniture and wall covering of their rooms had changed to different shapes and patterns. Roseanne was utterly surprised by it all and wondered how such changes were possible in the brief time they had left the palace. She had observed similar changes every time they went to bed, but was too tired to comment. Every time there was a different set of colours on the walls and the furniture cushions changed to match. The changes were quite subtle and blended well with the other items in the room.

'Do you think it's all virtual here as well?' she asked and he smiled.

'I suppose you are referring to the different patterns on the walls and elsewhere. I think it's all to do with micro robotics. What we call nano-technology back home. Here they must have it down to a fine art. That dust stuff must cover the walls. Even the furniture could be composed of them. I once read a book on the subject, also written by Doctor Longhurst. He said that anything can be composed of that stuff, and it can change its form into any other with a simple instruction.'

'That's impossible!' Roseanne exclaimed.

'Darling, nothing is impossible! You know, like our hospital robots. There must be a transmitter somewhere about that is linked to the palace Macron. I suppose the computer must be instructed by one of our young friends who came in here to make the changes for us. Either that, or a random sequence. However, I am sure we could try the system ourselves and see if our theory is correct,' he said and she viewed him in disbelief.

'You mean, all you do is ask the computer and all the decoration and furnishings in this room can be changed to one's personal liking? Are you sure we should try? I don't want anything to go wrong while we are here. Sarah might get the wrong idea,' she said.

'Just a little thing to prove the point.

'Computer, could you change this bedside table into a chair,' he said. While they watched the table slowly melted and buckled into the form of a chair of the original colour, but there was no cushion or hand rests.

'Darling, do you see what I mean. Therefore I must rest my case,' Mallory said nervously.

'It has changed into the basic format of a chair. If we wanted different colours or a soft cushion, I suppose we could choose from a set of standard designs, colours and textures by a simple code, and there must be a tremendous variation in size. By so doing small solid objects can be transformed into ten times their size with a more hollow construction,' he said.

Suddenly a voice with local screen came on with selections and they chose violet. In front of their eyes the bed spread and cushions would transform into a most beautiful violet texture.

'I see it, but I don't believe it. This whole palace must be like one living organism. I don't know if I can ever get used to the idea,' she said, still frightened by the ordeal.

'It's probably just the wall covering and some of the most used furniture. The process must save a lot on decorating. Personally, I think it's a neat idea,' he said.

'Shall we tell Jerry tomorrow, of our intention to have the implants and other changes, and we shall need special weapons for when we get back?' she asked.

'Only if you want us to go through with it. I don't know if the procedure is reversible, and if anyone of us decides to change their mind, we'll both look like ace idiots,' he said.

'I have given it much thought and think we should start our marriage as immortals, to assist our people on Earth and through-out Osmaron. Sarah gave me a full run down on the Javol's threat and I would like to be around to fight them off when the time comes. For now, you could do with ten years reduction and me, five in physical age,' she said.

'What do you think Carl and others will think when we return looking like teenagers?' he asked.

'They will think we had a great honeymoon holiday. We could always exaggerate a little about a visit to one of the best health farms. However, we should also try to get Carl converted like us. He is a very good guy, honest and conscientious,' she said.

'Ok, Darling. I am sold. I will tell Jerry tomorrow and the rest we can do when we get back. Now, let's have some shut-eyes,' he said.


That night they had the most pleasant dreams since their arrival on Eden. There was not the slightest sound in their room. When they arose early that morning cups of coffee were ready on the side table.

'Would you like me to run your baths or do you prefer a shower,' the computer asked.

'Shower please,' they both replied.

'Breakfast will be in one hour's time. Casuals may be worn,' it added.

CHAPTER 16

# Megotron conversion

As always, Jerry and his wife visited the couple each day at Sarah's palace. During that time they had breakfast together before leaving for their daily excursions. At that period of Eden's year there were few council meetings held and everyone knew most councillors, including Sarah and Lumak were away. In any event the Macron was quite capable of running things in their absence. Therefore all serious debating in chamber was held in stasis until she and the others returned.

Most of the six Ancients or Andromedan elders, including Lord Meron, were also away to a local uninhabited factory world assisting in its conversion for young human settlements. Those expected young human adventurers would consist mainly of engineers and scientists from Earth. They had been trained by Solarian Banking in Sol-Newtown and on Eden in their relevant fields. At that time many young people wanted a new life well away from the turmoils of Earth. Most of those were in their late teens and early twenties that had left families and friends permanently for their new life.

The Ancient's visit to those worlds, Melos III and Tyrrel II, was just for a month, while its new human inhabitants settled into their new lives. During that time they would be assigned their duties and estates. Secured portals were also being constructed to and from Eden City for their benefit. However, each couple, when married, would have the same privileges as anyone on Eden. From the time of their settlement they were all to be considered normal and mature Solarians with the usual benefits.

That morning Mallory and Roseanne decided to have a serious chat with Jerry before they went on their daily excursions.

'We have given serious consideration to everything you said and have decided to take the full treatment. We would therefore like to have the implants and any necessary reduction in age as appropriate before our return to Earth. This is mainly because we have much work to do on Earth and would like to be around and fully involved when the Javols arrive, if that's ok with you?' Mallory said.

'That's incredible news. It's nice to have you both on board. May I take this opportunity to congratulate you on that very important decision? This needs a stiff drink,' he said and one of the palace androids soon entered the room with a tray containing a bottle of vodka, lime juice, tonic and glasses.

'I hope you don't mind. It's a habit I just couldn't give up. I still have a drink or two on special occasions like this. Old habits die hard, eh!' A happy Jerry smiled while the android poured and mixed four drinks in precise amounts.

'Will that be all, Sir?' he said, before departing.

'Yes! Thank you, Carl!' Jerry replied. 'Let's hold our glasses and give a judicious toast to love, happiness, success and survival, to everyone throughout Solaria and beyond. Most importantly to the repair of our mother-planet, Earth, which is also an important part of Solaria.'

'To Solaria!' they cheered.

'You two mustn't worry too much about your fief here while you are away. I shall personally see to the construction of your palace. I didn't tell you, but architecture is one of my fortes. I shall send several plans in due course for your approval,' Jerry said. He then went over to them and gave them both a big hug.

'There is one more thing, however?' Mallory said.

'Anything, my friends... anything!' Jerry replied.

'I need some special weapons for my new soldiers on Earth. They must be made invincible and all weapons must be designed to self-destruct if they find themselves in the wrong hands. Perhaps a special code that can be initiated from base,' he said.

'Don't worry, Mal. We already have a range of such weapons. Those are called Plasma Projectors. They are made in two sizes, hand and mobile. Each contains its own internal nuclear fusion generator. They respond to implants or by a small button transmitter on the body of their user. If the carrier signal from the button transmitter is missing, which only has a range of one hundred metres or so, they will blip for a period of time before entering the self-destruct mode. Either that, or they will not function until once again in close proximity with their authorized user. It's all programmable. The system can be precisely adjusted to your needs. I shall also get you a battle Macron. However, all this must be kept in isolation from all others on Earth, because we wouldn't like any of it to get into the wrong hands. I shall arrange a demonstration before you leave.'

'Nice one! That will be great!' Mallory was ecstatic.

'In the mean time, we are to visit Mac in the city and arrange your conversion immediately. If you don't mind,' Jerry said.

'Can the process be reversed? I mean, if something was to go wrong?' Roseanne asked.

'Yes, my dear, everything is fully reversible. Don't worry, you have my word that everything will be all right!' Jerry stressed.


This time they took the most direct route to the Central Macron by portal from the palace. After their arrival Jerry had a few quiet words with Mac through his implants and she called the couple into a local office. Jerry and his wife, Sharon, waited patiently for them in the local reception area.

'I am pleased that you have decided to become one of us. Do you have any professional preferences? I would like to supply you with implants that are suitably programmed and tuned to the individual,' Mac said.

'I have spent most of my life in security, but I am also interested in science. It's a profession I could not have pursued when I was younger because of other commitments,' Mallory said.

'I am also in security and would like to be more efficient in the field, but I would also like to become a medic. In case someone got hurt during any of our future missions,' Roseanne replied.

'Well chosen. One scientist and a doctor, both agile fighters with the most advanced Martial Arts. You will be given the latest implants with many new facilities to be explained to you later. Even while we speak they are being programmed.'

'Thank you!' Roseanne said.

'Have you had any medical operations or transplants since birth?' she asked. They both nodded in the negative sense, nervously. Both felt like impatient children waiting for the dentist. Mallory considered his back damage from the  bullet he took for Jerry many years ago, but didn't have further repairs, despite scarring which played up sometimes.

'In that case, if you have no further objection, we shall proceed with the conversion. I would like you both to follow the operator and do exactly as she asks,' Mac said and another android woman entered the room wearing a white and blue uniform.

'Please follow!' she said and took them to another room where they were made comfortable with a virtual image projection of important places on Eden.

'You may wait here for now,' she said to Mallory. 'And you can follow me,' she said to Roseanne, who again followed her to another room. This time it resembled a large laboratory with many strange devices.

'Please remove your clothes for a full body inspection. Then you will wear this cap before entering the shower. It is to prevent your hair from getting wet. After a thorough scan you will be placed under the Psyrotron for a neuro-scan. After that operation has been completed, you will enter the Megotron chamber to be physically modified,' she said, in a most serious and matter of fact manner.

Roseanne removed her clothes, rings and earrings, then she went through a body scanner that searched for non-biological parts. Then her complete body was scanned, down to her skeletal structures, checking for any defects or malformations that would have been repaired or replaced during the Megotron's activation.

'Although you are in good physical health, your body will be optimised to an equivalent age of twenty-eight years. That is your present recommended optimum age. Further changes can be carried out with less trauma at a later date, after you have grown used to your new body and associated implants. Once those changes have been made, the bio-blueprint will be available for future changes,' she said.

Roseanne was then shown into the shower room where she was thoroughly cleaned. Then powerful blowers came on and she became dry in seconds. The cap was one of those tight fitting ones that pressed close to her scalp to conceal her hair.

'You may stand in the centre of this circle,' she said, while assisting her into position. The operator then went to a panel, a code was selected by hand and a large device descended from the ceiling. It resembled a large circular light with numerous concentric rings. The central part fitted closely to her head and covered her eyes. Another ring lifted from the floor to support her body and that part began to slowly rotate, anticlockwise. The moment the rotation began the device above her head also began to pulsate in brilliance, each ring having its turn in sequence.

After a short time, the lower ring which held her body changed its direction of rotation and the whole sequence was repeated until the process was completed. Then she was released and the units returned to their original places in the ceiling and below the floor.

'Do you feel all right?' the operator asked, as she assisted her by hand, before shining a small light into her eyes to observe her pupils.

'Yes, I am feeling fine,' Roseanne said with a worried smile.

'You are a very tough and brave one,' the operator said, with a cheerful smile.

'Please follow me to the Megotron,' she said and they went towards several caskets that were arranged in pairs along an almost vertical wall. From each casket were many flexible metallic tubes and other devices through which materials could enter or leave the patient's body. During complete body conversions some of those units acted more like mini portals that could transpose the whole with additions or different parts directly from bio-organ banks.

She was told to enter the first casket of the second pair, while the lid slowly opened. The inside was brilliant and translucent with many ridges, but basically took the form of the human body. Its micro robotics adjusted itself to fit the body precisely before entering areas within it during the scanning process.

When she entered, there was a blinding flash and much movement inside the unit while it adjusted itself to her nude body. From that moment on, microids took control of her body while the scanning process memorised every bit of matter therein. Once that was done, she was transposed to the other unit. During that time the implants were added along with the age reduction.

When she awoke she found herself in the second casket of the second set, feeling a little disorientated. The Megotron's door opened and she was assisted to her feet by the operator, once again observing her pupils with a bright light. She was then taken to another scanner for final body checks. After that process was completed a helmet was placed over her head to check her implants and many images appeared on a local screen.

The whole process took just twenty minutes and after another warm shower, her cap was removed and her original clothes returned to her. Afterwards she felt like a new woman of twenty-eight, but was still worried about after effects. It was all too easy and fantastic to be true, or so she thought.

'Your body has been thoroughly scanned. Every atom and memory has been recorded,' the operator said.

'Most incredible!' she replied.

'You look fine. Do you feel normal?' the operator asked.

'Like a new woman,' Roseanne replied.

'You are a new woman. Please follow me!' The operator said.

This time Roseanne was taken to a small computer room.

'Please put on this helmet and follow the instructions on the small screen. It will teach you how to use your implants. However, there is also a help program within your implants that can be accessed by you at anytime, so please learn the basic operational codes. Then you can train yourself at your leisure,' the operator said, leaving Roseanne with the equipment for the time being.

The operator soon returned to collect Mallory, who by now was very worried for Roseanne.

'Your wife's conversion has been completed. She is now in the training room, learning to use her implants,' she said and Mallory was pleased, although still nervous for himself.

He followed the same preparation as Roseanne, was scanned by the Psyrotron, but placed within the first of the first set of Megotron caskets. Then taken to the nearby shower where he was thoroughly washed before being physically inspected and scanned. Then his cap was removed and his clothes handed back to him.

'Your previous spinal damage has been repaired and all scar tissue removed. Now, you are in peak condition and your optimum age is thirty-five. Any further changes can be done in a simpler manner and with special drugs, after your new form has stabilized. Please follow me,' she said.

He was taken to a different training room where he was thought to use his implants. Mallory realised that he was the same person inside his head, but when he observed his body in the local mirror, he was about twenty years younger and the area of his bullet wound was normal.

'Ah! Ah! Ah! Ah! Wow! I don't believe it! Now none of my clothes fits!'

In the privacy of the training room, he removed his clothes to observe his muscles. The flab and bulge of his belly had all gone. He was now in peak fitness and all unwanted fatty tissue had been converted into solid muscle.

With excitement, he replaced his clothes and tried tightening his belt, but the buckle had to move beyond the minimum limit and could only have been fastened an inch from what he considered his new waistline.

He sat in front of the small screen trying to understand the program. It was in the form of three-dimensional hieroglyphics - two hundred and fifty-six in all - that had to be memorised. The first sixteen were crucial to the most frequently used menus in his implants. They were used to open two hundred and fifty-six main menus.

After ten minutes he had begun to use the first two link-symbols and his mind exploded into a massive three-dimensional cave. There he could observe many tags of information that led into other caves. He was now in the realms of physics and could enter any of the numerous sub-branches that represented different topics, to observe anything in detail. Although it was all happening in his mind, he could understand the instructions in English and other languages, including the strange three-dimensional hieroglyph. All that information was forming permanent links with his original mind and became as one with him.

Suddenly he thought of having lunch and the images faded away, leaving him still watching the screen, but with the added knowledge of his recent mental discoveries. He also found he could immediately return to where he had left the program while the information was still fresh in his mind.

'This is an incredible device. Let me memorise the help menu symbol and try it again,' he said and spent a little time on that one. He soon found himself in another tunnel. Most of the items he had been watching on the screen was now in his mind and within his mental cave. He scanned through the strange characters in his mind and as he did, they switched to two hundred and fifty-six menus of caves.

'So this is how it's done. I must also be a doctor of about two hundred and fifty-five subjects. I wonder if Roseanne has found the easy way to operate her implants,' he said, as the operator entered the room.

'You have found the easy way and so have your wife. Just a little more practice and you will learn to use the communicator and other functional modes. Those you can practise with your wife in private. However, your tests and training here are now at an end and I must now return you to Mac,' she said with a happy smile.

When Mallory set eyes on Roseanne she was young and very beautiful, and to her, he was young and quite handsome. He appeared to be in his mid thirties. With slight embarrassment they embraced and kissed each other.

Mac observed them carefully for a moment.

'Are you happy with things the way they are?' she asked the couple.

'I think it's a miracle. I still can't believe it,' Roseanne replied, ecstatically.

'In that case, I shall arrange for a portal to be assembled at your home on Earth. Your closest Megotron there is within Sol-Newtown and your internal implants can also be linked to satellite Eta in times of emergency. You can always find me here at anytime, day or night, so don't be bashful.'

'Really? Our own home portal?' Roseanne was ecstatic.

'I wish you both eternal life, success and happiness in all your ventures, and never forget your duty to the Greater Purpose, Osmaron, Solaria and Earth,' she said as Jerry and his wife Sharon entered the room.

Jerry went forward to embrace the couple. He and his wife, Sharon, had been waiting all this time for them outside, so he was happy when it was all over.

'Thank goodness! I told you everything would be all right. How do you feel now?' he asked, looking at both in turn with utter delight.

'I feel great. Just one little problem. My waist line has lost several inches and I feel like my bottom half wants to fall to the floor,' Roseanne said and they all smiled.

'Me too. We should have used our robes today. We shall have to get back soon,' Mallory said.

'Surely, not before we visit a local restaurant for lunch, and don't worry about your clothes, the palace androids can modify them for you,' Jerry said and they all agreed to go for lunch.

'Lunch? I can eat a complete horse. I am so hungry!' Roseanne complained.

They visited another local restaurant where they had a greater variety to choose from.

'I don't know much about you, Darling, but I want to eat everything,' Roseanne said. She filled three plates with a variety of everything on display.

'It's probably to do with the transformation. I feel the same. Anyway, horses are not eatable on Eden,' Mallory said and she laughed.

'Sharon and I decided to treat you to such a place after you had undergone your conversion. This is one of my favourite up-market restaurants and I am well known to the proprietor. He is also a professional jeweller in his spare time. Most of the people on Eden have more than ten professions at any given time. That way, we are seldom bored,' Jerry said.

'I think you both look great. Don't they, my husband?' Sharon said, while closely comparing their features to their previous ones and holding Jerry's hand.

'Yes, my dear. They look just great!'

'Thank you, Mr. and Mrs. Fraser. You are the kindest friends I've ever known. I only wish you could visit us frequently on Earth. Perhaps with our home portal that might be possible,' Roseanne said.

'We can arrange something through Sol-Newtown. In the mean time you will have to visit us at least twice a year and next time, please bring me some mangoes and more vodka. Mangoes are the only fruit we had problems growing here. Something to do with the climate and seasonal rainfall, but we are still working on it. We could grow them in environmental domes, but it's not the same as real sunlight. The bio-engineered one has never tasted right and there are so many different types on Earth, each with their unique flavours,' Jerry said.

'You just try to keep us away! Perhaps next time we could visit the palace directly from Earth?' Mallory said.

'For security reasons it's essential that you first visit one of the main stations on Eden. Then you can transpose to any palace, given the correct codes. However, most of those will now be within your implants, so you will not have the problems you encountered on your first visit. Once your home portal has been installed, the trip should take you only five minutes at the most,' Jerry said.

They ordered a variety of French and English cuisine with synthetic meats and settled down to another haughty meal. The couple had a ferocious appetite, which had been somewhat stimulated by their previous ordeal, but their new bodies also seemed to be more ravenous. It was probably just a reaction to the trauma of the transformation. Nevertheless their muscles were much larger and well toned as athletes.

After their first meal they were still hungry, so they had a second helping with pudding and custard.

When they arrived home that day they were greeted by the children and many others at Sarah's palace. They had prepared a special party for their coming across. Jerry then gave them each one of Sarah's special insignias. Those insignias were symbolic representations of the Greater Purpose and represented life throughout the Cosmos. It also said to everyone that they were now life members and noteworthy councillors of the greatest galactic empire.

'My dear friends, I shall cherish these moments and endeavour to return and visit you here at least once a year. All this has given us the greatest enthusiasm to complete our programs on Earth with utmost endeavour. So thanks again for everything,' Mallory said and they cheered.

CHAPTER 17

# Coup De Tat : Eden

'Not a ship in the sky over Eden City today!' Roseanne was surprised, while observing the clear view from the veranda of Sarah's palace.

'Could be they take time out for servicing and upgrades,' Mallory replied. He soon got on his mobile to Jerry.

'I know! Lennox just called me through the private palace link. Nothing is scheduled and with the exception of portals, Eden is on complete shutdown. Portals use a different system. This can only mean Mac is threatened.'

'From whom or what?' Mallory inquired.

'Mainly from computer viruses. They can be released by anyone trying to take over the system. Although Mac is immune to most types, one can never be sure of 100% protection,' Jerry replied.

'What happens now?' Mallory inquired.

'When Mac shuts down, she will port to a secured location several miles underground. There she will wait until receiving a special code from Sarah or Lumak.'

'Thank goodness she is safe for now!' Roseanne said.

'I am afraid it's up to us to take things back to normality.' Jerry was distressed.

'Who is in charge during Sarah's absence?'

'I am!' Jerry replied.


'I suppose... first we have to find out what it's all about. Whoever it is will go on TV to inform the public of their intentions, then we can plan a counter attack.' Mallory said.

'Whoever it is... chose the right time, with everyone of importance away from Eden. They also realize our Grand Lord will not intervene, being politically neutral. But, whoever it is will not get away with it!' Jerry was not amused.

'We always seem to follow and court intrigue whenever we go on vacation. First London, now here!' Roseanne said, while contemplating a most dangerous mission ahead.

Mallory parted her hair to check whether she had the mark of the beast inscribed.

'What's this, no 666?' he said and they laughed.

Soon the screen became alive with the face of a person. It was a generated image with voice sync.

**"For this caper I will be known as Underling. Everyone on Eden... you are to remain in your homes and palaces or be blasted by our Warrior Robots. They are armed to kill on sight. A computer virus has been uploaded making everything, including your Psyrotrons and Megotrons inoperative. So if you die there will be little chance of coming back.**

**This is just the beginning of our conquest of this galaxy. Don't worry, we will destroy those fearsome Javols for you. We have over 100 years for that and the best that money can buy. So be good and stay in your homes.**

**Portals have been reprogrammed to supply food and other essentials, but no living bodies. Not if you don't want to leave your heads behind.**

**End of message!"**

'The man has gone insane!' Jerry said, hardly believing the present situation.

The screen lit up again.

**"Our main reason for this Coup De Tat is to take over Earth for some serious culling. I intend taking out all their main cities, then towns and villages. That process should give life a better chance to survive.**

**We have developed a most deadly bacteria combined with a virus that only targets Inflates. It's based on the bubonic plague, but much more contagious. It will do the job in weeks instead of centuries. It will not effect Fertilates that were prescribed the Terminal Antidote.**

**I don't intend waiting around for 100 years, while all other life on Earth are virtually wiped out by mankind. As for you, Andromedans and Aliens, you are immune, so mind your business and please stay home. It's not your fight, anyway.**

**End of message!"**

'Wow! Another windbag. What can we do?' Mallory said.

'Were you guys given Locators? They combine with a communicator?' Jerry asked. He was now in his palace.

'We were giving a small key-ring device. Well, it looked like that. Is it the locator you speak of?' Roseanne said.

'Does it have a button in the middle with an inscribed imperial logo?' Jerry inquired.

'Yes, I think. The green, orange and blue segments,' she said.

'That's it. Before you can use it, it must be initialized and coded to your person. There is a machine in your palace basement. The children will know.'

'Go on!'

'There is a portal unit with a small slot for fitting the device. The portal only takes one person at a time. Enter the code for your unit. It's programmed in your brain implant. Look in the Coms menu under Portals. When the unit is tuned to you, a transposing satellite will be updated. Then you may travel to anywhere on Eden once you know the location of your destination.' Jerry said.

'Wow... that's fantastic! I didn't know that was possible,' she said.

'Beam me up Scotty!' Mallory interjected.

'Visit my palace as soon as possible!' Jerry said and passed on his location.


Both soon made their way to the basement in Sarah's palace while accompanied by Maggie, one of the palace children. They entered the necessary codes and were linked to one of the main satellites for Positional Transposition. PT for short. Now they could appear anywhere on Eden, given a suitable 3D location. Since that world had been thoroughly scanned over the years. That process was easily achieved.

Soon they appeared in Jerry's palace and were immediately invited for tea.

'I can never work on an empty stomach,' Jerry said.


'Somehow, he was able to have special robots made on Polion

to spec and despatched here without the knowledge of our security. This is a major flaw in our system that must be challenged. He must be using his own Macron to control them. So, we have to create our own computer virus to neutralise that system. I have given that task to Lennox.'

'My God! So he is really going for Earth?' Roseanne said.

Immediately a full 3D image in holographic form appear at the head of the table in a blank position.

'Wish I could join you in person,' Professor Khan (Ben) said.

'Is there an Antidote?' asked Jerry.

'Not sure, yet? And we can't process until we have a sample of the Bio-Bug. Currently I have several Primorphs and androids in most of the main cities, so it's just a matter of time,' Ben replied. He realized people had to be infected before he could analyse the disease to create an antidote. During that time many innocent people on Earth would die.

'Can you inform Carl, Chad and our people about the relevant dangers for us,' Mallory said.

'They have all been alerted. We cannot halt our present antidote operations. However, they can all be evacuated at short notice to Sol Newtown or a local Solarian Bank. All our branches are safe from such exposures,' Ben replied.

'How could he have visited Earth without the usual security checks en route?' Roseanne inquired.

'I agree, and there is no trace of him anywhere in the system. He has covered his tracks well,' Jerry said.

'For all we know, he could have travelled to Earth six months ago. This whole process could be linked to a timer. That way, his trail would be non-existent. Many of us travel to Earth on a daily basis,' Ben said.

'When do you think he will decide to set the bugs free?' Roseanne inquired.

'This appears to be a one-mans caper, using a hidden Macron somewhere on Eden. Release could be any time, if not already. The robots and other stuff here, on Eden, was meant to be a distraction while committing the crime on Earth. I am sure all portals are functioning correctly here. That could mean the bug has already been released,' Jerry said.

'All we have to do now, is sense a hot spot before it begins to spread. This could well be at a train station or airport. I am sure he will pay someone to release it. There could also be multiple release points at many stations, in many cities,' Ben said.

'It's location has been found. A computer virus was released to target his Macron. It should be down within the hour. It was hidden in one of our vegetable domes. All robot guards have been disabled. Soon, Eden City will be back on line. This was meant to be a timely distraction,' An excited Lennox relayed through his hologram.

'Now, it's all about Earth. Thank goodness we don't have to worry about Eden anymore. I feel so helpless being here, though,' Roseanne said. She never liked being outside of the action.

'Sorry Dear, this must run its course. The worst scenario, is that several canisters were placed in most of the major cities with timers to go off at the same time, making it difficult to control its spread,' Mallory said.

'Then, many will die!' she replied.

## CHAPTER 18

# Deadly Release

'I wish I was on Earth to assist. I have a bad feeling about this situation. I hope our guys back in the States are ok?' Roseanne was upset.

Mallory went closer to calm her. He wanted to call Carl back at the office, but all connections from Eden to Earth were down for the duration excluding secured ones from Sol-Newtown and Satellite Eta. That also included interstellar portals.

'Don't worry, Love. Ben has everything under control,' he said and she became more relaxed.

Suddenly Ben's hologram appeared on the main table, in front of them. Somehow that link from Sol-Newtown was not affected.

'We have heard of several large explosions in main cities globally. This indicates months of planning and implementation.' Ben appeared nervous.

'This guy really means to put on a show,' Jerry said, but was not amused.

'Some show, indeed. It started in the past hour. Now people are dropping like flies. This disease is so prevalent, that within ten minutes they fall with convulsions. The microbes literally eats them alive. However, we have received samples from our dedicated androids. They are currently being processed. The antidote should be ready within one week. One more thing; apparently our Fertilates are immune,' Ben said.

'Thank goodness, for that!' Roseanne could hardly contain herself.

'Not so, my dear lady. By the time we find the antidote and necessary vaccines, several million will be dead,' Ben said in his usual matter-of-fact manner.

'However, it seems the Terminal Antidote also works with this plague!' Ben added.

'Even so, millions will die?' Tears rolled down Roseanne's cheeks.

'Nevertheless, Europe, North America and Australasia has been spared. Not so for China, Africa and South America. I suppose those are the main countries responsible for high levels of poaching. Our mad friend appears to hate poachers, criminals and uncaring humans.'

'He must be a bloody genius to have created such a deadly bug that only targets our Infilates?' Mallory said.

'Do you know who he is?' Roseanne asked.

'No, and we shall never know. Even if we knew, what could we do about him. No one on Earth knows of this situation. The US President has been informed, but he is now one of us. Nevertheless, the outbreak has given him an excuse to inform his people and close borders. So the US will be safe for now. It's the same in Europe and other spared countries for now,' Ben said.

'Who do you really think it is?' Jerry asked, trying to pressurize Ben for an inkling.

'Incidentally, we found the body of Dr. Hal Seaton hanging from a most beautiful chandelier at his home. However, all computer information had been removed by a unique computer virus at the moment of his death. The intelligent virus was programmed to only target his data,' Ben said.

'Wow, what a clever guy. I met him once. His head resembled a Greek Centaur, with horns grafted so he would look less human. Knowing him, I am sure it's not the last we shall hear on this topic,' Mallory said, looking even more worried.

'You mean our Green Chameleon?' Roseanne could hardly believe.

'Also known as the Phantom in some countries. He devoted his life in saving Earth from its degenerates and cared little about its law and order! Now he is dead, I feel sad!' Mallory said.

'Yes! He was one of us and a great bio-geneticist. May his soul rest in peace for now. I only hope he will do better in his next incarnation,' Jerry said.

'You mean, you will bring him back?' Roseanne could not believe what she was hearing.

'Although he committed a crime against Earth, it was not against our Federation. We have no laws regarding Earth in this regard. Don't worry, we shall wash his brain during the rather painless conversion process. You will not recognise him. Neither will he recognise his past self even with horns! Nevertheless, records show that the last time he visited the Megotron chambers was before his anti-criminal capers on Earth. Therefore his memories cannot be reinstated after that time,' Jerry said.

'You mean, his new body will have no recollection of those deeds?' Roseanne was bemused.

'As far as we are concerned, he will be a new Dr. Hal Seaton,' Jerry said.

'Further, we have no real proof of his involvement in this crime. We cannot jump to conclusions without real evidence,' Ben said and they were agreeable, but not satisfied.


## BACK ON EARTH

'Sir, a call from the President!'

'The President?'

'Yes!' Carol Jennings handed him the phone.

'Hello, Commander Chad! I was given your name by Mallory. I understand he is now away on his honeymoon and is not accessible,' Arnold said.

'He is, Sir!'

'Well, that leaves just you!'

'How can I be of assistance, Sir?'

'This is a delicate situation. The less people know the better. You are a military man and know the score.'

'Yes, Sir!'

'A person or persons unknown have released the most deadly plague in several countries outside of North America. People are dropping like flies. Coded information is being faxed to you as we speak. Read this information and file it in a safe place. I stress, no one should know of this. You are to head a special military unit to guard our borders. Instructions have already been given to border police and airlines,' Arnold said.

'In that case, Mexico is the only real threat, Sir.'

'I agree! Canada will be out of the equation for now and all our ports are constantly monitored. Anyway, refugees will take many weeks to cross oceans. By then the infected will die. Apparently this bug kills within hours and is highly infectious, but only targets Infilates. We still have to protect all our countrymen and women,' Arnold said. Chad was speechless.

'As bad as that?'

'Yes! The most deadly in recorded history. My main worry is Mexico. South America has the disease spreading like wildfire.' Arnold sighed.

'My God! If it's that contagious and deadly, we can't take the chance to let anyone through, even with proper papers.'

'Agreed! Your mission will be a mission of death. You are to stop them from entering our country. We have bombers with napalm for that painful process.'

'We are going to kill them? Kill all those poor people, wanting a better life?'

'Can you think of another way? I am gripped by that very same dilemma,' Arnold replied.

'You are to safeguard an area near the border where they can remain for now. It will be an isolated camp. Other places outside of their main routes must be constantly bombed. That action will act as a deterrent to those using those places.'

'If the bug is that quick acting, all we have to do is create a firewall, while the infected die. They will only live for a few hours, anyway. After that time there will be no more crossing our borders. Because most of those areas in Mexico would be dead by then,' Chad said.

'First, you must have an idea of the rate of spread of the infection. This must all be timed before our bombers take action. I shall leave it in your capable hands. A military unit is on its way to you. You are to coach them well on this private mission. The Mexican president has been informed. And keep me up-to-date on an hourly basis.' President Arnold hung up.

## TWO DAYS LATER ON EDEN

Suddenly the hologram of Ben appeared before them.

'I have an update. The disease has been released by several

explosions and is spreading uncontrollably. So far over 200 million are dead in South America and rising. About the same number in Africa. Over 500 million in China, 50 million in India and rising. About 100 million in other places. This bug is much worst than we thought. It remains dormant in the human body for several weeks until triggered, giving the disease time to spread before it becomes active in the patient. We are not yet sure of the triggering mechanism. It could be some type of biological timer set for several weeks. So there could be a nano-bot link some-where in its design. The disease is now petering out.'

'So the explosions was just a trigger of some kind?' Roseanne inquired.

'Yes! It could have initiated a trigger virus!' Ben replied.

'With so many Infilates dead it's difficult to know what to say. I am utterly shocked! Thank goodness he saved a few countries. It could have been much worse if he targeted every country on the globe.' Mallory became very emotional and began walking around the large table. He felt so helpless.

'Although not an extreme global catastrophe, it has had a significant affect on those targeted countries. Poaching has somewhat diminished,' Ben added. He remained cool and objective.

Roseanne could not accept the situation of so many deaths and bursted out in tears. Then she ran towards the nearest toilet to spill her guts. Mallory soon ran after to console her.

'I think he made his point several times over. Anyway, numer-ous androids have been dispatched from Solarian branches to the countries involved to collect and innoculate against further infections,' Ben said.

'You mean to say, you have already created an antidote? We created the bacterial one. The virus and other parts are being identified and processed as we speak. However, the real killer is the Bubonic part. Since most borders and ports were closed to contain the spread, it was isolated. The only parts that worry us is the Mexican border. President Arnold has taken Chad into his confidence. He is now responsible for Border Control in that area.'

'You mean our Chad?' Mallory interjected.

'The same! His job will be to oversee that area and guide the bombers. A large firewall will be placed along that border the moment the infection crosses a certain point,' Ben said.

'I know Chad, he will do a good job,' Mallory said.

'Because of the quick-acting nature of this disease and it's predictability, it soon isolates itself by killing everyone of its carriers. However, we know very little about it's dormant life. There could be more outbreaks a year or so from now. Our gene-splicers are currently analysing for such answers. You will be updated again as soon as possible,' Ben said and disconnected.

'How could he do that? A single man can plan and implement so much suffering and Death?' Sharon said.

'He could have done much worse. Even to us here on Eden,' Jerry replied.

'Then there would be no one to bring the mad man back from the dead. What about all those poor millions that can never be brought back!' Mallory was not pleased.

'I suppose he must be very pissed off with the way Earth is going! He was one of my guys, you know. I knew him well as a brilliant geneticist, but never thought he would go to those lengths!' Lennox said.

'What about what he said about taking over the universe. Do you think it's possible now?' Roseanne inquired.

'No...! he is just another windbag trying to gain our attention,' Mallory replied. Jerry tapped his fingers on the table. He was in a most nervous disposition.

CHAPTER 19

# Nightmare Scenario

Andy, along with his father-in-law Dr. John Wilson and birth mother Cathy was on vacation in Mexico. That particular holiday had been booked by his parents well before his father's wedding. He had never mentioned any of those plans to his father, Mallory. Anyway, those holidays were scheduled each year, so he didn't regard it as an important item in his diary. Nevertheless, he enjoyed visiting new places and cultures, particularly South America.

'Have you taken the medicine your father gave you?' Cathy yelled.

'We leave in one hour, so pack your things. I don't want to hit the main traffic again. We arrive in Texas in 3 hours, if we catch our flight. I want no delays!' John yelled.

'I heard you both. Don't yell, you might wake the neighbours.' Andy shouted back, while watching the morning's TV in his hotel room. They were currently getting ready for their journey home having had a most enjoyable holiday in Veracruz, Mexico.


**'A most deadly Bubonic plague is now prevalent in Mexico City. From the little we know, thousands are dead or dying. At present no cure is imminent. It spreads like wildfire. Please remain isolated in your homes to prevent further spread of this very contagious disease. A further announcement will be made when we know more about this looming disaster,'** The newsman read.

Andy listened to the TV announcement, but could little believe what he heard until he was hit by the shock of reality.

'Plague in Mexico?'

He ran towards his parents, now packing their cases in the adjacent room.

'Mum! Dad! Plague in Mexico city. It's killing lots of people. They say it's unstoppable!'

'Really? You are not kidding?' John dropped the bundle of

clothes and ran towards the TV accompanied by Cathy and Andy.

**'As mentioned previously, a most deadly Bubonic plague is now prevalent in Mexico City. From the little we know, thousands are dead or dying. At present no cure is imminent. It spreads like wildfire. Please remain isolated in your homes to prevent further spread of this very contagious disease. A further announcement will be made when we know more about this looming disaster,'** The newsman read again, but it was also translated in British text.

'This changes everything!'

'Why, Love?'

'We can't get back by air. The Airports will be contaminated by now with moving traffic. We have to travel by car,' John said.

'But it will take us hours and hours in this stifling heat, Dad,' Andy was upset.

'Better suffer a little heat than be bitten by one of those bugs. It's not a pleasant death. I know all about Bubonic Plague. If this one is that contagious it will be here in the hour. This whole resort will become a ghost town by tomorrow, with dead bodies everywhere. I don't want that happening to us, so lets get packing. We take the hired car!'

'Whatever you say.' Cathy appeared unconcerned.

'Keep listening to the TV. We can't help until after we return to the States. That is if we are not dead before then. This thing is going to kill lots. It could be one of those bio-engineered bugs let loose by terrorists. But why Mexico?' John was sweaty and desperate. He loaded a water crate in the back of their hired 4x4 and went in for more. At least water was the most essential commodity for survival in that heat.

'But Dad, how could it suddenly appear in Mexico City like that, without any warning?' Andy asked.

'It could have been released by the recent explosion in one of their train stations. Terrorists these days are well-financed and quite clever,' John replied.

'My God! What if it spreads throughout South America, then the States?' Cathy became concerned.

'Our Border Control will isolate it, even if we have to burn every living thing in those areas. We cannot afford to let it through,' John replied.

'Then, how will we get through?' Andy asked. John became even more nervous.

'We leave immediately. We can collect groceries in a gas station on route. Get your things!' John was already behind the steering wheel. A small pistol was in the glove compartment.

'Why are you taking a gun, Dad?' Andy asked as he entered and viewed the open glove compartment.

'We don't know if wild beast are infected. What if our car breaks down and we are attacked. I have to protect my family. And you will when I am not around,' John replied.

'Dad, it will be spreading with traffic from Mexico. Many infected people will be using the main routes to the States!' Andy advised.

'Son, we have no choice... if we are to get home quickly. Put up car windows and turn the aircondition fully on. We will try to get gas masks at a local station. If not, we use several layers of cloth soaked in alcohol. That should help for now,' John said.

John considered the local airport for a moment but could not be sure of the spread of the disease. For all he knew that place could be the first infected by incoming flights.


## GAS STATIONS

'No one follows me in. Stay in the car and listen to the news. We only need a few items and a full tank. This vehicle is tightly sealed, so we should be safe for now,' John ordered.

John was soon back to the car.

'Locked up. Not a soul about!' He was furious.

'Perhaps there will be one open further up. I just hope we don't have to walk home?' Cathy interjected.

'How much gas have we left in the hired car?' Andy inquired.

'Enough for about 50 miles. They never fill them,' he replied.

'What about food and other things?' Cathy looked bewildered.

'At lease the disease hasn't reached here yet. But it's just a matter of time.' He made sure windows were up tight then drove away.

'There is one. Thank God, it's open. But a bloody long queue. Let's try another,' he said and drove off.

This time it was third time lucky. That gas station was in an inconspicuous side road. He filled up to the cap.

'How long will it take us to get home?' a worried Cathy asked.

'It will take us over 8 hours to the Texas border, if we go all the way by road. It's over 500 miles to Texas from here in Veracruz. Then we take our flight to DC,'he replied.

'Can't we get there any sooner?' Cathy was dismayed.

'May I suggest we travel to San Fernando up north and try to get a flight from there. It's only about 100 miles from the border. Flying across to Texas will be easier than crossing the border by car. For all we know it might be closed by the time we get there.' John said and drove off.

'Luckily we did not visit Acapulco this year. We would have had to travel through Mexico City,' Cathy said.

John remained worried and silent. Then a radio announcement broke into the music.

**'The whole of Mexico City is now under strict quarantine. Do not under any circumstance visit this city. The infection has spread far and wide. Please do not drive around and spread this disease further. All airports in Mexico have been closed to contain the disease. Traffic guards are now control-ling most routes near the borders of our country. We shall continue broadcasting as long as we can, while under quaran-tine. A population update is soon to follow.'** The newscaster repeated in English.

'This is serious business. I just hope we can make it home before this nasty bug gets to us.' John said. Andy was too upset to think of anything and began to cry.

'Can I call Donald? Please Dad! He might be able to help!'

'Isn't he on a special mission?'

'He might be back!'

'Call him then. Anything is better than our present dilemma,' John replied.

'He might be able to get hold of a military jet or helicopter. He is captain and is allowed to go on rescue missions. There must be many like us stranded in Mexico,' Andy said.

'Son, you are brilliant. I will contact our Embassy and get an up-to-date.' John packed the car in a local layby and began to check his diary.

'I have this address and number for emergencies and this happens to be the worst emergency of my life!' he said.

'Hello Andy. How is your holiday?' Donald inquired.

'It's finished. We are on our way home by car, but not sure if we are going to make it,' Andy said with a sombre voice.

'Let me talk to John.' Andy passed the cell-phone across to him.

'This is a very delicate situation, but I will try to help if I can. Our borders are now on high alert, so crossing by car might be a problem,' Donald said.

'We are moving north to avoid the plague. From what I can observe it hasn't arrived here in Veracruz yet and won't for several hours,' John said.

'In that case, keep moving north. I think several planes were laid on for a mass evacuation, but this disease is so contagious and deadly they grounded them. Now there is virtually no way out of Mexico and other bordering countries. I am afraid, you might be sacrificed for the greater good,' Donald said.

'I don't like the sound of that,' John replied.

'I shall try to lay on something at this end. We shall be broad-casting on several radio channels from Texas. Keep monitoring for a chosen location in Northern Mexico. However, you must hurry. We are not sure if the bug travelled to those places before flights were grounded. If all fails, I shall contact Commander Chad. He is now in charge of Border Control,' Donald said. Then he turned around to speak to Cathy.

'Chad is in charge of Border Control.'

'Uncle Chad?' Andy's face lit up.

'You do realize that when you get across the border you will be quarantined for several weeks in one of those camps. So also will be all you come in contact with,' Donald said.

'I don't care. All I want to do is get me and my family away from this terrible place and perhaps do some good at the borders,' John said.

'Ok, Doctor. Be careful. Leave it with me. I shall try to arrange something within the next few hours,' Donald said and hung up. John contemplated the dangerous journey ahead, with many cars overtaking and realized that sooner or later they would be overtaken by the infected.

'Get hold of cotton clothes. Tear into wide strips. Put about 5 layers together so we can breathe through it. Then douse it in spirits. Here is the small bottle I brought along. At the first sign of the sickness tie it tightly about your face and close your mouth. This type of Bubonic Plague has to be inhaled,' John advised.

After several hours John's cell-phone sang.

'John, its Donald!'

'Hello Donald!'

'I have been able to arrange a helicopter at a border post in Texas. Chad insisted that you were picked up on route. We have your route and destination, so carry on along the same highway. At approximately 35 miles from the border start blinking your headlamps. By then it should be dust, so your car will be quite visible from the air,' Donald advised.

'Thank you, Pal. I owe you a big one!' John was ecstatic.

'People, a helicopter is on its way. They will pick us up about 35 miles from the border,' he said to Cathy and Andy.


## ABOUT 35 MILES FROM THE TEXAN BORDER

'Keep on dimming that headlamp. The helicopter is on its way. It will be here soon,' John said to a tired Cathy. Andy was fast asleep at the back. His tiredness had passed the point of no return. It was 7:15 and getting dark with clear skies.

A car shrieked past, almost blowing their 4 x 4 towards the curb.

'Oh my God! How fast were they going!'

'About 100 MPH. That car was full of people!' Cathy replied.

'They must be trying to outrun the disease,' John replied. Andy stirred and was awake listening but yarning.

'But the bug is not here yet, is it?' he asked.

'Look in the distance. They just crashed and created one almighty pileup. Some cars are on fire. I must try to help if I can,' John said. He parked the car on the side with emergency lights and headlamp dipping, and collected the small medical kit he took along for such emergencies.

'Whatever happens, keep the doors locked and keep bleeping the headlamps. That helicopter will be here soon. Lock those doors and don't come out for anyone. Just wait here for the helicopter. If I don't get back, leave without me,' he insisted.

'You are going to help them now?' Cathy couldn't believe her husband's last minute decision.

'I am a doctor, so it's a risk I have to take. Pity I couldn't help anyone before.'

'No John! Please stay! We need you to get home!' Cathy and Andy cried.

'Dearest, my time has come, so I must go!' he insisted and quietly strolled towards the flames. She wiped her eyes and turned her attention to Andy in the back.

'Don't worry. Your dad has gone to help those poor people. He will be back soon,' she said.

'But Ma, there is no ambulance or fire engines anywhere. It will take forever,' Andy replied.

Cathy's cell-phone rang.

'It's me. I have just arrived at the accident site. This place is a mess with bodies everywhere. I am helping a few injured. However, we are all on a one way trip,' he said

'Where to Darling?' she inquired, innocently.

'That fast car and everyone in it were infected. Everyone was dying when it crashed. That means I am now infected,' he said.

'Where is dad's gun?' Andy inquired. Cathy began to search the glove compartment but no gun could be found.

There was a sharp crackle and John fell to the ground.

'My Darling! Oh my darling! Why did you leave us?' she sobbed. Both realized there was nothing they could do to save the day.

There they remained in a locked car with tearful eyes and taking turns dipping headlamps until the helicopter arrived.

## ON EDEN

Since Mallory was unable to communicate while on Eden he was oblivious to the rescue mission layed on for his son, Andy, and parents. In particular the death of John, Andy's father-in-law. That was until updated by Ben.

Once again Ben's image appeared.

'It has been a major disaster, but the infection has tapered out as predicted. This disease was meant to target major cities and towns. In that respect it has been quite successful. Infilates were the most affected, being resident in most of our cities, since the evacuation of our Fertilate families,' Ben said.

'So, the pandemic is slowing down?' Roseanne inquired.

'It is! Since we are now able to innoculate, it's days are numbered,' Ben replied.

'Any word about our families back home?' Mallory asked.

'I am afraid I have some bad news. Andy's father-in-law, Doctor John Wilson, did not make it. He went to assist during an accident near the Texas border and was infected. Sadly he was over 55 and did not take the Terminal Antidote. A loss of a good person,' Ben said.

'Is Andy and Cathy ok?'

'Yes, they were rescued by helicopter, thanks to Chad and Donald. They are now being quarantined,' Ben said.

'Oh my God! What a bloody disaster of all disasters!' Roseanne shouted and was again on her way to the toilet to bring up some more.

CHAPTER 20

# Two and more virtual minds

### ON EDEN

After the shock of Earth's global epidemic and its aftermath, they became more focussed and decided to concentrate on methods to overcome crime and terrorism. Mallory also realized that the Green Chameleon or Phantom would from now be out of the picture as far as Earth was concerned. Like everyone on beautiful Eden, he would be revived with a brand new body and given a new assignment. But they also realized he was much too clever to let things lie. A person like him would have planned his future years in advanced, even to the point of storing all information since his escapades on Earth.

'Mac is back on line. Sarah had hidden the special code within my implants to be released on such an occasion,' Jerry said.

'She is clever enough to have anticipated the whole episode?' Roseanne replied.

'Yes, she likes allowing such actions so we can learn from our mistakes. And we have learnt a lot,' Jerry said.

'That was only because she selected the right man for the job,' Mallory replied.

'Thank you both for having such great faith in this old ex-president. And thank utter goodness our USA is still around for my occasional visits, even though in disguise,' Jerry said.

'Thank Goodness for small mercies!' they shouted and drank a toast to each other.


That afternoon they decided to remain close to the palace with the children and practice their new implant modes like telepathy and communication in general. To them it was like buying a new computer without a clue other than a 1000 page manual. However the situation could be improved when two minds put their heads together.

They soon realised that young children on Eden were only given implants after the age of twenty-one and at their own request. After that time they would have had a full education and learned experiences in most areas of life. That was the present age of consent and any physical alterations other than those required for health purposes had to be taken by grownups. Nevertheless, it would have been a lot simpler to give young children those devices. Then there would be little need for long term schooling and university education.

Even so, not everyone were given implants. Implants were only available for those councillors of elite status. Those who directly influenced the society through their brilliant and caring efforts. Some of the special young with high potential were groomed for such tasks and chosen at the appropriate time. Those changes were usually associated with their honeymoon in much the same way that it had been with Mallory and Roseanne; signifying a complete new change in their lives.

The couple realised they now had a full vocabulary of many languages, including Sunolingua and the strange symbolic script of the Andromedans. That last one was used to select the main menus in their minds. The menus also included one that was associated with games, hobbies and leisurely activities. Those they could have used both in and out of their minds, with a personal sub-menu for choosing and adding their own programs.

Those latest implants increased their mental powers and potentials in excess of twenty times and all that data covered a wide spectrum specific to their own requirements, but some of it overlapped in relevant areas. They soon realised it was going to take them many years to cover the complete spectrum of choice.

After selecting the communications menu, they were soon able to select certain prerecorded names within their minds and add new names, or symbols and numbers to those existing names. However, just thinking hard of a particular name could cause a link with that person. The process was similar to memorizing a list of objects and numbers by associating them with bizarre objects and linking those objects into pictorial themes.

Entry to another's mind could only be allowed by the recipient, who could accept or reject the intruder at will. They could also transfer thoughts to each other directly as in speaking, but here again, access was required and even that could be terminated at anytime during the transfer. Thoughts could be transferred and downloaded thousands of times faster than speech and included images. In each implant were special image processors that could re-create the image as seen through the eye for transmission to outside equipment and computers. Those facilities made them proper telepaths. However, the transmission range was limited to just two hundred metres or what was considered to be shouting distance. That limited range could be extended indefinitely by special external boosters and satellites. Such a type of communication could be invaluable during any military campaign. The frequencies and protocols were tuned to the genetic blueprint of each individual, so the chance of crosstalk and external interference was virtually zero.

*'It will take you both a while to get used to your implants, but once you do, you will never want to return to your old selves. The first thing you must realise, is that they are secondary and almost external to your original mind.*

*'They are not yet properly connected to your natural mind, and initially require stronger links and imagery to turn them on. Once they are on, it's easy to turn any topic off by changing the current topic of interest into another like having lunch, tea, et cetera, or to simply relax your concentration.*

*'Such changes can be triggered by visualizing objects and forms not easily referred within your implants, and the device can also detect subtle changes in your brain waves.*

*'There is also a six-hour inbuilt timer for safety reasons. That facility will return you to your normal senses and back to the outside world after that time.*

*'When you create your own programs, you must use associative codes and images that are not commonly used in everyday life. I have a book of such bizarre images that you could probably choose from. There is also a table of possible icons within the help section of your implants. Check through them and memorize the relevant ones.*

*'Powerful links save you going through the main menus each time, and through the labyrinths of knowledge before you get to*

*where you want; because there are thousands of sub-menus and millions of subs of those, ad infinitum. But they can be flicked through in a fraction of a second once you get the routine right. However the most frequently used programs are kept in a more accessible menu.*

*'Nevertheless, your problem now is in entering any of the two hundred and fifty-six main menus instantly as and when required. When I started, I made the first sixteen my main library until I mastered them, then I selected another sixteen, and so on, until I covered the lot. Anyway, practice makes perfect.*

*'Once you become competent in their use, you will be able to exist in your own Virtual Worlds within your minds where you can practise real surgery on patients with your virtual doctors and nurses, design any highly technological device with as many laboratory assistants as you wish, complete complex calculations and procedures while asleep, play all types of realistic games and a lot more besides, and all that is without the use of Macrons. You know, Mal, Nano-technology can shrink the complete human brain down to the size of a pin head, with all its neurons, and these implants are much more complex,'* Jerry said and Mallory was astounded by their technologies.

That evening Mallory and Roseanne decided to work with their implants again and search through many of its strange labyrinths of information, until they could find any of the first sixteen menus at will. Then they decided to search through more specific areas of their new primary professions. To Mallory that was science and security and to Roseanne, medical and security. Even without their knowledge they had been given the latest implants with hundreds of virtual doctors in every conceivable field. Those doctors would be used only when they needed information in relevant fields.

Roseanne had entered the fifth menu, which was the medical one and soon found one of the sub-menus marked cures. From that main branch she searched through several branches until she came to the one marked, Surgical Operations. She followed that branch in alphabetical order until she came to the one marked humans and followed until she arrived at the Earth type. But they were also referred to as homo sapiens and other names that she was not yet able to understand, not having used the languages' menu.

When she went further into that tunnel, she found herself in an operating theatre with many other doctors standing close to a long table and wearing overalls, facials and gloves. They were patiently awaiting her arrival and she knew she was expected. As she entered, the cadaver was uncovered and she was handed a scalpel by the chief surgeon and shown her position.

'You took your time getting here, Doctor!' the senior surgeon said to her. 'Today, we perform an appendectomy, using the cruder method with scalpel and suture. A method currently used in some areas on Earth. However, it is still the only way into parts of the body, in the absence of more advanced technology. Therefore in the absence of robots and megotrons, it's a method that must also be learnt.

'You may proceed, Doctor Colman,' he said and Roseanne leant forward to make the first incision. Just before she started, Subliminals began to flash within her mind, showing layers of tissue, veins, arteries and capillaries. The smaller and less visible parts being magnified for a clearer view, until she arrived at the appendix which was coloured yellow up to the incision, which was marked with a blue line.

Every cut was clearly shown and marked with blue, all she had to do was follow the blue line with its slight changes until she arrived at the item to be removed. The path was now clear to her, so she made the incision and followed the lines. She removed the appendix and made the relevant stitches until the operation was completed. Then with further diagrams, she applied what was necessary and then a bandage.

'Well done, Doctor! It was a beautiful operation, well executed! Next time, you will be thought the more modern procedure with lasers, visuals, thermal's and controlled microids,' he said and the other doctors began to congratulate her. They laughed joyfully while removing their facials and gloves, then the program came to an abrupt end and she found herself lying on the bed and looking up at the ceiling, but still with vivid recollections of her experience as a surgeon. She wondered whether it all really took place in her mind or was perhaps one of those telepathic links to a hospital somewhere on Eden.

She turned to Mallory who was fully awake and held his hand.

'Darling, I just carried out my first appendectomy in my mind on a cadaver, with several doctors looking on and I did a good job. It was in a large hospital, and I suppose it was all in my mind. Afterwards I was complemented on a job well done. Can you imagine that? And I feel fulfilled as if I completed a very important task!' she exclaimed.

'Well, Dear, you are now a doctor, after all, and anything in this place is possible unless otherwise advised. So I believe you, because you were here all this time,' he said, with a grin of sarcasm.

'You are teasing me again. But it really happened. You wait until you begin to use yours, Mister Scientist!' she said and they both hugged and kissed.

Roseanne was now confident that she could perform that operation again on anyone with success, for the experience now formed part of her conscious self.

Mallory had found the science menu, which included subjects like nuclear physics, microidology and other branches of Nano-technology. Dimensional transposition as with portals and LPD dynamics he found to be quite intriguing. However, it also held a comprehensive library on every possible scientific topic. Since Roseanne's surgical experience he held back a little, fearing he would end up in some complex setting with clever scientists telling him off for being incompetent in their advanced technolo-gies. Then he realized such devices in his mind could not be abusive and were most likely part of a standard training routine.

At that moment in time, his main interest was in using his implants to aid his present missions on Earth. He could use them to record his reports, which could then be linked with his office computer, thus saving him much time in composing and entering such data. Then he realised that his present office computer was a special one that had been supplied by Ben and included a special interface for Brain Implants. That one also had a link with his local Macron and could also be linked to Central Macron on Eden. So he could now have full access to Mac and others via what they called H-wave communication.

After much practice, they soon realised they could link their implants together and experience fantasies in much the same way as they had in Jerry's V-room. However, they could also use each other's implants, as all mind tunnels interlinked when they were so connected. They would also have liked another V-room experience with Jerry and his wife before returning to Earth, just to sample the effects through their new implants.

CHAPTER 21

# Weapons and more weapons

The following day Jerry collected them after an early breakfast and took them to the Solarian Museum.

'This is the Hexolyte section. Most of the equipment here are over 2 billion years old. That's close to 1.5 billion years before the dinosaurs,' Jerry said and they couldn't believe their eyes, for the equipment appeared brand new.

'What are these strange metallic suits?' Roseanne inquired.

'They were containment suits used by the evil demon-like race called Hexolytes. Their living energies had to be contained in these special metallic devices. They once ruled most of the local galaxies and prayed on many worlds for their own personal satisfaction. Thank goodness, they have since become extinct,' he said and they swallowed hard on saliva.

After showing them around ancient artifacts from many worlds within Galaxy Osmaron and elsewhere, they were taken to the ammunition's section.

That museum also held the most modern types of weapons that could only be issued under special license to a privileged few. It was illegal for unauthorized humans to carry any type of weapon outside of the imperial palace and places where a very high level of security was needed. All such special guards were usually well trained and always under the scrutiny of their superiors.

As usual, there were many visitors to that particular museum, which was probably the largest in Osmaron. It held a comprehensive range of weapons over long historical periods and from all known civilizations. They included, present, ancient and extinct, within the local galaxies and associated globular clusters. As they walked through rows upon rows of the displayed weapons, they could observe many alien types, some of which Jerry attempted to describe to them in detail.

'What is that funny shaped one over there?' Roseanne asked innocently.

'It's a Pun'la'la gun from Selsii. That's a near desert world on the other side of our galaxy ruled by a type of reptilian. This weapon spouts a type of acid from their glands. It increases their effective range during hunting and can dissolve flesh down to the bone in seconds,' Jerry replied.

They soon came upon exhibits from Earth that covered the past ten thousand years of human history; from stone axes, arrow heads and boomerangs, to the small replica of a nuclear bomb. Where necessary their explosives and firing mechanisms had been removed for greater safety.

Mallory felt quite at home in that part of the museum. He could observe many items that he would have liked to include in his own armoury.

When they became tired of viewing the almost infinite display of weapons, Jerry took them by portal to another section. That particular area was inaccessible to the outside world by a very thick vault door and grade one security codes for clearance.

'This is where all our modern weapons are kept,' he said, while transmitting his code to the androids at the desk. Here again, there were rows upon rows of more weapons, but they were all brand new and still in their transparent packaging. A senior android came forward and opened another secured door which panned out unto a large test area.

'Please follow to the rear,' he said in sunolingua through their implants and they understood.

They entered a shielded training area and in front of the screen were many dummies and targets that could be adjusted on rails. In the distance to their right was a small obstacle course for accurate in-motion shooting.

'This first section is for testing the actual weapons and their operators for accuracy and other relevant factors.'

'This place is just what we need back home,' Mallory said.

'The obstacle course is fully computerised for checking the operator's response, agility and dynamic accuracy. While on this course you do not use a real weapon. It's a small weighted hand laser and you wear a special suit with inbuilt detectors that will measure stress and other biological factors,' he said.

The android went to get three plasma projectors and handed one to each of them. The weapons were similar in size to a small machine gun, but somewhat heavier.

Just below the handgrip was a small sphere that contained the nuclear excitor, but also acted as a counter weight when held. On the main body of the device and towards the rear of the barrel was a twelve-centimetre toroid that contained the hot plasma. Incredible magnetic fields maintained the plasma in motion close to the speed of light and at super high temperatures.

More plasma was constantly added from the excitor and liquid hydrogen capsule, until the toroid chamber was fully saturated. The charging process took about thirty seconds. At the end of that time the plasma would have attained a temperature in excess of one hundred million degrees centigrade. A temperature that would normally be encountered in the centre of stars. Jerry soon began to explain their operation to the couple.

'The excitor heats and focuses nuclei into the toroid chamber where they are accelerated and contained by intense magnetic fields. After a full charge cycle, which can take up to thirty seconds, you press the release mechanism. It is situated in the hand-grip and will cause some of the accelerated and super heated plasma to escape through a small window in the magnetic field within the nozzle.'

'It's quite heavy for a hand gun,' Roseanne commented.

'It's only a matter of getting used to. The amount of plasma per release can be adjusted from full to one tenth of full charge. Many prefer to use a setting of one fifth of full charge. That value gives enough matter per shot and enough time for plasma recovery between fire.'

'Our first plasma pistol!' Mallory held the weapon and began pointing it at different targets to get a good feel of the weapon. Jerry continued to explain the processes involved.

'How often do we recharge?' Mallory inquired.

'On a weekly basis for one-fifth firing. The small compressed hydrogen cylinders are clipped unto your utility belt,' Jerry replied.

'As much as that?' Roseanne inquired.

'The pressurized liquid hydrogen capsule should be replaced

every thousand shorts, working on the one-fifth of maximum charge basis. The nozzle is fully adjustable to narrow or wide focus. With this weapon, one can take out ten human targets, side by side at a distance of five metres with a single fire. You set nozzle spread to maximum output. However, at that maximum setting you will be required to wait for thirty seconds before you can release the same amount again.'

'So there is a limit?' Mallory inquired.

'But there is a limit with all weapons. You always have to reload. All data on these weapons are held within your implants under Military and Weapons,' Jerry said and they were astonished.

The android found them three shielded booths where they could practise. Mallory and Roseanne were shown the relevant buttons and adjusters to set the projector at one fifth, and the best way to grip the heavy weapon.

Jerry recommended a double hand hold, with the strongest hand on the trigger and the other, with the thumb underneath the toroid to add extra support. She fired at one of the dummy targets and the whole mass vaporised into a conflagration of sparks and smoke. The super-hot elements tore through the air and left a strange smell in its wake. The sight made her shudder. She then set the toroid window to one tenth nozzle size to minimize the plasma width and tried again on another dummy. This time a large hole was left where the plasma passed straight through. However the plasma tended to explode on contact, so the hole was shaped more like a funnel.

'It's unlike any gun I've ever used. There isn't even the slightest recoil, and it's so accurate, but it takes no prisoners,' she said to Jerry and they smiled at her choice of words.

'It has a small infrared detector that can automatically align to any heat source, including small animals. As always, you must have a good look at your foe, either through your implants or fixed sights, before you fire,' Jerry said.

When they were finished practising with those weapons, they followed the android and Jerry to another section where more weapons were stored.

'There are also plasma cannons that are based on the same

principle, but those are much larger and can take out an army at each blast, at optimum range and scatter. Most of our nuclear grenades are based on the same principle, to minimise radiation fallout and can be adjusted for yield and penetration. Some of our thermic devices so designed, can cut through walls and metal like a hot knife through butter. Those I shall show you in the other section,' Jerry said.

That day they tried numerous weapons until they entered the area where the armoured vehicles and clothes were stored.

'Here we have an induction suit that is also driven by a nuclear power pack. It uses super conductive coils throughout with high energy induction oscillators. While wearing this suit, it's advisable to remove all metallic objects like rings and earrings from your person. Although the fields act in front of the suit, metal objects on your person can cause distortions to the fields. Once activated, any conductive object in front will be rejected at great force and velocity or melted before touching the suit. It also works against plasma beams and normal metallic bullets.

'Wow! Non-Metallic armour!' Roseanne was intrigued.

'There is also an inbuilt bullet proof lining throughout for additional protection. Once activated, it can generate powers in excess of ten billion joules for short periods and can focus such energy on several objects at once. However, it can also fry exposed parts of the human body, so always wear the special helmet and gloves provided, and keep a good distance from other operators not similarly clothe.'

'We need some of those,' Mallory said.

'We have a range of more advanced suits that can allow one to fly and vector the individual through solid matter. Even to place them in a separate dimension of time and space, but those are reserved for other jobs and are not classified for Earth at this time,' Jerry said.

After they had tested most of the weapons and armour, Mallory made a list and handed it to Jerry.

Finally Jerry took them to a hanger and introduced them to another android responsible for the jet fighters. Those particular ones were called Vipers and contained no cockpits of instrument panels. Every aspect of flight and weaponry was controlled through implants.

'These Vipers can only be flown by those with special implants and contain a range of deadly plasma projectors and missiles. The most powerful missiles are manufactured on board by a small microid factory. Each one can be tipped with a small fusion bomb of intense destructive energy. However, they can be tailored to a specific yield and task. Here again all instructions are through your implants. Once you tune in to its central processor you become one with the fighter virtually,' the android said and they were further amazed.

CHAPTER 22

# Eden's domes

'You know, Dear, I have decided to return home in two days time. I don't know what's happening in our business back there and I am getting a little worried. I hope you don't mind. Anyway, excluding recent involvement with problems here and on Earth, we've had a great time. It will make our vacation here eleven days instead of the fourteen we intended, and we'll have the weekend back home to do our shopping, et cetera,' Mallory said. Yet, he was still worried about the plague epidemic on Earth, even when Ben gave assurances that things were returning to normal.

'You almost read my mind and that was without recourse to my implants. After all I've learnt since our arrival, I feel completely saturated with information and will need time for my mind to sort through it all. There is so much to learn and we haven't even scratched the surface. We'll have to visit again soon, particularly when Sarah and the others are around. I feel sad leaving Jerry and Sharon behind like this, but they are quite capable. He has been so good to us and seems to be a bit lonely at this time,' Roseanne said.

'Why doesn't he come home with us for a short time until Sarah returns? After all, this place runs itself in her absence and I doubt that anyone on Earth will ever be able to recognise him now. I shall put the question to him after I give him the bad news of our intended departure,' Mallory said.

'Since Mac's return, things should be back to normal,' Roseanne said, reminding him of recent troubles.

'Thanks! I almost forgot!'

'You know, we'll have to give a party in Sarah's palace for the children, Jerry, Lennox and their families. I wish we had seen more of the others. Pity they are all away at this time. I think we chose a bad time for our visit here,' Roseanne said.

'Jerry intends to take us to the Gaia complex of domes tomorrow, to see a few of Earth's endangered and extinct species. During that time we'll meet Lennox in one of the local administration buildings. He is in charge of that area. I mean the Bio-engineering projects. We might also meet that cursed Macron left in one of the greenhouses, by you know who,' Mallory said.

'Hopefully not the reincarnated mass murderer!' she replied.

'The reincarnated one is not a mass murderer. He has no knowledge of those dire deeds!' Mallory corrected, sarcastically and they giggled.

'One thing I missed on this planet is the sea, coconut trees and sandy beaches. Are there no lovely beaches on this world?' Roseanne said, disappointingly, while changing the plague topic.

'I think it's something to do with the life-forms in the seas and oceans. From what Jerry said, the smallest fish are like the most ferocious Piranhas back home, and those that don't bite use poisonous venom that affects the nerves and muscles. Most marine life here use quite deadly methods to acquire their food. I think they are now working on a plan to create an inland sea in one of the remote deserts, but it will be a while before we get sandy beaches and palm trees. The people here are very particular when it comes to conservation and will go to any lengths to assist the indigenous life,' Mallory said.

'I suppose we can't have everything in paradise, but all the same, I think it's a great place for bringing up kids and I hope I am not pregnant yet,' she said.

'I hope you are. We tried hard enough with our new olympian bodies,' Mallory said and they kissed and made love again. For some reason, their new bodies were supercharged with energy and emotion, and could not be controlled even by the most ingenious implants.

The following day Jerry took them to the Gaia complex of domes. So called because it represented Earth's environments in miniature. That area contained an array of super domes covering several square miles and only held land animals. The larger water creatures were kept in saline and non-saline lakes elsewhere.

Such pressurized dome enclosures were dotted throughout Eden and each complex was linked to the outside world through secured portals for added security. Such tight confinement was to prevent small creatures and microbes from escaping to the outside world. All observers could only enter and exit via the first level with personal transit cards. There were two secured levels and each was thoroughly isolated from the other, much like a dome within a dome.

The first contained observation platforms, which encircled the innermost dome, gave a reasonable view of the complete area from several standpoints. The second level comprised sealed transparent walkways that went throughout the dome, giving the viewers better access to the individual animals.

The next level would have taken them among the animals, but only androids were allowed through those portals for feeding and veterinarian purposes. However, food could be ported into several feeding points.

Each dome contained its own unique habitat that represented the creatures' original environment as close as possible. In most cases, three or more domes were linked together and connected to a central feeding dome. However, hatches and gates could be fully controlled by the zoological keepers to restrain carnivores whenever necessary.

Within the Gaia complex were seven domes. Six of which formed a circle around a larger central feeding dome. Here again, animals like lions, tigers, rhinos, hippos, elephants and others - many now extinct on Earth - lived together. The carnivores were fed on synthetic foods, being allowed to hunt their manufactured and disguised natural prey occasionally, while the herbivores ate normal vegetation.

They arrived at Lennox's building which was situated just outside of the complex and visited him on the fifth floor.

'Sorry I was unable to see you guys sooner. Because of our recent problems I was in the middle of a tricky project and couldn't get away sooner. Anyway, are you two enjoying yourselves on our beautiful world?'

'It's truly incredible, seeing you, Pal... and it's great to meet you again and in one piece. I thought you were a goner with Jerry and the others, when I saw the new's back on Earth,' Mallory said, while observing him from head to toes.

'Ah! You mean our last visit to the Martian domes. I didn't like that plan myself, but it was the only way to disappear without people asking too many questions.'

'Yea.. I understand!'

'Jerry told me that you had the full treatment. Well, I am very happy that you are now one of us. I will have some time off tomorrow, so perhaps we could get together at my place or yours to celebrate.' A young and happier Lennox said.

'We are having a small party at Sarah's place tomorrow evening. Sort of a farewell party and you must join us there. We haven't told anyone yet, but we have decided to return to Earth. Mal is worried about our projects back there and after effects of the plague,' Roseanne said.

'When are you leaving?' Jerry asked.

'Day after tomorrow. Probably sometime in the afternoon. We have to get cracking and I don't know what's happening back there with the business. Why don't you all visit us for a holiday when we have our new portals installed? You can visit via Sol-Newtown. The break will do you good,' Mallory said.

'That's a great idea. Perhaps after Sarah returns,' Jerry said.

'In the mean time, why don't you let me show you around my bio-complex. Then we can have some lunch and a little chat about old times. This whole area is dedicated to saving endangered species on Earth. Here, any creature can be created from scratch. We start with its mass, size, bone, muscle, shape and such parameters which are fed into the Bio-Macron. The prototype is analysed in Virtual Reality several thousand times per second, until fully tested. Then the Bio-Macron simply puts together the genetic code using a Gene Sequencer. Once that is done, microids link the numerous proteins together. The creature is then cloned and grown in a special synthetic womb that is prepared for the purpose. This place is used for the real endangered and extinct species. Then we repatriate them to multiply on Tyrrel II. It's a forest world similar to Earth.'

'Wow! You guys really do God's work for him here!' Mallory replied.

'And much more besides! After a few weeks or months we have a new life-form. However, we prefer to recreate the more natural ones, like Dodos and Mammoths. Those that were lost through extinction. Then when the time is right they may be returned to their natural habitats in the wild. That way a proper ecological balance is maintained within the proven food-chain. Unfortunately, we cannot return those here to Earth until the human population has somewhat diminished, which might take the best part of a century,' Lennox said with disappointment.

'Yea... I think someone agrees with you and tried to speed things up with the Bubonic plague!' Roseanne replied.

'Yea... Good old Hal always detested Infilates and criminals. He is about the most clever guy I ever met!' Lennox replied.

They took a local portal to one of the many domes that were populated with herbivores.

'The family of horses you see in the distance were sired by my mustang, Shiloh. We use them sometimes for hockey in one of the recreation domes,' Jerry said.

After he had shown them around the Gaia complexes, he decided to take them to the one called Tarran's complex. So they took another portal to that site. That one comprised five larger domes. One was filled with giant bat-like creatures.

'These are the famous Bat-vultures of Tarran. They look nothing like vultures and can easily fly away with a large child. Their talons are highly poisonous. They have small hands and powerful hind legs for landing, impaling and lifting their prey. They are now an endangered species on Tarran,' Lennox said and they observed the enormous creatures with trepidation. They resembled Gargoyles of the most vicious types.

'The others contain wild cats and giant sand-spiders that can devour a whole human in one go, but those live underground within caves and can only be viewed by remote cameras,' Lennox added. After he had shown them around that one, he decided to take them to lunch.

All the information of that visit was stored within their implants and could be retrieved through a suitable computer and made into videos for others to watch.

CHAPTER 23

# Goodbye paradise

As usual, any major changes in the palace routine could only be made by the Palace Macron, who would instruct androids and humans of those changes. Therefore an entertainment request had to be entered for Roseanne's party.

She had never communicated before with a Macron and wondered whether that experience would be one filled with dread and dismay. Nevertheless, sooner or later, it had to be done and better before she returned to Earth, so she entered one of her implant's menus. It was the one to do with communications. Roseanne took several tunnels through the labyrinth in her mind until she came to Palace Macrons. Then she followed from A to Z, until she found the Imperial Palace. She was instantly taken to a large reception area in that Virtual World of the mind.

'Can I be of assistance?' said a young man waiting at the desk.

'I would like to make a request for a party at the palace tomorrow evening, at eight p.m. That is the day before we leave for Earth,' she said.

'How many guests are expected?' the man asked.

'No more than thirty are expected and it will comprise dinner and the usual mix of drinks. Perhaps two bottles of champagne could be included for a toast,' she said.

'Any preference to food and drink?'

'Make me something Jerry and Lennox will like. My husband and I enjoy most of it anyway,' she replied.

'It all seems very straight forward, Madam Roseanne. Your party request has been cleared by myself and central, and will be on schedule,' he said and she suddenly found herself sitting on the breakfast table while steering at Mallory.

'Are you all right, Dear?' he asked, with concern.

'I just consulted the palace macron about our party and she's given us the go-ahead,' Roseanne said.

'Of course, Dear. I just realised... this is not Earth, and the robots and androids have to be instructed,' he said.

'How long have I been away? I mean staring at you like a mad woman?' she asked.

'Hardly two seconds. You just stopped eating and began to look through me,' he said.

Although it appeared like the best part of half an hour to Roseanne, her meeting with Palace Macron had taken only a few seconds in real time. She soon realised that communication could be greatly speeded within the mind and the imagery was just a suitable interface that she could better relate with.

'Do you know one of the things I would like to do today? I would love to walk through the gardens as far as I can go, and perhaps observe some of the fairy-like creatures,'

'And what is the other?' Mallory asked.

'I would have liked to visit the Osmaron City satellite,' she replied.

'Pity the Grand Lord and his crew is not around. I would have liked to have met one of the Supreme Beings of the known universe, but perhaps next time,' Mallory said.

'Why don't we take the kids for a picnic and say goodbye to this world and its beautiful flying creatures in so doing?' Roseanne said.

'That's a great idea. We can ask the kitchen staff to prepare some sandwiches and soft drinks. Since we are now probationary councillors, we are allowed to be responsible for them,' he replied.

'Gregory! Grace!' she shouted and the pair soon arrived.

'Would you like to join us on a picnic? We have decided to follow the route through the rear gardens and absorb the beauty of this place before we leave for Earth. Get some of the younger ones together and you can tell the kitchen staff to prepare some sandwiches and drinks for us to take along, and hurry!' Roseanne said.

The young children had no idea what a picnic was, but soon ran excitedly to the kitchen to tell the chief android cook. Palace Macron would have known everything about picnics.


They took the narrow path from the rear of the palace and followed until they came upon a field of giant flowers in full bloom. They were very similar to the ones they had passed on the day of their arrival on Eden.

Their fragrance was intoxicating and they held hands. She began to sing to the children some old Earth songs. It was "all things bright and beautiful, all creatures great and small" and a few other relevant rhymes. The children followed her words as best they could and when they were tired they rested for a while on the side of the path. There she spread a small picnic blanket and took the food out. The children's faces were red with excitement.

'I shall miss you all when I leave. But I shall be back soon. Should I bring you some presents from Earth when I next visit?' she said and they roared:

'Yes please, Madam Roseanne!'

'You must tell me what you like and I shall try to get you the same or something very similar. Perhaps Grace could make a list when we get back,' she said.

'I wonder where the little creatures must live. Do you think they have a nest like honeybees or wasps?' she asked, turning to Mallory.

'They are Cherubs, Madam. They live in the snow cliffs yonder. Their homes are built inside the chalk,' one of the younger children interrupted.

'They seem to be a lot more clever than insects and from what our implants said, they have a language and a form of culture of their own. They can also communicate with us, but because of our size and hearing, they are unable to do it directly. They seem to use a higher frequency and build their homes within overhanging cliffs. They are the symbol of peace, happiness and contentment, and Madam Sarah has used their image on all official palace documents,' Mallory said.

'Cherubs. How fitting? After all, this place is called Eden and they look so heavenly. Don't they? Like real angels in miniature?' she said.

After they had finished their picnic, one of the little creatures landed on a nearby flower and Roseanne got up and went closer to observe, followed by the others. They could see it project its long tongue to suck the nectar into a small expandable pouch just beneath its chin. When it was finished Roseanne nervously stretched her right-hand forward, close to the flower, and the creature landed in the palm of her hand. It observed her with its two large black eyes before gently bowing, as if to show respect to a giant God. She could observe its mouth move as if uttering a sentence, but she could hear nothing.

'Did you see that, Darling? It bowed and spoke to me, but I could not hear a word. Why was that?' she said.

'They must communicate beyond our audible range,' he replied.

'I wish I could hear what it said. Is there no device for translating their words?'

'Perhaps there is, but I don't think we should contaminate their society with our naive concepts of right and wrong. It's much better to watch them. After all, they are not human, are they?' Mallory advised and although disappointed she saw his point of view.

'As always, you are completely right. We try to see everything in human terms of greed and selfishness. Perhaps they are more advanced than us in that regard. Because they live peacefully in large communities without our vain technologies,' she said and the creature flew away, to meet its mate while turning around in mid flight to say farewell and she waved back.

'Goodbye for now my little friend,' she said and the children did likewise.

That day they spent several hours in the fields, observing the strange and varied fauna and flora of the planet and when Roseanne had seen enough, she felt a sense of contentment; a feeling at one and a joining with that world. Then she was ready to return to Earth and face its turmoil.


When they got back to the palace, Grace took them to a costume's room. It included many wardrobes filled with clothes of all types and sizes. Those were probably used by Sarah and others when they were on Earth, but would now be very handy for the party.

She decided to dress the children and teenagers in those outfits and would make the party a fancy dressed one from the Solarians viewpoint. However, the children found the whole thing quite exciting and were willing to partake to almost any degree.

She sent instructions to all those originally from Earth that were invited. They were to wear suitable Earth clothes for the occasion. Once Roseanne started a trend she tended to dominate and have her own way. Most of all, she wanted to shake the palace on the eve of their departure to Earth.

Roseanne and Mallory had dressed in their spare Earth clothes for the party. It was not their travelling suit, but party-clothes, and she wondered whether they would be frowned upon for wearing anything other than their official togas. She wanted to liven up the place to create a lasting impression. Anyway, that party was also meant for the young palace children and their friends, and was not an official one.

The imperial kitchen had prepared a variety of dishes, cakes, sweets and ice-cream for children and grownups alike and it was decided to start the children's party first at five p.m., equivalent Earth time. Then the little ones could retire at eight. However, the main party was to start at seven and continue well into the night.

When they arrived in the main hall the android band was playing a lively piece. It was one of their own compositions. Other androids began to serve snacks and drinks.

The children were having their own celebrations and were sitting around several prearranged tables to one side of the hall. The older teenagers and grownups were sitting on another set of tables to their right. Jerry then stood up to give the first toast to the couple.

'May I take this opportunity on this joyous occasion to congratulate Mallory and Roseanne - who are now respected members of our extended family - in their resolve to saving Earth from itself. May their future lives be filled with happiness, success and many fine children,' he said, and they cheered and drank a toast to the couple's future. Then Mallory got up to say a few words of his own.

'Despite the fact of our first brief visit to this beautiful world, we already feel fully at home here. It is also a fact that most of our friends now live on this beautiful world. Nevertheless, the time has come for us to return to the turmoil of Earth. Therefore, our sincerest thanks goes out to everyone, most of all Councillor Gerald, his wife, Sharon, and the lovely palace children, who have made our stay here a most enjoyable one. We wish we could return the same favours on Earth, but unfortunately, the present situation there is still quite volatile. However, should any of you wish to visit, consider yourselves welcomed at our home at any time.'

They cheered, but Mallory continued.

'Further, we intend to visit Eden at least once each year from now. So this is just a temporary farewell, since we have a very important job of work to do back there. Thanks again for everything!' he said and they clapped and cheered.

They danced to a range of mainly Earth-type music that had been adapted for the occasion, until they were exhausted. Then they sat and watched a humorous android play with a magician and a puppet who constantly lost his head and limbs. Also, the puppet was always sabotaging the magician's equipment and stole the show.

In great disappointment, the children's party ended at eight p.m. and they were escorted to their rooms by Roseanne and Mallory. Then the couple returned to the party. When the band stopped playing at twelve p.m., they stayed and chatted well into the early morning.

CHAPTER 24

# Earthbound

The morning of their departure was a misty one, which gradu-ally cleared into a most beautiful and sunny day. Since their stay on Eden they had not seen any rain. Just a dense morning mist that persisted until repelled by the warm sunshine. That mist and resulting dew tended to saturate all plants and surfaces.

Apparently there was no rain or snow on most of Eden so all indigenous life had evolved under those unique conditions. That was one of the reasons why sprinklers were used extensively in growing hybrids and other crops taken from Earth. However, water was in abundance in its seas, lakes and soil. Therefore most plants had evolved methods for storing moisture in their leaves, trunks and roots, which were usually long enough to tap into the water table.

By now their trolley and suitcases had been emptied. All items of food and drink were given to the palace kitchen, children and friends. Their travelling cases were packed with necessary clothes and items for their return journey. The ceremonious gold embroidered and laced togas were left in the capable custody of Grace, who would return them to Sarah for safe keeping on her return.

After they were dressed in their modified travelling clothes, they visited the children's rooms to say goodbye. Roseanne gave each a big hug and told them she would soon be back. Then they took two small suitcases towards the nearest portal and transposed to Jerry's palace. There they waited patiently with a cup of coffee while Jerry and his wife got ready to take them to Eden City.

'I feel quite sad seeing you leave,' Sharon said and hugged Roseanne.

They arrived later at the restaurant just before lunchtime and Jerry ordered one of his favourite three course meals. Then he took them to the central station.

'Your journey to Sol-Newtown will be automatic from here on.

Central Macron knows of your intended departure, so once your transit cards or implants are scanned, a route will be formed,' Jerry said.

'Thanks again folks for everything, and don't forget to visit, whenever you can. So see you soon,' Mallory said and they entered the cubicle waving as they did. In a moment they had vanished from that portal and had arrived within Sol-Newtown, Earth, seconds later.

They were promptly escorted to Ben's office while their cases were efficiently taken from them and already on their way to Oscar's trunk.

'You have?... pardon me for staring, but you both look so different. You obviously had a most enjoyable vacation, plus extras,' Ben commented.

'We did! I'm afraid we are now fully fledged Solarians.' Roseanne said.

'We have had our own type of excitement down here as well during your absence. Thank goodness it's behind us now. We lost too many though,' Ben said.

'Yes, pity we couldn't do more to assist,' Mallory said.

'Anyway, you have arrived just in time for an early lunch, so why don't we have a chat and some food. I want to know everything about your holidays,' Ben said, joyfully, changing the sad topic.

'Everything?' Roseanne queried.

'Only the parts you wish to tell,' he replied and they laughed.

'Only a little for us, thanks. We were just treated to a three-course meal by Jerry and Sharon, and we are on the brink of bursting, But we don't mind a small drink. Anyway, what's the news. Anything devastating happened to Earth in our absence, other than you-know-what? ' Mallory inquired.

'Could there be anything worse? And our Green Chameleon guy has died!' Ben replied.

'Yep, nothing could be worse than the plague. And despite everything, I feel sad about that guy, Hal. I wonder where his funeral will be held. I would like to visit and pay my respects!' Mallory said. He was also thinking of contacting his son, Andy, to console him for the loss of his father-in-law.

'I can find his address for you. Because of his anti-crime methods we think he should be given an appropriate sending off. He was always hell-bent on reducing Earth's population by killing off Infilates. He couldn't wait for their deaths in 100 years time because of lasting damage due to poaching and other crimes. However, his plague only targeted Infilates and criminals in many wayward parts of the world. So in a sense, he did us a big favour,' Ben said.

'Mass murder is never a good thing!' Roseanne replied.

'With all that's been happening, I have also been keeping a close check on your business through our Macron and Carl seems to have everything under control. But I can't say the same about the USA and USE governments. There has also been growing unrest among people since the infertility figures have been released. They think their respective governments have been doing too little to find a cure for the infected and are also contemptuous of those receiving the antidote. These feelings have been further aggravated by the plague. I believe we are in for a turbulent future,' Ben said.

'What is our President doing to relieve those problems?' Mallory asked.

'What can he do? I think they are waiting to see whether violence will escalate or the people get used to the idea. Any premature and poorly prepared remedy could further fuel the flames. So they are moving with a degree of caution,' Ben replied.

'We are expecting several crates of weapons from Eden within the month. Could you please give us a shout the moment they arrive? Portal engineers are also expected at our house soon,' Mallory said.

'I am happy that you have both taken my advice to accept a full conversion. Let me formally congratulate you both on that major step and greet you as a member of my larger family. You should also realise that this place is now open to you at all times. I have selected two local offices for you next door. Once the portal is installed at your house, you can use them freely as your secured offices. This place is impervious to outside spies and infiltrators, and is also beyond any of Earth's government jurisdiction and controls. To all intents and purpose, Sol-Newtown is an embassy of the highest level of autonomy by treaty,' Ben said.

He took them to view their new offices which were filled with a range of new technologies, but there were no robots or androids. Automatons were only used when necessary, and used only by senior members.

'Now, you both have your personal macrons that can link you to every world within the Solarian Federation. With these, you can find any information required with a single thought, once you get used to the system. They are also linked to each other. That also includes Oscar and all other ventures and operations throughout this and other worlds including satellites. They are fully accessible by implants, once your long range transceivers have been installed at your house. It comes with your portal,' Ben advised. They looked in wonderment at the small unit with many blinking lights. They were not like Central Macron, but instead much smaller and fitted neatly in one of the office corners, like some little black computer of alien design. There were no switches or buttons. Every control was only accessible through implants via the help menus in their minds.

'Oscar also had a full overhaul in your absence, with the inclusion of anti-inertia, but I am sure he would like to tell you all about it himself,' Ben added.

After they had coffee and snacks together, Ben took them to the nearest portal and they transposed to the area where Oscar was held. A helpful male android soon came along to assist them with their cases and guided them to Oscar's bay.

'Well, I never! Is this our original Roadstar? You look brand spanking new!' Roseanne exclaimed, as the doors lifted vertically.

'How are you, my dear friend? I have been told that you received a full refit and they were not kidding either. Do you appreciate those alterations?' Mallory inquired.

'Mal, I had very little say in the matter, but as you would say; I now feel on top of the world and that is while my wheels are still on the ground, and you won't be squashed against the seat in the future, whenever I take off at full blast,' Oscar replied.

'That's a very good addition and I see you haven't lost your sense of humour. What exactly have they done to you?' Roseanne replied.

'My memory and vocabularies have been extended some twenty times and they have fitted more powerful transceivers for a grater range. I can now transmit directly to you anywhere in Solaria, also through implants and your macrons. They have also given me a stronger personal male implant image. So we can converse more intimately, which makes me almost human, but it was all built around my original conscious core,' Oscar said.

'I don't know how I will be able to cope with two males in my life, excluding Carl at the office,' she said and Mallory laughed.

'I always say two males in the field is always better than one in the hand,' Mallory replied and she smiled.

'In that case, we should make a much better team in the future, to fight the evils of this world. Not to mention the evil Javols, in the name of the Greater Purpose,' Roseanne replied.

'I suppose, People, we better get home and see what Arthur has done to our garden in the mean while,' Mallory said and they entered Oscar.

'Oscar, please take us home,' Roseanne said and they waved to Ben as the car left the area. Oscar soon took to the air and very soon afterwards they were home.

'If you don't mind me speaking. I am surprised by the changes I now see in you both. Have you been similarly rejuvenated as myself?' Oscar asked.

'Yes, Oscar! We've also been given a full refit and servicing that should carry us for another twenty years or so, until our guarantee runs out,' Mallory replied, humorously and with a grin.

'In that case you must feel like new humans, and ready for some real action,' Oscar said.

'And you will see lots of real action soon, Captain Oscar!' Mallory replied.

CHAPTER 25

# The real struggle begins

At noon they arrived at the house, but Mallory soon realised that Carl had the keys. They went to the rear of the house and shouted to Arthur, their part-time gardener and handyman, but no one answered.

'Seems we are locked out. Any ideas?' Roseanne said.

'To avoid this problem in the future we need to rig our Macrons to this place and our implants to the electronic locking mechanism. In the mean time, it gives us a good chance to assess the security level of our new home and implement changes. After all, we'll be having a portal installed shortly in the basement and wouldn't like intruders getting a free ride to Sol-Newtown.' Mallory was not pleased.

'Now you are talking!'

'Yep. I am! So we better give it our best shot. The first thing we'll try and do is find a way in without keys. If we can, then our present security system is less than useless,' Mallory said.

They tried the doors and windows, but the metal shutters were on and access was almost impossible without high explosives. Slowly they made their way to the other two levels with a tall ladder, until they climbed unto the loft. They found one of the loft windows were not bolted securely and the shutter was not released.

'This is what I mean. Anyone, can climb up here and have easy access to our property. We need a timed system that operates all shutters automatically on all levels when there is no movement in the house. Also some cameras throughout the front and rear that can look for suspicious movement. I am sure our Macrons can handle the security if we had the shutter controls connected to a secondary system,' he said.

'Do what you think is necessary. It's our Earthly home now,' Roseanne said and slid into the house from that area in the roof.

Mallory made a few notes, they left their cases in one of the garden sheds and went to a local café for a snack. After they had discussed security matters he called a security company and made arrangements to receive one of their local reps. The couple didn't want to visit the business on their first day back, but had little choice if they were to walk into their home in a dignified manner.

'I see it but I don't believe... You both look awesome!' Carl exclaimed with utter astonishment as he checked them over inch by inch.

'Do you like what you see?' Roseanne said, posing like a real model.

'Unreal...!' he added and embraced them both.

'I hear you have been very busy in our absence. Thank goodness you didn't have to deal with the plague as well. Anyway, you just shout when you need a break, Pal,' Mallory said.

'And miss all the fun. Tell me something. What diet have you both been on? You look so incredibly young? Is it also available for people like me?' Carl said.

'We had a full body refit and you can have the same if you wish,' Roseanne said.

'Well, you both look fantastic!'

'I was worried for you guys back here, but there was little we could do during the crisis!' Mallory said.

'Yea, the plague killed a lot! Chad did a great service keeping it away from our borders. Apparently our Green Chameleon was responsible. He left a suicide note saying it was all his fault. Our favourite detective Calahan was not pleased with the outcome. Anyway, it's great to have you back. I moved to my flat two days ago and visited your place yesterday. Arthur, the gardener, is presently at the house on a daily basis and checks the place over whenever he is around. I think he had to visit his daughter recently. Some illness in the family. He is now back. Anyway, he also has my number in case of emergencies,' Carl said.

'We really came to say hello and collect the keys. By the way, you must come over to the house tomorrow with your lady, we brought back a few presents for you. I shall also be having a few close friends for dinner. Then we can have a little natter about important matters,' Mallory said.

'I just remembered. Chad wants you urgently. He would like to finalize the deal on the ranch. Why don't you call him now?' Carl said and Mallory immediately got on the phone.

'I am finally back from our honeymoon, Pal,' Mallory said.

'Did you have a nice time?'

'It was most enjoyable.'

'Not bad weather here either. I had a busy time with the plague and all that. However that military operation is now behind me and handed over to the medical people. Our President couldn't be happier with the outcome. I wanted to see you about signing some papers,' he said.

'Why don't you get you and your family down here tomorrow and spend the weekend with us? We can sort the papers out then. And by the way, have you still got those travel tickets?' Mallory said.

'Yes, they looked too beautiful to throw away,' Chad replied.

'Well, you can use them for as long as you wish. Just show them to the airline companies. They are programmed to the last route you took, so you must follow that same route. If you need to change inform them. By the way, what about my previous wife and son?' Mallory said.

'They should be out of quarantine by now. They were not infected. Anyway, thanks, Pal. We'll see you sometime tomorrow,' he said and hung up.

Mallory soon got on the phone to Cathy, Andy's mother.

'Hi Cath!'

'Hi Mal. Haven't heard from you in a while!'

'I heard about the dreaded problems in Mexico. Please accept my sympathies! Anyway, if you need a break, Please visit us. Chad and others are on the way for the weekend. It should make a pleasant change for you. Use the tickets I sent for travel. It's important, very important!' Mallory stressed.

'I will come! Thanks for calling!' she said and hung up.


Chad arrived before lunch and was taken back by the image of the younger Mallory Colman.

After many excuses, none of which having in any way convinced Chad and his wife, they had lunch in a local diner before going to the house.

'I shall have to open up to Chad before long. He's now getting a bit suspicious. The cunning old dog,' Mallory said to himself.

'How is our new place coming along?' Mallory inquired innocently.

'It will be ready in another fortnight or so. That is what I've been told by the big computer with the female voice. She reminds me of sexy Daisy and has similar mannerisms. Brother, I have never seen anything as fast as those robots and they never make mistakes. They move twenty times faster than us humans and most operations can only be observed with a slow motion camera. They are not anything like the models I've seen in the Automaton Museum in Washington. Where did they come from?' Chad inquired.

'We have our connections, you know. I shall let you into a few secrets when the time is right. Before that can happen you must be fully committed to our cause, which I shall tell you when we get home,' Mallory said.

'It must be some organization, Pal. To wield such power,' Chad replied.

'We are expecting several crates of the most advanced weapons in the next few weeks. Please let me know when your armoury is ready, so I can plan delivery,' Mallory said, as if changing their current topic.


The moment they arrived at the house they had coffee and after freshening up, Mallory called them into the main sitting room to join Carl and his girlfriend.

'Now that we are all together, let me say a few words to you in private. Mind you, our present conversation must remain only with us.

'Since our return from Planet Eden, many of our friends have wondered at our younger bodies. Well, on Eden no one ever grows old or dies. We were given newer bodies, not very different from our original ones and a lot more besides. Our minds have increased some twenty fold and we can now communicate telepathically with each other.

'You are not kidding?' Chad was astonished.

'There, they have the technologies to do almost anything, so that answers your questions,' he said. They looked at him with utter astonishment, thinking he was pulling their legs because of the way he and Roseanne looked, each being over ten years younger.

After all, where was this planet Eden and why did no one ever mention it before. Anyway, the whole story was too far-fetched to be believable. Nevertheless, Mallory continued.

'Now, for the more serious business, I have to show you a video I received from Professor Khan. After you have observed that film, you will be in a better position to ask questions freely,' Mallory said. Then he moved the large television screen and slid a disk into the slot while making small adjustments to the equipment.

The screen was composed of a special material that reflected light in such a manner as to give the impression of partial 3-D. However, their sitting positions were critical for best results. The image was the usual one of the Javols' destruction of Caefon in all its gory details. Many left the room in tears during the worst scenes of decapitation and absorption of little children.

The video was very realistic and all the people of that world had three fingers and one thumb on each hand but with penetrating sea blue eyes like Lord Meron.

'Friends, this was planet Caefon three thousand years ago, before our mutual enemies destroyed that world as they had every other world in the galaxy of Andromeda. Sadly, they are now on their way to our galaxy and Earth. They are expected here within about one hundred years and when they arrive, we shall follow the same faith as the poor Caefonites and others that went that horrible way.'

'My God. An Alien invasion!' Chad exclaimed.

'Although our plan is long term, many changes must be made on Earth and elsewhere within our galaxy before we are ready for the great battle. And fighting we must, if we care for ourselves, our children and their future generations.'

'You are right! We must preserve our species and way of life!' Chad was not amused.

'There are many advanced species within our galaxy, Osmaron, known to us more commonly as the Milky Way and they are actively involved in the preparation for the Javols' invasion.

However, at this moment our main duty is towards Earth. We are to recruit our best into the Special Squad and get our productive young trained in more advanced ways of technologies, away from the negative influences of Earth. Because I am afraid, the situation on our world will worsen in time.'

'You mean... Global Warming?' Chad inquired.

'That and other things. Those of you who decide to become committed to our cause in saving Earth, our galaxy and worlds beyond, must follow our mission with conviction, honour and commitment within the Greater Purpose.'

'I suppose there's a plan?'

'Yep! Our long term goal will be to destroy the Javols and return these galaxies and Earth to better times, where our families, friends and good people can exist in peace and harmony. Incidently, it's also our duty to save all other life. So we have a great responsibility to shoulder.'

'It's a major task. Do you think it can be done?' Chad inquired.

'I am sure it can be done. Now you may ask your questions?' Mallory said.

'So you really went to an alien world called Eden and we are also in real trouble and facing an alien invasion from Andromeda? Are they like us? Are they human with machines?' Chad said, while his hands trembled from fear and nervousness.

'The terrible Javols are shape shifting microids. A type of Nanobot life-form very much like our most advanced microid robots and composed mainly of metals. However, they require chemicals in our blood, biological tissue, metals and energy in its raw state for their own metabolic processes and to reproduce. Unlike our microid robots that are controlled by external computers, they are super-intelligent individuals and think like us, but with all the super abilities of microids. They are one of the best survivors in the universe, if not the best.'

'So we have to defeat the undefeatable!' Chad was not happy.

'They are also the most efficient predators. Because of the way they are constructed, they can change to almost any form of an equivalent mass and are immune to bullets, lasers and explosives. They can only be damaged by high energy plasma at close range, but can be infected by microid virus and a range of other subtler methods. Compared to us, they are truly invincible. That is why they have been so successful in removing all primal life from Andromeda,' Mallory replied.

'I don't know what to say. Seems to me that our work is well and truly cut out for us. These Javols make the plague look like sucking candy. Are there anymore people like you on Earth? I mean forming a part of your galactic organization?' John Friedman asked.

'We are it. My job among other things, is to begin the Special Squad to protect fertile families and curtail crime. At a later date we shall be advised further by the Solarian authorities who presently exist on Eden. We must prepare by first securing our race. Then we can begin the training program for our young. That is, until the time is right, which is a few decades in the future. Then we shall begin the fight against the enemy within Andromeda and elsewhere with the aid of The Son of Destiny.'

'Son of Destiny? You mean, someone like Jesus?' John Friedman inquired.

'He is all powerful and will lead us into victory. Those of you who wish to become Solarians will have to visit Eden for the necessary conversion, but it's not in any way compulsory at this time. However, only I can recommend you for that glorious promotion. Do we have a show of hands?' Mallory said. All hands went up with the exception of Roseanne's.

'Can't we negotiate with these Ja..vols,' Carl said.

'They do not like primals like us and see us as a useless species suitable only for food. Why should they negotiate when they can take it from us, anyway?' Roseanne replied.

'By the way, Lord Meron was an Andromedan. Jerry and the others are still alive and live in beautiful golden palaces on Eden,' Mallory said.

'I always thought something was not all together right about that accident. Now I know it was a put up job,' Chad replied.

'Yea...! Bloody Hell! So they are still alive! I wonder if our Green Chameleon is also alive. He could have been one of them?' Carl was intrigued.

'He could be? I wouldn't write him off yet! Anyway, I had a great time with Jerry, Sharon and Harry. You wouldn't believe the things they have on that paradise world. It's even more beautiful than the biblical paradise. Anyway, it's great to have some new members in our larger family. Now we need hold no secrets from each other. In a few weeks we begin recruiting our Specials. By that time the antidote business will be able to run by itself, with an occasional visit from us.'

'We don't have any choice now. It's war or nothing,' Chad said.

'I have chosen Sol-Newtown Dome for all future meetings that concern galactic business. That way, we can always be assured of privacy. I would like us here, to separate into two main groups. One to handle the advertising campaign and the other, to inter-view all possible recruits for background, basic tendencies and military experience. We don't want criminals in our organisation. Neither do we need greenhorns in senior positions. Because of those reasons I have decided to acquire some special equipment from Sol-Newtown, for which some of you will be trained. No Terminal infected are to be included in this campaign. That means people under the age of 45, present company accepted, of course. I'm getting to love my job!' Mallory said.

'Agreed, Sir!' John Friedman said.

'Roseanne, Chad and I will be assigned to tackle the interviews. Carl will be in charge of the advertising program. He will recruit whomever he chooses and that also includes us. Personally, I don't mind doing two jobs,' Mallory said.

'I will need another week or so to complete some work at the office. It's mainly to do with completing the database. Once that is done, the supervisors will be able to run things on their own,' Carl said.

'Those of you who wish to visit Eden with Carl in one week's time, please show your hands,' Mallory said and all hands excluding Roseanne's went up.

'I suppose we can take our wives along?' John Friedman asked.

'Only if they are of the same persuasion and agree to become Solarians. If it's going to be a problem now, you shouldn't worry. They might come around in time, and you don't have to take them along at your first visit. Simply say you have been sent abroad on special business for a week. If you can't make arrangements at such short notice, I shall be only too pleased to have them stay with us here in your absence. Once they are shown the video of horrible Javols I'm sure they will change their minds.'

'I see what you mean,' Chad was amused.

'You know, Eden is probably the most beautiful world in our galaxy. There, people live in golden palaces, everything is free and machines do all the repetitive and uncreative work. So I can guarantee that you will all enjoy your time there. In the mean while, I shall arrange special transit cards for you and open your new accounts in Solarian Banking,' Mallory said and they were happy and intrigued.

CHAPTER 26

# More important business

The following days were spent in the office, giving Carl a hand to reorganize the management structure of the antidote distribution, other business ventures, and in automating most of the processes involved. Since the plague, their program in some countries had significantly reduced, leaving just 5 billion Infilates to isolate, out of the original 10 billion or so.

They were also able to make direct connection with the computer through their macrons on Sol-Newtown. During those experiments, and to his surprise, Mallory found he could communicate with Roseanne anytime during the day directly through their implants. He would first enter his Coms Menu and think of her name or something they liked doing together. After that, he would find himself in her office and she in his. The process took place in their minds, using each other's eyes for visual reference. Both offices tended to merge as one in a seamless manner.

The imagery was so realistic, that to all intents and purpose they were in the same office, talking and touching each other. Almost any image, smell or taste could be virtualized in that manner and the implants had a special processor for configuring those realistic scenes.

During those periods a virtual cup of coffee was exactly the same as a real one and they felt satisfied in a similar way.

'This is truly incredible for slimming purposes, you know?' Roseanne said.

'I see what you mean. We can eat our fill of whatever we want and never put on weight. However we must remember to have real meals or our bodies will waste away. I know what we can do? We can place a nutrition alarm in our implants, to remind us when we require normal sustenance,' Mallory said and she agreed.

In their Virtual World, the players were always in synchronism with the scene and other players. That was for their mutual benefit and peace of mind during the communication.

They could now communicate by virtual telepathy, where senses of touch, taste and smell could also be realised.


While they were in the office the President's personal secretary called.

'Can I speak with Captain Mallory Colman, please?'

'Speaking! How can I help?'

'I am the President's personal secretary. Could you make it to Washington DC for a meeting on the twenty-eight?'

'I would love to! Can I also take my wife along?'

'Yes, Sir. That goes without saying. We shall see you then,' she replied and hung off. He immediately called Roseanne and told her the good news.

'My Dear, we have another visit to the White House on the twenty-eight. Can you make it?' he said.

'Of course I can make it, but I need some new clothes for the occasion. You will have to take me shopping with Oscar,' she replied.


Mallory had applied for special transit passes for Carl and his girlfriend, Chad and his wife, and John Friedman and his wife. They were to leave for Eden the moment Carl's task was completed. They were presently staying at Mallory's residence while assisting in different areas of the programme.

The following weekend a large black Roadstar limousine arrived at the house and two handsome gentlemen got out. They were wearing uniforms that were familiar to both Roseanne and Mallory.

'Can we speak with Commander Coleman?' one said and he was called.

'We have come to install your portal, Sir,' the other said and Mallory took them to the basement.

'This place is ideal for a V-room. That way you may conceal the true position of the portal. We have all the equipment in the car,' the first android said.

'Do what you think is appropriate, Gentlemen. I leave it all in your capable hands,' Mallory said and went back to his work.

Mallory smiled, when he realised how much simpler his colleagues' trip would be. Once the portal was fitted his intention of taking the new members by Oscar to Sol-Newtown would be unnecessary.

That portal point in the basement of his house was ideal for transporting members and special recruits almost anywhere, including Eden, or so he thought. He also knew through Ben and Jerry that his palace on Eden would be ready to accept visitors in a few more weeks. He hoped to visit with Roseanne on its completion and hold a grand party in commemoration of their generosity towards him and his wife.

With the aid of a special microid robot, it took the androids the best part of a day to fit the small macron and portals. Then they were optimised to the main portals on Eta, Mars and Sol-Newtown. It was then that he realised they could directly visit Mars instead, thus cutting out Sol-Newtown. However, Mars was only accessible in emergencies, because everyone still had to be thoroughly cleansed of Earth's bacteria before entering the main portal system and the cleansing equipment was only stored on Sol-Newtown and satellite Eta. In the mean time they instructed their colleagues as best they could about life on Eden.

Ben arrived directly by basement portal on the following Tuesday with the special passes for Mallory's friends. The moment he entered the basement the security bell rang.

'We have a visitor, Folks. I wonder if it's one of those intrepid galactic nomads,' Mallory said jokingly.

They went to greet Ben. The others, most of all Professor Friedman, were amazed by the concept of portal technology.

Friedman went to check Ben over, to make sure no limbs were missing and Ben saw the funnier side of his greeting.

'After all this time, I am only just getting the knack of portals. Yet, I've never heard of anyone losing a limb or dying during the process of transposition. If anything, it makes one look and feel younger,' he replied.

'You think the technology also includes a rejuvenation sequence,' Mallory inquired.

'That's quite possible. It could be using a special template. Hence the reason why all unwanted bacteria and degenerate cells are removed during the interstellar process.'

'Really?' Friedman was astonished.

'Anyway, it's great to see you are finally organized,' Ben said.

'And you must visit us anytime you wish. Consider this house as yours and you must please join us for dinner,' Mallory insisted.

'Put like that how can I refuse,' Ben said, while handing him a small box with the special metallic cards. Mallory opened the box and removed the cards and handed them around.

'Your route has already been programmed in these cards. You will further be advised of any changes in transit. Portal travel is strange at first, but once you get accustomed, it's a piece of cake,' he said.


Mallory and Roseanne saw them off from the basement portal the following morning and finally had the large house all to themselves again.

'Now, Dear, we can go to DC and do some serious shopping before we visit the White House at three p.m. Perhaps we could also visit Andy before we leave for home,' he said.

They got dressed in their best clothes, packed a small case and Oscar was called.

CHAPTER 27

# Another visit to Washington DC

They visited a few of their favourite haunts and did some shopping before taking lunch at a small cafeteria. Then they went to one of their favourite small hotels and booked in for the night. As they left, they were recognised by a few reporters who pounced on Mallory like hungry wolves.

'Captain Mallory Colman is now responsible for global distribution of the antidote for the dreaded Terminal Disease! Mister Colman, is it a fact that there is no cure for this ever growing pandemic? One that will most probably make the human race extinct within a hundred years or so?' the reporter inquired.

'All I can say is that, at present, a lasting cure has not been found. However, many scientists are presently involved in the program to find a cure, so it's only a matter of time.'

'Do you think such a cure will be found within this decade? Because by then almost everyone will be irreversibly infected?'

'Personally, I can't speak for the geneticists and microbiologists. We'll just have to wait and see. However, many countries are now involved throughout the world. So it could well be found within that time frame. In the mean while, we shall continue to supply the antidote to those that are not yet infected and further tests will be made available to those wishing them.'

'So there is a small chance?'

'A good chance! And by the way, to put the record straight, the antidote is a permanent cure for the disease if caught in time and taken regularly. Thank you all for now, ladies and gentlemen,' Mallory said, still being pursued by several reporters.

'That does it! Now you get your face on T.V. and all the crooks and hit-men know where we are!' Roseanne exclaimed and he suddenly realized he should have worn some form of disguise during this DC visit. Nevertheless, since his recent body changes on Eden, not many would recognise him as his older self.

'Anyway, they cannot find our home. We just have to be extra vigilant from now on. Particularly when we visit places like

Washington DC,' he replied.

At two thirty they were already at the White House and greeted by the President's wife who considered them to be different people. Then his personal secretary came and took them both into the Roosevelt's room where they greeted the President and several important scientists and senators. They were all surprised by the much younger couple now faced. Yet the President continued.

'Gentlemen and ladies, we are here together in an attempt to find some type of solution to the growing unrest and other problems associated with the Terminal Disease.' President Arnold said. They sat and remained quiet during his speech.

*Since the Bubonic outbreak the public have become more concerned for their survival. In the past weeks many of our politicians have received death threats by infected extremist. If nothing is done to appease this growing crisis, they may begin to take more drastic steps. Luckily for us, the infected (from the Terminal Disease) is still under 10 percent per capita of the population.*

*'Furthermore, many of us here have recently found, to our deepest regret, that we have joined the infected and still growing minority. Fortunately, most of us have passed the age of child-bearing. That responsibility now being passed to our children and grandchildren, some of whom, regrettably, have also been infected.*

*'Mallory, you being the global distributor of the antidote, and what a grand job you have done in such a shot time... Is there a possible cure around the corner?'* the president said and Mallory stood up to answer that question.

'Mister president, ladies and gentlemen, if we are to avoid further unrest, it is imperative that my words be kept solely within these four walls,' he said and abruptly sat down.

'Mallory, you have my word. You may continue,' the president replied.

'The Terminal Disease is of an incurable nature. It has been bio-engineered by a person or persons unknown. Its sole purpose being to reduce human population within more acceptable and sustainable limits. This is because the disease is also a type of cancer that only targets the reproductive systems in humans and destroys them permanently. Even without the knowledge of the infected.'

'My God! As bad as that?'

'I am afraid so. At least, that is what I have been told by a recent survey along with our most informed scientists and powerful computers.'

'So there is no chance of a permanent cure!' The President was not happy.

'There will be no cure for the infected. You will obviously appreciate the animosity felt by many conservationists, world-wide, by the ever growing human population and resulting problems of desertification and mass extinctions of rear species, not to mention certain limits imposed by global warming. Despite these ever mounting problems we humans are still reproducing as if there was no tomorrow.'

'I see!'

'I can only assume that a group of scientist somewhere on this world realized the problems faced and decided to take action to reduce human population to acceptable limits. Many of whom could have acquired the necessary resources to engineer such a disease. However, it will be very difficult, if not impossible, to point a finger at any particular group. Thank goodness, Professor Khan found an antidote in time to save our young.' Mallory said.

'Thank God for little mercies!' Arnold replied, but Mallory continued.

*'The anti-fertility virus itself has been linked to a synthesized type of human bacteria. Almost identical to the many forms prevalent on our skin and within our gut. The carrier bacteria can also mutate to the predominant types. That particular bacteria includes several types that have been engineered in one and can replace any of our more natural types. Once it touches the skin, it begins to break down the other bacteria for food, while replacing their functions. After an incubation period of about two weeks it becomes fully established through our bodies. By that time the viral part breaks off and is free to infect the genitalia and other relevant reproductive organs and their*

contents.

'*After the two-week incubation period, it is virtually impossible to decontaminate the patient, because of the difficulty of replacing that bacteria with the more natural and much weaker strains, and the persistence and prevalence of that particular one. Further, irreparable damage would have already been done by the virus. The only way is to bio-engineer an even stronger strain of bacteria without the viral part and replace the genitalia by implants.*

'*The antidote tends to isolate the genitalia and prevents the virus from taking effect, but does nothing against the parent bacteria. Personally, I think we can dismiss the possibility of any future cure and should concentrate our immediate efforts on prevention rather than cure. It seems that we are stuck with our present antidote method. However, it is not really as bad as it seems, if we begin adding it to certain foodstuffs and to water supplies after purification, etcetera.*

'*However, detailed analysis have shown this bacteria and viral system to have a limited lifetime. It should remain with us for another fifty years or so before mutating into a harmless type.*

'*Furthermore, this gives us a great chance to reduce our planet's population within more acceptable limits. We should now concentrate on our fertile or Fertilate families; for they are the future of our nation.*

'*Finally, all Fertilate families should be sent away from the cities to live in more secured areas. Their relocation is essential before the real violence begins. Because very soon the problems across the planet will begin to take their toll in stolen children, kidnapping and just basic jealousy from the Infertilate or Infilate types.*

'*Within our organization and with help from Solarian Banking, we have decided to form our own security group to tackle local unrest within our depots. But they will be thoroughly trained to combat opposition on a global scale, and will also tackle kidnapping and the larger organized gangs.*

'*Mister President, I think our only way out of the future turmoil on all fronts, is a strong course of action. We have to quell further unrest and criminal activities, otherwise there will be the inevitable break down of law and order in our major cities. It will not happen right away, but it's inevitable from our computer models. Then there is also the rising oceans and seas to consider as those waters begin to flood our coastal cities,'* Mallory said.

'Policing at a price, eh Mallory; packaged with your antidote distribution activities,' Senator Johnson replied, sarcastically.

*'No, senator. Our organization is a non-profit-making one. Whatever profits we make are ploughed back into the business and 10 percent is saved for contingencies. We are now planning hard for the future; in twenty years time when the streets will not be as pleasant as they are today. My consideration now is for human survival. Anyway, what's the use of money on a dead world.*

*'We would like to think of ourselves as a procuring force for all life on Earth. By so doing, we intend to work solely for the future of all endangered species, including our own, using computer models and projections. We currently use the most powerful Macron computers to get us answers within a 20 percent margin of error over a one-hundred years time scale. So we are in a good position to assist mankind, without the usual government procedures and red tape.*

*'Our band of Specials will be needed then and their services will be free to all Fertilates and law-abiding people throughout the planet. However, financial incentives and donations will be gladly received.*

*'Mister president, if present trends continue at their current rates, global policing will be necessary for procuring our Fertilates and with them the survival of humanity. We simply feel that our indigenous police forces are inadequate in those matters and the military is not trained for city streets. The antidote distribution is only part of the wider survival plan.*

*'Those are not just my conclusions, it's also the conclusion of Professor John Friedman and others, who have worked extensively with data received from different sources throughout the globe.*

*'Our Specials will be thoroughly trained and shall work for the survival of Fertilates and their children. We shall have a specific global independent army to take care of our future. To ensure*

*that our families and their children are made secure. To track down all criminals, particularly those child snatching and smuggling scum, and to make them fearful of our name. These are the goals we represent and I am sure not one of you will oppose our plans when we begin; for to whom will you turn to when things become intolerable, and I guarantee you, they will!'* Mallory said.

*'I have heard a similar story from one of our think-tanks, but they have been wrong before. However, I have great faith in Mallory, because he always delivers the goods, and on time. If we have little choice in the matter, and it is my opinion that Mallory is correct in his predictions, I think we should follow his guidelines and secure our Fer... Fertilate families. I like that word... Fertilate.*

*'His Specials will concentrate on our children and their survival, with all the necessary information et cetera. Leaving us to tackle the major unrest with our police and military troops. However, in the mean time we should try to find a cure for this accursed disease.*

*'I think we should assist Mallory for the sake of our children and their families, to form his special army. However, that matter will need a vote in the house.*

*'From the good work we've seen so far, I am sure Mallory and his organization is the best for that task.*

*'Is there any more input from anyone?'* the President said.

'Just one more thing, Mister President. It relates to our future election campaign. From what I see, we don't stand much chance of winning. Senator Humphrey has already begun promising things like a permanent cure for the disease and he has many followers. We now have to give the people something to believe in if we are to reduce our waning popularity,' Senator Johnson said. Then Mallory got up to speak.

'Mister President, so far our efforts in all this has been of success and speedy progress. Despite the numerous deaths due to the recent plague in Asia and elsewhere, the planet now has a successful antidote program and our best scientists are working on a permanent cure. You should also realise that the total infected of our population here is still holding at 10 percent, while elsewhere it's as high as 70 percent. That is all good news that should be brought to the attention of the electorate,' Mallory said.

'Well said, Mallory. You heard the man. Our campaign will accentuate our successes in the fight against the Terminal Disease. If handled correctly, we should also defuse most of the present unrest. One of our major problems in all this is misinformation and rumours by reporters and the mass media. Most are now under the impression that the disease is infecting everyone, which is not really the case. We must reeducate the masses and give them tips and updates, including a monthly progress report on the disease,' the President said.

Mallory and Roseanne left the white house for their hotel. This time there were no reporters about.

'My Dear, do you mind if I attempt to contact Andy before we get back? I must check that everything is ok with him and his mother, since the loss of his father,' he said.

'Perhaps we can also visit Donald and his aunt?' she replied.

He called the college and an appointment was made for the following morning. Mallory then contacted Donald's home and his aunt answered.

'Sorry, Mal. He had to return to NASA. Some new training mission or the other. Did you enjoy your honeymoon?' she asked.

'It was out of this world, and how was your stay at our place?' he replied.

'We had a lovely time and so did Andy. I think you'll find him a bit more grown up these days. I think it's one of those father and son things. He is a lot more like you than his mum,' she said.

'You must hold on to your travel card in case you want to visit us soon. The airline flight will be free if you show them that card and you and Donald are always welcomed at our place,' he said and she agreed.

The following morning they signed out of the hotel and took Oscar to Andy's college. This time Andy was a much happier individual and immediately hugged his father and Roseanne. Then he began eying them both.

'My God! You both have changed so! All the crinkles have disappeared. You look at least ten years younger and so does Roseanne?' he said.

'How perceptive of you, my son. We had an incredible holiday and went on special fitness programs. They have all the latest equipment and drugs to turn the worst Egyptian mummy into a beauty. Do you like what you see?' he said jokingly, while flexing his dense muscles and Andy smiled.

'I had to do an essay on the Terminal Disease and your name featured prominently in most of the books. I didn't realise you were such a popular person, Dad. When I told some of the guys in class that you were my dad they didn't believe me and had me doubting myself,' Andy said.

'Where are they now? These unbelieving thugs?' Mallory asked, jokingly.

'They are in biology class,' he replied.

'Well Son, don't you think we should pay them a visit, right now?' Mallory said and they both trotted off to the class, leaving Roseanne on her own. There was a tap on the door and they entered. Mallory was soon recognised by their master who immediately left what he was doing and came forward.

'Commander Mallory! What a pleasant surprise. I am Larry... Larry Stevens. I take the biology class.'

'You do?'

'Class please stand and say hello to Commander Mallory Colman,' he said and they immediately stood at attention.

'Hello, Commander Mallory,' they cried. Then Larry waved and they sat.

'You seem to have them under control. I had a meeting with the President and thought of stopping over to see my son and his classmates. From what I see, you run a tight ship, Larry,' he said, while watching the group of nervous students, who regarded his visit as the greatest thing since the recent one from the President himself.

'Work hard and take your daily dosage of antidote, because I might need you in my organization one of these days,' he said to the class. Then he thanked the master for allowing the interruption and they went back to meet Roseanne.

However, that wasn't the end of the story. Soon word got around that Mallory was on the premisses and the Head Master called his teachers together to give Mallory a proper greeting.

'Well, Son, is everything ok with you since Mexico?'

'It was distressing, but I am ok now,' Andy replied.

'Anyway, chin up! Give my regards to your mum. If you guys should ever need a break, you know where I am. We have to leave now, but whenever you want to visit, just say the word and hold on to your travel card. You may use it whenever you like.' Mallory then handed him an envelop. It contained a cheque for twenty thousand American dollars. Andy was to hand it to his mother. Anyway, his mother Cathy had promised to visit soon.

Andy was now king in his college. Even the known bullies tried to make friends with him.

CHAPTER 28

# A new challenge

After his return from Washington DC, Mallory was fully occupied putting together the rules and procedures for his new army of Specials. All that was accomplished in quick time with the aid of his implants.

Congress had voted unanimously for a special independent force to take care of their people when things got rough. Even so, the new military outfit was answerable to the President of the USA. Unknown to Mallory and others, except of course, Professor Khan (Ben), the USA President was also a Solarian and new about Jerry's survival. Even so, his family new not of his leaning towards Eden. Nevertheless because of his stance in such matters he was able to fund Mallory's operations and divert funds towards Fertilate housing and other relevant projects. The sole purpose of Mallory's Specials was to guard Fertilate families, chase criminal organizations, recover stolen children and act globally under the umbrella of the United Nations.

Mallory soon had a personal call from the President, thanking him for his ideas at their last meeting and asking him to visit the White House yet again to put his signature to a few documents. During that time he would meet others from the UN. Mallory had decided to visit after he had prepared the charter for his military organization.

'Roseanne, we are to visit DC again. Perhaps sometime next week. I think we should instal one of those portals in the White House, then we can travel at a moments notice and avoid the press,' he said, jokingly.

'You sure there isn't one already in the White House? Anyway, why should we deprive Oscar of his loopy fun, and the water bed in the hotel of our affections,' she replied with equal humour and suddenly the penny dropped.

'You seriously think Nicholas is one of us?' he replied.

'From Jerry's attitude and the way he spoke about our President, he must be. But in his position he can't tell anyone about his true following in such matters,' she said.

'I must say, you are one of the most perceptive women I've ever dealt with,' he replied.

'Darling, do you think I should were cream on our next visit?' she asked changing the topic.

'Like Sarah, that will suit you fine. In that case, you must remind me to wear a disguise when we are in public,' he replied.

'Since Eden, you already wear a partial disguise. Not many will recognize your new body as old Mallory Coleman, except those paparazzis,' she said.


Mallory's friends did not all visit Eden at the same time. Carl, his girlfriend and others were the last to go. Mallory's previous wife, Cathy, had visited and was shown the Javols video of death and destruction. As a caring nurse, she signed up immediately, which pleased Mallory. Carl and the others arrived from Eden somewhat younger than when they left and full of vitality and new implants.

Mallory soon received news that several crates of weapons had been dispatched and were awaiting delivery from Sol-Newtown. Since USA customs could not have been involved, the clearance papers had to come directly from the President. That matter was easily arranged by Mallory. The borrowed army trucks also had a military escort, complements of the President.

Their new military camp was twenty-five miles north east of Baltimore and covered an area of five thousand acres of grass-lands and forest. There were also areas of spruce and rugged hills ideal for training purposes.

The main block was only accessible by air and the whole place ringed by many razor-barbed fences, cameras and watch towers. That place was christened Warland by Roseanne.


'My Dear, the special weapons have arrived. We'll have to spend a few days with Chad in Warland to explain their operation. That is assuming he hasn't already learnt about them from his implants.'

'Believe me, he already knows. Chad is one of the most curious people I have had the pleasure to meet,' Roseanne replied.

'Before we leave, I shall also want to know exactly what types of implants each of our people have received, so I can place them in suitable jobs. This evening we hold a meeting to discuss those and other matters. In the mean time, those remaining here can assist with the antidote distribution,' Mallory said.

'Whatever you say, Boss!' Roseanne replied in jest.

'I am also worried about the gangsters finding out more about us, so it's urgent that we get training off as soon as possible,' he said.

'Chad reckons the main building and assault courses will be ready in another week. However, the armoury is ready and so is the security system. What do you want for dinner?' she said, abruptly changing the topic.

'And one more thing; I don't like you cooking every day for everyone, including myself. We shall have to arrange a cooking detail or take it in turn. Today I shall assist you in the kitchen,' he said, like a most considerate husband.

'Perhaps we should have a couple of the latest androids to do the job for us,' she replied, humorously. At that moment she saw an amusing change in his eyes and immediately tried to changed the topic.

'Just kidding about androids, Darling! Perhaps we should now have a full time cook and helper on the premises. We can well afford it, you know,' she added.

'Ok, you are the boss of this house and you make the arrangements,' he said.

'In that case, I shall call the agency right away and interview a few people,' she replied.

'Do you think that's a good idea? What about the basement? How do we explain portals and strange visits from alien worlds at anytime, day or night?' he said.

'The basement can be your private laboratory, where you carry out experiments on virtual images and suchlike, After all, you are now a scientist. So if they go there by mistake they will be none the wiser. Anyway, I know what to look for and they will both have to be trustworthy young people with good qualifications,' she said.

'Dear, I am also thinking of adding an extension to the house.

Perhaps another ten rooms for the occasional visitors. Ben, says he also wants us to assist Solarian Banking with limited accommodation for new recruits and in acquiring buildings for future Fertilate families. He reckons we should let them have such apartments for half the market rates, with no deposits. They would never refuse such an offer,' he said.

'Perhaps we should have a few of those apartments for ourselves. That way we won't have to extend our home,' she replied.

'You know, Dearest, in another two years or so almost everyone, excluding our present Fertilates, will be infected by the bacteria. When that happens, we shall have to begin distributing placebos instead of the real antidote. That change will be required if we are to get the uninfected population down to about thirty million in the whole of the United States, and just twenty million in the rest of North America, excluding most young below 20. At this time, close to a billion on this continent of North America receives it.'

'Now I know why you need your Specials!' she replied.

'Can you imagine what might happen if they discovered the master plan was to reduce our present global population from almost eleven billion to just five hundred million? From almost one billion in the whole of North America to below fifty million. A less than 95 percent reduction. Thank goodness, no one will be physically affected until they are too old to care about it one way or the other.'

'Yep! And people are growing old all the time! I suppose it's the reason why our Chameleon friend decided to kill off Inflates quickly. I wonder why he spared North America and Europe?' Roseanne said.

'He killed them to prevent further poaching and destruction to our planet. That's why he focussed on the third-world, and he was successful. Anyway, most were infected from the Terminal Disease in those countries, while here in the States only 10%. Very soon serious choices will have to be made. Most of it will be random, but the Macron has already compiled most of the relevant data from the returned testers and other information down loaded from the depots.'

'Talk about breaking eggs for the proverbial omelette! Thank goodness my eggs are safe for now. I wouldn't like to be any of those poor rejected young women!' She replied.

'Since everyone is tested, in three years many of the younger families will begin to worry when they find themselves unable to have kids. Then the real trouble begins. So we expect some real problems in about that time. Before then, we'll have to change back to the real antidote, but that won't matter, because they would have been irreversibly contaminated during the previous two years by the placebo, which also contains the disease in higher concentrations. That's when we shall have to isolate the real Fertilates and their families from city mobs and other groups, including criminals,' he said.

'Now, I understand why you are so keen on your Specials. Without them us poor Fertilate parents and our kids won't stand a chance,' she said.


Chad had since returned to the ranch to collect the special delivery of weapons. He was told by Mallory to keep them in their sealed cases until he and others arrived to officially open the base the following day. Subsequently, Chad and his wife arranged a small celebration for the occasion.

Mallory was also being irritated and nagged by the notion of the gangsters finding him or the special child, so he intended to get the whole training program on the road as soon as possible.

He now had to check Marlina's safety deposit box for important information on the criminal fraternity before visiting Chad, and to his delight there was one of Marlina's pink perfumed notes, that read:


**'Thanks for the donation. I have it upon good authority that Mr Darling gets his orders from one of the Mafia chiefs, now based in Miami. He used to be heavy in narcotics, up-market prostitution and gambling, but is now investing heavily in child smuggling and other associated crimes like naughty videos, mainly for the European and Asian markets. He owns five large hotels throughout Florida and two in Honolulu.**

**You are dealing with a very large shark, so be extra careful. His real name is Tex Nolan, but he may have several aliases.**

**Good luck, darling  xx**

**Please burn the evidence.'**

Mallory memorised its contents and tore the pink note in several small fragments. Then he threw them into the nearest rubbish bin.

'Good woman. You are worth your weight in gold,' he said as he entered Oscar.

'Lets go home via my old office,' he said to the car and they were once again on their way. He checked his old office and later his apartment from the roof of each building, but there was no sight of the hit-man's car or any of his accomplices, so he went home.

'He must be on another trail. I am sure my recent picture in the papers may have given him the opportunity of a change in his plans. He is probably now in DC awaiting my next visit at my preferred hotel, and of all things, the President's secretary has my new office number. I shall have to call her now and ask her to change it to one of the special ones,' he said.

'I shall get the line for you, right now,' Oscar said and the connection was made.

'How can I help, Captain Colman?' she said.

'There is a personal security problem with the number I've given you. Could you please change it immediately to this one, and erase all traces of the old one from your computer files? It's very important!' Mallory said and gave her the new one.

'I shall give the instructions immediately,' she replied.

'What would you like me bring you on my next visit. I owe you something nice,' he said.

'Don't worry about it, Mal. I do that sort of thing all the time. I will run a thorough security check on you while I'm at it and download your present profile and associated information with our current security codes. That way you will be able to update the information to your liking,' she said.

'That's fantastic! I owe you a big one,' he said.

That new number he gave her was linked through a diverter to Oscar, who could then take and connect, ignore or record such calls as appropriate. Even so, Mallory had to assume a worst case scenario and not visit that Washington hotel again until the nuisance was removed. Either that or wear a facial disguise.

CHAPTER 29

# Warland

The following day all six of them left for the ranch, they called Warland. They arrived early and Mallory insisted that Chad showed them every inch of its vast area from the air in the car called Oscar before they viewed the new buildings.

After they had spent the best part of an hour observing the outer perimeter, woods and hills, they decided to view the most secured building in the whole compound. It was situated centrally and well away from the other buildings.

There were still many robots about, adding extra fences, installing observation towers, around and above the main building. Many were adding the final touches, but most of their work was almost completed. The group landed and walked inside the main gate of the armoury.

'I have never seen a place more secure than this one. It's even better than Fort Knox. What we might have to do is pay a few good escapologist to try and find a way in and out,' Chad said.

'That's a great idea. Anyone in mind?' Mallory replied.

'I might have. Would you like me to arrange something?' Chad asked.

'My friend, you are now responsible for this entire training centre. Do whatever you think necessary for safety's sake. Remember, money is never a problem,' Mallory said.

'I shall do it then. Now let's visit the most secure part of the armoury. This is the largest room in the building and is placed central to the training blocks. It's really a room within a room. Its outer wall is several metres thick and made of steel reenforced concrete with anti explosive padding. The second is the same thickness but is even better reenforced and padded. The roof is of similar thickness and composition. So any attack from the air will be similarly resisted. We'll soon be installing powerful cannons and machine guns on the roof and elsewhere. Those will be linked to the war Macron computer.

'In the main armoury, there are two vault doors involved, each can only be opened by special card that is linked to the user's voice, finger, eye and face prints. However, that is not required with implant users, as the War-Macron computer can access their identification codes directly,' Chad said. Then he thought intensely through his implants and the first and second doors slowly opened.

'It takes a little while getting used to my implants, but I am getting better,' Chad said.

They entered the first area which contained weapons of every description that was considered non-lethal or neutral. They were on racks standing both sides of a wide passageway that encircled the central vault. There were long benches beneath with further lockers for storing the soldiers' equipment.

'In here there is also a separate oxygen supply in case of emergencies. It will supply enough for one person per week. However, there is an air circulation system that is driven by several fans, with inbuilt air-conditioning and filtration,' he said as they went towards the second enclosure and was flooded in bright fluorescence.

'This is the main vault. As you see, most of the real weapons are kept in here,' Chad added, pointing to racks upon racks of weapons.

'Explosives and more dangerous ones are kept in another vault a hundred metres down. That area is accessible only from this room and by special elevator and trap door arrangement,' he said.

'Where are the weapons from Eden?' Mallory asked.

'Your special crates have been left there for safe keeping. Shall we take a trip?' he said and thought again. A massive door slid across the floor and a large metallic elevator lifted until its lower part were almost level with the floor. Then they entered and were lowered into an even more secured area.

'This place is also nuclear blast proof and stored with cans of food in case of worst case emergencies. Here, there are specially monitored air filters and more oxygen supplies. We reckon we can store a thousand soldiers down here for several months,' Chad said.

'We need to collect a gun and suit while we are here,' Mallory said and they went towards a large metal crate and entered a card in one of the slots and the top sprung open. Mallory then took one of the boxes. Then they found a larger box that contained a suit and were soon on their way back to the surface. When they were finished, they went to the rear of the armoury building.

'This is the most secure firing range. The high wall prevents our outside operatives seeing what's going on in here. This is ideal for practising with our special weapons. To the right we have a survival range with simulated moving human targets and suchlike. All under computer control,' Chad said.

Mallory removed a weapon and body armour from their cases, checked the weapon over thoroughly before handing it to Chad and the others.

'What is it?' Chad exclaimed.

'This is the weapon of the future. It's called a plasma projector and uses no bullets, just a small container of liquid hydrogen and a nuclear power pack,' Mallory said, while explaining every part of the weapon and suit in detail.

'Whoops... when you said you were going to get us special weapons I didn't realise you meant those,' Chad said.

'Depending on the implants you received, you should already have their specifications. Anyway, let me give you a little demo at minimum setting on that target over there,' he said, aimed and squeezed the button. The first discharge melted a small hole in the target. Then he adjusted to maximum spread and the complete target was vaporised.

'They are good for a thousand rounds and the rate can be adjusted to fifty a second. I recommend five to ten per second on a minimum nozzle setting. In future, these types of weapons will only be issued to our best operatives on special missions. My two best weapons are the projector and dart gun with Amiterol darts to induce permanent memory loss... saves us killing the enemy outright, and the person can be suitably rehabilitated and retrained to take their place in society. However, they become dead to their past on a permanent basis and cannot be interrogated afterwards. Unlike guns and plasmas, these weapons make little noise and add to our evasiveness and stealth. The only problem with plasmas is they take no prisoners, so we have to make sure of our targets. If in doubt we use darts and we always have recourse to handguns and bullets. These small darts are just as accurate and there is a range for most purposes.

'The special suit of armour will destroy even the fastest bullets well before they touch the suit and also give a degree of protection from projected plasma.

'It's easy to use these weapons through our implants. However, greater care is needed when operated by an unmodified mind,' Mallory said.

When they were finished with that building, which had occupied most of their time, they went towards the main compound for lunch.

Within that compound were many buildings that linked together on several levels much like a shopping precinct. The largest of which was Central and contained an auditorium, hall for special occasions, cinema, theatre, game rooms, recreation rooms, a large internal swimming pool and outside, five outdoor swimming pools, tennis and squash courts.

Several of its upper floors were reserved for families and guests. However, the majority of soldiers were expected to live in the several barracks about a kilometre away. There was also a small golf course at the rear of the complex of buildings.

'This is truly an incredible place and makes your original setup look like a flower garden, and there is so much land left for future expansion,' Roseanne commented.

Around the Central building perimeter were shops, a restaurant and other facilities, making the area of the base fully self-contained from the outside world, being more like a large town. Nevertheless, there were no roads to the camp, so everything was delivered by helicopter or LPD transport. That would be until portals were installed.

At the top of Central were several satellite dishes and radar that were connected to every satellite and Macrons throughout the planet. That way the war Macron could eavesdrop on all wireless communications and inform of any unsavoury activities.

Mallory had thought of building a virtual war room for more realistic training, but later decided to postpone it until the training program became fully established. Having seen the level of security within the armoury, he decided to have a portal fitted within the underground vault, making redundant the food supplies held there. However, only special staff with implants would be allowed to use the lower levels.

After they had been shown all buildings, they went again to Central for the official opening ceremony.

A little area on the grass had been arranged for the occasion with covering, a table and a few chairs and Mallory decided that Roseanne cut the tape which was tied across the main entrance of the complex.

'I now declare this base open!' she yelled and they cheered.

CHAPTER 30

# Hal's First Resurrection

Dr. Hal Seaton had recently caused the death of over 5 billion Infilates on Earth. Leaving about 5 billion untouched by his Bubonic Plague. He would have liked to have caused more deaths, but such things never went the way as planned. The Infilate populations in the most advanced countries had not increased enough. Nevertheless as far as he was concerned, it was a success. He also realized he would be traced eventually and arrested. He never liked the idea of rotting in a highly secured prison on Earth. Anyway, his tasks on Earth could hold for a while as he turned his attention elsewhere.

Having been given the freedom of planet Eden in previous years with all its benefits, a more logical option was to get rid of his present body and opt for a new replacement. With his brain implants, it was quite possible to record all data since his last Megotron changes and store them in one of his personal Mecrons until required in the future. Further, since implants were still operational for many days after death, it was possible for him to hide and upload relevant information pertaining to his main memory storage without the attention of others. Then later he could update his mind as necessary over the ten-year period of his most recent exploits. Nevertheless he did not wish to clutter his mind, so he would hold such storage and use them only when necessary. That way, he could use this dying method, time and time again to evade the legal systems. Each time getting a brand new body without any attached crime.

'Where am I?' A dozy Hal inquired.
'You are in Sol-Newtown. You died, so we had to re-clone you. I'm afraid some of your post memories will be lost,' Ben replied.
'How did I die?'
'We found your other body strung up in your home. We thought you committed suicide?'
'I would never do that! Could be one of the filthy criminal gangs

I was chasing at the time. Those bastards will dearly pay!' Hal was not happy.

'Anyway, we have updated your new implants as best we could,' Ben said.

'Where is Lennox?'

'He was reassigned to Eden years ago!'

'Years ago?'

'Yes, and you were reassigned to Tyrrel II as chief coordinator, in charge of that world and its introduced flora and fauna,' Ben replied.

'I suppose that was a new.... world?'

'Yes! It is!'

'We would like you to return and continue your efforts there. You have many friends and colleagues there. They would like to see you back assisting the program.'

'What program is that?'

'Helping Earth's endangered species!'

'I see! In that case I should be back. However, I should return home for a while before I make the trip. I have thoughts and things to collect,' Hal replied.

'There is no hurry. You may take along one of our security guards in case you are attacked again,' Ben advised, but Hal was not interested.


Hal had briefly turned his attention away from Earth. Anyway, he had created a proven weapon that could always be improved against the Infilate population. He was convinced that next time no one would survive. Nevertheless with deaths of over 5 billion in those countries, the problems of poaching and nasty crimes had significantly reduced, so those problems could be placed on hold for now. He suddenly turned his attention to Javols.

Having viewed all his previous mind files, which included his recent capers and bubonic pandemic, he was now up to date on current events.

'Nano-bots! I hate bloody nano-bots!' Hal cried out, then took a well-deserved sip from one of his specially flavoured brews. He was almost addicted to tea in its many forms. For that purpose he had developed a range of distillers, electronic testers and cup warmers. Then he called his old friend Professor Powell.

'Powell, my man, how are you these days?'

'I'm ok, Boss! You sound a little different?'

'Sorry I couldn't contact you sooner. I died for a while. Some-one told me I hung myself on the chandelier, but I am not sure. Anyway, I know you had nothing to do with it, and I like my new body!' Hal said in jest.

Powell was silent, not quite knowing what to say or believe. He thought it was all impossible.

'Anyway, Pal, I must thank you for our recent successful caper. I have 10 mill bonus for you. I think you deserve it!'

'Thanks, Boss!'

'We have a new project. I don't mind spending one billion. That one is very important for our survival. That is, if you want your kids and grandchildren to survive!'

'As bad as that?'

'A lot worse. It's to do with an invasion by nano-bots. They will take a while to get here, but they are on the way. We have to stop them. We need a nano-bot bug!'

'Ok, tell me what I have to do!'

'First, I will show our Group of Thirteen a recording. That should shake them a little. Then we get them involved in funding our projects. That way, everything becomes legitimate and above board!'

'Sounds like a great idea!'

'Then see you at our next meeting!'

'See you!' Powell replied as Hal hung up.


'My first-body funeral will be on Friday. I must get out of this apartment before then and leave no forensics or sensitive equipment behind other than what I want the authorities to have. I wonder what I should wear for my funeral. Facial disguise is essential. Now I know how Lazarus must have felt.' Hal muttered, while pretending to be a police inspector on the scene.

He soon got himself another temporary apartment in a better part of the city. For some reason, he preferred New York, despite its hustle and bustle. He was more settled in this new existence and wanted to engineer the worse nano-bot bug ever created. One that would not target humanity or primals. Now it was necessary for him to learn everything there was to know about Javols.

Just like Hal had planned, he was considered a terrorist and blamed for the plague and other terrible atrocities against humanity. Nevertheless all his nasty crimes died with his burial. His funeral was visited by many, including Captain Calahan, Lieutenant Charles, Lennox, Ben, Mallory, Roseanne and others. Mallory knew it was not the end of that particular crime fighter. A disguised Hal in his new body, carefully observed the proceedings and people at his funeral and realized he had a few friends that cared. Those he owed little favours to sometime in the future.

During the subsequent meeting of the Group of Thirteen Hal had held on to his identity as one Dr. Hal Seaton. That was his real name. Others like Dr. Charles Manson, he had created for the benefit of the police during his previous escapades. Nevertheless many knew him as the Green Chameleon or Phantom. He could always change his profile and alter the police database at will. The name they new him as on Earth before was Dr. Charles Manson.

Hal continued to address the group of Thirteen.
'Gentlemen and ladies, I have it on good standing that there are aliens about. They are very advanced and come all the way from Andromeda. Apparently to warn us of impending disaster. That is the main reason for the technological changes and other factors of unrest here on Earth. However, they were not responsible for the recent bubonic pandemic. They appear to be benevolent and are willing to assist us.
'What have you been drinking?' Okeke interrupted, not quite believing in the subject matter.
'I know, it's difficult to believe in Aliens. But I have met several. Believe me when I say, they look exactly like us. I can prove to you this day that our Lord Meron was an Andromedan. I have his DNA profile. Although he is human, he is as alien as alien can be. Please take it from me, when I say there are aliens about!'

'Ok, please get us the evidence!' Okeke said.

'I want to show you a copy of a recording. It was taken 3000 years ago. It shows the destruction of Meron's home world by a nano-bot life-form called Javols. They are now on the way to our galaxy and will be on Earth in approximately 100 years from now. They are not like us and require our blood and other body nutrients for their metabolism. They are truly the most nasty vampire-like creatures in the universe and most difficult to destroy.'

'So what can we do?' Okeke inquired.

'We need funds to save our world! I want us all to devote the rest of our lives in saving our world. Therefore all donations will be accepted. We now know the source of all our problems. I intend to create the worst nano-bot bug in existence to destroy these Javols. However, we must begin the work now!' Hal said. Then he showed them the film on a nearby screen. They were extremely disturbed.

'Are we the only ones involved?' Okeke inquired.

'On Earth, we are the only ones, and we should keep it that way. The Andromedan survivors are working on weapons, but I think the only way to kill their swarms is by an infectious disease targeted only to Javols. That is why I need your financial assistance. I already have the premisses and staff. With many clever scientists in the field,' Hal replied.

'We should show a vote of hands,' Okeke said and all hands went up.

'The vote is carried, so from now on we focus on saving our planet from those nasty nano-bot creatures. Please supply us with the necessary files on Lord Meron. They will be held at the highest security. Next month we can continue our discussion on progress and any other relevant topics to do with our survival. Therefore I deem this meeting closed until the 13th of next month!' Okeke said and they left their seats fully aroused to partake in removing the Javols' threat.

'I thought you would pull them around!' Powell shouted in his direction.

'Now we have lots to do. You are to find us the best laboratory premisses along with some top scientists. You saw the film, now

I want you to go to Sol-Newtown for a Brain Implant. You are to select doctors within the nano-bot fields. I shall have words with Ben and recommend you. He will agree! You can also do with an age reduction. You are now 73, so a reduction to 25 will do fine!' Hal said and Powell was intrigued.


'Professor Khan?' Hal formed the image in his mind and in an instant was in Virtual Correspondence. His room overlapped seamlessly with Ben's office.

'How can I help?'

'I have a problem. I shall soon be returning to Tyrrel II to assist in that project, but is worried for the survival of Earth. I realize those on Eden are involved in suitable weaponry for the Javols' destruction. However, if they invade Earth in numbers we might not have a chance. Therefore, may I make a suggestion?'

'What is your suggestion?'

'I have decided to get all members of my Group of Thirteen involved in the creation of an anti-Javol nano-bot virus that will only target Javols. However, for this program to work I would like to recommend my friend Professor Kane Powell as president. He will be in charge of the necessary laboratories. Because this is an Earth program, it will be better kept well away from Solaria!'

'So what can I do?'

'I would like you to incorporate this into Solarian Banking for frequent inspection and project reports. If at all possible, I would like to recommend Powell for an age reduction along with an implant updated with relevant doctors in the nano-bot field. Very much like me, Powell is keen and wants to save his world. He is very wealthy and has no need for money.'

'He has had problems with us and the law in past. How can we trust him?'

'Like all of us, he had his setbacks! I think he is now a changed man. Anyway, he has a brilliant mind! You can always give him a young body with a young mind without the negative elements. I'm sure he wouldn't mind!'

'I see where you are coming from. Leave it with me. Anymore weapons against those Javols will be well appreciated. However, this project will be considered well outside of Solaria. Nevertheless it does not stop us from financial assistance!'

'No! It does not, and my mind will be at rest, knowing work is being done during my absence!' Hal replied.

'Ok, the decision is made. You will be informed about the interview. It's just a formality. However, he will have to undergo a full body change. His implants will contain everything there is to know about Javols. Since it's his first time, his memories will remain unchanged. That's the best I can do!'

'Thanks very much! I owe you a very big favour!' Hal said.

'How long will it take to fabricate?'

'I think within 10 years!'

'Ok, you have 20. This is because our people will visit Caefon in Andromeda about that time. They can test it on real Javols then!' Ben broke connection and Hal found himself back in his apartment. He had gained Ben's confidence and now had a mountain of finances at his disposal or so he thought.

CHAPTER 31

# Professor Kane Powell, rebel with a cause

Since the death of his wife over two decades before he had become a changed man. The slow and cancerous degeneration of his loved-one had taken its tole. During that time he had left his well paid professorship at MIT to take care of his wife. When she died he almost fell to pieces. Then he had to take a local job to care for his young daughter and son. There was another massive blow when his young son was killed in action. It was after that time that he could not refuse work and decided to play the system for whatever gains could be had, by good or fowl means. He had enough of all that political hypocrisy. After all, by virtue of his existence on planet Earth, part of that global wealth belonged to him. So he would take it by hooks or crooks for his benefit and those of his remaining family.

His first real public failure was on TV. He just couldn't hold it or keep up with that Doctor Jeffery Longhurst. Yea, and that Longhurst had proven him wrong over the years. Although he had to get to him through some unsavoury people for revenge, that canny doctor always survived. Thank goodness he was subsequently lost in space.

Then there was the badly planned kidnapping of Lord Meron. That Senator Cleary was the greediest person he had ever met. Always counting the cents. Good thing he and the gang were arrested before any real harm was done. Perhaps he should apologise to that nice guy, Meron, some day in the future, but incognito. Powell was not please with his past failed capers and had earned very little from them.

Powell's luck changed after that unexpected call from Dr. Hal Seaton. It was about blowing up one of Jeffery Longhurst's production plants.

'I got much satisfaction from blowing up that Microid Plant.

Sadly, the doctor was not there when it went up! Now I an not interested in revenge anymore. I have bigger fish to fry!' Powell murmured, while searching his desk draw for one of his better pens.

'Dam judge said I was a psychopath. When I had my psycho-assessment the bitch said I was normal. How can people be so wrong. Good thing I always had the best lawyers money could buy. Now I am free like a bird in the tree and soon will be back the way I was before all those turbulent changes. If she was alive, my wife Carol would be proud with my better changes in life. God bless her soul.' Powell murmured again.

'Dam Boss wants me to visit Sol-Newtown. He must be kidding about that age-reduction nonsense. He reckons those aliens have the technology. He must be well in with them to have such privileges. What a guy, to pull such strings. Professor Khan must also be one of them, being in charge of Solarian Banking. The largest and wealthiest organization on Earth. I must be slowly going insane or having a bout of dementia to consider all those options as real. Perhaps I should visit my doctor and insist on a full checkup,' Powell murmured some more, realizing his life was in a strange place, and wondered whether it was a change for the worse. Nevertheless he had little control in the matter. If it led to a better place with more rewards, so what the heck. Then he took a sip of cold coffee from his favourite black mug.

'At least, we completed the Boss's special suit, with a brand new fusion power-supply that could power-up for years. That one was of alien design. The special nano-bots were also improved. He was now truly an indestructible Chameleon. Pity he stopped beheading crims. I hate those vermin. I have however decided to retain all my best scientists for the new project. I don't like sacking my people. They are too important and earned their rights. They will get a good bonus as well. Perhaps 1 mill each plus a promotion. Yea, but if I have an age reduction, how will I explain it to them. Perhaps a change of name. Boss can say I had a heart attack and rig a funeral. Then he can introduce me as a genius in nano-technology. Yea, that will be the best way, if what he said about a new body was true. Then I will have a new name... but what about my daughter and grandchildren?'

Since Powell loved his family dearly he was in a dilemma. His problem was how to rig his funeral from a heart attack at work and become an important part of his family as a young man afterwards. Soon Hal got on line to him.

'I received an email from Sol-Newtown. You are due there on Wednesday at 10 am. Don't be late. I shall send a car to collect you. Everything has been arranged. Don't worry about family matters, I have a way to get you back in.'

'That was one of my main worries!' Powell said.

'I know! It's been sorted! Your funeral is being arranged as we speak. I don't suggest you visit!' Hal was adamant.

'I don't want to!'

'Good! Anyway it's also on Wednesday. At that time you will be given a new body in Sol-Newtown. Thank goodness you will have your original memories. So you will recognise me and all your old friends and family.'

'That was another of my worries?' Powell replied.

'You see, I always take care of my people. Nevertheless, I have taken the liberty in inviting all your old colleagues, so it should be a fun party. No expense has been spared for your wake. Pity you will not be there. However, there will be a video.'

'That's nice. I can watch my funeral at leisure while drinking a vodka and lime on the rocks!' Powell was intrigued and smiled.

'Your new name will be Professor John Simmons of London, in the united kingdom. It's a good enough name and a British one. So you will be known as John in future.'

'I like it!'

'The new Powell profiles has already been updated. So as far as the system is concerned he is dead and buried and so are his sins and crimes.' Hal said.

On arrival in Sol-Newtown Powell was promptly taken to a room for interrogation before the procedure. An operator in white overalls soon came to collect him.

'Mr. John Simmons?'

'That's me!'

'Please follow!' The operator said. The poor man followed like a sheep for the slaughter. When he viewed the equipment he almost fainted. Yet he just held on to sanity. He soon underwent the procedure with Psyrotron and Megotron. When he looked in the mirror he was aghast.

'Welcome to Earth, Dr. John Simmons!' he muttered and smiled. He was subsequently taken to a training room to learn the use of his new implants.

Despite the trauma felt by his close family and friends, he was 73, with a higher then normal probability of heart disease. So they accepted his death as due to natural causes. Nevertheless his large coffin contained his correct weight in sandbags. Since he was a member of the Group of Thirteen, a small monument would be erected above his grave and a new vacancy created for the 12th member. Which incidently would be for one young Dr. John Simmons. Hal was intrigued and called him at his new apartment the following day.

'Dr. John Simmons?'

'Hi, Boss. I remember your voice!'

'I supposed you must be very pleased with your new body?' Hal inquired.

'It's fantastic! Those guys in that place are like gods! The only problem is my clothes wont fit!'

'That's because they belong to old Powell! You should ditch them now. No memories of the old life, except family photos. Keep those in a safe place. Sort things out today and give it all to a local charity. You are now a new person. Powell is dead! You must forget that name and all its associations!'

'I can't help having some slight withdrawal symptoms.'

'The reason why I called is to set you up for your new family. You left a will. In it you gave lots of money to your family, including property. You also left money to a son from a previous relationship. His name happens to be one Dr. John Simmons. Your mother, I mean John's mother went to England and remarried there. You will meet them all at the reading. You should get to know them then.'

'Don't you think I might be too young for a son aged 25?' John said.

'No, he had that relationship at 47 and remarried late, as you know. You are his youngest and care about all your family. Your supposed sister will be very curious, but its quite normal. Not all fathers like to brag or spread news about extramarital relationships. You have to download all that stuff in your implants. I have sent you a secured CD with all that information. Learn it and act the part as a real caring brother.'

'I don't know what to say. It answers all my questions on my new life. Boss you are the most clever person I've ever met.'

Thanks for the complement, but you are the one doing the real work!' Hal replied and Powell accepted the half compliment.

The reading of Powell's will was held in a local hotel. Everyone was there, including Hal, who was Powell's executor. There were 32 people which included family and friends. Afterwards they laid on a buffet with drinks and hors d'oeuvre.

'You are my new brother, I presume?'

'It appears so! I didn't know I had a sister, or I would have searched. Anyway, it's great to be meeting you, Sis. I am Dr. John Simmons!'

'You mean to say we have another doctor in the family?'

'I suppose we must be a very caring family!' the young Powell replied.

'Don't remain in this expensive hotel. You must come home with us and meet the kids. They would enjoy having a new uncle!' she said and young Powell knew a solid connection was made.

He could now focus on the task of creating the most deadly virus on Earth. However, this time it would only target nano-bot Javols.

'Wouldn't I like to see a thousand of those nasty things fall apart like those infected by the worst plague!' He stretched his arms apart in ecstasy and yelled.

'Bring em on! Bring em on! Bring... em ... on!'

CHAPTER 32

# Another 13<sup>Th</sup> meeting

Mallory was chatting with Arthur, the gardener, when Roseanne shouted over the veranda.

'Darling a registered letter for you!' Then she threw it in his direction. He jumped about 5 feet and caught it in mid air. He opened it to reveal a bankers draft of 10 grand and another invitation for the 13<sup>th</sup>.

'That's very generous of them. I shall give it to a children's charity. They want me at the Hilton. That's in three days. I must check my diary. They can come in useful in the future. Those guys are full of knowledge,' Mallory muttered. Then he excused himself and went indoors.

'Was it important?' Roseanne inquired.

'It's the Group of Thirteen. Another meeting on the 13<sup>th</sup>. I find that group quite intriguing. I never know who they are. They seem to be all doctors and professors involved in saving the world, but they have no knowledge of the Solarians. At least apparently not at our previous meetings,' he said.

'Well, they are trying and that's the main thing. Perhaps we should enlighten them?' Roseanne was sympathetic.

'In some cases, I think ignorance is bliss. I shall inform them when the time is right!' Mallory was not sure in their case. Due to their ages, they were most likely Infilates outside of the Solarian survival plan. Nevertheless, he would keep an eye on them.

'At least, Okeke looked in his eighties, or so he appears,' Mallory replied.

As usual, Mallory entered that meeting well dressed and with briefcase in hand.

'Pleased to meet you all again!' he greeted and sat in his usual seat at the bottom of the long table.

'Mallory, thanks for coming at short notice!' Okeke said.

'Gentlemen and ladies, since our last meeting the situation had not changed significantly. However, our President has given my organisation the go-ahead to form a new army of Specials. They will take care of our families and remove crime from our streets globally. I want our world to survive the future crises due to the Terminal bug,' Mallory said.

'Anything we can do to help?' Okeke asked.

'Not necessary at this time. We have the backing of Solarian Banking and others,' Mallory replied.

'Hal, any words on the topic?'

'Yes, if I may!'

'Mallory, I think you are a great guy. Your plans are necessary for stability on Earth during this period of unrest. However, we have to think ahead in order to defeat the Javols. Yes, I am afraid we know all about their invasion. In future, you can feel free to speak with us on such matters. Also, I want you to know that some special people are now concentrating on a bug that only targets Javols. God help them, if they come in contact with any of us humans in future. I call it the Wand of Death. I intend infecting every human. Don't worry, we are immune.'

'You are currently working on such a weapon?' Mallory could not believe his ears.

'We are! One more thing. The demise of our Chameleon friend and Powell, has been greatly exaggerated. They are top scientists with others working on a special project to save Earth. And Mallory, please watch your back. Too many criminals are about these days!' Hal said. Mallory smiled, realizing those guys had fooled the system and were still alive.


When he arrived home that day he was more than pleased with himself.

'What's the matter with you today?' Roseanne inquired, but he remained silent for a while.

'I am going to have a Chinese. Let's order for everything. I have a great appetite!' he said.

'Something happened to you at the Hilton. Is it about the meeting?'

'Yep. I am afraid they know all about the Javols. They worked it out themselves,'

'They did?'

'I shouldn't be telling you this!'

'What? You got to spill the beans! That's what marriage is all about and we are on the same team!' Roseanne stressed.

'The Chameleon and Powell, the windbag, are still alive. They deceived the system. Apparently they are now working on an anti-Javols bug. One like the bubonic plague that will infect humans, but kill Javols. They have already started. Hal reckons they will destroy swarms of those nasty nano-bot Javols. What do you think of that?'

'You mean to say those guys were part of the Group of Thirteen all this time?'

'I think some are runaway Solarians, with Brain Implants and such like. They must be working on their own to save our world,' Mallory said.

'So who do you think this Hal is?'

'Dr. Hal Seaton, the Chameleon or Phantom. Take your pick!' Mallory replied.

'Oh my god! If anyone can do it they can. So from now we concentrate on our Special army, while they focus on developing a special bug that does not affect humans but infects Javols. That will be something to watch. Do you think Ben knows about them?'

'Who is to say, but I think he does. Now Ben has another option to kill Javols, incase other methods fail. Anyway, I would like all those guys converted and given new bodies. Some of the group are well over 70, you know. If they died we would loose all that experience. Over the years I have grown to like them,' Mallory said.

'We must never mention anything about them in future. We are Solarians and they are working for the benefit of Earth,' Roseanne stressed.

'I know, but on Eden he said he was going to take over the Universe and kill all Javols. Do you think he will do it?'

'I am sure we can stop him then. As for now that genius has a job of work to do for the benefit of humanity and Earth, so let him be for now. Anyway, a genius like him will let others conquer and rule the universe for him. Why buy a horse and walk,' Roseanne said.

'Ok, from now my lips are sealed!' Mallory replied.

CHAPTER 33

# Specials recruitment

Mallory got in touch with one of the best uniform makers in New York. He had given instructions for them to design several military outfits for different operations and duties. He wanted his Specials to be the best in the business and spared no costs.

The standard uniform was a gold braided black suit and hat to match, with central federation insignia on the hat. The winged insignia was also displayed on the left shoulder just above the military colours, and contrasted well against the black cloth.

All suits were well cut and bestowed on its wearer an air of dignity and power and a feeling of awe from their admirers.

The commando leather studded jackets were partially lined with bullet proof material, but was not as good as the standard bullet proof vest, which could also have been worn underneath the slightly oversized jacket. It held several embroidered emblems, including the winged Federation insignia across the left shoulder. The trousers were equally tough with screening wherever necessary.

There was also a range of standard fatigues and boots for jungle and desert training. The military fatigues and other gear were the most advanced and suited for survival in most environments.

The first few uniforms were made for Mallory and his other colleagues, with the exception of Professor Friedman and his wife. They were to take over the antidote distribution under Ben and Solarian Banking, while Mallory and the others concentrated on their new military careers.

Mallory had rented several small offices in the major cities for interviewing would-be recruits. Those were from the ages of twenty-five and below, with all travelling and other expenses paid.

He was pleased with the preliminary preparations, so he and Carl contacted the national and local press in most of the states, and the advertising campaign had begun in earnest.

The first adverts were meant to target the very young and those graduates that were interested in a military career and had the flavour of adventure tainted with national pride. Therefore the stars and stripes were included in those adverts.

Part of the first advert read:

**'Become a global soldier, using the latest technologies and weapons to face all those who threaten our country's stability and endanger life throughout our planet....**

**The Specials Force will go wherever they are needed to crush our mutual enemies....'**

There was also a sketch of a soldier in black wearing a bold insignia on his chest, holding a plasma projector and blasting a large military tank into vapour. In the distance were small LPD ships with similar projectors blasting the enemy's location. The whole scene was eye-catching and stunning. The idea was to catch the imagination of the young, most of whom were presently unemployed. From those he would mould the real fighters of the future.

Before Mallory began the interviews, he contracted a company to design several latex masks for himself and his colleagues. They were realistic and flexible, and tightly fitted the contours of the human face. The disguise was hardly detectable from real flesh and adhered close to the skin, allowing a modicum of facial movement.

With such disguises they could travel incognito to Washington DC and elsewhere with little worry from their enemies. He also knew his pursuers would never give up the chase, because failure was not one of the codes of their profession, but he had to forestall their advance until the time was right.

Mallory now travelled under the name of Captain John Williams and Roseanne as Clair Williams, his wife.

Unbeknown to their pursuers, they visited Washington DC again to sign the necessary documents, giving them the authority to form the Specials. It was then intended that the President visit the Warland camp in the near future to give it his blessings and the stamp of approval. By then, it was hoped, many soldiers would have been fully trained in military practice and drill ready for the grand occasion.

They left for home the moment they had the documents signed and Oscar was subsequently given orders to intercept all outside calls on the special lines. It was therefore not long before he intercepted an urgent call from a dubious male individual that was traced back to their usual Washington DC hotel. The caller insisted on speaking to Mallory by name and when Oscar insisted that he gave his name and number he was furious. He soon found he couldn't bypass Oscar and swore unmentionable words in anger before he hung up.

Slowly at first, calls came in from the adverts on several different free-call lines and appointments were made. It was not long before the lines became clogged with those calls and when he had a list of twenty thousand young recruits, the adverts were withdrawn. However, even after that time the calls still kept coming and a second list was compiled for interviews in several months time. That was after the first batch had been trained.

Training could only have been given to three thousand at any given time, so that was the number they expected from the first thirty thousand trainees. Then a different advert was placed for ex officers with a good military record and another list was compiled. The advert was withdrawn when their numbers reached a thousand. From that thousand Mallory expected to get two hundred good officers for training the recruits.

A different date was set for each city and Mallory and his colleagues dressed in their uniforms as captains and were taken by Oscar to the offices to complete the interviews. After the interviews they were given forms to fill and sign. Those would soon be posted directly to the main Warland office for processing. After those interviews they were sent acceptance or refusal letters and a commencement date, if accepted.

During this time Chad was busy organizing the barracks and interviewing some of his own civilian staff to run the offices and precinct shops. He also had to distribute three thousand sacks of clothes and bedding to the bunks. Their uniforms would be issued immediately before their graduation rally. It was thought there would be further dropouts during the training period.

The first to arrive were the officers. They came from all walks of life and many were in their late forties. They would live in the main Central building with their wives and families after their initial training. That was assuming they had been accepted after training.

Fifty at a time were airlifted by hired LPD craft from the local shelter, just beyond the last perimeter fence to the main precinct, and they were astonished by the enormity and character of the place.

Many had no idea what the Specials were and wanted clarification, so after their arrival they were assembled in the main auditorium for a general chat with Mallory and his colleagues, now without disguises but wearing their military uniforms.

*'My name is Commander Mallory Colman and these are my fellow officers, to whom many of you will be introduced later. Most of you are in a quandary as to the true nature of the Special Squad. Well, as our name implies, we are a special group of warriors and not answerable to anyone other than myself and the President of the United States.*

*'Our main concern is always to our country's security and that of saving our world from anarchy and organized crime. It is a truly enormous task we have ahead and each one of you will be trained to be as effective as three well-trained soldiers.*

*'Because of those requirements, you will be trained in all types of warfare until you are virtually invincible. When your bodies get damaged, we have the technologies to put you back together again in much the same as you were before, because we work with the latest technologies.*

*'There will also be missions to the Moon, Mars and away from the Solar System. Many of you will be trained as astronauts, to wage war in space, and will visit NASA and elsewhere as part of your training program. You will learn to use new top-secret ray guns that can vaporize a truck at twenty yards, with zero recoil, and body armour that cannot be touched by any number of high velocity bullets. Those latest weapons and armour are only for us and to be used only by us.*

'You have all been chosen because of your exemplary records as officers. Furthermore, because of the Terminal Disease, the time is coming when many fertile or Fertilate families will be open to abuse and violence. It will be your duty as fellow Ferti lates to assist those and their families.

'Crime is also on the increase and we expect little returns from an understaffed and unsuitably trained police force. We are not police and are guided by our own set of rules. When we are called, we simply clean the mess and move on. We must gain a reputation and be feared by all, but at the same time, not be considered as butchers or criminals.

'One of our first tasks will be to remove all crime syndicates from our country, particularly those dealing in human misery like child smuggling and associated crimes. We can have little sympathy for those. And the list goes on. There are also even more dangerous things happening outside of our Solar System. Those problems won't become apparent for several decades and I cannot even consider telling you about those problems. That is, until you have truly become one of us and is willing to give your life for this organization and your country.

'Those of you who are more than fully committed will become truly fulfilled in every sense of the word. Those that are less than fully committed, because of your families and outside interests, can still assist the organization. You can be on our reserve lists and assist when you are called, and we shall care no less for you. Who knows, one day you may wish to become a fully fledged member.

'Furthermore, you are not to worry about money and suchlike. Your salaries will be double that of the highest paid soldiers and all your expenses will be paid by Central and increased with each promotion. Finally, we expect a visit from the President himself in a few weeks time to inaugurate our base. Before his visit you will all be in peak condition.

'From the moment you begin your training, you will be considered as part of a family and each one of us becomes brothers and sisters to each other with the usual respect to our senior family members or higher officers. It doesn't mean that you cannot marry another special. However, when you are on duty, you *become soldiers. When you are off duty you do as you please within this compound, providing you are not a nuisance to others.*

*'You are allowed two months home-leave during each year, at the start of each season and with all expenses paid, and there is no escape from this camp during your training unless issued a special release by myself. However, we have many facilities in Warland and I am sure you will all be very happy here. If anyone of you would like some other facilities or wish to complain about anything, please enter your suggestions and grievances in the small boxes provided throughout this compound.*

*'You will now be issued with your personal folders and shown to your apartments. The included, little blue book of rules, must be thoroughly read and relevant areas memorised.*

*'Your training begins tomorrow, so use the remainder of today to organize and familiarize yourselves with this place and its facilities.*

*' Should you have any problems, please consult anyone of the many assistants in red uniforms throughout this building.*

*'Now you may ask questions,'* Mallory said.

'Sir, what sort of military training are we to expect,' a small soldier in the front row asked.

'Nothing too extreme. Just the normal training, but you must practise until you get it perfect. You all must master balance and coordination. Strength, although an important asset, is not strictly necessary with our brand of technology. You must all be able to cope under pressure, work as a coordinated team and be always loyal to your comrades,' he said.

Ten of the best officers were subsequently selected and inter-viewed again by Mallory and Chad. Those were selected to train the first group of officers. It took just one week to get them in shape to train the others. In another week there were enough officers to train the first group of recruits.

Each of the barracks were placed under the command of an ex army sergeant. Out of the initial thirty thousand applicants 70 percent was rejected and during the preliminary training another 50 percent was rejected for one reason or another. The remainder were to be sorted into three specialist groups after further interviews and training. The process was hard and tough but the rewards and incentives high. Those remaining would be trained as officers, for combat, surveillance and technicians sent on special courses in the local college. However, most would have had a basic knowledge of the other's duties.

After the first three thousand officers and recruits had been selected, the real training had begun in earnest.

CHAPTER 34

# Six of the best

'Can you believe this female? She is some Olympic specimen, isn't she? Her records say she was also a top runner but had stopped when she went into the army. Seems she hasn't lost any of her attitude and training,' Chad said, glancing at his electronic timer to check her current rate of progress.

'What's her name?' Mallory asked.

'She is nicknamed, Ebony Blade, because of her colour and attitude. She is also very clever at making quick decisions in times of stress. I was interested enough to check her army record,' he replied.

'Why did she leave the army?' Mallory asked.

'Some problems with her family. Some crooked developer tried to steal her parent's land for a pittance. After she and a few of her mates was finished with him he left the state, but that's a sad story. She left soon after to take care of her family,' Chad said.

'You must put her on my special list,' Mallory replied.

'The third behind is another good female. Also a good runner from school days and does a lot of athletics. Her forte in the army was M61 machine guns and flame throwers. She is nicknamed White Dragon. See how those six leave the rest of the field behind,' Chad said.

'I want those six for my personal missions and I need their files. I must have them!' Mallory insisted, excitedly.

'Here comes,' Chad said and transmitted all the data to Mallory-'s implants.

'Could you arrange an interview with those six for tomorrow? You can transmit me the details, later,' he said.

There they stood on the observation tower watching the group of female officers make their way through the endurance course with Ebony Blade in the lead and they appeared to him like female panthers tracking their prey.

After the first few training sessions, Mallory had selected the best six of his female officers for active duty and the best six of the male officers as reserve. They were to be used on his personal missions and use the most advanced weapons available.

He never liked mixing the sexes, as any form of sexual intrigue was a distraction in life-threatening situations. It also distracted from the real job of fighting the enemy.


Clara Boden, nicknamed Ebony Blade, was very dark skinned and a most beautiful human specimen. She was as fast and as agile as a feline and highly intelligent.

Tracy Cummings nicknamed White Dragon, was Caucasian, beautiful and fast. She had gained her reputation in the army with the flame thrower, but was also quite good with the machine gun.

Joan Kennedy was nicknamed Black Arrow and was effective with most weapons. However, she had won many competitions with the bow and was once a runner-up for the Olympics. She was also a helicopter pilot.

Nadia Wechsler was nicknamed Wild Falcon. She was once an air-force pilot and had taken part in several sautes when they were stationed in Africa.

Anne Astor was nicknamed Cold Fury, because she was quiet, calculating and vicious. She had little compassion for her enemies, but loyal to her friends.

Joeanne Sampson was nicknamed Still Warrior. She was probably the strongest and tallest of the women and was very muscular. She was an ex gladiatorial warrior and quite used to tough competition.

Most of those women had left the military for one reason or another, all of it valid and were now looking for an opportunity to make something of their lives. They knew little about Mallory-'s Specials other than what they read in pamphlets and adverts, and wanted to give it their best shot.


While sat in Mallory's office, they were dressed spectacularly in their commando outfits like formidable Amazonians. They waited patiently in a side room for Mallory's arrival. The door was left open as they shyly observed Mallory's approach. He waved his hand at the door and to their amazement it closed all by itself.

'Officers, please follow!' he shouted without even looking in their direction and they lined up and followed.

'At ease, and take a seat, we have lots to discuss. You may also ask questions if you wish,' he said, eying each of the women in turn.

His office had no paper or pens and there were no filing cabinets. With the exception of a strange looking black box in one of the corners. That office was more like a luxurious lounge. His desk was close to the window giving a view of the outside green through net curtains.

'Are you all here?' he asked and Ebony stood up to answer.

'Yes, Sir! All present and accounted for,' she said.

'Lieutenant Boden, you may resume your seat,' he said and she wondered how he knew her name, for they had never met before. Then she realized he must have glance through her file.

'I have read each of your files in detail and know you almost as well as my own family members. Is there anything more you think I should know,' he said, while shaking their hands in turn.

'No Sir, other than the usual stuff faced during life,' Ebony replied.

'I must say, Soldiers, I observed you guys recently on track and you left the whole field behind. So I am impressed with your physical abilities. However, my specials will need added qualities to survive in the field.'

'Always good to go, Sir!' Ebony saluted.

'Anyway, we shall see. How would you guys like to be chosen as my own personal assault force? Most of it is under cover and could be extremely dangerous. After all, we'll be tracking and dealing with the most hardened criminals. But you will be issued with the best weapons and body armour when necessary and there are lots of perks.'

'Perks, Sir!'

'Fast promotion, best civilian accommodation, best armour and weapons. Need I go on?'

'Sounds great, Sir!' Ebony replied.

'I shall give you just five minutes for that decision. I want you to discuss it and when I return with the forms I shall need an

answer,' he said and left the room. After five minutes he returned. They had discussed the matter and had agreed to accept.

'Sir, we have decided to accept your offer. It seems to be much
more exciting than military training, and we don't mind the
dangers,' Ebony replied.

'Don't worry, officers. There will be lots of training as well.
However, I am very pleased that you have accepted my offer.
This however places you at a much higher level of accountabil-
ity.'

'Accountability?'

'Yes! Please read the first sentence and place your right hand to
the side of your face to swear. Say after me, "I swear by every
rule laid down in this document, to obey and follow said rules
without question..." he continued and they repeated his words.
They then read and signed their forms and he congratulated them
again.

'Officers, you have now been given grade two security clearance. Your instruction book will explain your privileges, and I
shall get you your pass cards later. You will be taken to the
armoury later this afternoon to select some weapons. Shall we
say at two p.m.? That will give you enough time to freshen-up
and have lunch in the local canteen.'

'Will do, Sir!'

'You must wait for me outside the main armoury gate, and
please wear your present outfits. This meeting is now ended,' he
said and they all stood at attention and saluted and he saluted
back as they left.


As agreed, they waited for him outside the armoury gates and on
arrival the gate automatically opened and closed behind them as
they followed him into the yard. He waved his hands again at the
main vault door and it swung open into the first area and finally
into the central vault where most of the dangerous weapons were
kept. That area contained thousands of the latest military issues.

He waved his hand again at the floor and part of it slid aside and
initiated an elevator from below. It ascended until it was level
with the floor. Under his instructions they entered and it descended to a lower level. That area was just as large as the

ground floor but about one hundred metres lower.

'This is where the most important weapons and explosives are kept,' he said. By this time the women were quite nervous and in a quandary as to how he caused the highly secured vault doors to open by a wave of his hand, for there were no signs of magic eyes or sensors.

Then he took them to an area towards the rear, beyond the food stores and released the lid of a large wall cabinet. They were amazed by the share numbers of weapons and explosives.

'This area stores the super weapons. Most of them are nuclear-powered,' he said and the women's interest was greatly aroused.

'Guard the secret of this place with your lives,' he said. He followed to another vault door and waved his hand and they entered. This time the racks were filled with a different kind of weapon. Ones that the women had never heard of before.

'This vault has been specially built to resist nuclear explosions and this particular one has a thick outer layer of tungsten to resist even the hottest cutters known to man. You may each collect one of these weapons,' he said and handed one to each of the women in turn.

Ebony eyed the strange device closely but could not make heads or tails of it. She then assumed it was one of those long distant paint throwers that used paint filled pellets. Yet, it was heavier than she expected.

'They are called Plasma Projectors. For those of you with a knowledge of physics, hot plasma is accelerated in a strong magnetic field at velocities close to the speed of light. It is then fired unto a target when a small magnetic window is released within the nozzle for a fraction of a second.'

'Way, way, out of this world!' Tracy was astounded, but Mallory continued his explanations.

'The small sphere at the bottom of the pistol grip contains a nuclear powered supply which is used to ionize hydrogen. The small container underneath the toroid contains hydrogen in liquid state and at extremely high pressure. Hydrogen gas is then accelerated into the small toroid chamber through an automatic valve. This toroid stores more than a billion joules of energy when fully charged and takes about thirty seconds to attain full capacity. These weapons can vaporize a tank at twenty metres.'

'Gracious Lord!' Ebony exclaimed.

'Over here, we have the nuclear grenades. They can be timed from five seconds up to several weeks and adjusted from small explosions, to about a thousand kilotons of TNT. By so doing one can wipe out a small town with virtual no residual radiation.'

'Truly awesome!' Tracy exclaimed. While viewing the small spherical device in the palm of her hands.

'Don't worry, they are quite safe for now. They will only work when linked to you through your DNA. That process must be initiated by our central war Macron computer. Over here we have the chemical weapons. You are to also carry a small dart gun. The darts are filled with Amiterol or its equivalent. It's a drug that causes permanent loss of memory but with no brain damage or side effects. It's used mainly on criminals, to destroy their past selves without harming their bodies. I find it to be a more humane and desirable option than killing them. There is an antidote, but it can only work if administered seconds after the drug enters the body. It's mainly used for accidents. However other chemicals are available, in case we have to interrogate them.'

'Nice and kind!' Joan exclaimed, while sizing and inspecting the weapon.

'You will also have a choice of hand weapons and Coms sets. In this section over here, we store the special nuclear powered body armour. You may also take a box each.

'Body armour. Hope it's my style!' Joeanne commented.

'Finally, I would like to show you something of even greater importance,' he said and they followed to one of the corners of the vault.

'This cubicle we call a portal. Only very few people on Earth know of their existence. Consider yourselves extremely fortunate to be added to those few. Please leave your packages here and follow me into the portal. We shall be back soon.'

As they entered the door shut and they were engulfed by a brilliant whiteness for a brief moment. The women felt slightly disorientated and their knees almost gave way under their weight, but the strange feeling stopped when they began to move. They had been transposed to Mallory's house.

When they left the portal they were even more confused, for they were no longer within the vault.

'This is my home. We are now almost one hundred miles away from the vault and could have travelled the distance to Mars in the same time using the same portal. Come and meet some friends,' he said. They nervously followed him from the base-ment to the main living room, and to a small office towards the rear. There sat Roseanne, Carl and his girlfriend in their military uniforms. They were still taking calls from recruits.

'This is Commander Roseanne, my wife, and Commander Carl Marsden. Now follow me, soldiers,' he said and Roseanne and the orders were curious to find out what he was up to. He then took the women upstairs to the bedrooms.

'These three rooms at the rear are for you. You share two per room, but as you see, they are quite spacious with your own facilities. You will also have the run of the garden, horses, golf course and swimming pool and some facilities downstairs, but not all.'

'This is real luxury!' Ebony exclaimed.

'From now on, you are to guard this house and all its occupants from outsiders and I also want a detail to check the perimeter fences several times each day until we improve security. Now follow me downstairs,' he said and they went downstairs.

'These two rooms are also yours. They will be furnished with television and whatever else you need and the one next door will be your kitchen, to be used mainly for snacks. The cooks use the main kitchens and they cook for the whole household, so those of you who are free are welcomed to join us for dinner or have your meals in here at odd times, as you wish. Any questions?' he said.

'Will all this have a negative effect on our military careers, Sir?' Ebony asked.

'Good question. I would like to answer it after we get back to base. If you don't mind,' he said and they went back to the little office.

'Are you returning to base now?' Roseanne asked.

'Yes, Commander, right away,' Mallory replied, showing much respect to his wife in front of the strangers.

'In that case, I shall join you. If you don't mind,' she said and followed the group into the portal.

The portal was designed for ten average humans in a standing position and Roseanne felt a little cramped. She was also overshadowed by those women that were close to six feet tall and wearing thick commando outfits which made them look even larger than they were.

'Are you very busy, Commander?' Mallory asked Roseanne.

'I have to see Chad about an important matter, but it can wait for an hour or so,' she replied.

'In that case, why don't you join us. We should be finished in short time,' he said and she smiled.

They collected their weapons and were taken to the rear of the armoury building where the small shooting range was situated. Mallory took Ebony's Plasma Projector from its box, turned it on and began to show the women the settings and posture for best results. Then he aimed the weapon at one of the dummy targets and it vaporised. He then adjusted the nozzle and fired a sequence of pulses at another target and the hot plasma formed an array of holes through the target, until it was cut in two.

Then he explained the uses of the heavy armour suits to them and at the end of it all they were speechless.

'Now that you have a better knowledge of our potentials, soldiers, we return to my office for a further briefing,' he said and they followed like sheep to the slaughter.

Roseanne followed them to his office and separated when they passed Chad's on the way. He used the same hand signals to open the door and they entered.

'Can I please speak freely and ask a question, Sir?' Ebony asked, overwhelmed by curiosity.

'Yes, Ebony, please ask your question?' he replied.

'How does the door open for you whenever you wave your hands?' she asked and he smiled. The other women also smiled. Then there was a tap on the door and an assistant entered with seven glasses of orange juice and cola.

Ebony looked at the tray and observed the glasses were the exact number of those in the room, even their choices of drink was correct and yet, no one had been informed of their presence in that office.

'Ebony, Ebony, you ask a lot of questions. However, I shall attempt to answer that one as best I can,' Mallory said.

'I am a Solarian. Solarians are genetically improved humans. Call us stellar humans if you wish. However, we use technology to do almost everything. How old do you think I am?' he said, making the girls even more curious.

'I would say about thirty, Sir,' she replied.

'Well, you would be wrong. I could well be one million years old and look exactly as I do at this moment. However, it so happens that I am forty-seven, but I couldn't die even if I was run over by a lorry. How would you like to have such powers?' he said. As always Mallory was having fun with the girls and always enjoyed the dramatics.

'I find all this difficult to believe, Sir,' Ebony said and the others nodded in agreement.

'It is very difficult for me to explain certain facts to you. But I can assure you that you will experience many things in the future that will substantiate my answers. Yet, I haven't answered your original question.'

'No, Sir! You haven't!'

'My mind is linked to the main computer that run this base. Through its entirety I can do almost anything. Let me show you what I mean. Would anyone of you like another drink? Well, let's have two more glasses of cola anyway,' he said and within two minutes the assistant arrived with two glasses of cola.

'Now, I rest my case, Ladies,' he said.

'That is truly incredible. Are there many like you?' she asked.

'There are a few. We are to save Earth from within and without and you can be like us if you so wish; after you have given yourselves to our organization.

'As for now, we shall discuss you and your purpose in the scheme of things,' he said and they remained silent.

*'We face many problems in the future. As you know, many species have already been made extinct by mankind. Well, many have been saved and are on distant worlds, awaiting a time when they can be returned to Earth. There is also the problem of the Terminal Disease. Because of it, in a few years there will be riots and violence throughout the major cities.*

'*There is also global warming with the disastrous effects of the oceans and seas to our coastal towns and cities. All this will lead to misplaced populations and more turmoil.*

'*Finally there is also organized crime. Because of those reasons I want my own Specials. They will be the best and fight with me on many of the most important missions. They will have to be built like machines and fight like amazonian warriors. Those are you. I have also selected your male counterparts. However, those officers will be held on reserve and sent out to separate missions or used when we need greater numbers.*

'*Because of all those reasons you are to be always available at short notice. In the mean time, your real training will commence here at base. A gymnasium will soon be built at the house with a virtual image projector for simulating real battle conditions.*

'*When you are finished training, you will be the best fighters on Earth. However, you cannot be always fighting, so there is also the social aspects to consider. Therefore, living with us should provide a large degree of that part until your normal leave is granted. If anything, your quarters at the house will give you greater freedom, but it will not reduce your training in any way.*

'*However, boyfriends will not be allowed to stay at the house or visit for prolonged periods. After all, this is a military campaign. Nevertheless, if you have any social problems, please talk to me or my wife. We might come up with a solution to our mutual benefit.*

'*Now officers, please get all your personal effects together from your bunks. This time we travel by my Roadstar. You may wait for me in the main reception area downstairs in two hours time,*' he said and left.

'What a guy. Have you seen anyone like him before? Do you think he is a Visitor from another world?' Tracy asked.

'One thing I know for sure, he is not a normal person. He seems to be a lot more clever than anyone I've ever met. And those special weapons and portals... like things you read about in comic books,' Ebony said.

'But he is quite charming. I think I can fancy him. Pity he is already married,' Joeanne said.

'That had never stopped you before. Anyway, you heard the

man, no boyfriends are allowed during working hours,' Joan said and they giggled a little.

'At least we won't be in these stuffy military confines for much longer and that's a blessing. We won't be able to sneak into the boys section in this place, anyway,' Ebony said.

'I don't know much about you, but I am going to give this military effort my best shot. Boyfriends can come after,' Anne said and they shook their heads in agreement.

CHAPTER 35

# Microids and implants

Mallory and Roseanne were now the equivalent of professors in many subjects, including those pertaining to military procedure, surveillance, counter surveillance and much more. They were also specialists in their chosen fields which for Mallory covered the complete range of the advanced sciences. For Roseanne it was a most competent physician and surgeon in both mind and body. Therefore they spend many hours imparting their knowledge to their Specials.

They had it all within their advanced implants and much of the information had gradually dispersed throughout their minds during the ensuing weeks that followed. But for the necessary field experience, it had become part of their being and natural pool of knowledge. The complete process of filtration from implants to brain was an inbuilt program and  their implants automatically ran in the background, even without their conscious knowledge.

Mallory soon formulated a course for his specials. That original course he was to prove with his six Amazonians before extending its use to the base in general. However, he felt his special women were at a gross disadvantage without implants. Good communication and snap decisions were essential in the midst of battle and could sometimes outweigh share cunning, speed and agility. Implants could also increase their reaction speeds by altering brain processes, thus placing them within a virtual world with much quicker reaction times than even the fastest humans.

With such implants he could communicate with them directly and they could do the same with him, their colleagues and equipment. He pondered those thoughts and began to scan his implants for ideas until he found a suitable component. Then he designed a few of his own micro devices and dispatched the information to Central Macron (Mac) on Eden.

The items were further enhanced and manufactured on one of the special production planets called Polion II in the Solarian arm of the galaxy.

He also placed orders for thermal devices that could slice through walls and thick metal without the associated explosive effects, and small space cars, somewhat similar to the Roadstar, Oscar, but with tougher bodies and powerful protection screens.

The screens were based on the same system as the armoured suits and were fed by a much more powerful nuclear generator. Plasma projector cannons, plasma missiles and a range of smaller weapons, tracers and communicators were also included and all those special features with manual, could only be operated through implants for security reasons. Further, without any mechanical controls those ships could only be operated by those with brain implants and for security reasons they would be kept at Sol-Newtown when not in use.

Mallory had decided on a ten-room extension to his house, with the addition of a small gymnasium, landing pad and a dozen garages for automobiles. Those were to be built at the rear of the house and to one side of the garden with robots borrowed from Warland. The building Macron had been dispatched to his house and all the robots reprogrammed for their new task.

The girls took it in turn to patrol the fences and associated land around the house with the two small jeeps supplied by Mallory, and soon had control of the property and its many facilities. Roseanne also liked to have them around. They reminded Roseanne of herself when she was their age, and Mallory felt a lot safer from his enemies. When they were not working they played hockey and other games aggressively.

During that time several deliveries were made to their home portal, checked and transferred to the armoury. One of those deliveries contained the special devices he had designed. It included a new type of implant that could be administered to any human without recourse to Megotrons and Psyrotron scanners. Being of Nano-bot design, they were just visible to the naked eye, and could only be connected within the brain with micro robots that were specially programmed to complete the task on their own.

The micro devices were to be placed in a special solution and injected into an artery. Being the physician, only Roseanne could complete that delicate operation. Nevertheless, all six women had to agree to the micro operation before she could go ahead. Therefore Mallory called them and Roseanne together to discuss those ideas.

'Fellow officers, I have called this meeting to discuss an incredible idea that will concern you. That is, if you accept my proposal. However, you are not obligated in any way to accept this advise. Today, I received some special implants from Sol-Newtown. They were specially designed for untethered minds and will increase your mental capacities by at least a factor of ten, with a range of general subjects on survival and others. Those can be removed at anytime by a reverse procedure. However, I need your permission to go ahead with the operation, Ladies,' he said.

'What are these implants?' Ebony asked, even more confused than her other colleagues.

*'They are microscopic devices that can be linked to certain parts of the brain, to improve one's potential. They do not affect the normal person, and you will not be aware of any difference consciously or otherwise.*

*'They are first injected into an artery in your arm and find their way to the relevant area of your brain where they are connected to specific neurons by micro robots that are invisible to the naked eye. But for the initial injection, the process is completely painless and there will be no permanent side effects.*

*'These implants will make you telepathic, improve your coordination, turn you into a doctor in a field of your chosen subject and give you the ability to control our equipment and weapons by thought at incredible speed. This single feature will save you the efforts of manual controls and also more cabin space when piloting a space ship. It also makes such technology unworkable by normal humans, which is another safety feature from the security standpoint.*

*'Your brain capacity will be effectively increased, with extensive knowledge on many important subjects that will be constantly available for instant recall. Each one of you will become a super woman, and a doctor in her chosen field, and we have a*

*range of specialist subjects to choose from. So what will it be, Ladies,'* he said.

'So far you have been honest with us, Commander, so I shall accept your offer, if it will make me a much better woman and soldier, with no side effects,' Ebony said, and once she agreed the others did likewise.

'My wife will see to the operation. So I shall pass you over to her department,' he said. Roseanne then took the women away to a small private room she had prepared for such emergencies. It was like a doctor's surgery with a range of medical equipment that she had ordered from Sol-Newtown.

'I suppose, there is no time like the present,' Roseanne said, while opening a case. She retrieved six small medical syringes, six small bottles of a bluish liquid and a transparent plastic container. That one included a special nozzle for dispensing the correct amount of the bluish powder it contained.

'Ladies, please glance through the professional list and select one of the professions for yourselves, and please consider carefully your choices,' Roseanne said and the girls took a small pamphlet each. When they were finished filling in the enclosed forms, they had decided to become, a technologist, an astrophysicist, three medical doctors and one psychologist.

'Are you sure of your choices or would you like some more time to reconsider? Please look through the list again?' Roseanne insisted and they did as she asked, but their original choices were unchanged.

'Ok! However, these implants contain lots more peripheral information that you will require as fully fledged security offices and soldiers in the field. It also contains routines for administering first aid and such like,' Roseanne said. Apparently all six implants contained numerous doctors in many fields and could be selected during the training process.

Roseanne selected a coded vial that contained an implant and plugged it into the syringe. Then she discharged a fixed amount of the microid powder into the bottle of bluish liquid and shook the mixture. Finally, she pushed the needle into the bottle's cap and began to draw its contents into the body of the syringe while keeping the syringe in an almost vertical position. Then she gently tapped it and expelled any surplus up to the red mark.

'Ebony, please come forward and expose your arm,' she said and a brave Ebony nervously did as she asked. It was not the operation that worried her, she was just scared of needles. A small area of her arm was disinfected and the contents of the syringe injected into her upper arm. Within just three minutes they had all been injected.

'Now, I want you all to retire immediately to bed. You must draw the curtains in your rooms, switch off all lights and wear the eye patches provided for a minimum of three hours, which is the period of the operation. Make your rooms as dark as possible and relax your bodies while lying in a horizontal position and on your backs. It will even be better if you fell asleep during that period. The special drug will help you to relax. The process will begin in about seven minutes, so you should go and prepare yourselves for bed. I shall be along in three hours to check you,' Roseanne said and the girls left.

After the three hours had elapsed, she went to their rooms and awakened them. They were still quite drowsy, which was the side effect of the blue drug. However, its effect was diminishing.

They slowly walked downstairs and sat in her surgery for more tests, which was to do with their nervous system and related parts.

'Girls, how do you feel. Any side effects?' Roseanne inquired.

'No, Doctor. I am only a little drowsy,' Ebony said. She also checked their pulses and when she was finished, checked their pupils with a bright light, then she smiled.

'I think I shall fix you and myself a gin and tonic. I think we all deserve a drink, and the alcohol will help to disperse the drug,' she said and poured for them and herself.

'You are all in peak health. Now comes the difficult part, of learning to use your implants. I have some booklets that will assist you and I expect a small computer tutor from Eden within a week or so. However, if you need advice, please consult me or my husband. It's almost time for supper, so you may join us at the table today. Consider yourselves on sick leave until tomorrow. Doctor's orders,' Roseanne said and they went to prepare.

CHAPTER 36

# Another underworld recruit

With the aid of Roseanne and Mallory, the women warriors spent several days getting used to their implants, until they were able to communicate telepathically between themselves and their commander, Mallory. They also learned to master the art of remote control, with its many codes and sub-codes through their implants, until they were fully competent in controlling a wide range of computers. Since most complex equipment was controlled by computers, that aspect was very important during training. They need only to have learnt the most frequently used computer codes. By so doing they eliminated the need for writing lengthy reports or even the need for conversation during planning. All such information could be downloaded directly through their implants at many times faster.

However, they had not yet begun to use the other fourteen main menu items in their implants which included their master subjects. Those were outside of the Coms and their recent Help menus. They would concentrate on those after their current workload had reduced.

Over the past few days they were busier than in all their lives and there was still so much left to learn and practise. The women had also learnt to use their implants to control biological functions by artificially triggering the release of certain boosters like adrenalin and hormones, including enzymes that were sometimes required under extreme competition and stress. They could now be considered real Amazonians in every sense of the word, and could now outrun and endure limits beyond even the fastest Olympians.

Mallory had visited Marlina's safety deposit box and found another of her pink notes with Cupid's logo, which read:

**'Darling, one of my closest friends would like to give up her**

connections with a side of her business she dislikes. You met her once in a Miami hotel, with all those beautiful women and an occasional unwanted child. She was the one in charge. I haven't mentioned anything about you, but I think she could make a good recruit, with all those girls and freely available information. Please don't tell her of our association. She could be an ace, with many important connections.

Thanks again.

Marlina xxx.'

'Good woman. I shall leave a thank-you note in her other safety box with a bonus of twenty grand and try to visit the house of ill repute later today,' he said to Oscar through his implant. Then he tore the note into several pieces and threw the remains into the nearest trash bin. He visited her other box and left an envelope with a note and a credit card valued at twenty thousand dollars. The note read:

'Take good care of yourself.

M xxx.'


'Please take me to Miami, Oscar,' he said and the car was on its way. Mallory was disguised in his best latex mask, including a small moustache and wearing his distinguished military suit of black with many decorations.

The face-mask was tight fitting and took some getting used to its closeness. It fitted his face too closely and tended to accumulate sweat in some areas, with a tendency to itch after several hours. The use of the special cream provided had reduced those detrimental factors, but most of it was still experimental and he thought of ways to improve on the design.

He found facial itching extremely embarrassing in public, so he only used those masks when he had no other choice.

Unknown to their security, Oscar landed on the roof of the hotel and Mallory made his way down to the hotel lobby by stairway. He went directly to the receptionist and fumbled with his identity card, in the process accidentally dropping a one-hundred grand credit-card on the counter. He watched her overwhelmed by surprise when her eyes lit up and knew he had already been accepted at the highest level.

'The manageress will be with you shortly, Sir,' she said while entering a number on her computer keyboard. The manageress was soon out of the elevator and walking towards him.

'My name is Clair. Clair Nobel,' she said, taking his hand.

'I am Commander John Williams. Are you the manageress of this most enchanting place?' he said.

'I have never heard it described that way before,' she replied and giggled.

'I am the manageress and own most of it. Please follow me,' she said and they entered the vacant elevator.

'What is such a nice and handsome gent like you doing in a naughty place like this? I know you are not here for pleasure, but I shall go through the motions anyway,' she said and Mallory thought how perceptive she was.

'Anyway, you can have any of my special ladies. They are of all ages, colours and dispositions and we have a catalogue of their likes, dislikes and rates, depending on facilities and time. We aim to please our customers, you know,' she added.

'What about you. Are you available? I can make it worth your while,' he said.

'Me! What do you want with me of all people? I am in my late forties and well passed my sell-by date,' she replied.

'Perhaps I just need someone to talk to. A mother figure, if you know what I mean,' he said.

'Kinky! Are we? What have you got on your mind?' she asked, teasingly. The lift came to an abrupt stop, so they followed into her private quarters.

'I have a financial proposition I would like to put to you. However, before we begin to talk, I would like your assurance that we won't be overheard and that our conversation will go no further. There could be lots in it for you on a continuous basis, but you mustn't even tell your closest friends and family of our relationship,' he said and unknown to her, began to scan the area with his sensitive detectors for bugs and recorders through his implants, but could find no such devices.

'What is it... you would like to discuss with me?' she asked, while tapping a number into a local keyboard.

'I do not wish to be disturbed for an hour or so. I will call you when I am through with this customer,' she said and released the button.

'Now, we have privacy and some time to talk,' she said, going to a small cupboard and retrieving two glasses.

'What would you like?' she asked.

'Vodka and tonic, please,' he replied.

'I see you like things tidy and clear,' she said while pouring the drinks.

'I represent the government of our country. As a matter of fact, I am answerable only to the President of our country and cannot be traced or checked. I run a phantom organization that operates at the highest levels of security. There are major problems brewing in the wind and our task is to nip them in the bud before they take effect. Most of the serious ones will become apparent in about three years time. At least, that is what the clever computers tell us and they are seldom wrong. However, one of them relates to the rampant smuggling of children on an international level. One that will cause much pain and unhappiness to many parents in the future, to be further aggravated by the Terminal Disease.

'Clair, are you a patriotic person?' Mallory inquired.

'Yes, I suppose I am. Although my country hasn't been too kind to me in the past,' she replied.

'How would you like to spy for us? Pillow-talk with undesirables must abound in a place like this. All you need do, is train some of your girls to get information from hardened criminals. For that service I am willing to put you on a permanent retainer. Would you consider one-hundred grand per year, plus a bonus? The bonus can be for every delivery of important information, and the retainer can be increased once your service is more permanently established.'

'That's a lot of doe!'

'If you do agree, simply acquire two safety deposit boxes, one for my notes and one for yours and I shall give you a special number for calling me in an emergency. Take it from me, this work is very important to our country if we are to halt the increase in organized crime and improve the chances of our country's survival. So do I have your answer?' he asked.

'It's a mega decision for someone like me to make. Could be very dangerous, should one of my girls spill the beans in the future to any of our dangerous clients? If there was rich pickings for my girls they would go along with it. However, I can only give such duties to those that live-in and are fully dependant on me. That's those that have no real family or permanent boy-friends, and I will not be able to terminate their services and buy them off when they leave, or they might blackmail me in the bargain. You see how difficult your proposal is to put into operation,' she said.

'I see your problems, but we can give you special protection. Furthermore, you do not have to tell them the exact reasons why. They might be more susceptible if they thought it was for blackmail purposes on your wealthier clients, if you think the truth might drive them away. However, we are nothing to do with the police force and cannot get involved with petty law breakers,' he said.

'Perhaps you or one of your people could speak with them later. However, I would like you to give me a week to think it over and sample the waters,' she said.

'You have one week. You may contact me by the number on this card and please remember to dial it in reverse order, and here is a thousand dollars for your troubles,' Mallory said. He handed her two cards and left.

On his way home he visited Rosie's café and pretended to be a passerby.

'Two donuts and a coffee, please!' he said in a disguised voice. He knew Rosie always served the best customers herself, particularly the well-dressed males, so he pulled a chair from a corner table at the rear and awaited her arrival.

'How are you, Rosie?' he asked.

'Do I know you?' she replied.

'Sit down and be quiet. I am in disguise. It's me, Mal,' he said and her eyes almost popped out of their sockets.

'Ma... l!' she exclaimed, stopping her vocal cords in mid stream and continuing the conversation at twenty decibels lower.

'I said , be quiet! I thought of popping in to say hello to an old friend. How are you these days without my happy features around?' he inquired.

'You have changed! You appear twenty years younger, even with your disguise!'

'I had a refit!'

' I am not very happy. I am thinking of selling out, but no one wants to buy.'

'Why is that?' he asked.

'Business has dropped off a lot. I think it's something to do with the Terminal Disease. People think they might get infected by eating out in places like this. And it's not only me. Most of the other restaurants are also in trouble,' she said.

'Let me buy it from you. Then you can run it for me on a salary. Put something together and call me sometime soon. Here is one of my cards, and don't forget to dial the number in reverse. It's for security reasons,' he said and handed her the card.

'I don't know what to say. Are you sure you want to take on a loss? Or perhaps you know something I don't?' she said.

'You know, those attitudes come and go. Once they get used to the disease they will start using this place again. By then, many of your competitors might be out of business, leaving most of the trade to you. However, it might take a little while, even months, before your business improves significantly. Anyway, if you need me at anytime just call and we can arrange something,' he said.

'You are a godsend you know, and how is your wife, Roseanne-?' she asked.

'She is fine and would like you to pay us a visit sometime soon, but I will have to collect you because of security reasons,' he said.

He finished his donuts and coffee and left Rosie a much happier woman.


Mallory knew many people along his way of life and realized

they were in serious trouble because of the difficulties and changing times that were currently affecting every aspect of human society. People were worried for their future, which showed uncertainty where ever they looked. Further, the terms Fertilate and Infilates tended to separate Earth's humans into two factions, namely the wanted and unwanted.

He also realized that many of the people he knew would lose much more than their future families; they would also lose their future blood lines and genes. All those changes worried him, but he was a soldier of life and was also prepared for the inevitable, even when it was one he disliked.

If only humans could speak with one global voice and stop or limit procreation for a few decades, then they would survive the storm. However, Earth's humans were driven by hormones and other body chemicals which drove them in ways contrary to their long term survival. He spent some time contemplating those ideas and realized the Terminal Disease was the most humane way out of the dilemma.

CHAPTER 37

# Six new ships

After a hard day of training at the house, Mallory called his warriors together for a pep talk. They stood at attention in the back yard while he inspected them. Then he moved away, closer to the foundation of his new house extensions and began to speak.

*'You have passed your preliminaries with flying colours and are now capable of some real action. However, there is just one more test to go before you become competent in all spheres of activity and that is astronaut training. Because of your new implants that aspect has now become simplicity itself. Even so, you will still have to prove your capabilities to me in that aspect of our operations before I can issue you with your pilot's licenses.*

*'Further, our President will visit Warland in one week's time to inaugurate our facilities there and to inspect our troops. There-fore I would like our team to give him a performance that he will never forget. Perhaps we could put a small show together with our special ships.*

*'In view of your new capabilities, I have decided to promote each of you to captain. Please come forward and receive your stripes,'* he said. They each broke rank, collected their stripes, saluted and rejoined their group.

'At ease, Officers!' he shouted. 'Finally, I have received communication from Sol-Newtown regarding a delivery of several small Vipers. They are the most versatile fighting space ships. I wonder if you would like to accompany me to collect six of them today?' he said.

The women were full of excitement and curiosity and it didn't take them long to put their hands in the air, while Ebony came forward.

'Permission to speak for the group, Sir,' she said.

'As always, you may speak, Captain Boden,' he replied.

'We have considered your request. It is one that we cannot refuse, Sir,' she said and backed off to join her group.

'In that case, please lead your group towards Oscar,' he said.

'It was the first time they had travelled in Oscar at a high altitude and with the exception of Nadia, the first time they had been in a super fast ship. Something Oscar could only have accomplished when flying within the higher airways.

'Oscar, please take us to Sol-Newtown,' Mallory said.

'Yes, Commander, Mal,' he replied and shot vertically into the air. He made a few angular manoeuvres and was already close to satellite Eta. Then he dived towards the large dome as his ecstatic passengers held tightly to their seats. Oscar always tended to show-off a little with new passengers on board, but this time the G-suppression was on and they felt no physical discomfort. Only the psychological effects of the combined motions.

They were soon on their way to the docking area in Sol-Newtown and were even more impressed by the giant dome. They had obviously read about it and had even seen its picture on television, but never thought they would ever have visited that place from the air. Oscar landed in the first docking area, which was at level one. They could not enter the innermost dome. That action would have required complete decontamination of Oscar and his passengers.

To the rear of that parking area were about twenty ships. They were about the size of Oscar but even more streamlined and were a glossy metallic silver in colour and highly reflective.

'They can drive themselves, but I think they are better with two passengers each during special missions. I am afraid, we are to collect six of them. That means, you will each have to take control of one. The other ships can remain until we need them. They can fly under their own control, but will require landing coordinates from you to get home.

'You have been thought the relevant codes and operational procedures, so take your pick,' Mallory said.

'How do we get in, Sir?' Tracy asked.

'Once you know their numbers, it's easy. Here is a list,' he said and transmitted the special codes to their implants.

'I shall escort Oscar back home and I expect you to follow just behind and no heroics please, not until we prepare a proper exercise away from Earth. Don't worry, they virtually drive themselves and cannot crash,' Mallory said.

As the girls approached the ships their doors lifted and they entered. They remained silent while viewing the incredible virtual display panels for a while, trying to link their implants to the ships control cores. Once they made contact, they found themselves in Cyberspace, which was a truer representation of the ship's conceptual space. While there all normal motion in the outside world could be slowed from normal to a thousand times. Looking at it in another way, all their thoughts, conversations and actions could be speeded up by a thousand times. It was designed that way in order to react quickly during battle manoeuvres. The fastest response was only limited by the reflexes of the implants of the human operators and that was when they used manual. During automatic, every activity was controlled by the ships' computers while ignoring their human operations.

All battle ships were designed to work with a human operator at all times. Therefore, ships could not take the direct decision to fire weapons or harm anyone during battle. That decision could only be taken by its human pilot.

The main cockpit was designed for two human passengers in comfort and the seats could alter their shape for greater comfort. There were areas at the rear for four more passengers, food storage, clothes, weapons and suchlike. That area was only accessible through a small door between the pilots seats. The rear seats could also recline into four narrow beds.

Within the cabins were a few physical controls for passengers, including a large circular screen across the dashboard which gave a simulated view of the outside world with the relevant time differential when in motion. However, those with implants also had a similar perception within their own minds, with additional status indicators, symbols and suggestions from the main onboard computer. Those symbols and status indicators were also apparent on panels within the cockpit for those without implants. However, those models could only have been controlled by trained minds with implants, since there were no push buttons or visible controls of any kind for controlling those ships.

Their displays were comprehensive and included altitude, speed, target position, surface contour maps, long range and infrared scanners, spectrometers and a range of other detectors and stellar maps. They also included a large plasma cannon, a gravity projector or tractor beam. That one could be switched to attract objects of a lesser mass. There was four lasers, two forward and two aft. Also two plasma ejectors and plasma cannon along with a single nuclear grenade ejector that was not yet loaded.

The six small ships followed Oscar to a high altitude and descended like missiles towards the house. It took them about fifteen minutes to complete the trip of several hundred miles and they landed on the green at the rear of the house.

Their passengers were absorbed mentally by the incredible new concepts of reality in Cyberspace and had to slowly adjust to normality before they left their crafts.

'That was incredible and awesome! Beats any computer game I've ever played! It's like using one of those virtual war machines in the arcades, but much more realistic and a lot faster. No physical controls... Those are done by the onboard computer... just quick decisions relating to strategy, weaponry and survival. What an incredible machine?' Ebony exclaimed, full of excitement.

'That is true cybernetics, where the human mind is coupled directly to the machine and almost fully integrated and absorbed... even better than your brain to your own body through those special implants. Now you know the reasons why I wanted you to have those implants,' Mallory said.

'Yes, Commander, with those ships we can take on an army, even missiles will seem to approach us at a snails-crawl,' Nadia replied.

'I think we should put on an aerial show for the President, don't you? Perhaps a few loop-the-loops, near misses and so on. All coordinated via Eta and the Warland Macron. That way, every operation will be 100 percent safe. However, you will have to convince me that you can do it yourselves, which may require many hours of practice. What do you think, officers?' Mallory said.

The women gazed at him in utter surprise; for they were not experienced pilots. Only Nadia had experience with super fast aircraft and those were the more primitive machines with manual controls. Only Mallory had any real experience in space ships and they were the old Martian shuttles with minimal G-suppression. He had travelled to Mars that way more than a hundred times, co-piloting for President Gerald Fraser. He also had a few mining friends in Caefon Dome. He hadn't seen those particular Martian friends since his accident many years before. That was before he took the bullet that was meant for the President over a decade ago.

However, those new ships had almost full G-suppression to one thousand gravities. That was enough acceleration to crush any primal life-form into a splatter of liquified cells.

To avoid security problems while on Earth, those ships were grouped as class five LPD cars and filed as new deliveries from Sol-Newtown and were registered as such for use on Earth. Those undervalued specifications were only required for registration with the local police, customs and internal security. It also made it possible for anyone to drive them without the requirement of a special pilot's license after their temporary license had expired.

All ships boasted the multicoloured federation insignia in front as part of the outer coating. It was just visible against the glossy skin, and there were relevant identification numbers at the rear underside. However, those numbers were also constantly transmitted to checkout beacons and scanners during flight.

Once they were within the virtual mind of those ships, the girls could use them as they wished. However, they had to learn their true potentials and that needed practice during realistic and dynamic simulations and manoeuvres away from Earth.

'These ships are thirty times faster than the fastest LPD's on Earth, so they will take about two hours to get to Mars and two more for the trip back and that time includes slowing down for atmospheric entry, etcetera. However, the onboard computers will work all that out for you. They can respond so quickly, it's almost impossible for them to collide with any physical object. However, it doesn't mean to say you should take undue risks. The maximum speeds of comets and meteors is about 120,000 miles per hour, which is a snails crawl to those ships when in space,' Mallory said.

'Commander, can we travel to Mars for such an operation? I have always dreamt of visiting the red planet!' Ebony asked.

'I think we could take a practice run to Mars and visit Caefon Dome for lunch, if you soldiers agree. It's much better to practice in deep space and I know just the place. We could probably make the trip tomorrow with four ships and you could take it in turn to be captain of your particular ship. Will tomorrow be soon enough?' he said.

'Yes, Sir, but not soon enough!' Ebony said and saluted.

'In that case, we may leave at first light. So check your ships for survival gear and ensure there are six emergency spacesuits in the rear lockers. I shall need a report before we leave at six a.m.' Mallory said and left.

CHAPTER 38

# Ships to Mars

After dinner that day the girls and Roseanne checked over the ships and logged their contents into the House Macron. Then Mallory and Roseanne sat together in one of the ships and linked their minds with it's battle computer to learn more of its relative functions. Many battle simulations could be enacted within Virtual Worlds so created. They practised those manoeuvres until they became second nature to their responses.

The whole process was incredibly smooth. It reminded them of the V-room technology that was used on Eden. However, the ship's type of Cyberspace was tuned specifically for dog fighting, ducking missiles and fast-moving objects and suchlike.

After a while they broke off contact with the ship's mind and kissed each other like they hadn't done for weeks.

'I love you more than ever, My Love. Pity we are so busy these days. We are always on the move with someone or for something or another. Anyway, I have an idea. Are you very busy tomorrow?' Mallory said and she was intrigued.

'I still have some important parts of the present campaign to complete. I also wanted to see Chad about the President's visit and new recruits. But I suppose it can wait for a day or so,' she said.

'The girls have decided to put on an aerobatic display for the President and his associates, but have little experience with the new fighters, so I decided to take them for a practice run to Mars. I will be happy if you could join us and be my copilot. It could make a break and we can visit some old friends of mine in the Caefon dome,' he said.

'Mars is very far away by ship, isn't it? How long will it take?' she asked.

'At a steady cruising pace, it should take us close to two hours to make the trip there and about the same again for the return journey, following the standard spaceway. That is if we don't decide to leave the girls there and take the Martian portal back home. However, It would be nice to spend a little time at Caefon Dome to check on a few old friends. We were in the air-force together and met again when we became shuttle pilots.'

'I heard of Caefon dome. It was visited just before Jerry and others supposedly got lost in space.'

'The same! Some of my old friends moved there with their wives and families and are now involved in mining for the Spirox Mining Consortium. They own the whole complex. My friends run and train their new groups of asteroid miners. It should make for an exciting trip and the experience could come in useful,' Mallory said.

'Ok, in that case count me in. While we are having a break, why don't we take Carl and his girlfriend along?' she said.

'You tell them for me when you return,' he replied.

'I suppose we'll require to take along some food and perhaps a few bottles of whisky, rum and vodka for those hardened miners?'

'We'll see what we can rustle up, otherwise we'll go to the late-night supermarket or place a Tele-order, if we have to. By the way, we leave at six a.m. tomorrow morning. Don't worry about anything, it's perfectly safe,' he said.

'Nothing in this universe is perfectly safe!' she replied.

The house was awakened at four a.m. and they began filling the empty cupboards in the ships with food and drink. Those cupboards were lined with a thick sponge rubber material which expanded on its own accord to fill the empty spaces when closed. It was perhaps formed by microids and were also triggered by changes in oxygen levels. That way nothing remained loose during transit.

After the items were loaded they dressed in their travelling outfits. They were made of a light nylon fabric with the colours of the Specials and the Solarian insignia. Then they had a haughty breakfast before assembling in the main office.

Carl and his girlfriend was allowed to spend several minutes to learn the different modes of control, but most of it would come to them during the long flight.

*'We should pass about ten shuttles on our way to Mars. Three*

*freight and two combined passenger and freight. As you may soon observe within your implants, the spaceway goes around the Sun and links with Earth, Mars and Mercury. It's like a large invisible tunnel, two million miles in diameter, and linked by small tunnel branches that lead to the planets of our solar system.*

*'It took about ten years to clear spaceway of all asteroids and orbiting debris, and there are many space beacons and scanners at critical areas throughout its length. However, because of planetary motion, its ellipsoid, or perhaps near toroid route, is not stationary in space and has to be repositioned every sidereal month or so.'*

*'Our ships' computers have all the relevant information within their data banks. May I suggest I lead the squadron for a while until we enter spaceway. If there are no questions, let's take our ships out,'* Mallory said and they walked towards the ships, took their seats and waited for him to take off.

The sun was rising above the horizon when all five ships lifted into the air. They followed Mallory's ship at normal air speed through the local skyways until they approached satellite Eta, then they took a new route in the direction of satellite Gimbal which was in another orbit. That route took them close to the Moon where they would catch the Lunar branch of Spaceway, sometimes called the Martian Way by the more hardened space travellers.

'Here we are. Now we can open up, but watch your indicators. This is also a training mission and I don't mind any of you overtaking me. Bon Voyage!' Mallory shouted with a consenting smile from Roseanne who was also linked within Cyberspace.

At that time the total Martian population was only about sixty thousand and most of them included hardened miners and their wives. All children were usually sent to Earth to be registered and schooled. Children that were reared away from Earth had zero status and were considered aliens. All such aliens required special papers to visit the mother planet. However, if their parents were born on Earth or on one of Earth's satellites, their parents could apply for naturalization before they were six months old. Then their country of origin were taken to be their parents country of origin before moving to Mars. Nevertheless, since Solarian Banking was considered a separate organization by treaty, it could absorb its own people even without those papers.

Because most miners were Baptists, originally coming from North America, the Terminal Disease was a late arrival within Caefon Dome and its parent company made sure the antidote was freely available there. Nevertheless with the exception of a few vivacious contract engineers, the mining inhabitants of the dome were very religious and with little criminal intent. Even so it had its own police and internal security, and was regarded as a separate world with its own judiciary.

Miners worked hard and played hard, making the Caefon population a highly volatile one, and many were constantly on the move to and from Earth. Many thought it was to do with the claustrophobic effects of the pressurized domes and the pink and uninviting look of the planet. Not to mention the reduced gravity and constant fear of the dome collapsing on itself if something went wrong with the pressurization system.

However, there were several other factors involved and one of them was the price of food and clothes. They were double the usual prices on Earth and not always of great variety. Many Martian parents also wanted to visit their children who were schooling on Earth and experience family life in the more pleasant settings on the beautiful green and blue planet.

Then there were the Baptists' conventions, where they would immerse the young and newcomers to the faith. Ceremonies concerning the use of large quantities of water were better conducted on Earth, where the liquid commodity was in abundant supply and still relatively free.

Furthermore, because of the difficulties, danger and stress of their work, all miners had a month off every three months, so most shuttle passengers consisted of such individuals, either visiting Earth or returning from their vacations.

The population of Caefon Dome had peaked at fifty thousand, with an additional ten thousand contract engineers in the southern quadrant.

Trips to and from Mars were twice the cost of intercontinental flights on Earth. While flights on LPD passenger shuttles were one-fifth the price of jet airlines. Those included flights driven by fossil and chemical fuels which were very rear and extremely expensive.

The dome had been built about fifteen kilometres from the Solarian cluster of domes and was owned by several independent mining companies from Earth.

As they entered the invisible tunnel of spaceway, Mallory projected a virtual image of the Solar System to the other ships and the computer plotted the best course between both planets. The journey so far had taken them less then fifteen minutes and their bodies had not been affected by those excessive G-forces or weightlessness because of inbuilt G-suppressors. Those neutralizing fields had the same affect on acceleration, since those forces were indistinguishable from each other.

Mallory had decided that the girls have in-flight training at one of the lay-byes behind the sun. That part of the route was further out from Mercury. That area was supposed to be free of debris and meteorites and ideal for interplanetary dog fighting. For those exercises, they would set their plasma projectors to minimum and shields to maximum. That way, no damage could be done to their ships or passing shuttles.

It took them another forty five minutes to arrive at the place called The Solar Cross. It contained a small scientific space station with several warning beacons shaped like a cross. It was on the other side of spaceway to the layby and closer to the sun than Mercury.

'Get ready for reverse drive! Convergence with target area begins now!' Mallory said and all the ships began to decelerate at once. Then they were in the test area observing Mercury like a small half disk against the much larger solar inferno.

'We fight two against two and I shall be referee. You are not to use your lasers, and plasma projectors are to be set to minimum. Points are scored for direct hits and I will take note of your evasive tactics. Remember, the computers will take over if you are in danger. Now, change over to manual. You are now in control of your ships. Enemy ships take your positions close to Mercury and at the intersection shown!' Mallory said, and Carl and Ebony was on their way to the small world.

'Ok, People, let me explain our present operation scenario to you. We are to break through the defences of Mercury and capture that world for our glorious leader. However, you are required to knock out all surveillance and fighters before you can survey the planet and find a suitable place for the mother ship to land its troops. The mother ship happens to be me. Get to it!' Mallory shouted and Joeanne and Nadia with their copilots, Anne and Joan, followed on an intercept course to Carl and Ebony's fighters, both primed and waiting.

The two supposed invaders could clearly observe their stationary targets in their sights, aligned their weapons and fired, but to their disappointment their opponents had predicted their move and disappeared. To their further surprise, they had reappeared directly above them and as they did Ebony and Carl fired. Joeanne and Nadia could not have taken any evasive action in the intervening milliseconds of time and their two ships were counted as destroyed.

'Fighters, return to base!' Mallory said and all four ships returned to their original safe positions.

*'Never under any circumstances remain a sitting-target for anyone. Whenever your target moves, you must do likewise. Each of you must fight within an invisible sphere of many grids. That sphere is within 3d space. You must randomly move from one part of the grid to another, under computer control. That way you become a difficult target and can still observe every move your enemy makes. The size of your sphere can be altered to fit your circumstances, those of your environment and your closest fighters. Further, no two spheres can ever coincide, unless both ships are in identical positions. Since your battle computer will calculate those changes and parameters, you may consider yourself safe during such operations. Therefore the chance of any two ships ending in the same spot within space is too small to worry about during battle and that aspect is allowed for by the computers. Also remember, your fighter can only evade an enemy*

*while in motion. Further, even if ships collide they will simply bounce off each other.*

*'Kill the grid only when you are sure you can surprise the enemy and that step must be quick and decisive. Remember, these ships are super fast falcon Vipers, with almost zero inertia. That means, they can move a hundred miles in any given direction during the blink of an eye. After I am satisfied with this exercise, we can do some dog fighting. Then we will see how quickly you can out-think and outmanoeuvre your opponents and their plasma beams. Now I'm going to download a battle sphere to each of your implants,'* Mallory said and they resumed their previous positions.

This time they created their virtual spheres and fought in and out of the complex matrix, surprising and being surprised by their targets. Mallory had relaxed the rules to ten hits each and at the end or one hour's practice they were in full control of their machines and weapons. By that time Ebony had taken five hits, Carl six, Joeanne six and Nadia four. Nadia was ahead in that operation.

'This is incredible. No matter where we are, the positions in the grid in our minds is always precise,' Roseanne exclaimed.

'And that applies to any motion in real and virtual space. For higher accuracy you may increase the size of the spheres to virtually any size and use smaller sup spheres and grids for even higher resolution. Also, with practise one can jump within different sub spheres as and when required. With these ships we are almost  indestructible and the best on Earth.'

'I think you guys are getting to like this game. Perhaps I should bring on some nasty Javols!' Mallory said.

'Please bring em on, Commander!' Roseanne replied.


'Now, I see what you mean, Commander!' Nadia shouted with utmost enthusiasm.

'Sorry, People. We start killing Javols in about 20 years. So you have a long wait. However, I can guarantee you that you will all be with me during that first battle,' Mallory replied.

'Won't we be too old, Commander?'

'No! You will just be as you are now. We have the technology to change you back to you youthful selves. But you must be fully committed. When the time is right you will be given that gift,' Mallory said and they remained silent and in awe.

'We can do some dog fighting over Mercury if you wish. The rough terrain of that planet should make for an interesting flight pattern,' Mallory said.

They dived towards the dark side of the planet and circled around until they touched the terminator, that part where the darkness met the light. They could observe many small domes on the dark side, just within the terminator and large arrays of solar panels on the brightly lit side. There were also an observatory and long distance radar installations.

'I think we are soon to be entered into their logs as five UFOs. I hope we haven't scared them too much,' Mallory said.

'How can anyone live on such a dead and desolate world?' Roseanne asked.

'Wherever there are places, there will be people. I think most of them are scientists drilling for rear metals. Mercury is supposed to be the place for the next mining boom. They must be from the station we passed back there and I bet some of those scientists are prospecting for the owners of Caefon Dome,' he said.

After half hour of manipulating their ships Mallory thought they had done enough for one day.

'Ships, to Mars!' he shouted and they left the dead world and its small settlement behind and flew off in formation towards Spaceway.

CHAPTER 39

# Space rescue

In another half hour or so the Martian disk filled their viewers as they dived towards Caefon Dome. Their systems were too advanced to link with Caefon's landing routines, so they followed Mallory towards the docking area.

During their brief descent they could observe many of the miners' ships leaving the area. There seemed to be much activity on the air waves that could not be attributed to normal operations. It gave them the impression that there was some type of emergency down below.

Mallory wondered whether it was anything to do with their unexpected and sudden arrival above the planet. However, they had appeared too quickly to have been the subject of such a lengthy emergency process which required preparation.

Just before crashing into the dome, to everyone's surprise they halted in mid air and hovered in a triangular formation. The traffic controllers were amazed by their swiftness and even thought they were being attacked by UFOs.

'This is Commander Colman from the USA, Earth, on a special practice mission. We request permission to land and have a drink with an old friend by the name of Captain David Anderson. He is one of your main flight instructors,' Mallory said.

'Who are you?' the operator asked again nervously and in disbelief. But Mallory didn't have to repeat himself a second time, as such information was always recorded. The operator soon regained his composure from the initial fright induced by the strange ships overhead and sent a call to Captain Anderson, known to all as Andy.

'Sorry, Sir, but we caught your trail back there and thought you were a cluster of UFOs. We have seen quite a few of them over the past decades. The miners call them God's observers.

'For your information, Captain Anderson says, if it's the one he and his crew used to call Hitchhiker Mal, to give him a wide berth.

'Anyway, you guys are beginning to scare the people down here, so if you can, please tune your guidance on the second beacon for dock two. Please wear your suits when you leave your ships. There are a few pressure leaks and most service robots are out of action,' he said.

'Hitchhiker Mal, eh,' Roseanne said and giggled.

'One day I shall tell you all about it,' he replied.

The five ships queued in line and followed the guidance beacon to land within one of the four docking areas of Caefon Dome. They entered the main reception area through two circular metallic doors of the pressurization chambers and were greeted by the dome's mayor and several other officials.

As Mallory lifted his space helmet, he was immediately recognised by his old friend Captain Anderson.

'Mal! Is that really you? You look even younger than when I knew you!' Anderson shouted.

'Andy, how are you? Long time no see!'

'I am even better for seeing you. Come and let me introduce you and your guys to the Mayor and some other important people. Then we can have a quiet chat about our present problem,' Andy said. He introduced Mallory to the officials and both went to one side for a chat, while Roseanne continued with the formalities.

'Mal, you have visited us on a very bad day. We have five trapped miners on Thor's Anvil. It's a medium size asteroid about two miles long, and shaped like a blacksmith's anvil. There was an explosion near the mouth of the main entry-well and the whole entrance has been blocked. Their mother-ship has detected faint signals from a region about a hundred metres from the well. That part is along one of the branch tunnels, but Mother-seven can do very little to assist because of the motion of the meteor. It spins like a top about an arbitrary axis once every thirty seconds. There are also a few loose rocks in the vicinity.'

'Wow! Seems quite serious?' Mallory was concerned.

'Even our best ships will take three days to make the trip and the miners have just enough oxygen for two more days. We've got to do something. Those particular miners are well known to us all and one happens to be our Mayor's son,' Andy said.

'I think we might be able to help. Where is the position of the asteroid now? Show me on a map,' Mallory said and Andy took him into one of their main operations room which was part of the docking facilities.

'It's just about here, between the orbit of Jupiter and ours. Mother ship will have the exact position coordinates.

'Noel, please contact Mother-seven for their coordinates,' he said to one of the operators who was in timed communication with the distant ship. From what Mallory could see the mother ship was about ten million miles away. That meant light would have taken about two minutes to cover the distance to and fro, so the communicator had to send a set of three replies and some-times several answers each time with options. Two for if the answer was either yes or no and one for, don't know. They could nest such questions and answers with the aid of the predictive computer.

Such transmissions could continue for the full period of the emergency and they made corrections from the information received, by more corrective feedback. It was a type of predictive communication that Mallory had never encountered before. Since they had no H-Wave technology it was one of the ways to overcome the time distance due to light speed. However, that method had improved to a fine art by space miners over the years.

'It will take our ships fifteen minutes to get there. How many are in danger?' Mallory said.

'There are just five. Mother-seven is now about three-hundred miles from their location. She hasn't made a decision to leave their present position. They are at their third drop-off point in the belt.

'For your information, several groups of miners are dropped-off at several mining points within that area of the belt and are collected again after several days, corresponding to the period of their shifts. All have communicators, but the portable surface dish was damaged by the explosion and is now covered with rubble. Joseph and his group also have hand communicators, but they are only for local communication and will not travel through the dense material of the asteroid.'

'I understand!' Mallory replied.

'See what you can do, Pal. They will be forever grateful to you and your team,' Andy said.

'I want a complete drawing of that asteroid, its rotation, mass and other relevant criteria. Then I want a close-up of the damage,' Mallory said as his group entered the room.

'Group, we have a rescue mission on our hands. This is all the data I have at present. Whatever we say, it's going to be highly risky. We can use our tractor beams to shift the boulders and rubble. That means we'll have to go on full inertia when we use the T-beams. If we don't have enough mass to compensate, we could be dragged unto the spinning meteor with disastrous consequences. This will be a good test of your skills. I shall lead the rescue and update you while on route,' he said to them through their implants. Then downloaded all available maps and information to their implants.

'Can I come along? I am familiar with the system and might have a few ideas of my own,' Andy said.

'If you don't mind sitting in the rear cabin. Some extra weight might come in handy when we use the tractor beams and we have space for another three passengers. Andy, we need three more volunteers!' Mallory said and Andy left the room and returned promptly with three more sturdy miners.

'You'll require suits to walk through the lower pressurized dock, and unfortunately, we have them in the ship,' Mallory said.

'Don't you worry about them? These are Martians through and through, with zero Earth status and are used to working with low oxygen and corresponding pressure levels. They never visited Earth for the birth registration formalities. Anyway, the pressure in the dock is about half normal, with close to one-third oxygen. They can handle that environment for days with oxy-pills,' Andy said.

'In that case, please follow us,' Mallory said.

When they entered the ship, Andy could not believe his eyes. There were no controls of any kind, just a large screen with many moving images that he could not even recognise. It was a new type of technology that he and his friends had never seen or heard of before. He remained with them for a while, observing every detail until their restraining harnesses automatically clamped their bodies into the seat. It was then that Andy went to join his companions at the rear.

The ships lifted off and flew in the direction of Jupiter. Their scanners and reflective shields were fully on as they followed one of the safer mining routes to that part of the Asteroid Belt. If there were any particles, the leading ship would have taken the flak. The ships decelerated as they approached the mother ship and Mallory transmitted a signal to say he was part of the rescue from Mars.

It took them just over fifteen minutes to arrive at the rescue sight. Even Andy could not believe that they had made such a long trip in that time, with zero inertia effects from extreme changes in velocity.

Ebony and Carl's ships were selected to take on the wounded miners, and Roseanne was to see to their wounds, if any. That was assuming their suits had not been punctured by the debris from the explosion.

Mallory's idea was for all the ships to match the peculiar motion of Thor's Anvil. He was the only one that would use the tractor beam to try and lift the material blocking the entrance of the well. Once the boulders were away from the surface of the meteor the others would blast the large particles with plasma beams set to automatic targeting.

However, Ebony would use her lasers for freeing areas of rock to release the larger boulders during the lifting process. The whole operation had to be precisely timed and accurately targeted.

When the well was cleared, Mallory and Andy could enter and make their way to the stranded miners, who it was hoped would be waiting at the forward tunnel some hundred metres or so from one of the well's entrance.

Many thought the explosion was due to a rogue explosive device that had been accidentally left behind during previous prospecting. However, those miners knew their business well. They also followed procedures that made sure such accidents were uncommon. That was the reason why others thought it was due to sabotage. It was then that they decided to pass the blame onto one of the miners called Joseph. Since they had heard of the Terminal Disease there was much unrest in a highly religious society and Joseph had a reputation for being a playboy.


'Ebony, if I fail to lift the largest rock, you will have to release your inertia suppression and assist me with your tractor beam,' Mallory said.

'Yes, Commander. I am ready!'

'Get ready. I shall target the right peak first. Use your lasers to cut around that area while I increase pull and try to release it.'

'On it!'

'Carl and sniper ships, adjust plasma beams to medium nozzle and get ready to blast rock!' Mallory shouted.

'Ready and waiting, Commander!' came the reply. Mallory released his inertia suppressor and instantly matched the rotational dynamics of the Anvil, to target the large rock fragment with the intensely concentrated beam of gravity. The net effect was to bring both bodies together and the lighter one tended to move more energetically through the weightless environment of space towards the larger one. However, as a safety precaution, the strength of the beam was set to the equivalent mass of the ship and could be monitored and adjusted during the lifting process.

He transmitted the pulsating G-beam to the rock, while the ship compensated for small changes in rotation. Many of the smaller boulders shot upwards towards his ship as he immediately released the beam and moved away from their trajectory just before possible collision. The snipers had them in their sights and they were soon scanned and blasted into dust.

The main fragment was still in place and probably weighed as much as ten tons while unstuck. He tried again and again, lifting more of the smaller fragments into space, until only the three main ones were left remaining. Those three were firmly wedged into each other.

The explosive device must have been placed just below the overhang at the mouth of the well and triggered a rock slide from above. However, if that was the case there would be much more debris at the bottom of the well, even after those rocks had been cleared.

Ebony had enough of the delay and dived towards that main fragment of rock, chipping away at its surface with her lasers and slicing large chunks off, while Mallory did the lifting. The process was slow and dangerous, but the larger fragment was beginning to shift, which could allow the other two similar fragments to fall into the well and create even a worse blockage.

Ebony had to use her G-beams to assist Mallory to lift all three into space at once. The computer did their calculations and both beams optimised for mutual pull. Then they were slowly lifted away from the anvil and placed into a local crater.

'Commander, I think I've got the knack of the G-field generator. I can now match the forces pound for pound,' Ebony said.

'The field needs precise control in intensity and positioning for accurate manoeuvring of the objects being lifted, and it takes a little while getting it write in your implants,' he replied.

The inner well was still blocked by debris which prevented access to the miners. Tractors could not be properly aligned in such close proximity to the inside of the well. The beam would have been deflected by matter all around that area of the well, which was about fifty feet deep.

'We could use our plasma beams to melt the loose debris. Such material should take up less volume in molten form and be lifted away from the entrances,' Ebony said.

'It might work, but if it doesn't, we'll have to wait a while before it cools and it would then be impossible to shift. There could also be thermal blowback towards the miners. We need another option.... If only my ship could fit inside the well.'

'Get a fix on the diameter of that well,' he said to Ebony who responded immediately.

'Three and a half metres, Commander. Just half a metre to spare and it might taper to a point inwards. It will be a close thing Commander and you will need very precise matching of your motion with that of the meteor. I shall be fifty feet above you, in case you get stuck,' she said.

'Thanks for the overwhelming vote of confidence,' he replied.

Mallory maintained his position close to the well while the

computer rotated his ship until it was pointing directly into the black well. During that operation it had to precisely match the rotation of the Anvil. Then the powerful search lights came on and the ship slowly entered the black and dusty hole.

'If we get stuck, you might have to use two tractors to get us out. Here we go,' Mallory said.

As they had assumed, the well did taper inwards, but so did the front section of the ship. Their ship had gotten as close as twenty feet from the pile of debris. Mallory adjusted his G-beam to half the width of the diameter of that part of the well. He switched on to grab and began to move the ship away from the debris, lifting most of it out of the way and into space to be vaporised by his colleagues.

Three of the ships settled down on the anvil and Mallory, Carl, Roseanne and Andy floated down the well. They found the miners all crouched together in a narrow area of the tunnel in constant prayer. Those miners were well trained in the use of their oxygen supplies and had adjusted to the bare minimum survivable requirements in the hope of a rescue.

One sluggishly got to his feet to greet the strangers, who he realised were not miners, but stretched out his arm none the less. Words were said, but nothing was heard through the nonexistent atmosphere of the asteroid. Roseanne came forward to shake them to their feet and check them over, but they were all in good health.

The explosion had occurred when they had entered the mouth of the tunnel. Obviously timed to go off when they were safely away from the well. However, it would have been a real disaster if the Specials hadn't arrived on Mars to assist in the rescue.

They were escorted to the well and used the tractor beam to lift them gently along a line. All of their equipment was left behind to be recovered later by the mother ship.

The miners wore heavy mining suits with two large oxygen tanks on their backs. Everything about those miners and their equipment, even their mother ship, was antiquated. Mallory wondered how it was possible for those miners to land on such a rotating body, with such antiquated equipment. Yet they were hardened miners with many tricks up their sleeves.

Several of the members of their parent company on Earth were in financial difficulty and that aspect reflected in their holdings on Mars, which still relied heavily on outmoded equipment.

They were just able to squeeze through the small cabin door to the rear of the ships and were unable to fasten into their seats, so the seats were adjusted into beds and they rested horizontally on route. That position also distributed their heavier masses more evenly in the artificial gravity of the ship.

Those poor miners carried close to a ton of equipment on their persons and that was excluding the bulky semi automatic cutting and drilling tools. Luckily, they worked under near weightless conditions in space.

'All the men have been rescued and appear ok.' Roseanne advised.

'A job well done! We fly past Mother-seven to signal everything is ok and head for the red planet,' Mallory said.

He immediately transmitted a signal to Mars through their electro-magnetics. They could have used H-wave, but that form of instant communication was unknown to Earth and Martian technology and could only have been used between their own ships and Solarian bases.

'Our rescue mission has been successful. Prepare to receive five healthy but shocked miners in fifteen minutes,' he said, as they dived towards that part of space.

CHAPTER 40

# Martian celebrations

This time they landed in Dock 1, which was at the highest level of the dome and closer to their hospital. The five miners were stripped of their heavy suits and rushed to the observation bay, while assisted by many of the specials. Although in slight shock from their ordeal, they were young and in the peak of health.

Roseanne removed a small device from her first-aid kit and scanned each in turn. She simply removed their clothes from the waist upwards and pointed the device in the direction of the patient's chest. As if by a miracle, it displayed every parameter, including lung capacity, blood pressure, infections, vitamin deficiencies and arrange of other parameters, including when they had their last meal. She pressed another button on the hand-held device and read out a list of possible cures.

'John is a mild diabetic, but all the others, although slightly anaemic, appear ok,' she said and handed small printouts to their doctor, including prescriptions.

They embraced the Specials, most of whom were giant women and wondered whether they were from Earth; for they had never seen the likes of their technologies before.

The dome had also been informed of the successful rescue by them from the mother ship and had already begun to prepare a large celebration for the visitors.

The Mayor and two of his senior officials formed the welcoming procession that patiently waited outside the hospital until the five miners were given a full bill of health. Then the miners and their rescuers joined the procession amidst much joy and cheer. Finally, they made their way towards the main civic building which was also at that level of the dome. They were soon taken away to the more pleasant reception area within that building.

'Cheers everyone to our incredible rescuers from Earth with their magnificent vessels,' the Mayor shouted and the crowd lifted Mallory and others of his group above the crowd. They had no choice but to proceed with the noise and confusion.

Suddenly it was night on that part of Mars and the lights of the domes came on, showing that part of the planet as a small lighted diamond within an almost dormant landscape. It was sometimes even visible from earth through powerful telescopes.

Caefon Dome was built in one of the largest meteoric craters, and was over a decade old, having been constructed to last tens of such decades. Its many shopping and entertainment arcades mimicked Earth's in every detail, with several churches on each of its three uppermost levels for its many Baptist denominations. Because of the way it was constructed, several more floors could be added beneath the dome with the numerous robotic diggers and tunnellers they had at their disposal.

At ground level was a minor lake surrounded by a small forest. The lake was the main depository for all affluence from the dome, with automated sewage filtration and purifiers. The process was further assisted by certain genetically engineered grassy plants and bacteria during filtration. Finally the pure water was pumped into holding tanks. Most of their reclaimed water was retrieved from certain areas of the Martian surface by mobile drills.

The residue or manure was formed into pellets and deposited through the small enclosed forest of fruit and vegetable trees by conveyors. The complete bio-system of the dome was self-sustaining. However, the area of the park and lake stank, and for that reason were sealed off from the main areas.

Unlike Sol-Newtown, there were no robots to repair its outer surface. However, due to the less chemically active atmosphere, there were virtually no corrosion of external metals. There was even less from severe sandstorms which had not occurred in that part of the planet since the dome was built.

Internal transport was via LPD trains on each level, aided by elevators and escalators. The dome was not the most peaceful of environments, as all sounds tended to reverberate across its transparent circular walls.

Mallory was called to the auditorium to give a short speech, accompanied by Roseanne who followed him to the rostrum. The Mayor was the first to congratulate them on behalf of his people.

'Commander Colman, and his special force should be congratulated by all of us, for saving the lives of five of our dearest
friends and most experienced miners, including my own son. By
providence, he and his Specials visited our world at a most
opportune time, with ships faster than anything we have ever
seen. I dread to think of the alternatives, if they were not around
or able to assist in such a tricky and dangerous rescue operation.'
The crowd cheered.

'Many of you have seen Thor's Anvil and the rescue as it was
relayed to us from Mother-seven, and know of the difficulties
faced. Because they risked their own lives to save some of ours,
I hereby make them permanent members of Caefon Dome.
Therefore, I am to give them each one of our golden medallions.
It is the symbol of our Order of Miners and bestows on them the
status of interplanetary miners.' The crowd cheered again,
showing their overwhelming gratitude.

'Without any further ado, I would like Commander Colman to
come forward to collect our medals of appreciation and perhaps
say a few words of his own to us, in view of his kind assistance
during our time of need,' The mayor said and Mallory got up and
walked to the rostrum to collect the medals.

'Mister Mayor, good people of Caefon Dome, my wife Roseanne and fellow officers. We came to Mars with the sole intention
of practising a few intricate exercises and manoeuvres with our
new ships. We also intended to visit an old friend in this dome,
but had never expected or planned for a rescue mission of such
complexity. Luckily, we had a range of special devices on board
that helped us to accomplish the task well within the time limits
allowed.

'Having observed your accident log, many of you are always at
great risk as space miners. You do your labours in a much more
hostile environment than below the surface of large planets such
like Earth. In light of those problems and my newly acquired
membership of your esteemed order of miners, I have decided to
place our Specials at your disposal for all such difficult and life
threatening rescues. However, I must stress, only life-threatening
situations, please. You may then contact us directly at our main
base on Earth. Further, should you require any advice, assistance,

or political representation on Earth, please inform us of your requirements. Our organization has links with the President of the United States of America and carries much clout, even with the UN.' They were ecstatic by that knowledge and could not stop cheering, so he placed his arms out and they were silenced.

'I must once again, on behalf of my colleagues here and our organization on Earth, thank you at the bottom of my heart, for the great honour of accepting us as members of your community,' Mallory said and left the rostrum with the ten medals. However, as the Mayor got up once more to continue his speech there was a disturbance close to the main entrance of the auditorium, as three strapping miners entered holding a younger miner in his early twenties.

'This is the bastard that laid the explosives!' shouted one of the three.

'We should string him up here and now in public, to teach others with similar notions a lesson,' shouted another.

'Arrest that man for his own safety!' the mayor yelled above the crowd and several police surrounded him and took the fellow away, leaving his three captors arguing among themselves for not having taken more drastic action sooner. This was because the young man had pleaded guilty to the crime. They were also the fathers of four of the rescued miners.

'We shall hold an enquiry tomorrow at eleven a.m., Martian time. During that enquiry all the evidence will be brought forward and charges made. Then the prisoner will be questioned,' the mayor said, with an air of authority and fairness.

'He has already confessed to the crime, your honour,' said one of the three miners.

'In that case, he will state them publicly and not under duress. Then a suitable sentence may be passed,' the mayor replied.

After the commotion was over Andy took Mallory and his colleagues to his apartment on the second level of the dome. They were to meet his wife while the girls took three trolleys and went to collect food and drink from the other ships.

'Mal, here is my wife, Alex,' Andy said and introduced Mallory, Roseanne and his companions to his wife.

'How is my godson, Andy? I haven't seen him since he was a little nipper,' Andy said.

'He is still in DC with his mum. He is now in college and doing well,' Mallory replied.

'You know, Mal. I never expected you to look so young. It's like you stopped aging years ago. I would like to know the special diet you are on. If that's what it is,' Andy said and Mallory smiled.

'You don't seem to look much older yourself, Pal. That's what a happy marriage does for a man,' he replied, evasively.

'Some say the lower gravity of Mars reduces the aging process by 20 percent, but there is no real evidence to prove that theory. However, our oldest population has only lived on Mars for about thirty years, with frequent trips to Earth,' Andy said.

'What will they do to the chap that planted the explosives?' Mallory asked.

'He was the brother of one of the young girls chased by Joseph, and they are highly opposed to sex before marriage in these parts. This is not modern USA you know. Here, everyone has to obey strict rules of brotherhood, morality and conscience if we are to survive. If you ask me, Joseph was asking for it. If anything, he should be the one that was arrested, and many would see it that way; so I suppose the lad will be given a severe reprimand and prevented from mining for a couple of years or so. Probably, sent to work in the sewage farm for the duration, which I won't recommend to anyone.

'If there is further trouble, Joseph will be banished to Earth for good,' Andy said.

'As drastic as that!' Roseanne commented with sarcasm, not realizing Martians considered their beautiful home planet to be a type of prison.

'Roseanne, with these people here it's a cultural thing. To most miners, Earth is the most ungodly planet in the whole of the universe,' Andy replied and she probably agreed.

It took Ebony a little while to get used to the lower gravity of Mars, while wielding the trolleys to the elevator and down to Andy's apartment.

'The Mayor wants us all to visit his place at eight for dinner. Then I would like you all to spend the night here, with us in this apartment. It will be a little cramped, but we have lots of blankets and three rooms,' Andy said and Mallory transmitted a thought to his group, asking them if they wanted to spend the night and they said yes.

'We will be pleased to stay the night, but we must leave first thing tomorrow,' he said. Mallory then handed each of his group their medallions and they accepted them proudly.

They were dressed in their travelling suits for the Mayors dinner and decided to walk the distance to his apartment. That was preferred to waiting for the old LPD tram-cars which were quite intermittent in their arrivals and departures. They took with them several bottles of vodka and cans of food for the Mayor.

The following morning they were up at dawn and had breakfast together before preparing for their departure. Andy had already told his colleagues at the dock and another assembly of miners were waiting to see them off.

It took them just over an hour to return to Earth and another fifteen minutes through its dense and sometimes cloudy atmosphere. But they were in no great hurry, since most of their training had been accomplished.

CHAPTER 41

# The President's visit to Warland

*'Many New York parents and citizens have been shocked by the recent increase in child snatching. Some children are being stolen from their parent's arms in broad daylight and in sight of bystanders. The gang or gangs involved use large crowds as cover and threaten their victims with machine guns. They take the children to one of several nearby cars for a quick getaway.*

*Over the past week alone, there has been over a thousand such cases and the situation is worsening, with little help from an already stretched police force. Mayor Conwallice's office has been picketed during the whole of last week by frightened parents, but he says the city just haven't the extra funds and resources to expand the present campaign to all areas. He advised parents with young children to be extra vigilant and ensure they are kept out of crowded areas of the city...'* Roseanne read the discomforting article in the local newspaper as the phone rang.

'I wish we had our Green Chameleon back to lose a few heads,' she muttered.

'One moment please! Darling, it's for you!' she shouted and Mallory linked through his implants. He had a special line coupler that was connected to the Macron for handling such calls telepathically.

'Clair! Good you have called,' he said to Clair, the owner of one of the legal prostitution hotels he visited earlier. She had decided to become one of his spies on criminal customers.

'I have been trying to contact you since yesterday evening and didn't bother to leave a message on your machine. I have decided to accept your deal and have some information for you. I left it in one of the boxes. You better take these numbers and addresses down. They are for the boxes. Please use number one for my notes to you. I must go now,' she said nervously, as she recited the information and hung up. He went over the drinks cabinet and poured them both a glass of lemonade topped with a little rum.

'Love, she is in charge of one of the largest pleasure hotels in Miami, where most of the criminals visit to let off steam. I think I have recruited her as our second inside spy. She is an important part of the child snatching ring and might give us the inside information we need before we take them out,' he said.

'I have just been reading about it and that type of crime seems to be on the increase. You must be very careful, Darling, they are very dangerous people,' Roseanne said.

'Love, they may be good, but they haven't our brand of technology or realistic disguises,' he replied.

'Pity our Green Chameleon phantom is not around these days to take care of those nasty criminals!'

'Yes, pity! I think he is now on more important business to save our world, so this crisis we are to solve on our own!' Mallory stressed.

Mallory did visit the safety deposit box that same day and received several photographs of criminals involved in the paedo-smuggling ring. However, he now had to put together a planned operation to neutralize their evil efforts. Since they had to prepare for the President's visit, it was not the best time to take them on. Therefore he decided to ignore that problem for now and concentrate on the preparatory work before the President's arrival. That important operation would consume their efforts for the next few days.

After dinner that day Mallory called his Specials together.

'My Specials! May I take this opportunity to congratulate you on your impressive skills during our most intricate Martian operations and thank you on behalf of the organization for an operation well done?'

'No problemo!' Ebony said and the others nodded in agreement.

'I have decided for us all to take a holiday tomorrow, so you may visit your families if you wish. Use Oscar if you need special transport for the day. He will also enjoy the experience with you in tour.'

'Oscar! Sounds fantastic!' Tracy interjected.

'It's the car!' Ebony corrected and Tracy appeared disappointed.

'From the day after, we assist Chad at the base to get the troops shipshape and perhaps plan a tournament in addition to the parade and aero-display. I was thinking of a real dogfight. It could probably be arranged with three of you against another three using the small LPD's on your armoured suits. That way you can fly about the base with plasma projectors set to minimum. With all your recent experience, you should now be able to use your implants to control those weapons and suits automatically, so we should be able to stage some real entertainment for the President and his crew. The base Macron can be your backup and take over in case of any problems. Anyway, think about it and let me know what you plan day after tomorrow.'

'Will do!' Ebony said.

'Anyway, I think the President will be more impressed by such a performance, so if you decide you must try and give it your best shot.'

'We shall! We have thought about it and the answer is yes!' Ebony interjected.

'Then that's settled! If you do decide to visit your family and friends, you must walk tall and look proud in your uniforms. I want everyone including Mr Public to be proud and respectful of us, Specials, and we must also set an example. They must look up to us as a symbol of order and strength in a period of uncertainty and insecurity. Further, if any of you or your families happen to be in any type of trouble, we are all in it together, so please ask for help and we shall tackle the problem together.'

'Thanks Commander!' Anne interjected.

'I recently received your new accounts, which are held with Solarian Banking for obvious reasons. These are your relevant account numbers,' Mallory said and transmitted the private numbers to each in turn.'

'Money! Glorious money!' Tracy said.

'You can draw funds through any bank and most large organizations and stores have direct links with our bank. Any questions?' he added and Ebony placed her hand up.

'Commander, we would like to have a party and invite a few old friends,' she said.

'Ladies, if you want a party you will have one. From what I've been told, the new building's conservatory has recently been completed. Why don't you check over the ground floor and see which rooms may be used?' he said.

The following evening the women had a most exciting party that took them most of the day to organize. On that occasion most of the senior officers were invited.


When they arrived at Warland the main yard was filled with columns of troops marching and training for the President's arrival. They were all dressed in the blue uniforms of the recruits which had their buttons and braiding arranged in the same manner as the black suits of the specials.

'At ease!' Chad commanded and they dropped their automatic rifles. The small ships hovered above their heads for a while, six glistening silver specks in the early morning sun. They made a few complex loops at several times the speed of sound to make their presence felt and landed in one end of the field.

As the doors lifted vertically, Carl, Mallory and the eight women left the ships and walked towards Chad and the recruits. They saluted him and he saluted in return. The recruits were subsequently dismissed and couldn't hold from cheering the visitors and their superior flying skills.

'Now, you have over five thousand fans. Very soon they will be sticking your photos on the heads of their bunks,' Chad said in a happy frame of mind.

'Sorry, Pal, we have not been around for the past few days, we had to visit Mars and do some training of our own in a less hazardous environment. However, as you have seen, we are now ace flyers and fighters, so we have decided to assist you for the remaining period,' Mallory said.

'I see what you mean. I just hope you don't scare the President and his band of merry men away by your keen efforts,' he said, while staring at Ebony and the other Amazonian women. They were wearing their plasma projectors and other utilities on broad belts. Those women stood in a solid queue and appeared invincible.


The president arrived in one of those large black LPD limousines and his entourage in another, and both landed on the large platform that was prepared for the occasion. Their flight to the base was controlled by the local Macron for security reasons.

When he got out of the large car, he was greeted by Mallory, Chad, Carl and Roseanne, who stood in line close to the stairs. The president's company also included his wife, three senators, three senior officers from the three main branches of the military and other senior officials and advisors. They were taken towards the main building and shown the different utilities and facilities of the base.

'I must say, Mallory, it's quite an achievement for any private venture these days. I wish our people had such training facilities in our most modern bases,' the President said.

'We are financed by Solarian Banking, Sir, and most of our equipment are designed and manufactured by our people and androids in Sol-Newtown Dome and elsewhere,' he replied.

'Did you know that Sol-Newtown is outside of our jurisdiction? It's to do with a treaty we signed with the President of Solarian Banking several years ago. Jerry knew all about it, God bless his soul. Since then, all their major buildings were to be considered embassies,' he said.

Mallory then took them to the main armoury and acquainted them with his stocks of weapons. Finally, they were taken out to see the parade and inspect the recruits. There were about five thousand arrayed in the main parade grounds.

When they were finished, they were taken to a small sheltered pavilion where refreshments and seats were in waiting. Here they would witness the main events.

Suddenly there were several sonic booms as three small ships of unknown origin darted towards the pavilion several times faster than the speed of sound. They were followed closely by three more, firing what looked like ray guns. The President and his group could not believe their eyes. The three ships did three spirals at enormous speed and the other three travelled through the spirals they made with the disturbed and ionised air above forming circular wisps of mist.

As if by magic, they disappeared from their predicted positions, to be followed by more sonic booms. Suddenly they thundered towards the pavilion from six different angles and stopped in mid air just before they crashed into each other, leaving the President and his group even more astonished and slightly shaken by the ordeal. There they remained in mid air, as one huge ship of six separate parts, moving and rotating as one solid object. Then they broke away and the dogfight began again, yet no one won any direct hits. Their ships were too swift and their pilots quick and evasive.

The ships landed in two different parts of the grounds, and their warriors left to wage war against each other, three to three. Ebony took her position in the centre between both ships, while Nadia blasted her with a small machine gun. She delivered twenty rounds per second. Ebony stood her ground while the bullets melted against her pulsating armour and fell to the ground at her feet.

The president was impressed, suddenly realising that it was not an invasion from outer space, but instead, to do with the planned show. Ebony's suit flared into activity as her miniature LPDs came to life and her body became mobile vertically through the air. She darted upwards and alighted on one of the taller trees for shelter, catching Nadia with a plasma beam and throwing her off balance.

The battle went on for a good fifteen minutes as the women fought on land and in the air. It continued until they descended towards several dummies, taking them all out during the descent. Then six small land-rovers that stood in their way were vaporized from their path. Then they floated several feet above the ground and began to move that way towards the pavilion, while being cheered by Mallory, the President and others.

'What an impressive performance, Mallory? I saw it but I couldn't believe such technology was possible except in comic books,' the President said.

'At ease, Specials! You may come forward to greet our President!' he shouted and they walked towards the small pavilion.

'You must tell me the name of your weapons supplier. They are truly invincible Amazonians,' said one of the military chiefs.

'If women can fight like that, I would like to know how our best men will fare,' a male official said. Then Mallory got up to say a few words.

'*Mister President, may I take this opportunity to thank you and your distinguished company for taking time off from your busy schedules to honour us with this visit.*

'*You have seen the capabilities of our Specials and know of our intentions to maintain peace and order, but most importantly, we are a rescue organization. Nominated by all to rescue lost children and those that are beyond the help of the other organizations, including our main services like the police.*

'*As Specials, we are committed to the security and safety of all Fertilate families throughout the solar system. So to many, we shall be known as the first real army of the Solar System. Because of the enormous tasks we have set ourselves, we shall also have to become the best in all things, for we must be respected as well as feared.*

'*Within our organization there are no males or females, just fighters for the future survival of our species, those that are endangered and of our still beautiful world...*' Mallory said and when he completed his speech thousands of hands clapped. Even the President and his group stood up to cheer.

They knew that the survival of their families were dependant on Mallory's independent organization and from what they had seen, that organization was not an easy one to defeat and had earned their trust.

CHAPTER 42

# Chasing criminals

When Mallory visited Clair's safety deposit box in Miami again, he received another envelope with several more photographs and a note. The photos were those of women criminals and one of a wealthy man outside his stately home with three of his little children. He gave the impression of a loving father, and Mallory assumed his family knew very little, if anything about his illegitimate operations. Mallory took the note and began to read its contents.

*'These women are couriers that carry kids over to Europe and Asia on false papers. The innocent looking gent is the big boss himself. You wouldn't believe it, would you? He is a Texan. His family used to be very big in oil at the turn of the century, until the wells dried and they missed out on LPD concessions. He moved into his new line of business about ten years ago, having become successful in gambling, porno and other crimes of a less violent nature. Despite appearances, he is no saint and has an army of hoods and bouncers that will do virtually anything for a price. He is now a powerful man with many strings in high politics, so be extra careful,'* the note read.

Mallory stored the data in his implant, including the photos and discarded the information in much the same way as he had done on previous occasions.

He had reprogrammed the Macron to assist in his criminal surveillance and investigations, aided by Oscar, and was now once again becoming the enthusiastic sleuth and hunter that was his second nature. He had been away from the job he liked most for a while and missed the exhilaration of the chase, the stalking and finally the kill. Now he also had several trained and hardened fighters to assist him in that most important of all operations, namely; the destruction of those who wanted his life and caused misery to so many innocent families, by stealing their little loved ones.

'Oscar, I think Michael Cockburn and his guys have given up

the chase,' he said.

'I've been checking and we've not been followed since we began these checks. He must have been satisfied with Lord Khan's explanation,' Oscar replied.

'What do you mean by calling Professor Khan (Ben) by the "Lord" term?' Mallory inquired.

'I thought you knew, Mal. He was recently made a Lord by the Grand Council. It was for all his enduring efforts in saving our world,' Oscar said and Mallory was surprised.

'So we can't call him Ben anymore!' Mallory was disappointed.

The Macron computer had linked into the main government computers including the one used by the UN, clandestinely. Therefore, he now had lists of the worst dictators and largest gangs on the planet including the Texan millionaire and his political associates. At least, those he frequently met in the course of a year. His name was Tex Nolan of Nolan Enterprises and most of his legitimate businesses were covers for those of lesser legitimacy and money laundering.

Mallory had purchased the latex company that manufactured the face masks and had their type patented to prevent criminals getting their hands on such unique disguises. As a scientist, he had also given them some good ideas for improving the original designs. He also realized such disguises could be used by Fertilate families in the future, particularly when visiting dangerous areas of cities. Such masks could change a young person into someone several times their age to avoid attention.

The later samples were almost indistinguishable from human flesh and showed better facial movement. However, they still had the problem of itching when the mask was kept on for long periods of time in hot and humid weather.

A special powder and associated cream was soon devised for relieving those irritating conditions and was to be applied to the face before the mask was fitted. However, it was intended to use more porous and absorbent materials in future designs. Soon those masks would be available to every special and young

Fertilates who had to visit certain areas of the city that were controlled by Infilates, but hopefully, they wouldn't be needed for several years.

   Later that evening, Mallory called his Specials together. They met in one of the new rooms at the rear of his house for further discussions.
   'I received a letter from the President this morning. He thinks our outfit is the best in the nation and would like me to personally convey his thanks to you all for putting on such an incredible show. Chad has also incorporated our new program for training the most advanced recruits.'
   'That's nice to know, Commander!' Ebony interjected.
   'Now we come to the part that concerns our own future program. Tomorrow you begin your surveillance training. We are to catch and neutralize some criminals as soon as possible. The process will teach us a few lessons and sharpen your investigative techniques and analysis skills.'
   'More brain training,' Joan commented.
   'I suppose most of it is already in our brain implants?' Ebony inquired.

   The following day they split into two teams. Carl, Ebony and Tracy left for Kennedy Airport, while Mallory and the others visited the busiest streets of New York to observe their enemy's territory. Roseanne and Carl's girlfriend remained at home to mind the operations headquarters.
   Wherever possible they would relay important visual information through their implants to local boosters which were usually sited at the top of Solarian Banks. They used Satellite Eta and Gimbal for further boosting and global coverage. Those could further relay important information to Oscar and their War Macron, for Roseanne and others to analyse.
   Carl and the two women were wearing disguises and stood near the counters to observe those single passengers with babies and small unhappy children. They took their surveillance efforts patiently and in turn, until Carl decided to check over the whole airport while the two women were left to view the passengers.

It was almost lunchtime and close to the departure of a European flight when they observed a suitable couple. Despite heavy makeup, the woman was recognised almost immediately by Ebony, who was at the time sipping a cool drink with Tracy.

'Well! I never? Who do you think is the one in the blue at the counter with the little kid?' Ebony said, while carefully observing the woman.

'She looks like the second picture in my implant, but with lots of makeup and she is already on her way to the boarding section for the flight to London,' Tracy replied.

'Don't worry! Our facial recognition system will find her later.' Carl said.

'Pity we can't do anything about the kid here and now. Boss doesn't want them disturbed in any way. I only wish they could have been followed and arrested at the other end. At least one poor family could have been saved a lot of unhappiness and misery,' Ebony replied.

'I suppose they have been doing the same thing for months, with a range of forged passports for each one of their disguises. It would be useful to know their different disguises and overseas contacts?' Tracy said.

'Boss is working on contacts in UK Customs and elsewhere with the help of the President, but it might take a few weeks before we have freedom in those ports. Meanwhile, we learn as much of their operation as we can and try not to do anything that might arouse their suspicions. We are also to learn the complete layout of this port in case we have to move quickly against them and there are also four more important airports like this one,' Ebony replied.

'I think our Macron, Tron, uses our eyes through the implants to check this place in its entirety, so we'll be informed of any changes, immediately,'Tracy said.


Carl and the two women spent the whole of that day in Kennedy Airport while the others under Mallory's guidance followed the busiest areas of New York City.

By the end of that day the Macron was programmed with lots of information on the areas they visited but little on the gang members.

After dinner that day Mallory called them together again for a discussion on progress.

'*The work is tedious but necessary if we are to penetrate their operations and find the kink in their armour, their weakness and strengths. However, this is phase one of our operations. During this phase, we observe and learn like ordinary civilians.*

'*Before we can even begin to fight back, we have to link with our operatives in Europe, or their complete operation will retreat underground only to pop up elsewhere again with greater vigour.*

'*From information received, we have learnt that the gang operates a fleet of old cars that are registered in legitimate names. From computer reports, most of the names belong to missing people and some of the cars are frequently stolen and sometimes end up in crushers or set on fire to cover up evidence. So that end is virtually untraceable. It is also implied that they operate many safe-houses in New York, including hotels, old abandoned buildings and nurseries. They use those for holding the children for short periods before their journey is arranged. We need a list of such places.*

'*New York is also the stop-off point for most of the other states including California, so it's the city where we must concentrate all our efforts for now. Then, there is the other route across the Canadian border. They must also involve qualified nurses and doctors to supply the necessary drugs. So that's another stone to be unturned.*

'*Their so-called transit parents are few, for safety reasons and they are very professional in their disguises and methods, with knowledge of several languages and the immigration system. They must also have a range of safe-houses in Canada and England, where they can get new documents for their trip back home.*

'*They obviously leave nothing to chance, and must be capable of choosing any of those places at a moment's notice. From computer analysis of their clothes, we are now certain that they carry small non-metallic calibre weapons. Those can be hidden in the soles of their shoes, which will not be easily detected by scanners. They could also be using micro-bombs or small plastic explosive bombs disguised as powder compacts and such like, so beware... you are dealing with a nest of vipers,'* Mallory said.

Their surveillance of the gang continued for another two weeks, during which time Mallory listed most of the components of the gang and their hideouts. They also received much invaluable information from Clair. She had planted bugs in all of the girls rooms that were radio-linked to a range of recorders in the basement of the building.

However, Mallory had always realised Clair's girls to be the week link in that chain. He just hoped her clandestine operation would not be detected until his surveillance work was completed. What if one of the girls were affiliated with the gang from the start? But that was a risk worth taking to crack the ring of misery and so he thought.

Mallory had also noted the frequent visits of a male member of the gang. He was one of their trouble shooters and kept reputation as a bouncer, but coercive soldier was a more appropriate description. His name was Marrio Carillo, nicknamed Spaghetti Man by his associates because of his liking for pasta in its many forms. He had also taken a liking to one of her new girls. One Molly Bennet from New York. She was a lovely brunette in her late twenties. Mallory soon warned Clair of their close associations and meetings and she took note.

Soon after the airports were checked and the gang's routines noted, Carl and his girlfriend were sent to London, England, as an advisor to Scotland Yard. They were also intent on cracking the gang and there was also growing unrest in that part of the world.

Having read several of Mallory's articles on the Infilate problem, they thought his advice would be invaluable to their own operations. Mallory also wrote several letters to Presidents, Prime Ministers and high ranking officials, pointing out future problems if early plans were not set in motion.

On his arrival, Carl began the European Recruitment Agency and an advertising campaign was initiated to train European Specials. The situation in Europe was at least two years in advance of America and was worsening on a weekly basis. Violence was now a way of life with many warring factions. The Infilate problem had now begun and Fertilate families were being molested and abused in public. However, Mallory could not send any of his troops over until he had diplomatic clearance from the authorities. Nevertheless, many travelled under the cover of essential Solarian Banking employees to assist in secret.

CHAPTER 43

# Marrio - Spaghetti Man

Marrio's presence at the hotel made Clair quite nervous. Although she hadn't involved Molly in her small group of spies, there was always a slight chance that Molly may have overheard or even found something to arouse her suspicions. She could also have been one of Marrio's plants that was placed there to spy on their opposition. Since there was no honour among those criminals, they would go to most lengths to remove any of their competition and in the process leave behind a most gory message.

Although the hotel was mostly owned by Clair, several local companies had smaller stakes in it's gambling and she wondered whether anyone of those companies belonged by proxy to the wealthy Texan. Nevertheless, she knew all of her partners well and they were contented in the way she ran the hotel and most of all its yearly profits.

Molly had only been with the hotel for three months. That was two months before Marrio began his regular visits. When Mallory observed the liaison, he immediately informed Clair of the problem. At that time he did not wish to arouse the couple's suspicions by installing one of his operatives at the hotel. Nevertheless he advised Clair to halt all spying activities until she was given the all-clear. Anyway, Mallory now had most of the information he required on the gang and was concentrating his efforts on Europe, which was the tail-end of their current operations.

Clair had written a letter to Marcus Darling regarding the use of her hotel for the purpose of paedo-smuggling. He was the one that paid her for the stolen children she sheltered while in transit. She informed him of her intention to discontinue that side of her business because of frequent visits from the local police and other law-enforcement officers.

The letter was written convincingly and Marcus was furious. Any such changes to his well established links would be of much inconvenience at a time of flourishing business and such secure places were quite difficult to find at short notice. He soon had words with his boss, who had more words with his hatchet man, Marrio.

'One way or another, you make sure she tours the line or take her completely out of the picture. I want this matter resolved!' Tex barked.

'Yes, Boss! It's going to be a piece of cake!' he replied.

Marrio was to lean on Clair and use whatever means necessary to win her over. If that course was too difficult, he was to kill her and figure out a way to buy or take over the hotel.


'The boss is not very pleased with you breaking one of our important links, not to mention our previous agreement. You know you are in a unique position here for the tourist trade. So many little kids from all over the place are passing through, not to mention all the rewards that you have been receiving for a very small piece of the action. I told him I would talk you around, so he's given you a couple of days to make up your mind, and I don't do failure.'

'You must be kidding! This is my business and I do what I like!' she exclaimed.

'Hear me woman! I don't ever fail!' Marrio said, overstressing the point.

'You cannot threaten me in my own place and in front of my own staff. Get out or I shall throw you out!' Clair shouted, but he remained as cool as ever while sipping his drink.

'You run a very nice place here. One that my boss would like to get his hands on, so you better be more pleasant to your paying customers, Lady,' he replied with sarcasm. Then one of his hoods grabbed one of the waitresses and pointed a gun to her head.

'Down Mo! This is not the time for action. I'm sure the good lady will come across and be a lot more polite to us in future,' he said and his gun man released his captive.

'Polite to a trumped up hood like you. You must be bloody drunk!' she replied, now quite furious.

'Don't you worry, I'm leaving? But before I go, just a word of warning; this pleasant hotel of yours has been allowed to exist for a while. I wouldn't like to see it and your customers collapse into a pile of rubble one of these lovely days, so be sensible, lady, and do what we ask for your own good,' he said and walked away, throwing a note at the counter on his way out.

He came back the following day to see Molly, his girlfriend and made a few more threats to the staff. Molly was already waiting for him at the bar.

'I had a few words with your boss lady, yesterday. I had to warn her about leaving our outfit,' he said.

'I didn't know she was. I wonder what she's up to... I mean, to turn down such a lot of dough for just holding a few dirty little kids for a couple of days each time,' Molly replied.

'She may have found herself another set up. Could even be one of our main competitors? If you know what's good for you and your friends in this place, do some snooping around for us. See what you can find out about outsiders trying to cache in on our patch. There could be big bucks in it for you,' he said and left.

Two days later they got together in the hotel bar and Molly handed him a small device.

'This is what I found in my room. It was hidden behind the bed. What do you think it is?' she said.

'It looks like a bloody bug. I will give it to one of our guys for analysis. If it's a bug, that means all our conversations has been recorded by her or someone else, even the competition. It sickens me to think that all our personal conversations and bed noises are being listened to by some bloody perverted cop... laughing at me behind my back. Good thing, I never discussed business or I am sure I would have been called in before now. She must be in with the cops. That must be the reason why she has been acting so strangely recently. Have you seen any strange faces about?' he said.

'Nothing out of the ordinary. Come to think of it... a military guy visited a few weeks ago. I thought it was a relative, because she saw him personally. She never spoke about him since, but he was not a cop,' she said.

'The boss won't be happy with the present situation here, you know. Once cancer starts it has a way of growing and contaminating everything. This will need some drastic action, even a bit of surgery to remove the tumour. Here is a hundred bucks for your efforts. You did well, but I must rush,' he said and left in a hurry, leaving Molly in a mild state of panic and not quite knowing what the outcome might be.

Molly realised the lives of her friends in the hotel was now at great risks, so she decided to visit Clair and inform her of Marrio's intentions. After all, Clair had helped her since she arrived from New York, lonely, broke and homeless, and it was the least she could do to repay her kindness.

'I am sorry for disturbing you. Can I have a word? It's very important,' Molly said and Clair allowed her into her drawing room. She had a small apartment of her own on the third floor.

'Marrio found what looked like a bug behind my bed yesterday and has taken it away. He thinks you are in with the cops and I am sure he will show the device to his boss and when they get suspicious our lives here won't be worth a dime. I thought I should warn you immediately,' she said. Clair nervously listened to her story and began to nudge her out of the room.

'Thanks for letting me know. I will see what I can do,' she said and went directly to the phone to call Mallory. It was Roseanne that answered the call and immediately passed it on to Mallory.

'Commander, Colman. I am in real big trouble. One of my girl's boyfriends happens to be the member of the gang that you have been after. His name is Marrio Carillo. Well, she says he found one of my bugs behind her bed and has taken it away. He also thinks I am in with the cops and will give that impression to his boss, who at this moment is after my hotel. I don't know what to do. Can you help me?' she said in a most miserable state.

'I know this chap Marrio and of his liaison with your girl Molly. They have been under surveillance for several weeks. One of my operatives and myself will visit you later today. I shall be disguised as your elder brother Joseph from Nebraska. No one will know of his existence and we have prepared false papers and a mock farm incase they decide to check. My other colleague will be playing the part of my wife. I shall carry a brown leather briefcase with a red handkerchief in my shoulder pocket. My wife will be tall and dark. See you soon,' he said and hung up.

'Ebony, we have a special assignment together. One of our spies is in trouble,' he said.

They took Oscar and were away towards the hotel in Miami. Oscar landed on the roof and they made their way towards her apartment unseen. He knocked on her door, she checked the image on her screen and opened the door.

'That was quick. Please come in, Brother!' she said, but was in no mood for jokes.

'We came via the roof to get our stories right before we made a proper entrance at the reception downstairs. It might be a good idea to tell the desk to expect a visit from your brother, who is on holiday in Miami and has decided to look you up,' he said.

After they rehearsed their story she called the desk and Mallory and Roseanne once again went to the roof and took Oscar towards the local car park at ground level.

They entered the hotel and walked towards the receptionist.

'Nice place you've got here. Is my sister Clair around?' he said, while chewing some gum and she immediately contacted Clair who was soon to join them.

'Joseph! You are a sight for sore eyes! ... and this is your new wife? It's so good to see you after all those years!' Clair said.

Yep, Sis! Please meet Clara!'

'You haven't changed a bit! How is the old ranch these days?'

'Holding up! It took us quite a while finding where you were. I have been stuck to the farm for far too long. I thought I would treat us both to a break. It's our first time in Miami,' he said, in a countrified accent.

'Why don't you both remain here with me for a few days? I have lots of space upstairs. That is if you don't mind,' she said.

'That's great, Sis. We had problems finding a good department in this busy city of yours and the one we got is in a small scruffy hotel and very uncomfortable, with closely breaking waves. If only we knew before,' he said.

'Forget about the money. Your stay here will be on the house,' she said.

'Only if you are sure, Sis. I don't like to take advantage,' he said.

'I insist. We have so much to talk about and I would like to catch up on old times,' she said.

The whole show looked very realistic and most of her girls, including the receptionist were taken in by their performance.

CHAPTER 44

# Hotel explosion

Mallory and his Specials took it in turn to guard Clair's apartment. Unknown to the hotel staff they would enter and leave via the roof of the building each day wearing different disguises.

Although Mallory had taken all necessary security precautions, he knew the gang would try to get her sooner or later. He subsequently had all the weak areas of hotel security strengthened with the help of her own people.

Molly had changed her mind about Marrio and decided to assist Clair's so called brother and wife. She would inform them of any unusual deliveries or strangers, and so also would the other girls.

Having done as much as he could, Mallory decided to have another serious chat with Clair for her own safety.

'In future, everything that enters your apartment must be thoroughly scanned. We have installed a special piece of equipment for that purpose. You are to place all packets, parcels and letters in the tray and press the red button. The object will be automatically scanned for several residues and also be x-rayed for weapons, miniature devices and bombs. The unit can also recognize micro-circuitry and such like.'

'Really! I don't wish to be a prisoner in my own place!' she commented.

'I must seriously stress the importance of this measure and this rule applies to everything including your presents, shopping, purses, handbags, parcels, letters and those belonging to your known visitors... and never let your handbag or purse be left alone, mislaid or lost. It might be a lot safer if you took nothing with you whenever you left the building. Also, be careful where you shop and what you bring back.'

'I will try!' she replied, but was not happy.

'Any questions?' Mallory inquired.

'No! You've done enough. I am sorry for dragging you and your people into all this, but I had no one else to turn to. I never thought I would ever live to see the day when I became a prisoner

in my own place. I only wish you catch those bastards very soon,'
she said.

'We have to neutralize the whole gang worldwide. That means
a lot of planning and a timed operation if we are to prevent some
slipping through the net. However, we'll get them all within a
month or so,' he replied.

The gang's leader had decided Clair had become too great a risk
for his organization and she was to be terminated forthwith by
whatever means available. The contract was given to Marrio in
whose territory the problem had occurred, but he passed it on to
one of his juniors.

Having observed the hotel for several days, they soon realised
the security was too difficult to curtail and he didn't want to show
his face in that place again until the deed was done. Then it
would give him the greatest pleasure to see the tears and sadness
from their downfall and he didn't mind uttering the occasional
abuse to rub salt in the wound. That was before he took over the
building, with all those women to choose from.

The weapon would have to penetrate security and also deliver
a message before she met her end and it would be even better if
her brother and wife were very close by at the time it took effect,
and so he thought. Finally he decided on a letter bomb, using the
latest micro-explosive to be embedded in a small plastic card.
Many people still sent such notes with invitation cards, so there
was a high chance that it would penetrate security and be
delivered to its recipient.

It was timed to go off the moment the card was removed from
the accompanying letter, giving her enough time to read the first
few lines. By then it would be too late for her to throw the device
or run away from it before she felt its fatal impact.

The previous day Clair had met an old friend at a party in town
and was looking forward to her date that evening. Therefore it
was no surprise when she received a letter that was delivered by
courier and addressed to her, personally. Above the address read:
'From a loving admirer.' It was taken by one of the bellboys to the
main entrance of her apartment. When she read the envelope she

was overwhelmed by excitement.

'Wow! It must be Harry. He told me he was going to get in touch,' she murmured to herself.

At that time Mallory and Ebony were observing an old video on wild life. It was about the survival habits of a previously extinct animal and they were intrigued by its incredible size. It so happened to be the African Rhino.

'I think we all need a drink,' Clair said, as she entered the room and Ebony got up to assist while she delicately opened the envelope. She removed the small card and began to read the letter.

**'You have tried to double cross me once too often. Now it's your time to visit hell....**

**Very bad luck, Bitch!**

**Marrio.'**

There was a blinding flash to be followed by an enormous bang, with blood, severed flesh and bones being sprayed in all directions away from the centre of the explosion. She hadn't any time even to cry out or throw the card away. She was stunned in her tracks by the unexpected letter and in that split second she may have just had enough time to say a short prayer. Whatever remained of her body fell to the floor in a pool of blood.

Ebony was about two metres away and Mallory four when it happened. She had one of her right arms blown off in the blast, along with the drink she held and had acquired many lacerations throughout her body. Mallory was lucky to get off with a few minor cuts and bruises. He immediately called the emergency services and then Roseanne in case they were delayed.

Very soon the place was swarming with police and they were all taken to the local hospital. This time Roseanne played the part of his half sister and he was allowed to leave the hospital a few hours later, still a shaken man.

'Woooo! That was close, Dear. I thought I was a gonna! Thank goodness the weapon was engineered for a single target. Even so,

Ebony was not too lucky,' he said to Roseanne.

'You must be very careful, Darling. These people mean business and Marrio will not lose face with his boss,' she reminded.

Mallory had returned to the hotel to calm the people there and ensure that business went on as usual. When he arrived many of the girls were in tears. Everyone loved Clair and were indebted to her for taking them off the streets. She had worked like a slave for many years to acquire the hotel, and had made a few undesirable moves along the way and her present one happened to be her downfall.

If only he knew of the letter. Why didn't she use the scanner? Why are some people so impulsive? Those were questions Mallory asked himself time and time again, while trying to accept the enormous shock to his system. However, what was done was done. The clock couldn't be turned back, so he was to let bygones be bygones and continue the program to get the criminals, relentlessly. Nevertheless, that experience almost knocked him off his perch and reminded him of his previous experience with a bullet in his back. Thank goodness he was not hospitalized for several months as before, with more broken bones and other long term problems. It was then that he remembered the immense resources and technologies that were presently available to him through Solaria.

Mallory soon gave orders to his other Specials to be stationed at the hotel in case of trouble with Marrio and they immediately took their positions throughout the building. They were also keen on revenge when they heard of Ebony's severe wounds, but she was now out of immediate danger, although with the loss of an arm. They were all working under cover with disguises and carried basic firearms under their clothes.

Marrio believed in hitting while the iron was still hot and enjoyed taking advantage of their weakness, so it was not long before he called on the hotel with three of his best. As he entered, Molly rushed towards him with her fist in the air. She just couldn't suppress her anger any longer and began laying into him with her bare fists. He held both her hands and turned her about her feet until she was unable to move, yet she fought back with words.

'You bloody bastard. You didn't have to kill her... and do it like that. I thought you only wanted to take over her operation, but you have murdered her. I am going to get you if it's the last thing I do!' she said, still resisting him until he threw her away from him and straightened his pinstriped suit.

'You shouldn't say such words without proof. I can have you for slander and there are lots of witnesses about. Anyway, I wasn't even in the vicinity when she lost her head,' he said, glancing at his grinning henchmen. He then went close to her and began to whisper.

'Anyway, she had it coming. I just reported things the way I saw them to the boss, with some inside help from you. So don't start mouthing off to me about rights and wrongs. You are in all this up to your pretty little neck as well, and don't you forget it,' he said, while removing a handkerchief to wipe her tearful eyes. She remained silent for a while and straightened herself before running up the stairs to get away from him, still in a rage.

'Who is in charge here? Tell them I would like to talk business right now,' he said to the chief barman as his three men took their positions within the restaurant.

Mallory soon entered, accompanied by three of his Specials. He moved towards Marrio while the other women went towards each of Marrio's men, marking them as targets.

'You want to speak with me?' Mallory inquired.

'Only if you are the new boss!' he replied.

'I am her next of kin, so that must make me the new boss,' Mallory said.

'My boss wants this place and is willing to give you a good price for it. What do you say?'

'I must decline your boss's offer. I have no intentions of selling and if he has any similar plans for me, he can forget it. Tell him that his kids and wife on a certain ranch in Texas won't be worth a dime if he tries anything here. You can also tell your friend Marcus Darling that I am also on his heals, and will get him one of these days. These days, I play two for one,' he said, leaving Marrio in a daze, and wondering how he knew so much of his organization.

'So you've got contacts! Tell me, who the hell are you working for?' Marrio asked, unsatisfied with the outcome of his present conversation.

'That's for you idiots to find out! You think you are smart, but you have no idea who you are dealing with!' Mallory replied.

Mallory snapped his fingers and in less than a second Marrio's three colleagues were relieved of their weapons and lying on the floor.

'Next time you won't be so lucky. You better take your useless filth away now and don't forget to pass on my message,' he said. Marrio's eyes went red with anger and hatred, but he could do nothing. He and his three men were covered by Mallory's women and they meant business.

Mallory had already fitted sensitive cameras and scanners throughout the hotel and had been nominated the legal owner of the place. At least, he had taken over her major share of the business until his current operation against the gang was over. Then he would hand it over to her real next-of-kin.

The whole performance was rigged to annoy the gang and catch those responsible for Clair's death. Roseanne was to get close to Molly before the snare was laid to catch Marrio, who at that time was seldom seen in that part of Miami.

CHAPTER 45

# A healing miracle

After Clair's funeral, Mallory paid another visit to Ebony in hospital. He knew she was not the type to accept the boredom of any hospital environment, so he took her lots of her favourite fruit and a virtual games microdisk. It had a special interface unit that linked directly with her brain implants. She was pleased to see him but remained firmly fixed to one side of the bed and what remained of her severed arm was bandaged.

'And how is my best captain today?' he asked.

'Commander, I am still a bit woozy from loss of blood, even with the transfusion. I am sorry for letting you down like this, but they took me by surprise. I thought she had the letter scanned, but that was too much of an assumption to make on my part.'

'I am as much to blame as you. It's just a small setback and I am sure you will be ready in a week or so,' he said.

'I don't know about that, Commander. I think I've come to the end of my military career. I've never heard of a one-armed soldier before on active duty, have you?' she replied and turned her head away in disgust.

'When do you think you'll be ready to move out of here?' he asked, ignoring her feelings of self-guilt.

'In about a week's time to convalesce, but I shall have to return here twice a week for them to check the wound and start planning for an artificial limb,' she replied.

'Make it sooner rather than later. I have a big surprise in store for you,' he said and she turned around in curiosity, wondering what the surprise would be as the nurse entered.

In another week and with the exception of the still sore and painful parts of her upper right arm, Ebony had almost fully recovered. She was therefore ready to leave the hospital when Mallory and Roseanne came to take her home.

After another two days at home he visited her in her room for a quiet chat.

'Can you walk?' he asked.

'Yes, Commander. I've been practising. It's all those days in bed, and the special drugs make me dizzy. However, the local pain reliever your wife gave me seems to work a treat,' she replied.

'In that case, put some loose clothes on. I want to take you somewhere by portal,' he said and she was out of bed in a flash and getting ready. They entered the basement portal and found themselves in Sol-Newtown Dome. Once they had been disinfected, they took another portal and found themselves in a large room with many androids operating advanced equipment. An operator came forward to greet Mallory.

'Please take care of her for me,' he said and she was taken to another room where her clothes and bandages were removed and her complete body scanned for abnormalities. She was then asked the usual questions, to which she answered yes to implants and no to artificial organs. A tight fitting cap was placed over her head and the remainder of the severed arm left on her shoulder was placed in a small container of warm jelly-like substance. The rest of her body was placed in another similar material. Most of it was brushed onto her body until it became a separate skin above her own. Then she was placed into one of the Megotron caskets and the lid shut.

For a brief moment Ebony wondered where she was. The place was filled with every conceivable type of equipment of alien technology. She had always trusted Mallory and knew it was for her own good, so she went along with the operator's demands.

The operator pressed a few buttons on a large console and the device began to scan her complete body, checking for deformities, but memorizing every cell structure down to sub-molecular levels. Then it began to repair her damaged body. Several tubes were inserted into her severed arm and biological substances were deposited, to be modified and put in place by special drugs and millions of microids. They would use the recordings of her good arm to build the old, with a small change in size to compensate for her right-handedness. Once her complete body had been scanned by both devices, she could then be re-created from scratch and brought back to life; for that was the power of Solarian technology.

The flexible metallic tubes within the outer part of her arm soon became active and so did the localized transposers and microids, until her arm was completely regrown. She could just detect a warm sensation throughout her body. Despite her severed arm, she always felt the sensation that the arm was complete. That was until she looked and observed the bandages.

Because her arm had recently been lost, all the neuro pathways were still in tact. Otherwise it would have been necessary to retrain her in their use to regain the precise coordination of that arm, assuming it had remained unused for long periods.

When she was removed from the Megotron she glanced towards her arm and couldn't believe the sight she beheld. As if by some form of incredible magic it was normal and drooping by her side. She looked at that hand and its fingers while flexing each joint, but it was perfect and all pain had gone. Even the lines in her palms appeared the same as before. She was astounded by it all. Ebony, had heard of cybernetics, where artificial limbs and organs could be added, but this was much more advanced.

'Please follow me!' the operator said.

She was placed under the Psyrotron and her brain completely scanned. The Macron now had a complete record of her mind and body and she had been completely repaired including the addition of better brain implants with all of her original programming. That later change had been made to standardize the process.

Ebony was taken to another bath where the jelly-like substance was completely removed from her skin.

When she met Mallory she couldn't resist placing her arms around him. She hugged and kissed him on the cheek and he was a little embarrassed but knew the way she felt.

'How do you feel?' he asked.

'I feel great. I still can't believe it's possible for a machine to regrow a complete limb in such a manner, with no changes or scars whatsoever. You've given me back my life! It won't drop off in a few days, will it?' she replied in jest and he laughed.

'No! I can guarantee you it wont!' he replied.

'You are all such a strange lot, Commander. Whenever you get close to a door you simply wave your hands and it opens and you always carry everything in your head, like you were a super genius,' she said.

'Ebony, the curious one. Are you not able to use your implants to hold such information in your head? Anyway, I can open doors and such like because I have grade one security clearance,' he replied.

'Where is this place?' she asked, out of curiosity, but Mallory declined to answer that question directly.

'I cannot tell you it's precise location for security reasons. However, you will know when you are given grade one clearance in a month or so. I hope you don't mind? However I can assure you that it's out of this world!' he said.

'I am sorry I show too much curiosity, Commander, but I would like to fit in more precisely in our outfit. It's not a bad human quality, you know,' she said.

'You must be patient and in time everything will be revealed,' he replied.

'Commander, I understand. However, I thank you from the bottom of my heart for giving me back my arm and my life. Now I know what you meant when you said any damaged body can be repaired,' she said.

'Believe me, when I say that we are all one and the same organization and working together to get our endangered planet back on course.'

'I know, Commander!'

'The machine has memorized every molecule in your body and every bit of data in your mind, including your implants, so if you are seriously damaged at anytime in the future, you will be repaired and renewed. But in the case of serious accidents, we must return your body to the device immediately via portal. If not, and you die, you will be assigned a completely new body based on the previous recording, with a loss of all your previous experiences from that time. That is why we must return our special operatives to a local portal if they are severely damaged. However, you must first be scanned by the machines in order to be brought back from death.'

'What about our other warriors?' she inquired.

'I have ordered for several special ambulances with portals from head office, but it will be several weeks before they arrive. In the mean time we are to use the portal at our house.'

'I see!'

'Your transit card will get you to the repair centre by portal immediately, but you will have to break off one of its corners. That will tell the system you are in real trouble. If not, use the emergency code in your implant.'

'Thanks again for everything!'

'Are you ready for work?' he inquired.

'Yes, Commander. I want to see an end to those bastards as soon as possible before they do more damage, if you don't mind me swearing. I have a lot of time to catch up and I feel like a new woman,' she replied.

'In that case, we have a celebration this evening to commemorate your new arm. The other girls will be shocked, so I want it to be a surprise. You will have to return to bed and hide that arm from them until the party is ready, then we can surprise them,' he said.

'I like it, Commander. It will be great fun and I will wear something special for the party. I can't wait to see the expressions on their faces when I show them my new arm,' she replied.

CHAPTER 46

# Goodbye Charles Morang

As far as the girls were concerned, Ebony was expected home later that day and a party was being arranged for her homecoming. At least, that was the impression Mallory gave them when they arrived home that evening. Ebony was already upstairs and in her room and getting ready. Mallory's game was going to be a great surprise to everyone and relieve the stress and uncertainty felt by her group.

Roseanne knew about the situation and had done most of the cooking, including baking one of her favourite cakes with no help from the kitchen staff. She could have called the caterers but wanted to sharpen her culinary skills for a change. Anyway, she felt she had a part to play in Ebony's home coming.

When Oscar arrived in the driveway that evening, Mallory left Oscar to fly off and park at the rear of the house.

'Where is Bony?' Nadia asked, disappointingly, as he entered the room. They tended to call Ebony by that pet name.

'Isn't she upstairs in her room?' was his casual reply.

'In her room?' Tracy shouted as they took to the stairs and busted into the room.

'No one told us you were home. How are you, Girl?' shouted an over excited Joeanne.

'Not too well. Still a little groggy, but I am getting there,' Ebony replied, innocently while putting on the pretence.

'You girls better go downstairs and I'll follow in a minute or so. I have to get dressed with one arm,' she said and they kissed her and left.

Soon after, Ebony appeared in a beautiful party frock with both hands held behind her back and while the girls cheered she lifted her arms above her head. The girls, including Roseanne, couldn't be more surprised. They went towards her to check the arm, its flesh and veins, but everything was in place including the hand and fingers without a single scar and she had full control of every digit.

'It's a bloody miracle. How can that be? We saw it missing when we visited you in hospital, and now it's all grown back to normal?' Anne said.

'I took her to a special place today and they repaired it. I told you once that I always took care of my special Specials. So don't any of you worry about such things in the future. Now, lets enjoy the party,' Mallory said.

'Repaired it! She's got a brand new one without even a scar where the original one was missing. I would like to know where that place is?' Tracy commented.

The following day and while they were all in the hotel, Mallory called Ebony into his office. She still had her right arm in a sling. It was to make the others in the hotel think she was still incapacitated and getting it ready for an artificial one. However, word soon got around that the severed arm had been stitched back on and no one asked anymore questions. At that time it was common knowledge that such operations were possible, although not always very satisfactory from the patient's point of view. That was due to difficulties in connecting nerve endings and the numerous blood vessels without the use of microids.

'We both have a job to do. It will be your first real termination and I want you to learn the procedure precisely. Whenever possible, we try not to kill the victims body, people are always useful. Further, life is precious and should never be wasted.'

'Understand, Commander!'

'Anyway, although we can kill the body of a life-form, we cannot kill its Identity. Similarly, when we use special drugs, we do not kill the body or the individual's Identity, only certain areas of memory.

'One Charles Morang has received a contract on me by the head of the gang that we are after, so I laid a dead-end trail for him to follow while I got on with more important business. Now it's his turn and a loose-end we have to tidy up. For this mission, we take along dart guns and super-browning nine millimetre automatics with two clips of armour... and wear bulletproof vests. Also, double check all communication links with Oscar and base. There must be no mistakes during this operation.

'On it, Boss!' Nadia exclaimed. She took point and was dying for some payback. Ebony stood back as her second. She had not yet fully recovered from the trauma of the explosion.

'Meet me on the roof at five forty-five p.m. Our watches will automatically synchronized through our implants,' he said and she left to make the necessary arrangements.


Oscar had taken them to the roof of Mallory's original office building and they cautiously made their way down the stairs to his old office. Slowly he scanned the door and its frame for any telltale signs of a forced entry, but there was none, so he asked Nadia to stand several metres away in case the door was booby-trapped while he unlocked it and entered.

As the door inched open, it creaked a little, giving Mallory expectations of worse to come. The place was in darkness and the creaking set his teeth on edge. He stretched his hand to one side, flicked a switch and the lights came on to reveal a bare office in much the same way as he had left it weeks before. He waved his hand towards Nadia and she entered, followed by Ebony.

'These people are after me, personally. He wants to get me face to face. Even say a few words before he pulls the trigger and blows me away. Perhaps a requirement from his boss as part of the contract. The last words I am expected to hear or something like that,' Mallory said, while Ebony and Nadia checked every-where for bugs and hidden explosives.

'It's clean, Commander!' Ebony said while pointing one of her small gadgets in each nook and cranny. Then he lifted the phone and called reception.

'Girls, it's Mallory. I am back. Was there any messages for me?' Mallory inquired. Mallory had visited the office twice from the roof since the new receptionists and had acquainted them with two free Chinese takeaways.

'Yes, Mal. The same chap called again this morning. He has been back a few times. There are also messages and letters,' she replied.

'Place them in the box and I will collect them later today,' he said. He placed the phone on-hook and turned to Ebony.

'I don't expect them to do anything this time of day, but I want them to know that I am back and the office lights should be a good signal. We'll leave in a couple of hours time, just after dark. Here is a key to box number thirty three at reception. I want you to go downstairs and plant a bug underneath the receptionist desk. She should have left by now. Then you can bring me the contents of that box, and check all envelopes for letter-bombs before you return,' he said. Ebony immediately froze when he mentioned the words "letter bombs", as her past experience came flooding back.

'My girl, there is little chance of you finding a bomb in any of those envelopes, but you have to get used to the idea and overcome your fears. You've got to get back on that particular horse time and time again, so the sooner you climb the saddle, the better you'll feel. Anyway, Nadia can accompany and assist you. Use your special tools!' he said and they left. She soon returned with a stack of letters and some notes left by the receptionist. He carefully read their contents. Most of them were just security assignments and bills. There were five calls by the hit-man and other phone calls from the same source.

'We'll be based here for a while until we neutralize those guys, so we must pack some food tomorrow and begin a normal routine from the roof. That will force them to visit us via the reception and stairs,' he said.

For some unknown reason there were two teams involved and Mallory thought that the price on his head may have increased. However, they knew not of his associations with Clair's hotel. During that time, some kept an eye on his old flat while the others kept a round-the-clock surveillance of his office from the street outside.

When they realised his office lights were on, they immediately called whoever they were working for and he was on his way.

'How did he get in while you were watching the place?' Charles said in anger.

'I don't know boss. A large Roadstar flew overhead and we didn't see it leave. Could have been his car that landed on the roof?' one of his men said.

'A Roadstar? How can a nobody like that own a Roadstar?

Private investigators, even with their pictures in the papers, don't earn that much money. Perhaps he found himself a rich widow? That would answer a lot of questions. Anyway, we know he is back and he has not returned to his flat since, so that can only mean he is living with his rich woman.'

'Could be, Boss!'

'Joe, you will return to his flat and inform us the minute he shows up there. The other two of you will meet me here tomorrow morning and we must try to get a fix on the Roadstar number. We must get this contract over by the weekend. People are beginning to think of me as an incompetent enforcer, but I haven't given up a job yet and this one won't be my first,' he said.

Mallory and Ebony had prepared the office for the following day.

'We can't spend too much time on this operation with Marrio about, so we'll end it tomorrow morning. We use nerve gas and dart guns, but carry your Browning Automatic, just in case. We should both wear our usual masks with internal nasal filters, and turn away from the poisonous vapours when the capsules explode.'

'Got it!'

'You will wait in the street outside and on my signal walk towards them to ask for instructions. Could be, it's your first visit to this area and you want to find a street? When they lower their window, break the cap from the capsule and throw it into the car. It will explode the moment it hits the floor, but be ready to use your gun if things don't work out as planned or you'll have to dart them.'

'Sounds easy enough!' Ebony said.

'I have arranged for a collection van. If things work as planned, they will all be taken away to the lunny farm for rehabilitation and new identities. I will do the same with Charles after I've got some information from him about his boss and other colleagues. It's the only and most humane way,' Mallory said.

'What are we to do about those outside your old flat?' Ebony asked.

'When they are all in the van, we take Oscar over there and you play the same tricks on them. If it worked once without a hitch, it will work even better the next time around. Anyway, we should know from Charles more about their organization,' Mallory said.

The following morning Ebony arrived early to check the area and made sure she kept hidden from the view of Charles and his men while observing their every move, which she constantly reported to Mallory through her implants. When he was ready, he phoned reception to say he was in his office and ready to receive all visitors.

The three assassins, including Charles, arrived outside the building at ten a.m. Charles whispered some instructions to the other two and walked towards the entrance. Mallory was immediately told of his movement and prepared for his visit. Charles obviously wanted to do the job himself for his own personal satisfaction. Soon he was on his way upstairs and tapping on Mallory's office door.

'Please come in!' Mallory shouted and he entered.

'You don't look like the one with his picture in the papers. Are you the detective called Mallory Colman?' Charles asked. Mallory broke off the top of the small gas capsule and pretended to be inhaling part of the small container, but accidentally dropped it on the carpet while placing a handkerchief to his nose.

'You will have to forgive me, but I have a terrible cold and my nostrils are completely blocked. Did you say you wanted... Mister Colman?' he said, giving himself some time for the invisible gas to take effect.

Charles was a big hulk of a man and he hit the floor with a loud thud. However, the effects of that particular nerve gas was only temporary and would begin to wear off in a few minutes, so he taped his mouth, then both his hands and legs together and placed his body in a sitting position on the Settee. Nadia was waiting as backup in one of the office corners with dart-gun in hand.

Once Ebony knew Charles had been subdued, using all of her feminine and seductive charm, she walked towards their car and tapped on the window.

'Hi guys, can you lovely gents show a lost girl the way to Rochdale Road?' she said, while braking off the cap and dropping the capsule into their car. Unluckily for her the driver saw the item fall and picked it up to hand it back to her. Like a flash she pointed the gun at the face of the one closest to her.

'You can keep it, complements of Mallory Colman,' she said, while waiting for the gas to take effect. Then she darted each of them, removed the darts from their bodies and were on her way to Mallory's office. They fell asleep with fear in their eyes and would awake with a headache and permanent loss of memory.

Ebony entered the room as Charles regained consciousness. He moaned and groaned and Mallory walked towards him and peeled the tape from his mouth. Then Mallory removed his own mask to reveal his true identity.

'So you are the silly bugger that's been after me?' Mallory said, while fidgeting with his dart gun. The door opened and Ebony entered the room while Nadia approached.

'Boss, I've taken care of the two in the car outside. They are now asleep as babes and completely changed persons,' she said and giggled a bit.

'I seem to have missed all the fun!' Nadia complained.

'There is more fun to be had with those outside my flat!' Mallory advised.

'What have you done to my men, you bitch?' Charles yelled and Mallory turned towards Ebony.

'Good!' It'll teach them not to be rude to ladies,' he said and turning to Charles he took the other gun from his pocket and placed it on the table.

'Tell me, you fat bum...' he said, but was interrupted by a slightly nervous and sweating Charles.

'Charles... My name is Charles Morang,' he said.

'Tell me, Charles Morang, what would you do if you were in my shoes? And I want an honest answer,' Mallory said as he lifted his Browning Automatic from the desk and began to load a full clip.

'You would have been dead by now and I would have been across the state-line,' he replied, even more nervously.

'As we are on the path of truth and honesty, how many other men do you have tracking me and where are they now?' Mallory said, as he took a silencer from his pocket and began to slowly screw it onto the barrel.

'Just one more. His name is Joe. I swear on my mother's grave. He is waiting outside your flat,' he said.

'Just one more question before I splatter your brains all over this desk. Who gave you the contract on me?' Mallory said, while continuing to slowly screw the silencer onto the gun. Then he turned towards Ebony.

'Please call the cleaners for one more body,' he said and Ebony immediately got on the phone. The whole performance was too much for Charles and he began to chatter like a parrot.

'It was Sunny Durante. He is second in command and in charge of all operations in this state. Tex Nolan is the boss and is based in Miami and Texas. He likes gambling and pornography. They thought you knew too much and there was an unexplained incident in London just before you left. They put two and two together and your name came up each time. They have powerful contacts in Washington, particularly in the FBI and can trace most people to rub them out and you are a big loose end that can jeopardise the organization.

'What else do you wish to know?' he said.

'You have almost said enough. Any others following in your footsteps?' Mallory asked.

'No! There is no one else. They only had a hundred grand reserved for this contract and I am the one they chose. Nothing personal. Now that I have assisted you, would you please allow me to return to my wife and kids?' he pleaded.

'Let me get you right. You are saying that if we let you go, you'll forget all about us and cancel the contract?' Mallory asked.

'Yes! I'll even do that much, if you let me go,' he pleaded. Mallory nodded his head to Ebony and she fired a single dart towards his fat abdomen. Mallory knew the terms of his contract and such contracts were non-retractable , could not be rescinded and irrevocable. He could never have reneged on such a deal and remain alive.

'Let's check his papers. We have to find his family's address. This is one dad that will never go home again to his kids,' Mallory said.

'I feel so sad! I'm almost in tears!' Nadia jested.

'Me too!' Ebony replied, pretending.


All local members of his gang had been neutralized and collected by special transport. They would take them to the rehabilitation farm where they would learn a new career and given new identities. However, that was not going to be the end of the story. Such well known criminals had many contacts and they would miss him if he wasn't available within a few days. Therefore, they had to move swiftly.

The criminals wives and next-of-kin soon received letters of sympathy from Sunny Durante lawyers, but they were really sent by Mallory. Each envelope included a cheque for one hundred thousand dollars and the letters read:

*'With much regret, I am to inform you that your husband was recently reported as "missing in action". Because of the circumstances of his death, we are unable to supply a body at this time. However, we sincerely wish the enclosed money will go towards solving any current financial problems. We shall inform you the moment his body parts, if any, are received. The State Department has also been informed....'*

It was a situation that their families could do very little about. Even the police could not have responded without a body, but the finger was nevertheless pointed at Sunny Durante by those who knew. However, in such cases their wives seldom knew of their true criminal occupations, so the letter gave the impression that they were involved in some other clandestine pursuits for the government. Knowing the secrecy of such organizations many did not bother to check.

Nevertheless those offenders were still alive and would be reeducated to pursue a non-criminal existence without knowledge of their families.

CHAPTER 47

# Molly's plan for revenge

Soon, Mallory had acquired rough profiles and habitual characteristics of the most important members of the targeted gang. He had also received information from the Group of Thirteen regarding the illicit bio-organ criminals and they were also under surveillance by a trained group from Warland. Those were some of the first to be trained by Chad with Mallory's assistance and also included his six male Specials.

All such gangs were plaguing humanity and were to be terminated forthwith, but Mallory didn't like taking their lives in cold blood, so whenever he could, he had new jobs arranged for them within Solarian Banking. Those were mainly in off-world mining, well away from the Solar System. Nevertheless, they would first be injected with a high dose of the Amiterol type drug, which erased almost all of their past experiences. It was an amnesia inducing drug with no side effects. However, all of their long term memories relating to certain areas of their past were lost forever. Its effects was almost the same as amnesia caused by being hit a heavy blow on the head. However, the latter was not always permanent.

Having been changed into new individuals, they would spend several weeks on a rehabilitation farm or ranch with special trainers and equipment, where they would learn their new skills and be given new identities. They could then begin a new life well away from their previous haunts and with no knowledge of their past associations. As far as the past was concerned, their present characters never existed. However, to them, they were still the same conscious beings, and would experience the world in much the same way as any amnesiac patient, but without the constant reminders of that previous existence.

The process of psycho convergence worked for all, friends and foe alike. The only ones that suffered were their families, including their innocent children who were missing a parent. In some cases, their wives knew the score, and when they failed to return home, realised they were dead. Either in the bottom of a river with weighted pockets, dissolving in a bath of acid, or left dead with a damaged face and without hands in an alleyway somewhere, where they could not easily be recognized or identified. Usually such bodies were completely scrubbed and left without any forensics or other forms of identification, because those were the ways of hardened international criminals. In some cases all their organs were removed and frozen, while awaiting a patient for transplant. Those criminals even made money on their dead victims and double-crossers. Criminals never gave their DNA to the police and because of certain laws their DNA could not be processed without their permission.

They never left any identification or evidence behind since almost anything or anyone could be traced by biological residues. Credit and transit cards were also prone to computer analysis, so they were always discarded. Those were the rules of their initiation in that their bodies were thoroughly cleansed after death.

In Mallory's case, those that were conditioned would never see their family and friends again, and even if they did, what purpose would it serve. Since they were taken away from Earth, they could not have recognised them, anyway. It was harsh treatment for harsh crimes, but the only humane one, if Mallory was to put an end to such offenses against humanity.

Marrio and his local hoods were next on Mallory's list. The hit man and his assistants had been taken out of the way, which gave Mallory time to concentrate on the real criminals.

In London, Carl and his specials had traced most of the gang with the aid of Scotland Yard. They had placed several operatives in key positions, aided by electronic bugs and suchlike and were finally ready to move on Mallory's command.

'Hi, Mal! How are things at your end. I called to say everything is ready at this end, so make your move when ready,' Carl advised.

'Got you, Pal! How are things in London? You like my Croydon hotel?' Mallory asked.

'It's fantastic and completely free. I had no idea Solarian Banking owned so many hotels. It will make life a bit easier for us. Not that the money worries us now,' Carl said.

'Since we are now Solarians, it all belongs to us, anyway. Bloody posh, isn't it,' he replied.

'Anyway, I've got to go. Another appointment with Under-cover,' he said and hung off.

Mallory and his special women were permanently based in Clair's hotel. That place was where they expected Marrio to make his takeover move.

Roseanne remained at the house, which was now their operations base and neutral territory that was unknown to the gangs. From there she could coordinate the operation in several distant places at once.

The hotel staff had taken well to Mallory and accepted that he was the brother of Clair. They also respected him for the way he took on Marrio and his men and won.

Molly was quite eager to assist and wanted to make amends for Clair's death. She realized that she was partly responsible, so Mallory called her into his office for a chat in the presence of Ebony, who still played the part of Mallory's wife.

'Molly, I think you like being here with us, don't you?'

'Very much!' she replied.

'Well, you should seriously consider the alternatives. You are either with us all the way, or you are out of this place. I'm sorry, but too much has happened over the past weeks and this chap Marrio is still around and will be making his move again. So what is it to be?' Mallory said.

'I am very sorry for what happened to Clair and I sincerely wish I could bring her back, but I can't, so I'll have to make it up to her one way or another. Whatever you want me to do to get that bum, Marrio, I will do. And I don't want any payment until I know for sure he is one dead dude,' she replied.

'My organization, which is much larger than Marrio's, wants us to take out Marrio's outfit before he tries to do the same to us. Will you help?' Mallory said.

'Your wish is my command, Boss! But I would like to kill the bastard myself!' she replied.

'Don't be too hasty. Leave the trapping to us, it's our profession. You mustn't do anything to jeopardise our operation. Just do precisely as you are told. You can always kick him while he is down.'

'Ok!'

'I think he still requires your special favours. After all, you are a very beautiful woman and I think he had a crush on you before, but I don't think he is the type to remain with a good woman for long. Anyway, you are in a key position for him to get information on this place, so he will approach you sooner or later.'

'Ok, I can play that game!' She replied.

'You will be our bait to lead him into our trap. You must give him the impression that the present management here is in a mess and the girls and staff here hates my guts. He will then plan a take over which will involve taking me out as soon as possible. You must feed him with a wrong time table of my movements and tell us his plans. Then when he makes his move, we'll be ready and waiting for him,' Mallory added.

'I will do it for Clair and my conscience,' she replied.

'Here is the address of a local café he frequents. I think the place belongs to his boss, but they sometimes use it as a meeting point. Pay an occasional visit to that café. He or one of his guys will observe you.'

'I will!'

'Wear this ring at all times. It's a direction finder. If you find yourself in trouble, just press the stone and it will begin to transmit your position to us. You must also wear these earrings, they are bugs that will also transmit your conversations to us. All information will be remotely recorded in one of our surveillance vans. They will begin to transmit the moment you touch them with your finger and will stop after an hour or so. You need only touch anyone of them again, to continue. Pretend to scratch your ear lobes,' Mallory said and she took the three items.

Molly visited the restaurant in the shopping precinct several times, until she was observed by Marrio himself. He soon joined her at the table and began to apologise.

'I didn't know you came here? Can I join you for a moment? Something I would like to explain,' he said.

'It's a free country,' she replied and looked in a different direction to where he stood.

'I know you are very mad with me, but it was business. If I didn't, someone else would have been given the job and I would now have been a dead duck floating in the river. I would like us to become friends again. Honestly!'

'Friends, you are not kidding!'

'I am not kidding! Are you going to give me a second chance...-?' He continued and Molly stared directly at him.

'I was on my way to the hotel and thought I would take a different route today and do a little shopping. Then I felt a little empty and decided to try this place, but I had no idea you would be here. If I knew I would have taken the other street and I have no desire of becoming your friend again. Is that enough explanation for you?' she replied.

'Sorry, I didn't mean to probe. I was just making conversation,' he said.

'That's all right. I am quite used to being pushed around. If not by you, by my present boss,' she said.

'That one tough son of a bitch, and his Amazonians are just as bad,' he replied.

'And a right bastard too. He takes any of us girls on demand. He calls it sampling the goods before the customers. Whenever he snaps his fingers, we have to jump or we are kicked out the door into the streets,' Molly said in a sad tone of voice.

'If that's the way you feel about him, why don't we join forces and rid the world of such a pervert. My original promise to you still stands. The only reason why I did not return is because I had another more important job for the boss.'

'Really?' she showed interest.

'What do you say?' Marrio asked.

'What do I get out of it and how would you do it? He is a very clever man, with spies everywhere and his Amazonians are still around. They floored your men the last time,' she replied.

'My men were caught by surprise. Next time they won't be so damn lucky. If you help me in this, I could make you in charge of the girls, with a percentage on all their takings. But I have to discuss all business arrangements with the boss first. After all, it's his money,' he said.

'You arrange something with your boss and let me know. If the percentage and position is a good one, I might accept your offer,' she replied.

'Leave it with me and I'll see what I can do. Meet me here at the same time in two days, and make sure you are not followed.' Turning to the manager he said:

'Charlie, her order is on the house,' then a very pleased Marrio left to join his men in the car outside. Unbeknown to them the complete conversation had been recorded.

CHAPTER 48

# Goodbye Marrio

Mallory had spent the following day briefing Molly for her meeting with Marrio.

They met in the restaurant as arranged and Marrio appeared to be in one of his cheerful moods.

'I've been able to get you a good deal, but the boss says it will only be valid if you give us 100 percent involvement in getting this thing sorted,' Marrio said.

'What is the deal?' she asked.

'It's 10 percent of all the girls' takings and you can become their supervisor under me as their boss. I will be there for a while until my boss finds a legitimate manager to run the finances,' he said.

'In that case, I accept your bosses offer, but I'll need something in writing, in case you or your boss change their minds. And no funny business trying to bump me off for my share,' she replied.

'You know I can't put such a deal in writing. You have my word on it and as a token, here is ten grand as down payment for your assistance,' he said.

'Thanks, that will do for starters. I've already got you some important information. Most days he remains in the office until eight at night. His three female guards leaves the hotel by seven and returns again just before nine. That gives you two hours to do the job. It would be a lot easier if you and your men visited via the roof. That way, no one will see you enter, but the security there will have to be neutralized,' she said.

'That's very useful information. Try and get us a sketch of the roof, showing scanners and sensors, and keep observing their routine. Try and visit me here at lunchtime every two days and watch that you are not followed,' he said.

Molly took the money. She considered it blood money and intended to share it with the other girls when the operation was over, so she hid it in a safe place.

Mallory had recorded all their conversations and was waiting for Marrio to arrange a date. He had also got himself a lookalike android from Sol-Newtown that would take his place in the office on the day in question. That was while he and three of his specials hid outside the office for a surprise assault. The other three would remain on the roof to prevent their escape.

It was another one of Mallory's planned military exercises, where all six of his personal specials were involved. However, Molly was given limited information and knew nothing about Mallory's real purpose or those of his Specials. As far as she was concerned, they were another gang and Clair's brother now ran the outfit.

Mallory always explained his methods to Molly before briefing her with false information. In any event, he always knew their conversations and had her tailed, just in case. Instead of waiting for Marrio to make the first move, Mallory had decided to set a date for Marrio's visit. He had to give him the impression that he was to remain in his office very late on two particular evenings during the week.

Once again Molly visited Marrio to supply him with plans of the roof and inform him of any changes in their routine.

'I know for sure he'll be taking stock and doing some bookkeeping next Thursday and Friday. I overheard him talking to someone on the phone. From what little I heard, it could have been his boss, because he was quite tense when he finished the call. Barking at everyone within sight. Anyway, he has to get the place ready for a visit in the next two weeks or so,' she said.

'I knew it. I bet you, he is not Clair's lost brother, but part of another outfit. The fool doesn't realise he is organizing the place for us until we take over. My boss is still running a check on him, but so far we've come up with nothing. He has covered his tracks well,' Marrio said.

'Personally, I think Thursday will be your best day. Friday being the last working day, tends to be a little busy. Many of our clients get paid on that day and like to visit us to unwind. I can call you from the hotel before seven to let you know whether it's on or off. Anyway, the decision is up to you, because we might not have such a good chance again for months,' she said.

'I agree. There is no point in waiting any longer. If you think

Thursday is the best day, that's good enough for me. We'll have to steal an LPD motor to land on the roof, and we don't want any active scanners when we arrive. We'll give you some special filters to put over the receivers. It will reduce their range to about five metres, which is where he usually parks his Roadstar and we can park fifteen metres away, well beyond its range,' he said.

As agreed, Molly placed the filters over the receivers and called them to say everything was going to plan. It was one of several devices that scanned the roof of the hotel and received information from local cars that were passed on to the main security computers which were linked to the police and customs.

Having received the call from Molly, Marrio and three of his men arrived soon after eight p.m. They used a thermal cutter to get through the roof door without the special card-key and were soon on their way to Mallory's office on the fifth floor, via the stairs. That route was seldom used by clients as they preferred the elevators.

Marrio also didn't want the police to think he had inside assistance, in the event of any investigation.

The trap had been carefully laid for Marrio and his men, and the net was soon to be sprung.

Mallory placed the lookalike android in his office chair and awaited their arrival with three of his specials in an adjacent room. The android would notify him the moment they entered.

As expected, they knocked before entering and as they did, fired several bullets at the one sitting at the desk. Their guns were fitted with silencers so most of the noise was made on impact with the metallic body of the android, who began to pick the fragments of metal from his clothes. He then got to his feet, and by then Marrio's men were taken by fear and began to retreat. However, Mallory and his three specials quietly arrived in the room at that time and fired darts simultaneously at Marrio's three companions while Mallory pressed his gun to Marrio's ribs from behind. The three men were instantly disarmed while the drug took effect.

'A gad-damn robot! I should have known this was a set up. It all went too smoothly from the start. I will get that bitch if it's the last thing I do!' Marrio yelled.

'Call the van for these three. They seem to be already asleep. Marrio will take a slightly different route with us, but first we must put him to sleep,' Mallory said and Ebony happily came forward, pushed a device against his arm and pressed the trigger. He was asleep in less than a minute.

'You and Nadia come with me.'

'On it, Boss!'

'Tracy, I want you to take Joan and Anne. Remain in the street outside. It's just a matter of time before his other men show up, and when they do we must be ready. In the mean time, Ebony, Nadia and I will take Marrio away to be scanned for more information. There is much we can learn from him about his boss and others of the gang. Expect us back in two hours,' Mallory said.

Marrio was assisted to Oscar and they were taken to the house. From there they took the portal to Sol-Newtown.

They were thoroughly cleansed biologically before being taken to another portal for the Psyrotron room.

Just after they arrived, Marrio regained consciousness.

'Where am I? What are you going to do with me?' Marrio shouted, trying to resist another one of the special drugs that were administered to him. That one allowed him small and slow movements. He had to be conscious while being scanned by the Psyrotron.

'To save us a lot of time in asking you lots of silly questions, this device will scan your brain and record all of your past experiences for further analysis by our computers. The drug will make your mind relax and your body will remain rigid during the scanning process,' Mallory said while giving the operator a signal to begin the scanning.

Marrio stood immobile in the centre of the strange room as the device descended towards him.

Several minutes later all of his memories were in the Macron computer.

'I don't know where I am, but this is beyond anything I've ever seen and you are not who you say you are,' he said, still trying to resist the drug.

'We are members of a large interplanetary organization, with the sole intention of saving Earth from people like you. However, you shouldn't worry. Your wife and two children will be well taken care of, financially,' Mallory said.

'What are you going to do with me?' he asked again.

'We are not going to kill you. Instead, we are going to erase all of your criminal memories and give you a new life and a new identity. Sadly, you will never see your family again. But you are still young. I am sure you will meet another woman and have another family. Neither will you recognize any of us in a few minutes,' Mallory said.

'Please, you can't do that to me. I'll tell you whatever you wish to know. Just release me!' he yelled.

'I'm sorry, Pal. You are much to dangerous for that and by killing Clair you sealed your own faith,' Mallory replied.

Mallory then nodded to Ebony and she administered the memory drug. That drug would erase all of his most dominant memories, leaving behind his basic self. He was then taken away to a rehabilitation and training farm where he would be given a new identity and career. He would then have most likely been given a clerical job in Solarian Banking or perhaps on a mining planet.

Marrio's other companions arrived outside the hotel several hours later and were asked directions by two lovely women. A small gas container was dropped into their car, to be followed by two targeted darts and another two men were loaded into the van and dispatched for rehabilitation.

'Molly, come and look at some pigs!' Mallory yelled. She rushed out of the hotel to observe those two fast asleep in the back of the van. She spat in the face of the closest to get the rage out of her system.

'We got Marrio. He will never be a gang member again,' he said and she was happy.

'Now and finally, poor Clair's death has been revenged,' Mallory said and she nodded in agreement, but with sadness.

CHAPTER 49

# The main assault

Mallory had written letters to Tex Nolan and the other main members of the international paedo-smuggling gang. They included detailed photos and mentioned about what had happened to Marrio and his men, while asking them to desist from their criminal activities or they would follow the same faith.

Although those criminals had become quite nervous of their future due to Mallory's recent successes, his letters were completely ignored and their operations in New York and elsewhere increased. They had also placed a reward on his head of 1 million US dollars, dead or alive.

Mallory was good at disguises and never remained in any place long enough to be traced. Nevertheless, during that time he kept well out of the news. Anyway, he was presently doing the chasing and any of the headhunters he met on the way were swiftly neutralized.

At least the gangs had been forewarned of Mallory's intentions. Neither did they realized he was the Private Eye that took out the people in London.

Mallory had seriously tightened security about the hotel and decided to use that place as a front for his operations in Miami. He had an extra team of specials brought in to guard the hotel and its perimeter on a twenty-four-hour basis.

Tex and his organization had attempted to acquire more information on Mallory, but each time they came to a dead end. The man called John Williams had pretended to be Clair's brother. He was using her own surname and had been identified as a small farmer that turned to crime after he lost his farm to the bank because of his inability to pay back a modest loan.

If only he, Tex, knew of this John Williams' problems with the bank, he would have paid that bank loan back himself and twice over. At least that would have got the guy out of his hair for good. Now, he is absorbed by revenge towards all his criminal competitors.

At least that was how Tex felt after he found he couldn't get Mallory by fair means or foul; not even to join is own organization. Nevertheless, something had to be done to rid him of that thorn in his paw, including negotiations. He was undermining most of his lucrative business operations. Not to mention, getting rid of one of his best men, namely Marrio Carillo.

Finally, Tex thought the only way was to take him out permanently, even if it meant levelling the hotel and all its occupants with explosives. He called a meeting with a few of his best guys and the job was given to another gang that specialised in that side of the business, namely, demolition.

Mallory's plan was not a complex one, but depended on the most advanced robotic technologies ever devised by the Solarians. As a Solarian Director, he had full assistance from Sol-Newtown and Central Macron on Eden, and they could furnish him with all his required technologies to defeat the criminals and maintain the survival program on Earth.

Mallory's idea was to replace all of the gang leaders with lookalike androids covered with synthetic flesh and emotions that were indistinguishable from their real counterparts. Those could then be given specific instructions by Mallory or his Macron. However, the only way his cunning efforts would have been achieved was to have each of the gang's most senior members scanned by the Psyrotron, in much the same way they had done with Marrio. That way their complete psychological profiles, experiences and memories could be recorded and downloaded into their artificial duplicates.

In order to accomplish that great feat, they would each have to be captured in secret, scanned and replaced without the knowledge of any of their families and associates. Then the androids could be programmed with their subtler behavioural patterns. Afterwards, their replacements could be controlled at will by Mallory's operations Macron. The technology of such devices were so advanced, that it was impossible to tell the difference on the outside, and those androids were more advanced than humans and had several Macrons to assist in their tasks.

After that part of the operation had been completed, all stolen children subsequent to their replacement, could be returned to their real parents. That was after their arrival at the London branch, which would at that time be in the hands of Carl's Specials. That way, the American gangs would be non-the-wiser and the operation could continue until every relevant participant was known by Mallory. However, only the most important members of the gang would be brain-cleaned and sent away for rehabilitation. That replacement method would prevent other criminals from moving in to fill the vacuum if the criminal organization suddenly disappeared. The only problem was due to the immediate inconvenience and loss felt by the child's parents after such kidnapping. However, the children would be returned the moment they had arrived at their final destination.

It was a good thing the criminals kept records on the kids and their relevant destinations. That was because payments had to be made to many throughout the route towards their final destination, and they didn't destroy the records on completion of each delivery.

In time, it was hoped that the less significant criminals would disband once they realised their business was on a downward spiral, with additional pressures from the police and others, including Mallory's Specials. However, that would only have been possible if they were pursued relentlessly by the mass media and Mallory's Specials. Anyway, those small fish would not have had the know-how, potential or finances to continue such a complex paedo-smuggling organization.

Mallory was also building his own intelligence network within the fringes of most criminal organizations. It was to find those leaders of high potential and to smash them before they became large enough to affect the system.

He and his specials considered all such criminals like virus waiting to affect the body of humanity. His Specials were like antibodies that was ready to take action at the slightest indication and destroy them before they had gotten a foothold and begun to reproduce.

The second part of Mallory's plan was to create greater animosity between those gangs and the public, by inducing them into kidnapping the son of a well-known politician. Such a kidnapping, backed by the correct type of publicity, would have engendered much public hatred towards the paedo-smuggling gangs.

It was also essential that such a kidnapping was brought to the attention of the President and congress. The government would then become involved and put greater pressures on the police and other law enforcement organizations, including his own Specials.

Once the child was returned by Mallory's organization, they would also receive much coverage in the mass media and be subsequently acknowledged by the planet as a leading law enforcement organization. From that moment on, his specials would be considered an international force to be reckoned with.

However, Tex Nolan, Sunny Durante and Marcus Darling was next on Mallory's replacement list. Joeboy Hazard, who had survived the Chameleon's wrath, was not considered an essential cog in their child smuggling operation and was left to his own desires. He was the type that did anything for money and such people were also quite valuable to Mallory for inside information at a price.

Once the main pillars of that criminal organization had been removed, it would collapse soon after, or so Mallory thought.


It happened on the way to his large Texas ranch, after leaving the Rodeo in a local town. As the car turned a bend they came upon an accident involving two old cars. There were three bodies stretched out on the roadside, with a woman weeping over one.

'Stop!' he shouted to his driver.

As his large limousine came to a halt, the tearful woman came towards them.

'Please sir, can you help? I think my husband is dying. Could you please call emergency or take us to the closest hospital?' she pleaded. However, by then it was already too late for Tex and his driver.

The crying woman removed a gun from her handbag and a small gas capsule was thrown into the car. There she waited with her hand to her nose while the immobilizing gas took effect. Tex was subsequently unclothed and replaced by a lookalike android which was now dressed in his clothes. The limousine was then taken several miles in the direction of his house and left in a small ditch, with the driver asleep at the controls.

The lookalike had not yet been fully programmed to Tex's basic characteristics. That would come about an hour later, after Tex's brain had been fully scanned by the Psyrotron. Then the lookalike would be updated from a local Macron.

When the driver awoke, he found himself still at the controls of the car and in a ditch at the side of the road. The memory of the accident soon returned and he assumed it was a dream caused by his own accident and by too many glasses of wine at the restaurant that evening. He turned his head around to check his passenger in the rear seat, but his boss was fast asleep. He assumed it was all to do with whisky and the hectic rodeo celebrations of that evening and reversed the car out of the ditch. By then the android had been fully programmed to Tex's more subtler desires and dislikes.

'Where are we now?' the android Tex inquired and sat up.

'We are now entering the drive. Don't worry, you'll soon be home,' the driver said, without the slightest knowledge of the switch.


Marcus Darling was next on Mallory's agenda. He would be more difficult to capture and replace, being always in the presence of his gang of gamblers and thieves. However, he had to visit the toilet sometime during the course of each day and that was when he would be captured.

It was another busy day in his little casino and there were three disguised and unknown visitors with much money that was greeted generously by his senior staff. After they had gambled at the roulette for a while they went to the bar and bought some more drinks.

During all this time they were checking the building and Marcus's movements. Soon afterwards, they found the staff toilet which was only used by Marcus, his few important staff and special visitors. Mallory remained in that room and locked himself in one of the cubicles. He would be informed of any changes by his colleagues outside by implants. They accompanied the disguised lookalike, also wearing a mask.

As Marcus entered the toilet, Mallory was at the sink and like a flash fired a tranquilliser dart at his fat belly.

'You remember me, swine. You and your men insulted me once. Now its time for some payback,' Mallory said and he couldn't stop staring at Mallory, while he removed his disguise to show him the face of the detective he had once tied to a chair.

He was a very large and fat person and Mallory expected the drug to take at least two minutes to take full effect. So he removed his other gun to ensure silence during that time. A signal was sent to Ebony and soon her android entered the toilet, was undressed and their clothes and disguise changed over.

'I think our friend has had a little too much. The burger fainted on us. Don't worry we'll be back to reclaim our winnings,' Mallory said to the manager and they left.

Marcus's large fat body was taken out through the door in the same disguise and clothes of the android that had entered an hour earlier. No questions were asked as they escorted their fat and apparently sick colleague through the door. The new Marcus remained in the toilet for the best part of an hour, until one of his men came looking for him. By that time his lookalike had been fully programmed.


Sunny Durante was next. He was based in New York and also managed a large hotel there among other things. He was the brains behind most street crimes, including the street gangs, their hideouts and safe houses.

He was also involved in the bio-organ gang, but that part of his business became too difficult as hospital security improved. However, he hadn't given it up completely; just shelved the operation until someone with the relevant know-how and finances came along.

Sunny was in his hotel room when his turn came. There he sat on the side of the bed in a dressing gown and with one of his favourite prostitutes. He picked the phone up and called room service.

'Make it a bottle of best champagne, and make it right away!' he said and hung up.

The disguised waitress soon arrived and was told to uncork the bottle, which she did and began to fill their glasses. She waited for them to sip their drinks and fired her tranquilliser guns at each in turn. Sunny tried to rush her but she was too quick for him and retrieved a real gun which she placed towards his head.

'Now! Now! Sunny, be a good lad and relax. That way the process will be painless,' Ebony said and he fell limp to her feet.

They became dizzy and both fell to the floor at about the same time. The switch was made and when the prostitute awoke she assumed it was the champagne; for the bottle had been emptied in the sink. By that time the lookalike had been fully programmed to Sunny's tendencies. Orders were subsequently given to Carl in London and the gang's operations there was neutralized and replaced by Specials.

All that remained was the kidnapping of an important child. For that special job, one of the grandsons of New York's Mayor, Conwallice, had been chosen to fulfil their requirements. The Mayor's son was a young senator and that would surely have taken matters to the President and his Congress.

CHAPTER 50

# The end of a gang

The mock kidnapping was arranged by several lookalikes. It took place in Washington DC and in broad daylight. The child was simply snatched from his mother's arms in a city that was hitherto known as one of the most secure in North America.

That incident shook Washington DC and like an earthquake rippled outwards until the ensuing waves rocked the whole of America. The news media was the first to be alerted by the police.

As usual, no notes or phone calls had been received during the first hour, which made it the case of a stolen child with an even slimmer chance of recovery. The only consolation was that such children were not killed for ransom as was the case with most genuine kidnapping.

The police and customs had become more active than ever they had been for years. Houses were searched and known criminals arrested and questioned, but by that time the child was already in Europe. The well-programmed lookalikes had sneaked him out of Washington DC by a special route and had taken special transport to one of the criminals' hideout just outside London.

The original European members of the gang that had been so far ignored, were subsequently captured, drugged and taken back to their London office where they were sacrificed. To make things tidy, their memories were erased and explained as a condition of their capture. They were then replaced and held under surveillance only to be re-arrested publicly by Mallory's specials. The child was then supposedly captured from one of their safe houses before arranging delivery to his parents.

Mallory and a nurse joyfully accompanied the child to the passenger shuttle that was to take them directly to Washington DC, amidst many reporters and flashing cameras. This time he wore no disguises and made it his point to get as much publicity as possible.

'Sir, it's great that you have foiled the plans of one of the largest paedo-smuggling gangs in Europe. What have you to say on that topic?' the reporter said.

'All I can say to you people and parents with young children, is to be extra vigilant and report neighbours and others with young children that they are not expected to have. We can do our jobs a lot better with your assistance,' Mallory said.

As they arrived at National Airport, Washington DC, he was greeted by many officials, his wife Roseanne, Chad and his six female Specials. They were all wearing their best uniforms and making the most of their national publicity.

While all this was happening, Carl and some of his senior operatives were being interviewed by British television and congratulated for a job well done.

Mallory and his group were subsequently met by the President and some senators, including the father and mother of the child. They could not restrain their tears of happiness when he took the child from the nurse and handed him over to his mother. She was also filled with tears of joy. All those images were collected on camera by numerous networks and transmitted throughout America and elsewhere at peak viewing time.

Crowds of people accumulated throughout the streets of the capital to greet the motorcade on its way to the White House. Mallory and his Specials were taken directly to the White House where they were commended by the President for their act of bravery in rescuing the child and for bursting the international gang. For their benevolent actions in the face of such dangers, they were each rewarded with the Congressional Medal of Honour. Mallory did not appreciate the manner in which he had received the medal, After all, he had created the scam to neutralize the growing danger of paedo-smuggling and to get the public more aware and involved. However, he realized that the publicity of his organization outweighed everything else, so he accepted its results. Nevertheless, he was happy when that particular file was lost in his archives. Anyway, creating such important situations were not possible without breaking a few eggs.

Mallory remembered his previous visits to the White House. That was when he promised he would do everything in his powers to assist all Fertilate families and now he was back being commended by the nation for what he had set out to do. Now, his efforts and commission were doubly reenforced by the rescue of the child and the capture of the gang of child snatchers. He would now hunt the remainder relentlessly until they were no more.

The less important members of the gang who observed the news had suddenly become nervous. Their lookalike bosses, unknown to their subordinates, had received changes in their programming, telling them to move into more legitimate enterprises and from then the international ring of paedo-smugglers had been broken permanently and began to dissipate. However, the power at the top of the gangs remained. If they were suddenly removed a vacuum would be created and others could have taken over their criminal operations. By such a clever method most of Earth's master criminals were substituted by clever androids who were in turn controlled by powerful Macron computers.

Every bit of information on those criminal organizations would in future be relayed by those lookalikes to Mallory's Macron who could then transmit new instructions for them to follow.

Mallory could now concentrate on Fertilate housing and other projects that would be required in the years to come. He was also quite relieved that he was no more a target for those criminals.

Carl remained in London where his recruiting progressed.

Chad continued to train his specials in Warland, USA, with the aid of Mallory and his six female specials.

Roseanne was in child, and remained at home where she took on the role of Chief Controller of Base Central on all their special missions during the days of her pregnancy.

CHAPTER 51

# Satan's Bug

Old Powell was dead and buried. The Group of Thirteen soon built a monument with epitaph and he was soon forgotten. His new version in the form of the 25 year old Dr. John Simmons soon took his place. Through Solarian Banking and Professor Khan's help they had acquired a large laboratory with over 100 specialist in many fields. Those included his dedicated scientists. However no one on Earth knew that level of nano-technology at the time. So he had his work cut out.

Dr. Hal Seaton was back on Tyrrel II taking care of many endangered species and creating new ones to replace those extinct on Earth over the past millennia. He would draw the line at Mammoths and Neolithic Man. The planet's evolution had diversified too much since their existence. As far as he was concerned they would now be contaminants in the food-chain. He was always a professional to the letter. Nevertheless he now considered himself a Solarian and would stick to their long-term plans while they worked in his favour. As far as he was con-cerned, Sarah and her cronies, with their long braided robes, were doing a great job. That meant he could focus on more important matters. He also realized that one could conquer the whole universe without the knowledge or help of the most clever mice or ants.

Dr. John Simmons (Powell) found everything he needed to know about Javols within his brain implants. Even the original blueprints by the Andromedan, Professor Andra Safarar. They decided to name their new business MIMMIC in commemoration of Andra's failings. That name being the acronym for Microid Induction and Motivation by Microwave and Intercellular Communications. As with Professor Andra, who created those deadly monsters named Javols over 3000 years before, they thought they would be the ones to cause their demise.

Since they had no Javols for their valuable experiments, they had to create a few. Hopefully with similar tendencies and motivations. Those would seriously hate humans and would attempt to devour them with extreme prejudice. There was also their most deadly nano-bot sprays that could take a body apart in seconds. They made ancient mythological creatures like the Gorgon look like the most cuddly pets by comparison. Those would be fabricated several hundred feet below ground within the central part of their MIMIC laboratories.

'I'm back for our 13th meeting. How is everything?' Hal inquired.

'Great, Boss! We have started putting the technology together. I will download to your implants after I've finalized my current plans,' John (Powell) said.

'What plans?'

'I have an idea for a perfect specimen. We can create similar Javols, but with non-removable Brain Implants. Then although fully functional, we can control them to any degree by microwave transponders or by other systems depending on environment. We can even make them friendly, to be anti Javols.'

'You mean with a "love human" template?'

'Something like that!'

'Then they will be like our slaves! That will be fantastic! I shall focus on those concepts as well. I shall get Lord Khan to fit an H-Wave communicator on your building. Then we can communicate more frequently between worlds. If we can accomplish those plans we will be able to save the universe from those filthy and disgusting bastards! Then our Javols' most deadly spray will include a microid virus to take nasty Javols apart instead of primals like us!' Hal was very pleased.

'I'm sure we can do it within 10 years!'

'Well, we have 20, so take your time and make it perfect. I have arranged another 20 billion from Solarian Banking. Lord Khan is now responsible for us, so expect a visit from the great man and myself in the near future!'

'I hope we have something to show by then,' John replied.

'Early days, so do your best. See you at the meeting. Have to go!' Hal disconnected.

'Mallory was present at that meeting on the 13th, by the Group of Thirteen. He explained further plans for his Specials and removal of criminal gangs. However nothing of a technical nature was discussed.

'Gentlemen and Ladies, I would like to recommend those of you, over the age of 45 for an age reduction. Over the years I realized how much you sacrificed for our troubled world, with little rewards. Since you are not part of any criminal organization, I think it necessary for you to have such a reduction. Since I would like you all to be among us much longer, with your permission, may I contact the relevant people for that purpose!' Mallory said.

'An age reduction, eh! Any interested parties?' Okeke said, and many hands went up.

'Mallory, we shall supply a list at our next meeting. In the mean time please keep us up to date on progress. We have an over-whelming interest in our world's future,' Okeke replied.

'And Mallory, please watch your back. We have much work in the future to save our world from those nasty Javols!' Hal interjected.

'I shall!' Mallory replied.

Nevertheless, since they were only interested in a modest age reduction, they would be supplied with special medication until the time was right for Psyrotron and Megotron body changes.

# Epilogue: The real struggle continues

### Earth time... AD 2074

Several years had passed since Mallory had formed his international group of soldiers called The Specials. In the intervening years most of the major gangs had been subdued. However, Infilate terrorists of many beliefs and inclinations began to grow throughout the planet and assassinations and violence became commonplace. Most of the coastal cities, including Miami was presently covered by water. However, New York and Washington were turned into walled cities with an array of sealed underground tunnels and bridges to the main land. However the waters were still rising and would continue until the planet cooled significantly. Extreme flooding also caused the displacement of populations, leading to further extreme violence.

Mallory's wife, Roseanne, was now a mother of three beautiful children, two girls and one boy, and in charge of all operations' coordination on Earth.

His eldest son, Andy, had spent his first year in the air-force, having passed the entrance examinations with flying colours and they had been together several times since.

His six female Specials were now in charge of their own Specials and when they were not on special missions also assisted Chad to train the best. After their arrival from planet Eden with new implants and bodies, Mallory gave his six girls each a house of their own, but they also had concessions on Eden. They were now Solarians and like Mallory, were looking forward to their permanent retirement to that world.

Planet Earth was in even greater turmoil than she had been in previous years and all that was due to the irresponsibility of mankind combined with the stresses of that time.

Nevertheless, Dr. Hal Seaton and Dr John Simmons (Powell) continued their anti-Javols experiments. They had two types in mind; The friendly anti-Javols soldiers. Those were to be designed to Andra's original specs, to be the best warriors in the known universe, but on our side. The other type would extract Javols' memories and take their place. The latter would be called Mind Probes. They were not soldiers, but were copiers. Nevertheless they could defend themselves in emergencies.

All those nano-bot warriors were unable to breed and procreate new versions of themselves. Neither could they be copied and manufactured outside of special production plants. For their production on Earth, special Class 5 equipment had to be imported from Planet Eden and other Federation worlds. This was all done via Lord Khan (Sarah's father Ben) who had a vested interest in Earth's survival.

Many young Infilate families felt rejected when they realised they would never have children. As a result, many couples resorted to suicide while others began to take action against their respective political systems that had let them down so badly in the past. Then again, there were those who turned to terrorism. They thought force would pressurize those responsible and give them what they wanted. Top of their list was finding a cure for the Terminal Disease. However, Mallory's target of five hundred million human survivors on Earth had almost been reached. That was when the last count of Fertilate families were taken in the winter. Therefore, the antidote distribution was suddenly wound down and handed back to Lord Khan.

Mallory's own antidote distribution building was converted for use as a latex mask production plant and everything that was relevant to the antidote distribution was transferred to Sol-Newtown. Anyway, the distribution system had become fully automatic and tablets could be acquired from most stores.

Jealousy and hatred of Infilates toward all Fertilate families increased, until they and their children were harassed, abused and assaulted in the cities' streets. That was when they were moved away from the most densely populated areas and rehoused in domes and new apartment buildings that had been prepared for them during the previous years.

Mallory's specials were very active at this time, establishing safe areas, guarding those families and assisting in the rehousing program. Soon, the cities were only inhabited by Infilates and criminals. They soon became no-go areas for the young.

Over the intervening years Solarian Banking had purchased numerous buildings and farms worldwide for the housing of Fertilate families. Many domes and accommodation complexes had also been built for that purpose. It made the supply of antidote a lot easier, since it could be added to the water supply and food supplements, thus making the process invisible to Fertilate populations.

## A child in trouble.

Mallory had recently taken a holiday break on planet Eden with his family. Its purpose was to view his new palace and visit his old friends like Jerry and Harry Lennox. On his return, he was relaxing at home when the phone rang.

'Mal, sorry for this interruption. We have received an urgent message from Lord Khan. It concerns the special boy in England. His father has died. Here is the complete file,' Ebony said and transmitted the data through her implants. Ebony had taken control of operations in their absence and they were still on holiday at home.

Mallory carefully scanned through the information and turned towards Roseanne, who was playing with their eldest child called Clair.

'Darling, the boy's father is dead and his mother is having an affair with a much younger man. I shall have to ask Carl to assign two of his best operatives to that house in case they decide to move,' he said and immediately contacted Carl, who was now head of European operations.

'I wonder if he knew of his wife's affair before he died?' Roseanne asked.

'I don't know, but the way things are going, we might have to take the kid away and find him a new home,' Mallory replied.

'That might be tricky. You know the laws in Europe regarding adopted kids and child snatching,' Roseanne warned.

'We have already arranged papers for George Peterson, Son of Destiny. The moment his security is threatened, he will be taken away and placed in one of our special homes for children of his age. He is too important to be left alone with such parents,' Mallory replied as the nanny entered the room.

'Mam, it's Charles, he is playing up again,' she said. Roseanne got up from the Settee and made her way upstairs to his room, but soon returned.

'Darling, Charles wants to see you about a broken toy or something. Please talk to him before he goes to sleep. Our son seems to require more than his fair share of attention these days. It must be due to all the time we spend with his younger sister,' she said.

'Kids that age are quite difficult to handle. They require more than their fair share of love and attention,' he replied, while on his way to see his little boy. Mallory had now become a father through and through and now had a second family that he cherished in every way. Even so, the strange destiny of the Son of Destiny was foremost in his mind.

## Two years later.... August, AD 2076.

'Darling, I have received a communication from Sarah. It concerns a new world called Melos III within the Bi-Setti system. She wants you to become Chief Councillor of the complete system.

Apparently, that's where she intends to place most of those young Fertilates from Earth desiring a new interstellar life with much excitement. The population there is only twenty thousand, but it is steadily growing and a city is being built. The nearby world, Polion II, is one of Solaria's most important of manufacturing worlds.

She thinks your influence there will be important to the young and it could be a prestigious position if you accept,' Roseanne said, full of excitement.

'Really? When can we leave?' Mallory replied, jokingly.

'I am serious, Darling! They want us for that job and I think the change might do us good. Most of the real work here is now at an end and we can't control the violence, which seems to worsen each day. Anyway, we can return any time we wish.

Carl, Chad and the others can handle current operations on a global scale with Lord Khan's assistance, and I think we are getting a little bored with the present status quo. The only problem could be the kids' education, but these days that's not a problem with implants and suchlike,' she said.

'Are you really serious about going? We will have to leave this place and everyone we know behind, and for God knows, how long. Then there is the aging problem. Next time we return we'll be exactly the same, while they might age another fifty years,' he said.

'You are always good with disguises. I'm sure you'll find a way. Even if it means a reconversion in one of those Megotron chambers,' she replied.

'In that case, we might have to stage an accident like Jerry's. After all, we can't tell Andy, Donald and the others of our intentions to live on a distant world many hundreds of light years away. Then there is Ebony and the rest of our specials to consider. They are like family and I would like them to have a say and be given the option to join us. However, such a change could be a very exciting one. Imagine, building an organization on a completely new world from scratch.' Mallory said.

'Now, I see the twinkle in your eyes, which means you are interested in the challenge. We can always return in disguise to Sarah's country house during our occasional visits to Earth. Obviously, this house will have to be signed over to Solarian Banking for safe keeping, but Andy and others could use it after the portal has been removed,' Roseanne said.

'I would like to discuss this matter with Ebony and the others, face-to-face, before I come to any decision.' Mallory replied.

'Ok!'

'Why don't we invite them for dinner this evening?' Mallory said.

'If you want, Darling,' she replied and immediately transmitted a coded thought to her Coms set.

'They have been contacted and will be here by seven,' she added.

Ebony and the other five women were still single, but most had boyfriends, including Ebony.

Only the six turned up for dinner that evening. They had obviously sensed something of a more serious nature in Roseanne's tone.

'Ladies, before we settle down to dinner, I would like to mention something of importance. I have been asked by Sarah to become Chief Councillor of Bi-Setti. It's a stellar system seven hundred light-years away. I wondered whether you would like to join us as co-councillors, advising in its administration. I am sure Sarah wouldn't mind. However, I have not decided on the position yet.'

'An alien world!' Ebony inquired.

'Alien, but with mainly young Earth humans! Just consider what I have said and give me an answer in a week or so. If we accept, I am sure we'll be able to return if we find conditions there unsuitable. That will be during the usual probationary period,' Mallory said, and the girl's eyes lit up with excitement when Mallory described the system to them in greater detail.

'A complete world to choose from and mould to our liking, within the Solarian context. Will we have full say in its administration?' Ebony said.

'In a democratic manner, with the exception of the usual Macrons. I think our roles will be mainly to do with the young human population. Most of those are taken from Earth as students and trained to work on the local manufacturing world of Polion II and elsewhere, including the Solarian navy. If we accept, we'll also have to train all new recruits from Earth.'

'Sounds like a great experience to me!' Nadia interjected.

'From what I heard the world is young and has been converted by robots to be like Earth. It was one of the main planets used for the evacuation of endangered life from our world. So it's full of our forests and wild life,' he said and they were amazed.

That evening they talked about the new challenges faced on the distant and young world of Melos III.

It was not long before they voted for the change in residence. However, they would have to give up their boyfriends, homes and properties on Earth and in such a manner as not to arouse suspicions. All of their homes, with the exception of Mallory's, were already owned by the organization, so that aspect minimised future problems.

'I think I might have an idea on the subject of our disappearance.' Ebony said.

'I hope it's a good one!' Joan replied.

'What if we fitted a portal on our yacht and set the ship on fire, or blew it up with everyone on board. After all, there must be many criminal enemies about with such notions for our downfall. That would make our permanent disappearance more legitimate. Before the fire or explosion was triggered, we would have returned back to this house and on our way to Eden. What do you think?' Ebony said.

'I think it's brilliant! However, we'll have to make sure that the local people saw us go onboard, including the children,' Mallory replied.

'We can't take the children, Darling. It might be too risky,' Roseanne said, defensively.

'Ok, we simply replace them with lookalike androids, and make sure everyone is properly introduced to the local police. Don't you think they might like a visit from one Commander Mallory Colman and some famous members of his team?' Mallory replied.

The decision had been made and they now had a flawless plan for implementing their disappearance.

Soon after, Ebony and her female companions returned to live with Mallory and Roseanne as they had done previously. The usual arrangements were made with Sol-Newtown for the lookalike androids, including one for Ebony, and another for dismantling the portal at the house after they left.

Ebony was expected to baby-sit in the house and remain in control of communications during the operation.

The yacht was rigged with enough explosives and a small portal fitted. When all the preparations had been completed, Mallory sent a message to the local police in Miami, for that was where his yacht, Sun Flower, was moored. He informed them of his visit to observe their crime busting methods. They were pleased to show him and his company around, even to take him and his group to sea and observe an arrest of smugglers, but he declined that particular invitation.

After they had spent the morning with the police, they left for their yacht. Afterwards, they made sure the yacht was three miles away from shore in deep water and at least half a mile from the closest ship before their plan was set in motion. It was to look like their enemies had planted a large bomb on the ship that was timed to go off several minutes after the engine was started.

Mallory first tested the portal by sending Roseanne, the girls and lookalikes through. Then he said a painful prayer of forgiveness, including a mention of his son Andy; for not having been a better father and other friends like Rosie, whom he knew he would never see again. Carl, Chad and other Solarians would be informed in due course and could join him if they so desired. Finally, he checked again to see that there were no boats or divers in the area before initiating the device that was set to a thirty-second timer.

It was a large explosion that vaporised the complete ship and its contents, leaving their loved ones to mourn the loss of the greatest fighters in the struggle for order and freedom in the history of Earth.

To be continued with
**Son of Destiny**

# The Chronicles of Galaxy Osmaron Series

The Chronicles of Osmaron series point a way to one of our possible futures. In this future, technology is more advanced. But our real problems come from another galaxy, where another human species have accidentally created the ideal nano-bot type soldier that went bad. They are truly unique in the sense that they are almost indestructible, can copy and replicate almost anything, can live for ever, can reproduce their own kind and require living organisms like us for food. At least that was the unintended nano-bot type demon that came out of the mould after their second and final experiment.

Those nano-bot Javols went on to destroy all major animal life, including their creators, within Andromeda and are presently on their way to our Milky Way galaxy. The most advanced in our galaxy, who are non-human, decide to fight back for the survival of all naturally evolving life, but have to first inform lesser civilizations like us of the impending danger.

Before we can confront the demon Javols, we must first advance our technologies to Class 5. This is about 100,000 years more advanced than Earth's present levels. During this period Earth undergoes many changes due to Global Warming and human overpopulation, but manages to survive the onslaught.

Wars will rage, but apparently ubiquitous humans will always find ways to survive and win the day.